The Legacy of the Unborn
A Novel of Lovecraftian Horror

The Legacy of the Unborn
A Novel of Lovecraftian Horror

Silas K. Henderson

Published by Tekrighter LLC 2020
The Legacy of the Unborn

Cover designed by the author
Images are under license from Shutterstock.com

This book is a work of fiction. Names, characters, places, and incidents either are products of the author's imagination or, in the case of historical personages, used fictitiously. Any resemblance to actual persons, living or dead, or actual events, is entirely coincidental.

Silas K. Henderson

Printed in the United States of America

First Printing: June 2020

ISBN-13 978-1-7331140-4-2
ISBN-10: 1-7331140-4-1

Dedication

To the memory of Howard Phillips Lovecraft, a troubled, beautiful soul, without whom this work would not have been possible.

Table of Contents

CHAPTER 1 1

CHAPTER 2 8

CHAPTER 3 21

CHAPTER 4 27

CHAPTER 5 40

CHAPTER 6 45

CHAPTER 7 58

CHAPTER 8 67

CHAPTER 9 77

CHAPTER 10.. 92

CHAPTER 11.. 99

CHAPTER 12.. 111

CHAPTER 13.. 128

CHAPTER 14.. 141

CHAPTER 15.. 148

CHAPTER 16.. 156

CHAPTER 17.. 169

CHAPTER 18.. 176

CHAPTER 19.. 190

CHAPTER 20.. 199

CHAPTER 21.. 205

CHAPTER 22.. 209

CHAPTER 23.. 226

CHAPTER 24.. 234

CHAPTER 25.. 249

CHAPTER 26.. 256

CHAPTER 27.. 261

CHAPTER 28.. 266

CHAPTER 29.. 283

CHAPTER 30.. 296

CHAPTER 31 300
CHAPTER 32 316
CHAPTER 33 318
CHAPTER 34 320
CHAPTER 35 321
BEFORE YOU GO... 322
ACKNOWLEDGEMENTS 323
ABOUT THE AUTHOR... 325

"Behold now behemoth, which I made with thee; he eateth grass as an ox."

Job 40: 15

CHAPTER 1

The Statement of Dr. Ebeneezer Warman
Manhattan State Hospital, Ward's Island, New York City

January 1, 1932

I write this affidavit at the behest of Dr. Oglethorpe. He thinks it will be therapeutic; as he puts it, it will help me separate fantasy from reality, and hasten the day I will walk out of here a free, if not an altogether well, man. I doubt that will remain his position after he reads it, but I really don't care. It is important to get the facts of the case on record, even if my peers consider them ravings. Dyer will support me, despite ongoing efforts to discredit him, and, sooner or later, the information that Henderson is suppressing will come to light. And it will give me something to do, for the days here are long, but blissfully monotonous for the most part. It's not a bad place to grow old in, all things considered. It is as safe and secure as anywhere for one who knows what I do, and I am well treated.

My name is Dr. Ebeneezer Warman. Until recently, I was a general practitioner with offices in Lenox Hill on 67th Street in New York City.

The Legacy of the Unborn

My patients, mostly neighborhood residents, were largely women, though I am neither a gynecologist nor an obstetrician. So, it was no surprise when Sarah, my receptionist, buzzed the intercom late in the afternoon last September 25th to inform me that a lady wished to see me. It was an annoyance, however. I was just finishing up for the day and I still had my rounds, after which I was planning to leave for a weekend's fishing in Montauk. I told Sarah to ask the lady to make an appointment for next week.

"But she says it's a personal matter, Doctor." Sarah's voice on the speaker was scratchy. "Her name is Mrs. McDowell."

I pushed the intercom button. "Evelyn McDowell?"

"Yes, Doctor."

I considered. Evie was a friend, not a patient, and it was not a bit like her to arrive at my office without calling or wiring ahead. I hadn't seen her and Colin for a couple of months, but that was not unusual. We had been quite close in college; I am sure that Evie seriously considered me as a prospective husband until she met Colin. Luckily for me, I fell out of the running after that—I couldn't compete with the *ubermensch*.

I first became acquainted with Colin McDowell in medical school at Harvard. We belonged to the same study group. It didn't take me long to realize that Colin was an extraordinary person; while I and the other group members were struggling to keep up with our first-year subjects, Colin was studying for a Ph.D. in addition to his medical degree! His intensity was incredible—he seemed to have time for nothing but work and would tolerate imperfection neither in himself nor his associates. I believe this was the principal reason that our study group was so effective—none of us wished to face Colin ill-prepared. As we became better acquainted, I discovered that Colin did indeed take his leisure, but it was as rigorously scheduled as his work. I introduced him to Evie, whom I had met at a social to which the Wellesley women had been invited.

"Send her in," I told Sarah.

I opened the door, for I had no wish to make her knock. One look at her face as she came down the hall told me there was trouble indeed.

"Come in, Evie, and sit. May I get you anything?" She shook her head.

Evelyn McDowell was a beautiful woman. Her face was almost too perfect. The soft, blue eyes, pert nose and delicate mouth were superbly balanced and ideally accented by her creamy skin and flaxen hair, which she kept short in the modern style. She wore a white dress with a single black band that ran diagonally from her left shoulder across her full breasts, then curved round behind to terminate at the ankles, deftly marking the path a man's eyes would take upon observing her. Her matching turban-style hat, black leather purse and shoes complemented the outfit faultlessly. Automatically, she smoothed the dress over her rump as she sat in the leather wing-back chair facing my desk, then began fumbling for a cigarette. I offered her one from the inlaid mahogany box on my desk and held the lighter for her. Her hands trembled, and she took mine in both of hers to hold the cigarette's tip to the flame. The tears in her eyes were not from the smoke.

I perched on the edge of my desk and waited for her to speak.

"Eben, I've come to you about Colin," she said. "He's not been home for three days!"

I hoped this wasn't what I feared it was—another woman.

"He's not been staying at the office?" I knew Colin had an apartment there, for use when he was working late.

"Miss LeMay said he's not been in."

"Have you called Rockefeller? You know how he is when he's involved in the lab."

"Yes. They haven't seen him for weeks."

That was unusual.

She looked blankly at her cigarette, then started to rise. I handed her an ashtray. She flicked her cigarette, then held the ashtray in her lap.

3

"I've been twice to the police," she continued. "The first time I couldn't get past the sergeant. He told me they couldn't do anything until Colin had been gone for two days. If I'd known that, I'd have lied and said he had been!"

"But Colin's stayed away longer than that before, Evie,"

"Yes, but he's always been at the office or the lab, Eben. I couldn't find him at either place!"

"Isn't there anywhere else you could check?" My earlier fear was returning.

She thought a moment. "Possibly at the Settlement House," she said finally. "I don't know if they have a phone. But there's no reason why he would want to stay there for three days!"

"It's worth a try," I said. "What's the name of it?"

"The College Settlement, I think. It's somewhere on the Lower East Side. God, I'll feel so foolish if he's there!" Her face was alight with the hope in her eyes.

You shouldn't feel foolish, I thought, but didn't say so, as I reached for the Manhattan directory. The College Settlement House on Rivington Street did have telephone service. It required only a moment to contact them. Unfortunately, McDowell wasn't there either.

"Have you seen him recently?" I asked the woman on the line.

"No," she said, "I hope he's not deserted us. He's not come for his regular clinic for several weeks. His receptionist says he's gotten our messages, but he hasn't called back. If you see him, please tell him we need him."

I assured her I would and rang off, troubled. I told Evie only that Colin wasn't there.

"You said you went to the police twice." I reminded her. "What happened the second time?"

"I told them they had to do something. They told me a man named Henderson was handling the case, so maybe that sergeant did do something after all. But Henderson wasn't helpful. He told me he'd look into it, and then he asked me a lot of questions about Addison Strangways."

"Who's Addison Strangways?"

"Colin's tenant," she said. "He's a doctor who takes the office on the bottom floor of Colin's brownstone. We don't know him, really. Colin took his practice for him once when he went on vacation. Henderson seemed to think he'd done something."

"Done what?"

"Wouldn't tell me. I asked him if he thought he'd done something to Colin and he said no, not really."

She reached for her purse again, so I got her another cigarette and held the lighter again. She looked at me gratefully.

"Are you sure you wouldn't like a whisky and soda?" I asked. "One wouldn't hurt you."

"Is that a prescription, Doctor?" She tried to put levity in her voice, and failed.

"Yes, it is," I said, "for both of us." I got the bottle of Canadian from the cellaret, and two glasses. After pouring a couple of fingers in each, I diluted them with a spritz from the gasogene, and handed her one. She took it in both hands and drank off half of it. I saw the color slowly come back into her face.

"Eben, at this point, I've no confidence in the police. I think this Henderson's not telling me everything. Is there anything you could do?"

I took a swallow of my drink and considered, as the whisky trickled down my throat and warmed my stomach. My fishing trip was long anticipated, but that wasn't the sticking point. I wondered if there was anything I *could* do.

"I could talk to this Henderson, I suppose, although I've no reason to think he'd tell me any more than he would tell you."

"Would you, Eben? You're a man, he might tell you something he wouldn't tell me."

I didn't like the implication of that. "Now, Evie, I'm sure Colin's all right. He's probably chasing some wild goose in his research and he's gone off somewhere without calling you. When you called Rockefeller, did you talk to Carrel?"

"No, just to somebody in the lab. Do you think Alexis might know where he is?"

5

"It's worth a try. Dammitall, call everyone he knows!" *It'll keep you busy, at least,* I thought. "How are the girls taking it?"

She stubbed out her cigarette. "Not too badly. They miss him at dinner and ask where he is, but I've just put them off. They don't see a great deal of him anyway." I was sure I detected a hint of disdain in her voice.

"Well, I'll tell you what," I said. "I'll go downtown in the morning and see this Henderson fellow and try to find out what's going on. Meantime, tonight you call people. Maybe you'll find him, and I won't even have to go. All right?"

"All right, Eben. I'm sure I'm just a silly woman and he's really all right, just as you say. But you will tell me everything that Henderson says?"

I regarded the silly woman, whom I knew had a baccalaureate from Wellesley, and sighed inwardly. Damn Colin McDowell for a louse, anyway! Part of me hoped, reluctantly, that something was really wrong.

"I promise, Evie, I'll tell you what he says," *if I think it won't upset you further,* I added mentally. "I've got my rounds now—why don't you come on outside and I'll get you a cab."

She finished her drink and handed me her glass and the ashtray. I put them on the desk along with mine, still half full, and offered her my hand. I held her wrap as she slid her willowy arms into the sleeves. Her perfume wafted over me, and I wanted to embrace her from behind, to comfort her, but I resisted. I got my topcoat, then opened the door to the hallway and motioned her to go first. Her shoulders were slumped as she walked toward the door.

Dammitall! *Colin McDowell was really a louse,* I thought, as I watched her slink down the corridor.

Silas K. Henderson

CHAPTER 2

The Statement of Dr. Ebeneezer Warman

Saturday, September 26th, 1931

After my rounds, I called Harvey and told him I'd be staying in town after all. I suggested dinner at Louis Sherry's, late, but he told me he'd already dined on his way home. He sounded tired, didn't even inquire why my plans had changed, so I didn't press him. I stopped by Otto's on 86th for a sandwich, and was home in bed by eleven.

Evie called early Saturday morning, about eightish. She'd no luck in finding anyone who'd seen Colin for the last few weeks, never mind discovering his current whereabouts. She entreated me again to brace the redoubtable Henderson, and I told her I would.

After ringing off, I bathed and shaved, pulled on an old pair of gaberdines and a flannel shirt and went downstairs to the newsstand on Third Avenue for a *Tribune* to read with breakfast. The news was depressing. The Collings murder was still in the headlines, as was the series of killings perpetrated by the fiend dubbed the *New York Ripper* by the newspapers. Neither case seemed anywhere near a solution. I wondered whether Inspector Henderson was involved with either, and how his involvement might reflect the way he received a meddling doctor. No matter. A promise was a promise, and besides, I was beginning to think something serious might have befallen Colin.

I rang up police headquarters and asked for Inspector Henderson. I was speedily connected.

"Henderson." The voice was clipped and gave the impression that he had somewhere more important to be.

"Inspector Henderson, my name is Dr. Ebeneezer Warman. I am a friend of Mrs. Evelyn McDowell's. She has asked me to discuss your handling of her husband's disappearance with you."

"You a friend of the husband's, too?"

"Yes sir, we met...," he cut me off.

"I'd like very much to talk to you, Doctor. Can you be here in thirty minutes?"

"That's a little quick, Inspector, I..."

"An hour, then. Would you like me to send a car?"

"No, that...," he rang off, leaving me with the distinct impression that if I was not there within the hour, he *would* send a car.

I washed the breakfast dishes, then changed into proper attire and caught the downtown train. As always, the ride was noisy and bumpy, but for quick, reliable transportation about Manhattan, it is impossible to better the elevated lines and subways. Thankfully it was Saturday morning—the train was not crowded. By the time I disembarked at Grand Street it had begun to rain, so I hurried along, clutching my topcoat at the collar, and finally dodged through the dark, wooden double doors of 240 Centre Street.

After shaking the water from my fedora, I gave the sergeant in the lobby my name, asked for Inspector Henderson, and was told to wait. Five minutes later, I was approached by a short, rat-faced man in a rumpled brown suit. His oversized nose and ears and bullet head, covered with a brownish-gray fuzz, made him look even more rodentlike. His tired eyes regarded me pensively.

"You Warman?"

I acknowledged that I was.

"Henderson. Follow me."

He led me to a small office on an upper floor. It was furnished with a metal desk and filing cabinet and was horribly untidy, with papers strewn about everywhere. I am a smoker, but even so, the fetor emanating from an overflowing ashtray, exacerbated by the stifling heat from the room's single radiator, caused a momentary wave of nausea to ripple through me.

"Sit." Henderson gestured to an uncomfortable-looking wooden armchair facing the desk. He lowered himself into a battered swivel chair behind it, which groaned in protest, setting my teeth on edge.

I removed my hat and coat and looked vainly for a place to put them, then sat clutching them in my lap. The moisture from my coat was seeping into my trousers, and the chair had one leg too short, so it rocked back and forth. This was going to be a most unpleasant interview.

"Smoke?" Henderson extended a battered package of Phillip Morris, then lighted one for himself when I shook my head. I most definitely did not want to share that ashtray!

He leaned back in his chair. "So, you know this McDowell." It was not a question. "He the kind to skedaddle on his wife and kids?"

"Hardly, Inspector. He might forget to call home if he were going to be late, but I doubt he'd stay missing for days."

"What kind of bird is this egg, McDowell?"

I considered a moment before answering him. "He's a most extraordinary man, Inspector. He's a respected physician and scientist. He's reached the pinnacle of every field he's ever involved himself in. He's worked with some of the most respected scientists in the world, including Dr. Jung in Europe. You'll not find a more distinguished gentleman in the city."

"But you don't like him." He leaned forward a little in his chair.

"I didn't say that."

He stared at me silently. His eyes, no longer tired, drilled into mine, and they made me feel distinctly ill at ease.

"I've known Colin since medical school," I continued, to break the silence. "We see each other a few times a year, mostly at professional functions. Once in a while I have dinner at his house."

10

"The wife invites you."

"Yes, Inspector, she does," I said, daring him to make something of it. "She's also been a friend since medical school."

"You know an Addison Strangways?"

"No. Ev..., that is, Mrs. McDowell, told me he's Colin's tenant. Do you think he's involved?"

"What about Dana LeMay?"

"She's Colin's receptionist. She..."

"He fucking her?"

This has to stop!

"Inspector. I am here to find out what you are doing to locate Dr. McDowell. I..."

"He fucking her?"

I rose. "Perhaps your superior will be more helpful, Inspector." A stride took me to the door.

"Sit, Doctor." I reached and grasped the door knob. "Please," he said.

Turning back to face him, I saw that he was sitting on the edge of his chair, contemplating me soberly. His eyes had regained that weary aspect.

"Please," he said again.

I sat.

"Doctor. I have to ask these kinds of questions. I want to find him, too. I need to know what sort of man he is, if you want me to do that for you." He stubbed his cigarette out in that nasty ashtray.

"I do not know whether Dr. McDowell has been intimate with his receptionist, Inspector. I hope not, for his wife's sake."

"But he's the type."

I didn't answer. I didn't need to. This was one shrewd little man.

Henderson shook another cigarette from the pack and lighted it. I wanted one too, badly, but I would not deal with that disgusting ashtray. I decided to wait until I was out of there.

"I don't know what happened to McDowell, Dr. Warman. I can assure you this case is a top priority with the department. You don't know anything about McDowell and Strangways?"

11

"No, Inspector, I don't. I first heard of Dr. Strangways just the other day when Mrs. McDowell mentioned you'd asked about him."

"Well, who are McDowell's pals?"

"I don't think he has any real friends. He has colleagues, people that he works with. For a long time, he's worked with Dr. Alexis Carrel at Rockefeller Institute."

"Who's this Carrel?"

"He was the Nobel laureate in Medicine in 1912, Inspector. For his work in vascular surgery." I was suddenly very irritated with this vile little man. "Colin McDowell has worked in his laboratory for many years."

"I thought McDowell was in practice, not in research."

"He is in practice. He conducts research in his spare time."

"Doctor let me assure you we're doing all we can to find Dr. McDowell. We..."

He was brought up short by a plume of smoke arising from his desk. That wretched ashtray had caught fire! It was the first time during our interview that I'd seen him at a disadvantage, and it was evilly satisfying. I took the opportunity to leave as he was trying to stub out the smoldering butts with his handkerchief without spreading the conflagration to the papers on his desk. Ruefully, however, I realized I'd given Henderson far more than he'd given me.

I rode the elevator down to the lobby, then paused to take a cigarette from the case in my inside pocket before venturing outside. As I was lighting it, a woman's voice spoke up beside me.

"How are things with Henderson?"

Clicking my lighter shut, I scrutinized her. She was youngish, perhaps in her middle twenties, and had curly dark hair tucked under a red beret. Her face was not unattractive, but an excess of make-up tended to detract from her looks rather than accent them. Big mahogany eyes, perched above a nose slightly too large, met mine frankly. Her red skirt was a bit too short and her white blouse a bit too tight for her Rubenesque figure. She seemed ready for me to rebuff her, but her demeanor suggested she'd have another verbal sortie prepared if I did.

"How do you know I talked to Henderson?"

"Saw you going upstairs with him. Thought I'd wait until you came back down and talk to you." She extended her hand. "I'm Sally Barton."

I took her hand and found the grip as forthright as the gaze.

"Dr. Warman. What's your interest in Henderson?"

She glanced pointedly at the sergeant, who was beginning to take an interest in our discourse. "There's got to be a better place to talk," she said.

I thought a minute—it was nearly lunchtime. I asked, "Do you like chop suey?"

She grinned, and her entire face lit up. She was attractive, after all! "Let's go!" she said.

We headed outside, then walked downtown on Centre Street towards Chinatown. On the way, I learned she was a reporter for the *Evening Graphic*. I knew it as a tabloid of dubious reputation, with *avant garde* political views, animosity towards organized medicine and other mainstream groups. It promulgated sensationalism, though I must confess its lurid headlines and dramatic, front-page photos of politicians and other celebrities caught in compromising positions enticed me to buy more than one copy.

The rain had escalated to a downpour when we reached the venerable Port Arthur, Miss Barton's choice of restaurant. I opened the door and motioned her to precede me up the stairs. The mingled aromas of soy sauce, cabbage, and other aromas unique to Chinese cuisine engulfed me and I was suddenly starving. I gratefully shed my sodden topcoat and fedora, and followed a waiter to one of the inlaid pearl mahogany tables overlooking the Mott Street balcony.

I raised an eyebrow at my companion. "Chop suey?"

"Chow mein!" She said. "It's the best in Chinatown. We'll only need one order for the two of us, unless you're really hungry."

I gave the waiter the order, then nodded to Miss Barton. "You still haven't told me why you're interested in Henderson."

"Did you know he's in charge of the New York Ripper investigation?"

"No. What's that to do with you?"

"Henderson has a reputation with reporters. It's harder to get news out of him than it is to get a cab on Wall Street on a Sunday morning. He's been known to throw reporters in jail just for trying to talk to him."

"So, you want to get thrown in jail?" I was beginning to like this young woman.

"No, silly! I was hoping you were chinning with him about the Ripper case and I could get some news from you."

The waiter arrived with a large teapot and two small, handleless cups. I poured some for Sally, then myself. As I picked up my cup in both hands, to warm them from the chill imparted by the rain, the sweet smell of jasmine engulfed me, causing tears to flow.

"I'm sorry to tell you I wasn't , 'er, chinning with him, about the Ripper case. I don't know much about those murders, other than what I've read in the papers."

"Then you know the cops haven't got to first base. They're saying they have some leads, but nobody can find out what they are."

I watched the rain spattering on the windows overlooking Mott Street, and deliberated. The last thing I wanted for Evie McDowell was bad publicity—she had enough to endure with Colin's sudden disappearance and two young children. On the other hand, I had only Henderson's word that Colin's case was a priority for him. Maybe some publicity would do Colin some good. I made my decision.

"Tell me what you know about the Ripper case, and I'll tell you why I went to see Henderson," I said.

She hauled her oversized purse into her lap, rummaging inside until she produced a marble-covered notebook with a pen clipped to it, other objects falling out on the floor in the process. After picking up her things and depositing the purse (really a small satchel) back under her chair, she placed the pen behind her ear and paged through the book to nearly the middle. She read for a moment.

"He's a sex fiend. He's killed three women so far, all uptown. The bodies were cut up pretty bad, more than it took to kill them, I think, but I've got no corroboration on that. People are really worried, because this kind of thing generally doesn't happen in that kind of neighborhood."

"I knew that from the papers," I told her.

She gave me a sour look. "Well, I've got the names and addresses of the women, and the dates they were killed. I don't have much else, mainly because Henderson's in charge. I told you, he doesn't talk.

"Who were the women?"

"The first one was a Mary Courtney. She was a housewife— husband's a department store manager. She was found on Central Park West a couple of weeks ago. She'd been walking her dog."

"Go on," I prompted.

"The next one, a week later, was Eileen Trulove. Her old man's Simon Trulove, the shipping tycoon. She was killed right in her apartment, which is really scary!"

"Any idea how the killer got in?"

"Nope. The last one was Katherine Willoughby. She was a rich dame too. Her husband's a big-shot uptown attorney. They found her body Thursday morning in Turtle Bay."

I made a mental note to ask Harvey if he knew Willoughby.

"She was killed in her own backyard." Sally shuddered. "It's pretty terrible, isn't it?"

"Were they all about the same age?"

"Yeah, late twenties, early thirties, all pretty ritzy." She paused to take a sip of tea. "What's your angle in this?"

"I don't know that I have an angle in this. A friend of mine turned up missing. His wife asked me to talk to Henderson, since he's apparently been given charge of that case as well. I've had the same experience with him as everyone else has. Didn't tell me anything."

"What's the friend's name?"

"Dr. Colin McDowell. He has an office on Park Avenue."

"That's the neighborhood this bird has been working in, for sure. You think the Ripper has anything to do with him being missing?"

"I don't see how," I said. "Apparently, the Ripper preys on women exclusively. Unless Colin surprised him at his work, or something..." I had a thought. "When was the last killing?"

She looked at her book. "Thursday. Just a couple days ago. When did your man go missing?"

"His wife told me he didn't come home Thursday night." I did not like where this was leading at all. I hesitated, then said, "Henderson asked me about a man named Addison Strangways."

"Who's he?"

"He has an office in Colin's building. Mrs. McDowell told me that Henderson asked her about Strangways as well."

"Now that's some news," Miss Barton said, whipping the pen from behind her ear and scribbling in the notebook.

We stopped the conversation as the chow mein arrived—two large platters, one piled high with crispy fried noodles, a second heaped with chopped meats and vegetables in sauce. There was also a large covered bowl, full of white rice. Miss Barton was quite correct about the portion size; this was ample for both of us. We ladled out food and poured fresh tea, then spent a few minutes satisfying our hunger. I used a fork, but I noticed Miss Barton was quite adept with chopsticks.

"You must eat a lot of Chinese food," I observed.

"A fair bit," she admitted. "It's cheap. If I go by myself, I always have some to take home."

I surmised that she was not recompensed munificently by the *Evening Graphic*.

Clearing my throat, I said, "I don't mind you printing the story of Colin's disappearance. I rather want you to. However, I would appreciate it if you didn't interview his wife. I know as much about the affair as she does, and it's going rather hard with her, right now." Miss Barton gave me a strange look.

"That's fine," she said. "But after it comes out in the papers, somebody's going to try to talk to her, you know."

"I suppose. I'll warn her."

"You have no idea why Henderson's interested in this Strangways?"

"No, I don't."

Sally flipped her notebook to a fresh page. "Well, if you want a story about your missing pal, you'd better give me some background."

I gave her Colin's name and address, and some of his educational history.

"What kind of a doctor is he?" she asked.

"He primarily works with people who have mental and emotional problems, nervous breakdowns, that sort of thing."

"A head-shrinker."

"That's one way of putting it, I suppose." The *Evening Graphic* did not demand first-rate writing skills of its journalists, I surmised. "He is also a research physician."

"What does that mean?"

"That he tries to create new therapies for the disorders he treats. He is a top-notch chemist and pharmacologist."

"Pharma...?"

"That means he tries to create new medicines. He's working in the laboratory of Alexis Carrel at Rockefeller University, who is a Nobel laureate"

"Oh, okay" She scribbled dutifully in her notebook. "What else?"

"He runs a free clinic for the less fortunate in a Settlement house on the Lower East side."

"What's a Settlement house?"

I knew quite a bit about the Settlement movement, thanks to several excellent sermons by Reverend Shoemaker. I told her that the movement had originated in the London slums during the last half of the last century. Its basic premise was for collegiate men to commandeer a building and "settle" in a poor neighborhood, and use their education and skills to aid and instruct the neighborhood residents, while simultaneously learning how the common people lived, away from the affluence and privilege the settlers had known up to that point in their lives. The idea caught on rapidly in America, where women as well as men quickly established settlements in the poorer areas of most of the larger cities and in depressed rural areas as well. The settlers offered classes in English, writing and music, lectures on subjects both practical and abstract, and organized clubs, exhibitions and other activities to bring more refined pastimes to the people they served. The settlements tended to attract more women and children as clients than men, and they came to depend on the settlers for many basic needs—medical care and legal assistance, to name a couple. With its high population of immigrants, the Lower East Side was a natural magnet for the movement.

"Wow!" she said. "This bird is really something! When does he sleep?"

"I suspect he considers sleep a waste of time," I told her truthfully.

"Well, I've got more than I had when I got up this morning," she said philosophically. "Maybe more than anybody else in the city's got right now. I thank you for that, at least."

"What are you going to do now?"

"I've got a meeting this afternoon with a copper. I think he likes me. Maybe I'll get something out of him about Henderson's leads."

"You're going to publish the news about Colin?"

"I'll sure give it to the city editor. I don't know if he'll run it or not, unless I can link it to the Ripper. A lot of people go missing in New York, you know."

"But they're not all of them prominent people."

"You'd be surprised," she said. "Remember Judge Crater?"

"But Colin doesn't have any gangster connections..."

"...that you know of."

I frowned. She was right. What did I really know about Colin McDowell, anyway?

We made small talk as we finished lunch. I learned that she was single and a New Jersey native who'd moved to Manhattan to attend secretarial school. She'd gotten a job with the paper to do shorthand and typing and had worked her way up to reporter.

"I still get the flower shows, the obits and the women's stuff. But I've brought in a real story or two, too. If I get the lowdown on these Ripper killings when nobody else in the city can, they'll have to take me serious, for sure."

I took the check from the waiter. Seventy-five cents. I could see why an aspiring young female reporter ate Chinese a lot. She held out her hand and I gave it to her.

As I helped her with her coat, I said, "Let's stay in touch. I really don't know what else I can do about Colin, except maybe talk to some of his colleagues at Rockefeller, and I expect the police will do that. Maybe you can ask your police friend this afternoon."

"I'll let you know," she promised.

We parted company in front of the Port Arthur. The rain was still falling. I decided to head for the Bowery and splurge for a taxicab; I wouldn't have to wait for the train. I resolved to spend the rest of the afternoon in a hot tub, then in bed.

The Legacy of the Unborn

CHAPTER 3

From the notebook of Sally Barton

Saturday, September 26, 1931, 12:30 p.m.

It sure was a stroke of luck running into Dr. Warman. I never would have gotten Henderson to talk, but Warman sang like a canary! I'm certain I've heard of this Addison Strangways, but can't remember where. I've got a couple of hours before I meet Moscowicz, so I'm going to run by the paper and check the morgues to see what we've got on him.

Saturday, September 26, 1931, 2:00 p.m.

I was right! Here are the articles.

The Legacy of the Unborn

July 12, 1926—*New York Evening Graphic*

Prominent Obstetrician Accused of Assaulting Patient

The prominent obstetrician, Dr. Addison Strangways, who has his office in an exclusive neighborhood in the East Sixties, has been accused of assault by one of his patients. Dr. Strangways was arrested late last night and released on his own recognizance early this morning. A source in the Manhattan District Attorney's Office confirmed that Dr. Strangways will be prosecuted to the fullest extent of the law.

February 9, 1927—New York Evening Graphic

Obstetrician Cleared of Charges

The Manhattan District Attorney's office confirmed today that it had dropped all charges against the prominent obstetrician, Dr. Addison Strangways, who was accused of assault by a former patient. Evidence of the accuser's mental imbalance presented at the trial by Strangways' attorney caused the judge to dismiss the charges as baseless. "As far as I am concerned," said the Hon. Justice Stephen Hill, "Dr. Strangways is totally exonerated of any wrongdoing." It is unknown whether the Doctor will return to his practice in Manhattan's exclusive Lenox Hill neighborhood, or if the charges have damaged his reputation sufficiently to make that impossible. It is also unclear at this time if Dr. Strangways will seek legal redress against his accuser.

Either I can't read between the lines, or Strangways tried to diddle one of his patients, then got some wise guy shyster to get him off the hook. He's obviously taken a powder, or Henderson would have slapped him in the Tombs by now. No wonder Henderson's got him tabbed for a sex fiend! Now I've really got some questions for Moscowicz. I need to remember to do some more digging on Strangways, too.

Saturday, September 26, 1931, 4:45 p.m.

I'm sitting here at the Bellevue Inn after my gab fest with Moscowicz, staring out at the turrets of the hospital across the street. This case gets stranger and stranger, and not just because of old Addison Strangways!

I wondered why Moscowicz wanted to meet here instead of downtown, since he works out of Centre Street. I figured he didn't want it getting back to Henderson that he was jawing with me, especially if I wrote something I wasn't supposed to know about. Turns out that was only part of the reason.

Moscowicz said five o'clock, but I got here a little early. Sure enough, he hadn't arrived yet. The Bellevue Inn is a tiny place, but it does a real good business because it's close to the hospital, and it's likely to be crowded at any hour of the day with interns, nurses and other medical types. It's a great place to pick up gossip about Bellevue.

What they say about Chinese food must be true, because I sure was hungry again. I had Pete make me a double-decker and got an egg cream to go with it while I was waiting for Moscowicz. I had most of it gone and a cigarette lit by the time he blew in.

It wasn't hard to know when Moscowicz came in. Even if I hadn't been watching the door, I'd have known when everyone else turned to look. Moscowicz is a big guy —I mean, a really big guy. He probably played football or something when he was a kid; it looks like he used to have a lot of muscle but now it's mostly fat. I had gotten a table instead of a booth because you can move a table. Moscowicz, he could never squeeze into a booth, no way.

I waved and he saw me and came right over. He's not a bad looking Joe; his nose and ears are as big as the rest of him and I suppose he's what you'd call homely, but just looking at that mug of his makes you smile, and he'll smile right back when he sees you.

He was smiling now. "Good to see you, Barton," he said.

That's one of the things I like about Moscowicz. He'd call a male reporter by his last name and he don't treat me no different because I'm a dame. I think he likes me, though.

"Hey, Moscowicz! Waddaya know?"

He grabbed the chair, turned it bass-ackwards and sat. I guess that must be more comfortable for him than perching on the edge and trying to get those long legs of his under a little table.

"Not a damned thing," he said, answering my question. "What's up with you?"

"Just looking for the latest scoop on the Ripper killings. Thought you might know something."

His face got a little less jovial. "Thought they had you on cat shows and stuff like that, Barton. Why are you fooling with this Ripper thing?"

"C'mon Moscowicz, you know why! Why ain't you pounding a beat no more?"

He plainly wasn't happy. "That's Henderson's case, not mine."

"Why do you think I came to you? Can't get nothing out of Henderson."

He sat silently for a minute.

"You want a cup of joe?" I asked him. "You like it regular, right?"

He nodded. I got up and went over to the counter to order. I could have waved for the waitress, but I wanted to give him a minute or two by himself. I knew I was putting him on the spot.

I watched the waitress pour the coffees and add milk and sugar to each. I carried them back to the table and gave him his, then sat and lighted another cigarette.

"I know Henderson's on to Addison Strangways," I told him, wanting to get him off the hook a little. "I know Strangways had some sex trouble a while back, too. That what put Henderson on to him?"

"I think," he agreed, "Henderson don't talk to us cops anymore than he talks to you reporters, you know."

"He got anything else on Strangways? Or is he just fishing?"

"Maybe. Scuttlebutt is, all the victims were connected with Strangways. Maybe patients, or something. That didn't come from Henderson. Or from me," he added.

I consulted my notes. "I hear the victims were cut up bad. A lot more than it took to kill them."

"Well, I guess there's a reason they're calling him the Ripper," he said, "but I don't know anything about the condition of the bodies. That'd be in the coroner's reports, and Henderson's got those locked down tight."

"What about a bird named Colin McDowell?"

"What about him?"

"He's missing. Missing since the same night the Ripper got his last one, and from the same neck of the woods."

"Missing? You don't say!" Moscowicz's eyes brightened.

"You know him?"

"No, but I've got me a missing person, too. Or a found one, that is, with nobody to claim him. That's what I wanted to talk to you about."

I nodded at him to go on.

"Guy was spotted by the beat man in Chatham Square in the wee hours Friday morning. Half-naked, beat up, generally in a real bad way. We brought him up here to Bellevue. He's here right now, in a coma." He said *comer*. "Think he's this McDowell?"

I thought about it. "Probably not. Chatham Square's a ways from Park Avenue."

"You know this McDowell?"

"No. But I know somebody who does," I added. "How come you ain't heard of McDowell?"

"Is it Henderson's case?"

I nodded.

"I told you he doesn't talk, even to cops." He took a drink of his coffee. "When can we get this guy up here?"

"How do you know it's a guy?" I teased him. I shouldn't.

"Whatever." He didn't think it was funny.

"I can call him now."

25

He thought a minute. "Look," he said, "Joe's not going anywhere, including the cemetery, the docs say, for the next few hours. I was going home after this, for a rest and a change of clothes. I been up since five a.m."

I felt sorry for him.

"Can you call your guy and have him here by, let's say, eight?"

I nodded.

"You got my number," he said. "Call if he gives you trouble, and I'll handle it."

"I don't think he will," I said. "This McDowell is his pal."

"Good," he said, getting up and putting the chair back. "So long, Barton."

"So long, Moscowicz." I watched him walk out the door to First Avenue.

I know he wants to go out with me. Maybe I should go. He's a good egg, Moscowicz is.

CHAPTER 4

The Statement of Dr. Ebeneezer Warman

It was after 2:00 when I finally returned to my flat. I was cold and wet, and the interview with Henderson had left a bad taste in my mouth. In the bathroom, I turned on the hot water in the tub full blast, then shed my damp clothes while the room filled with steam. I ran the water till it turned cold, then let it run a little longer until the temperature in the bath was just tolerable. I climbed in and slid down until the water rose to my chin. It was just right, hot enough to actually lower my blood pressure, and produce a feeling of light-headedness, but not quite hot enough to scald.

I must have dozed. The water was nearly tepid, and I do not usually like to let it get that cold before I either run in more hot water, or get out of the tub. I did the latter, and as I opened the bathroom door after drying off, I heard the phone ringing. I thought briefly about letting it ring, then it occurred to me that it might be Evie. I hurried to pick it up.

It was Harvey. He had symphony tickets for this evening, did I want to join him? Of course! We arranged to meet at Town Hall at 7:30; we would discuss where we would go for our post-concert victuals later. After hanging up I reflected that, even though my fishing trip had been spoiled, it was fortunate that I had arranged for Prather to cover my rounds for the weekend. I could have a bit of a vacation, after all! I resolved to celebrate with an afternoon nap, a luxury in which I am seldom able to indulge.

The phone was jangling again. I had that wooly-headed feeling that arises from being startled out of a deep sleep; it took me a moment to locate the handset on the nightstand. I'm afraid I wasn't very pleasant as I answered.

"Yes."

"Dr. Warman. It's Sally Barton."

"What do you want?" I grumbled. I was still waking up.

"I have some news, Doctor. Maybe about your pal, Dr. McDowell." That woke me.

"What about Colin?"

"I talked to that policeman friend of mine, like I said I was going to at lunch. He has a man here at Bellevue they found roaming around in a fog Friday morning. He's hurt kinda bad. Moscowicz, that's my pal, thinks you should take a look at him."

"When?"

"About eight or so?"

Damn! "What time is it now?"

"Almost six-thirty."

I had really been out! There was no way I was going to do this, and be able to meet Harvey for the concert. I briefly considered telling her to call Evie instead, then I was ashamed.

"All right. Where shall I meet you?"

"There's a little place called the Bellevue Inn right across from the hospital on 1ˢᵗ Avenue. I been here most of the afternoon—Pete must think I'm gonna move in. You might as well meet me here."

"Very well." I rang off.

Naturally, I couldn't get Harvey on the phone. He must have left early to have a bite, or run errands. I called the box office at Town Hall and left a message that I would try to arrive late and pick up my ticket when I got there. Then I set about getting dressed and out of the flat.

28

The rain had all but stopped, but it was still damp, and the city had that unpleasant, sweet sewer smell that comes after a rain. I took the el down to 23rd Street, then headed east to 1st Avenue on foot, where I saw the great, crenellated hulk of Bellevue on the east side of the street, looming before me. It took only a moment to locate the tiny coffee shop on the other side.

Sally was at a table in the back. She rose to greet me.

"Waddaya say, Dr. Warman!"

"Hello, Miss Barton." I made no move to sit down. "Where is this fellow who may be Colin McDowell?"

"We gotta wait for Detective Moscowicz. He shouldn't be long. Have you eaten? They have swell double-deckers here."

I realized that I had not eaten since our lunch in Chinatown.

"I suppose I should have something, at that. Double-deckers, you say?"

"The best in town, and only 45 cents. Cost you six bits, anywhere else. I'll get 'em."

She signaled the waitress and placed the order. I smiled. I really was beginning to like this independent young lady.

The sandwiches arrived shortly and were indeed, as Sally put it, swell. By the time they were consumed, we were Eben and Sally instead of Miss Barton and Dr. Warman.

"Oh, here he is." Sally said.

I looked toward the entrance and saw one of the largest men I had ever seen, coming toward us. He stood at least six foot six and went over three hundred pounds, easily. He was dressed in a rumpled brown suit of good manufacture (he must have had them custom made) and wore a white shirt with a nondescript tie. He appeared somewhat acromegalic, with the characteristic large features and protruding jaw. He was smiling broadly (at Sally, I suppose) as he made his way to our table.

"Moscowicz, waddaya say!"

I rose as he approached.

"Dr. Ebeneezer Warman, Detective Moscowicz of the New York Police Department," Sally said.

My hand was engulfed in his. I winced involuntarily, but his grip was firm, not painful.

"Glad to know you, Doctor," he said. "Thanks for coming."

"If you have found my friend, Detective Moscowicz, it is I who shall be thanking you."

"Well, I don't know about that, Doctor. This egg turned up about the same time your friend disappeared."

"Well, let's go take a look at him, Detective. I have a concert ticket waiting if this isn't Colin."

Sally left money for the sandwiches on the table. I wanted to protest. I probably had ten times the funds that she did, but I thought she would take it rather badly if I didn't accept her treat, so I kept silent. We went out and crossed the street to Bellevue.

Darkness had fallen. We headed for the center drive and entered the hospital complex through a tunnel, then continued past a low gray building on the left. The saccharine, metallic smell of the East River made my stomach roil as we walked a long block in front of the main hospital building. We passed under an awning to enter a lighted doorway.

A fellow in a starched white hospital jacket greeted Detective Moscowicz.

"Hello, Moe, waddaya know?" He leered as if he was terribly clever.

"Hello, Eddie," said Moscowicz. "We've come to see the John Doe you admitted the other night."

"We finally got him moved up to the ward after you left this afternoon, Moe. I'll get Miss Fisher to take you."

Moscowicz protested that we could find our own way, but Eddie summoned a young woman in a nurse's uniform.

"Take these good people to see that fella we sent upstairs this afternoon," Eddie told her. She smiled a smile that would melt an ice block, and led us away.

I, for one, was glad she was with us. I had been to Bellevue only a few times, and while I knew it was big, I don't think I had an appreciation of how enormous it truly was until that evening. The place was a city within a city; Miss Fisher led us through several interconnected buildings and we rode on two different elevators. I was certain that I could not find my way back to the door we entered by. She showed us into a huge ward, which contained about two dozen wrought-iron beds, half on either side. A large ladder, with a man perched atop it, was set up in the center of the room. He was busily engaged in replacing a bulb in a light fixture at least fifteen feet overhead. Miss Fisher stopped, then moved to the side and squeezed through the narrow space between the ladder and one of the beds, rather than walk under the ladder. Moscowicz stopped also, then looked at us ruefully.

"What's a guy to do?" He said. He had to turn sideways and duck to fit under the ladder. Sally and I looked at each other and grinned, then walked under the ladder as well. *One for all and all for one*, I thought.

We approached a bed near the far end of the ward. The figure huddled within was very still. I could see that his heavily bandaged hands were on his stomach; they had obviously been placed in that artificial position. I held my breath as I moved closer so I could see his face.

Moscowicz stared at me eagerly.

"This is not Colin McDowell," I said. "I have never seen this man before in my life."

Moscowicz looked downcast. "Well, I should have guessed it wouldn't be that easy," he said.

The man in the bed appeared to be in late middle age. He had leathery, weather-beaten features, as if he'd spent considerable time outdoors. Dark hair peeped out from bandages wound around his head. His face was bruised and lacerated. I regarded the chart at the foot of his bed.

"Whoever this gentleman is, he's been badly treated," I said. "Was he beaten?"

"We think so," said Moscowicz. "He had a bad bump on the back of his head, like somebody sapped him, and his hands was all banged up like he'd been in a fistfight. They took a ton of splinters out of them, like maybe he was fending off somebody with a board. When they found him, he had no shoes even. His feet were cut up something terrible. This day and age, people will still kill you for your shoes."

I motioned them away from the bed, out of the patient's earshot, after perusing the chart. "Well, he's in a bad way," I said. "He may have a brain injury. The doctors here have him on a large dose of Luminal to keep him sedated. He may not live the night."

"That's too bad," said Sally. "Helluva way to go, in a place like this, nobody even knows your name."

Her dispirited tone made me sorry I'd spoken so clinically.

"On the other hand, he may pull through after all," I reassured her. "The brain is a funny thing. It can shut itself down when it's been badly abused, sometimes for days, weeks, or even months, while it heals. Then the patient wakes up like nothing was ever wrong with him." I turned to Moscowicz. "Is there anything else I can do for you, Detective?"

"I don't think so," said Moscowicz. "I'm just sorry it's not your pal."

"I'm sorry, as well, Sergeant."

"Just because Eben couldn't identify him for you doesn't mean you don't owe me one, Moscowicz," Sally said.

"What do you mean?" He eyed her suspiciously.

"The coroner's office is here at Bellevue, ain't it?"

"So what?"

"So howsabout a look at the coroner's reports on the Ripper's victims?"

The lady had brass!

"I don't know about that," Moscowicz said.

"C'mon.," she pushed him, "maybe Eben here can tell you something about it you haven't figgered out yet. He's a sawbones, you know."

Moscowicz and I spoke simultaneously.

"It's not my case..." Moscowicz said.

"I have a concert to attend..." I reminded her.

"Then you can't get in trouble for spillin' the beans," she said to the detective. Where was the logic in that? "C'mon, Moe, do it for me," she wheedled. She turned and looked at me soulfully with those big, brown puppy dog eyes of hers. "It'll only take a few minutes, Eben," she said, as if Moscowicz had already agreed to the plan. "Moscowicz, waddaya say?"

The big detective plainly did not want to go along with her, but, just as plainly, was very reluctant to tell her no. I thought I knew why.

"If you find out anything, you can't print it," Moscowicz said. "Henderson's too good a detective not to figger out where it came from, and I'll be back pounding a beat."

"I won't print it unless I can verify it from another source. Then I'll quote that source instead, and you're off the hook. Waddaya say?" She had him, and from the look on his face, he knew it.

"I can't swear that we'll be able to get them," he said, "but I'll see. Let's go."

She looked expectantly at me. I hated arriving anywhere late, especially to a concert, where I'd have to wait in the lobby until intermission before being allowed to my seat. I glanced at my watch. No matter what I did, I was going to be late. Maybe I could meet Harvey for supper afterwards. I must confess I had a somewhat morbid attraction to this Ripper case.

"All right," I said, "but I want to be out of here in an hour."

"Swell! Let's go!"

Miss Fisher had left us while we were examining the man in the bed. We were on our own.

"We'll have to get back outside," said Moscowicz. "I can find the morgue from there."

We wandered out into the hall and back to the elevator, which we rode to the ground floor, where we found an exit to the outside. After Moscowicz got his bearings, he confidently led the way back toward First Avenue, then to another entrance to the hospital complex on 29th Street. We soon found ourselves in front of a desk occupied by a white-coated functionary, smoking a cigarette and reading a magazine with a garish cover that depicted a buxom young woman shying away from an evil-looking oriental threatening her with a large curved knife.

"Are any of the medical examiners on tonight?" Moscowicz asked him.

He looked bored. "Steinman is. He's busy, though. Doing an autopsy."

"I'm Detective Moscowicz. I need to see some autopsy reports. Do you know when he'll be through?"

"Got a buzzer?" the man asked.

Moscowicz showed him his badge.

"He should be finished soon. He started a couple hours ago. You can go in, or wait here."

"We'll wait," said Moscowicz. "Steinman can't help us till he's done with his cutting, anyhow. Where is he?"

The man waved at a set of double doors. "Room three."

Moscowicz gestured to us to follow, then proceeded through the double doors. "The autopsy rooms are down here," he said.

We followed a long, dreary hall, painted institutional green. Lamps in cages hung from the vaulted ceiling every few feet and the walls were penetrated by double doors at regular intervals. Moscowicz peered through a tiny window in one set.

"He's in here," he said; "we'll just wait till he comes out."

I was tempted to remind him that I'd only promised him an hour, but I decided to keep silent for a little while. It was only a few minutes before the doors swung open and a short fellow wearing hospital scrubs appeared.

"Steinman?" said Moscowicz.

"Moscowicz! What brings you here at this evil hour?"

"We'd like to see some autopsy reports."

Steinman regarded the three of us carefully. "It can't wait till tomorrow, or Monday?"

Moscowicz shook his head.

"I can't stay to interpret them for you," Steinman said. "I'm already late for an appointment."

I knew how he felt.

Moscowicz indicated me with a beefy arm. "This is Dr. Warman. He speaks your lingo."

"Which ones do you want to see?"

"The ones for the Ripper killings."

Steinman looked at Moscowicz critically, not responding right away. Then he said, "Okay, I'll pull them for you. You can use my office. Just leave them on the desk when you're through and I'll put them away tomorrow."

We followed the little doctor down the hallway. He indicated a door with a frosted glass window and said, "This is my office. Go in and make yourselves comfortable. I'll be back in a few minutes with the reports."

We did as he suggested. After we had closed the door behind us, Moscowicz said,

"I'll bet he knows this is not my case. If he says anything to Henderson, I'm in trouble."

Sally came over to him, took his hand in both of hers and gazed sweetly at his face with those deadly brown eyes.

"I really appreciate this, Moscowicz."

The look the big detective gave her was truly pathetic.

There were only two chairs in the office. Moscowicz motioned me to the desk chair and Sally to the other one. As he perched his large frame on the edge of the desk. I reflected on the daily difficulties of living in a world too small for you. Momentarily, the door opened and Steinman entered, carrying three manila folders.

"I told Henry to put on a pot of coffee for you. Just ask him and he'll show you where it is." He handed me the folders. "I assume you'll know what to do with these. I'm going to change and go patch up my love life. Need anything else?" He looked at each of us in turn. "Very well, then." He left the office.

I regarded the three hefty folders. No way was I going to meet Harvey for an *aprés* concert meal, if I had to wade through those.

"I have to make a phone call," picking up the receiver on the desk.

"You want we should leave?" asked Moscowicz.

I shook my head. It was only a moment before I had someone at Town Hall and left a message for Harvey, with my regrets. I was going to have to patch things up with him tomorrow, too. Then I lighted a cigarette and took one of the folders.

Almost two hours had passed before I had finished reading the three reports. Both Sally and Moscowicz had tried to do likewise, but the former gave up quickly upon encountering some photographs of the post-mortem. Moscowicz persisted for a while, then volunteered to go for coffee and sandwiches. Sally decided to accompany him, so I was left alone with my reading.

It was certainly gruesome stuff. I had never seen the particulars of the original Jack the Ripper murders, but I couldn't imagine anyone doing a more thorough job of evisceration than this fellow had done. All of the internal organs had been meticulously removed as if for a dissection, arranged in a definite pattern around the bodies and of all things, *sprinkled with salt*! That certainly conjured up a disturbing association. Then I noticed a certain organ was missing from the crime scene in the case I was reading about. I reached for another report to see if a pattern was there, then for the third. It was there, all right. My blood turned cold.

The aroma of coffee filled the room as the door opened to admit my companions. Sally deposited a white paper sack on the desk in front of me, along with a cup of coffee.

"I didn't know how you take your joe, Eben," she said. "I hope regular's okay."

I really didn't feel like eating, given my current reading material, but the coffee was welcome. I decided to say nothing about my discovery until I had thoroughly examined all three reports.

Finally, I was done. I put down the last report and cleared my throat. Sally and Moscowicz looked up expectantly.

"This is a very demented individual doing these things," I began.

"Is he a sex fiend?" asked Sally.

"I don't know, really. Criminal pathology is not one of my specialties. But I don't think so. If there was just one victim, I'd say it was someone who was very, very angry at her. Since it's three, so far, it might be someone who's very angry at all women."

"What makes you say that, Doc?" said Moscowicz.

"Because of the violence done to the bodies, after death. The ladies appear to have been killed most efficiently in each case, with a single knife thrust, directly to the heart through the ribs from the back. The rest of the damage appears to have been done *post mortem*."

Sally shuddered. "Those pictures..."

"He cut them up pretty bad," Moscowicz agreed.

"Yes, he did. The medical examiner thinks that there was first a flurry of stabbing at the dead bodies, followed by a more protracted and meticulous episode of evisceration."

"You mean he gutted them," Sally said.

"Essentially. The organs were removed and left outside of the body, as in an autopsy. But there was one organ that was never accounted for at the crime scene in any of the three cases," I paused. "The uterus."

They looked confused.

"But why would he take that?" Moscowicz said.

"My God!" I suddenly had a horrible thought. "Strangways was an obstetrician!"

"So?" said Moscowicz.

I tried not to look at Sally. "I wonder if any of them was pregnant?"

A cold silence suffused the room. I reached inside my jacket for cigarettes, took one out and lighted it. The other two did likewise.

Finally Sally broke the silence, "If they were pregnant, wouldn't that be in the report?"

"Not necessarily. With the uterus missing, and if the woman was in the early stages, given the damage done to the body, other signs of pregnancy could easily be missed, especially if the doctor wasn't looking for them."

"I wonder if we could find out?" said Sally. She turned to Moscowicz. "You said they were all Strangways' patients?"

He shook his head. "I don't know. I think they might have been, but Henderson isn't talking."

Suddenly Sally said, "I can find out! I'll talk to their husbands!"

Both Moscowicz and I looked at her with disapproval, but she seemed not to notice.

"I can maybe confirm a lot of what we found out here tonight from the husbands! Then you're off the hook if I print it, Moscowicz!"

I decided I did not want Sally Barton's job, now or ever.

"I'm not sure that any of this has gotten me any closer to discovering what happened to Colin," I said, rearranging the reports in their folders and stacking them neatly on the desk, "but I really need to be getting on." I rose, stretching my muscles, sore after hours in that chair.

"Sally, can I take you home?" asked Moscowicz.

She waited a moment before answering. "I don't think I'm going straight home, Moscowicz. It might be kinda hard to sleep for a while. Especially after seeing those pictures! Ugh! But thanks for asking."

I was gratified that she included that last, but nevertheless, the big detective looked as if someone had hit him in the stomach. I realized that I was no longer sure whether I liked Sally Barton very much at all.

We left the morgue and walked out to First Avenue, where we said our goodbyes. I left them in front of the hospital and I struck off for the train on Second Avenue, and home.

Silas K. Henderson

CHAPTER 5

From the notebook of Sally Barton

Saturday, September 26, 1931, 11:30 p.m.

After Eben left, me and Moscowicz talked a while in front of Bellevue. He wanted to take me out for something to eat, but something to eat wasn't what I wanted. What I wanted was a drink, and I wasn't about to take a flatfoot to a speak, at least not somebody I didn't know well. He had a real hangdog look on his face when we finally split up. I'm going to go out with him real soon, even if I have to ask him.

I didn't feel like drinking alone though, so I thought I'd head up to the fly beat and see if I could shake some company loose. Besides, I wanted to ask around and find out what news was on the street about the Ripper killings. I had the feeling that, after what Eben told us about the autopsy reports, I had the makings of an exclusive.

I walked down to 23rd and caught the cross-town car, then hopped on the Sixth Avenue el. In spite of the hour, the train was crowded. It was nearly midnight; the shows were letting out and people heading for a late dinner—some, I'm sure, were just now venturing out for the first time tonight to take in a night club or a speak. This was what I really loved about New York—even in the middle of the night, it's just so alive, and it was comforting to have all those people around me just now. If I shut my eyes I could still see those damn pictures from the autopsy files. God! How could one person do that do another?

I got off the train at Times Square. As I came down the stairs from the platform I was squinting against the glare of the marquee lights that lit the streets as bright as daylight. I had to shove my way through the crowd to make my way north along 6th Avenue. At 47th Street I turned toward the Hudson, and the crowd thinned out immediately. I picked up my pace. It felt good to stretch my legs after all the time I spent cooped up today, in Bellevue and on the train, so I really hoofed it. After a few blocks, the green globes of the old Tenderloin precinct glowed a warm welcome ahead. I turned right into the brownstone directly across the street and followed a dark flight of stairs downward. I pulled open the heavy door to the basement and the smell of cigarette smoke, mixed with coffee and sweat, rushed out into my face. Typewriters rattled like a regiment of tommy guns and the jangling of telephones was so loud as to set your teeth on edge. I smiled. I was home!

The basement room, lit by a bunch of naked bulbs dangling overhead, was crammed with as many cheap wooden desks as it could hold, with just enough room left to walk between them. Each desk had at least one typewriter and a phone, some had two of each. Each desk was manned by at least one reporter, either pounding madly on the keys or shouting into a receiver, the fingers of the other hand jammed in his ear so he could hear the person on the other end of the line over the hubbub. This was the fly beat—the district reporters' headquarters. These are the guys who are supposed to get the scoop on any big story that breaks in the district, then phone it to the rewrite man in the city room, allowing the news to hit the street as quickly as possible, and get it all done without letting the other boys know a thing about it. Sometimes it actually happens that way!

Marc McGrath waved as I sidled among the desks. Marc's been here nearly forty years and knows as much about the goings-on in this

City as anybody alive. I smiled inwardly. I'll bet he didn't know what I did about the Ripper.

I scanned the crowd, looking for Charlie Killarney. I knew he'd be here, but not where—only McGrath and one or two others have regular desks; for the rest, it's catch as catch can. Finally, I spied Charlie and caught his eye, brought my hand to my lips and threw my head back, downing an imaginary shot. He nodded, then pointed at the phone and grimaced. His editor, most likely.

Charlie is fat, old and bald, and I love him like a father. Sure, he tried to discourage me from trying to be a "real" reporter, but I really think it was because he didn't want to see me get hurt. When he figured out what a thick skin I had, he changed his tune and started to teach me what he knew. Never gives up trying to get under my skirt, either, the old goat! He hasn't been around quite as long as McGrath, but he knows a lot, Charlie does.

By the time I got to his desk he was hanging up the phone and reaching for his coat and hat. We didn't even try to talk until we got out of that basement; we'd have had to yell to be heard over the ruckus. On reaching the street, we both turned right by unspoken agreement, and walked a quick block. Down a flight of stairs, a rap on a door and a peephole sprang open. No password was needed—Charlie Killarney was known by every doorman in Midtown, and more than a few knew me, too. Inside, the speakeasy smelled like wood, leather, tobacco and hooch; I hope when I die that smell's in my nose! Alf had 'em waiting by the time we reached the bar—a shot and a chaser for Charlie and a rye highball for me. Charlie knocked down his shot standing at the bar and signaled for another, then picked up both glasses and the bottle before following me to a table.

"So waddaya know, Barton?" Charlie was wheezing like an old Model T from our brisk walk here.

"A little, Charlie. How you been?"

"Terrible!" said Charlie. "I told Hurwitz, I gotta get off this night beat! It's killin' me! Start comin' in nine to five; eatin' and sleepin' reg'lar. I been with that rag long enough, they owe it to me!" He downed the second shot, topped off again, then extracted a cheap cheroot from an inner pocket of his jacket.

I smiled. Charlie'd been singing that tune as long as I'd known him and he was as likely to give up the night beat as Henderson was to give me an exclusive.

"What do you hear about the Ripper, Charlie? Anything new?"

"I told you last I saw you, you shouldn't be digging in that, Barton! It ain't nothing for a frail!" Having lit the cigar, he tossed off another shot and half of his chaser. " 'Sides, it's Henderson's case. Nobody's got bupkes!" He paused, then cocked an eye at me shrewdly, " 'Cept you, maybe?"

I don't know how the hell he does it, but I've seldom been able to hide anything from Charlie. Oh, I wasn't going to tell him what I'd got, but I knew there was no way to keep him from knowing I had something. That's why he's the reporter he is.

"Maybe." I said. I took a swig of my highball, then lit a cigarette to give me a little time. I knew I had to give him something if I wanted anything back. "Maybe a missing person case that ties in." I told him about Colin McDowell.

"You think this doc caught the Ripper at it, and maybe the Ripper got him too? Pretty thin, Barton, pretty damn thin!"

"Who was it told me a good newshound runs every lead, no matter how thin, Charlie? Where did I hear that?"

"I wouldn't know," said Charlie with a perfectly straight face. He downed yet another shot, refilled, then tried to pour more into my glass. I covered it with a hand and waved to Alf with the other. Another drink would be good, but straight whiskey I didn't need.

"Has anybody got anything from the husbands?" This was what I really needed to know—I didn't want to hash up old ground, and I could use some pointers on how to approach them.

"Not much," replied Charlie. "Courtney's a nervous wreck, still in the hospital, last I heard. And Henderson's supposedly wised up Willoughby about talking to the press. He might be worth a try anyway, though." He paused to drain his glass again, then added, "I hear Trulove's mad as hell. Not talking to nobody no more."

"Mad?" I prompted him.

"As hell! I hear he took a poke at Evans from the News."

"How come?"

"I guess Evans asked him some pointed questions about what he was doing when his wife got the shiv. Didn't like it nohow."

"Anything there?"

"Maybe. Maybe not. Maybe a dame would have a better chance to find out than a Joe would." He looked at me again. "What else you got, Barton?"

"Nothin'," I lied.

"Yes you do, Barton, you know you do. You can't keep old Charlie Killarney in the dark."

Maybe it was the booze, or the stress, but suddenly, I got it. "Oh, get off it, Charlie!" I told him. "I think you say that whether you think I've got something or not, just to see if I'll look guilty. Don't you?"

Now he was the one who looked guilty! Sonuvagun!

"Well, you really shouldn't play poker for a livin', Barton," he said.

I grinned. I'd learned one of his tricks, sure enough.

"Maybe you shouldn't either, Charlie. And you shouldn't drink any more of that rotgut if you want to get home tonight."

"Maybe you'll just have to take me home with you!" The old lecher smirked.

It didn't sound like a bad idea, though I knew he'd misunderstand if I said yes. It was just that, even after two strong highballs, I still couldn't get those damn pictures out of my head.

CHAPTER 6

The Statement of Dr. Ebeneezer Warman

It was well past eleven when I reached home after my discouraging excursion to Bellevue. I was tired, and out-of-sorts, the result of twin disappointments—that the unknown patient was not Colin, and missing the concert. I was also deeply disturbed by the autopsy reports. As a doctor, I have seen my share of trauma, some of it deliberately inflicted, but this Ripper case was unusual in several respects. Despite the violent, almost random, stabbing of the bodies, both the manner of death in each case and the comprehensive eviscerations had a fiendish deliberation about them, something very difficult to reconcile with a random street thug who held a grudge against women. And what delusion could account for the misappropriation of the *uteri*? I could well imagine why Henderson suspected Strangways, a doctor, although I could not conceive of anything that could cause one who dedicated his life to the good of humanity to go so terribly wrong. Again, I wondered if any of the unfortunate ladies had been pregnant.

The Legacy of the Unborn

In my younger days, I had occasion to terminate a pregnancy for a young woman who convinced me that she had made a great mistake and that it would be a hideous injustice should she suffer societal opprobrium as a consequence of her actions. Since her pregnancy was not too far along, I had little moral difficulty with the operation, and even less fear that I would be held to account for it either in this life or in the hereafter; both the lady and I had a vested interest in discretion, and were of a social class where such things would not be investigated very closely. But I was mightily sorry for what I had done when I observed its subsequent effects. Even though my friend initially expressed her undying gratitude to me, I watched as she developed a great *melancholia* over the next several weeks. She tried to carry on with her former life, but it was no good; she gradually withdrew into herself, abandoning her friends and activities she had once found diverting. Her demeanor steadily worsened until, impelled by pleas from her mother (who had been a willing party to our scheme) and my own worries, I confronted her. She told me that she had nearly given up hope of ever having a normal life again and confided that she often woke from a sound sleep to the noise of a baby crying; while she understood intellectually that this was a delusion, it nevertheless took its toll. I tried to tell her that the fetus we had terminated wasn't really a child yet, that she had nothing to feel guilty about, but I could see that my argument had little effect. I recommended a good psychiatrist to her mother, and it was well that I did. The doctor was able to prevent her suicide, but the unfortunate girl still resides in a psychiatric hospital and the prognosis is not favorable. I do not blame myself for any of this, for I truly believe that the lady wanted that pregnancy to end very much, but in light of subsequent events, I cannot help but wonder how much worse it could have been for her, social opprobrium and all, had the child been born instead. When asked to perform the same procedure again some years later, I politely declined. I have always regretted that I did not say no that first time. Could the unfortunate Strangways have had a similar experience, or one even more tragic, which had unhinged him somehow? It might bear looking into.

What was I thinking! I became involved in this affair because of Evie's concern for Colin; why get wrapped up in this Ripper business? That was a police matter. I decided that a little help sleeping would not be amiss. I took my cigarette case, a snifter and a bottle of cognac into the living room before retiring. I couldn't get those autopsy reports out of my mind, however. I was more than a little tipsy when I finally went to bed; my sleep was troubled and filled with dreams, none of which I could remember upon waking.

It was my custom to meet Harvey for church each Sunday. That morning, I really didn't want to go—cognac causes a more painful hangover than most alcoholic beverages, and the one I woke to was full blown. But I knew I was already in Dutch with Harvey, and should I be absent from church with no explanation, the situation would only worsen. I dragged myself out of bed into the bathroom and began the ablutions necessary for my transformation into social acceptability. I swallowed a bromide and a couple of aspirin, resisting the temptation of a prairie oyster—it wouldn't do to arrive at church smelling like a distillery.

The congregation met at the civilized hour of eleven, so I had ample time. A pot of black coffee made me feel well enough to attempt a little breakfast. That in turn, made the idea of getting into my church-going apparel much less repugnant.

Services were at Madison Avenue Methodist, at 60th Street. I found the day to be glorious as I stepped out onto 66th Street, cool and clear with a steady breeze off the water. Now I wanted to skip the service for an entirely different reason! Maybe I could convince Harvey that, aprés luncheon, a stroll in Central Park would not be amiss. It took a regrettably short time to walk approximately a dozen blocks between my flat and the church. I entered and looked toward the pew we customarily occupied, and sure enough, there was Harvey. He was turned around, chatting up a young woman in the pew behind. I did not recognize her. As I approached them, I could see that she had that look on her face—the one that so many young ladies acquire in Harvey's presence. He doesn't seem to realize what his looks do to women, but his thin lips, pencil mustache, aquiline features and jet-black hair worn slicked back would be envied by many a film star. Any number of belles in Manhattan would love to snare him. He cast a deprecatory glance in my direction as I sidled in next to him, then continued his conversation with the young lady as if I had never arrived. Fine. I expected as much after last night's debacle. The organ announced the beginning of the service. I picked up the hymnal and found the proper page.

The service seemed interminable. The chill emanating from Harvey was palpable as Reverend Shoemaker droned on and on with one of his political diatribes, which had become more frequent of late. His effort to make religion more immediate and relevant to our lives, I supposed. As he expounded at length on our sacred duties to the disenfranchised during these difficult times, a dull throbbing began in my forehead, just above the eyes. The aspirin was wearing off. And no chance of getting any hair of the dog at lunch, either. The wages of sin!

Finally, the last hymn was sung. The day seemed even more glorious than before as the crowd slowly flowed out into the sunshine on Madison Avenue. Harvey complimented the Reverend on a fine sermon as we passed him on the stairs, then he stalked off toward 59th Street. I had to trot to catch up.

I was puffing as I drew abreast of him. "Child's all right?" I asked.

He stopped suddenly, spitting me with that falconoid glare of his, which has intimidated many a witness.

"I trust you have a very good alibi for last night?" His voice dripped ice.

"I think so," I replied, "if you'd care to listen to it."

He considered, making me wait. "Child's is fine," he said at last. "Let's go." He was off again at a lope.

We reached 59th Street, then turned west. Harvey's pace hadn't slowed one whit, which made conversation inopportune. I resolved to enjoy the walk. As we approached 5th Avenue I realized my headache had subsided again, doubtless the result of the large infusion of oxygen into my blood occasioned by our rapid pace. Walking north on 5th toward Grand Army Plaza, we met a beautiful sight; the sun reflecting from Edwardian façade of the Plaza Hotel had turned that edifice a pure, gleaming white and each of its myriad of windows scintillated with its own rainbow, the multicolored bands appearing to waver in the cool breeze. It was a rare moment and, out of the corner of my eye, I could see Harvey relax as he too was captivated by the spectacle. We stopped and just drank it in—at times like that I would not trade my humble flat in Manhattan for a sultan's palace!

Finally, the spell broke— Child's doorway was just a few steps away. We entered and took a table. As we sat, I could tell that Harvey's demeanor had softened appreciably.

"Well?" He cocked an eye at me after we had given the waiter our order.

"It's a long story," I told him.

"I have time. Let's hear it."

"Well, while you were held in the thrall by the world's most beautiful music last night, I was swilling cold coffee in a dirty little office at Bellevue, reading the autopsy report of a young woman who'd met a most grisly demise...," I saw that I had his interest.

I retrogressed and told him of Evie's visit to my office on Friday evening, and of Colin's disappearance. He was acquainted with Colin peripherally while we were at Harvard, but, involved with the rigors of law school, he had little discourse with my medical friends. I told him of my visit to Henderson, which made him smile; apparently his legal work had brought him into contact with the little ferret and he liked him about as well as everyone else seemed to—that is to say, not at all. I described my first meeting with Sally, my introduction to Detective Moscowicz and my subsequent activities at Bellevue.

By the time I had finished my narrative, lunch had been delivered and consumed. Harvey carefully fitted a cigarette into a long, ebony holder, lighted it and took a deep satisfying draw.

"That's quite a tale," he hissed as the smoke poured out of his nose and mouth. "Much too elaborate for you to have concocted as an excuse to miss a concert date, and too easily verified." Always the lawyer, Harvey. "What's your next move?"

"To go and see Evie, I suppose. She was going to canvass Colin's acquaintances to see if anyone might help."

"D'you really think there's any connection between McDowell's disappearance and this Ripper business?" asked Harvey.

I shuddered inwardly. "I really don't know. I hope not. It was Miss Barton's opinion only because the murderer has been operating in the general area of Colin's office." I laughed shortly. "Mine also, for that matter. I think it would be a rather large coincidence that Colin should have surprised the fiend at his work."

"Not if the fiend is McDowell's tenant, as Henderson seems to think."

I thought about it a moment. "Dammitall, Harvey, it just doesn't work. The police have presumably been through Strangways' office, which is the most likely place where a confrontation between him and Colin would have happened. If they'd found anything, you'd think that Henderson would have told Evie or me!"

Harvey shook his head. "Henderson doesn't talk. Not to suspects, colleagues, witnesses or bereaved family members. Not even to the District Attorney, at least not until his case is made. Believe me, I know."

Since Harvey Harrigan was one of the shrewdest criminal lawyers in the city, I believed he did know.

"You're probably right about Strangways' office having been tossed," Harvey went on, "but what about McDowell's? They may not have looked there as yet."

"True enough." I said. "Maybe I should have a look. Might be something there to give a clue as to what's befallen him." I eyed Harvey. "Want to come along? You have more experience in matters like this than I do."

He sighed. "You're going to think I'm getting even for last night, but remember, Eben, you were supposed to be out of the city all weekend. I have an engagement later this afternoon that's likely to run well into this evening. I'm truly sorry, because I would really like to help you with this."

I cocked an eyebrow at him. "Another young lady?"

"Yes, but you needn't worry. She's very young indeed. Six, today in fact. Mums and daddy will be there as well, don't y'know." He smiled. "It's my niece."

Harvey's sister lived in Pelham Bay—he had quite a jaunt ahead of him.

"In that case, I'd best let you get on." I shook my head at him as he reached into his jacket. "My treat. To atone for last night."

"Nothing to atone for, Eben." Harvey said. "You were just following your noble calling. But I'll let you pay, anyhow!"

I tossed some greenbacks on the table, then followed him outside.

He turned to face me and extended his hand. I took it and squeezed.

"Don't forget that Kreisler is playing Tuesday week," he said. "I had to call in some serious favors to get those tickets. I shall be awfully cross with you if you're not there."

"I'm looking forward to it."

He put his other hand atop mine.

"Let me know what happens with the search for your friend, Eben. I'll do all I can to help."

"I know you will, Harvey."

We disengaged our hands. I watched a moment as he walked back toward 59th Street, then I tuned and headed uptown towards Central Park.

The McDowell residence was on 67th Street between 5th and Madison. I could have gone straight up 5th Avenue, but, truth to tell, the day was a grand one and I was little anticipating to this meeting with Evie—I knew she would have called me had Colin returned, or had she gotten any positive news from her interviews. I decided to walk uptown through the park.

I crossed Grand Army Plaza, tipped my hat to General Sherman and entered the park through the Scholars Gate. The shaded path was crowded with strollers; solitary men and women like myself, couples and even whole families, most decked out in their Sunday finery, out to enjoy this rare warm day in September. Here and there were men in rougher, grubbier garb, some sitting or lying on the benches that flanked the walkway, others shambling aimlessly along, doubtless awaiting the waning of the sun and the coming of the nighttime chill with dread, for the park would be their hostel for the night. It was these poor devils, victims of the declining economy, whom the Reverend had referred to in his sermon this morning.

When the path split, I decided to go right; the other way would take me further west and deeper into the park, and while I was not in a great hurry to get to my destination, I didn't want to dally. Before long, the breeze carried the earthy odors of the zoo to my nostrils. The crowd became denser as I neared the zoo and I had to take care not to trip over the many children frolicking about. I briefly contemplated buying a bag of chestnuts from a nearby vendor, but reconsidered; I had eaten lunch only a short while ago, and really, it just wasn't chestnut weather yet.

As I walked by, I glanced into the cages; most of the animals were out in the fine weather and the children were, of course, fascinated with them all—wolves, bears, tigers and camels alike. I did linger for some time at the enclosure housing old Caliph, the hippopotamus, watching both the children and adults who were feeding him apples and whole loaves of bread, a resounding "Ah!" arising from the crowd each time he opened his cavernous maw.

Finally, I succumbed to the call of duty. I saluted old Caliph, hoping he wouldn't expire from acute dyspepsia before the day was out, then headed east, exiting the park back onto Fifth Avenue at 64th. From there it was only a short walk to the McDowell residence.

The McDowells occupied a fine Beaux Arts townhouse just down the street from the mansion of the dowager Mrs. Vanderbilt. The limestone edifice was well-appointed with ornate cast iron accouterments, generally befitting the great man who owned it. I could not hear any chimes through the stout walnut door when I pushed the button, but, through the heavy beveled glass, I saw Evie approaching. As the door swung inward, the smell of her perfume, intermingled with that of last night's dinner, wafted over me.

"Eben. It's good to see you. Come in, come in."

She was dressed in a rose-colored frock with lace at the sleeves and bodice, and a hemline that came just below the knee, a church-going outfit if I ever saw one. She was exquisite, as usual, but her eyes revealed the strain she was enduring, despite her makeup. I followed her from the vestibule down a long, richly paneled hallway that smelt of wood and lemon oil, into the living room. She motioned me to a seat in a lushly upholstered armchair and seated herself on a matching settee opposite. She removed the lid from a polished wooden box on the glass table between us, removed a cigarette, then held the lid while I took one too. I lighted mine with a slender silver lighter that sat next to the box, then held the lighter for her. This was getting to be a habit.

"Have you found anything?" I asked her.

"No. I called everyone I could think of. No one's seen him for several days." She took a long, shuddering drag. "Did you get anywhere with Henderson?"

"Not really. He asked me questions about Addison Strangways, same as you. But at least he let on that the police are looking for Colin." That last was not strictly true, but I wanted to give her some hope.

"That's something, at any rate."

I paused, considering the best way to make my next point without alarming her.

"I spoke to a friend of mine," I said at last. "She's a reporter. She's willing to give Colin's disappearance a little publicity. Maybe that will help in finding him" There was no way I was going to bring those Ripper killings into this conversation.

"Oh!" She exclaimed, her cigarette ashes landing on the white carpet as her hand flew to her mouth. "Colin won't be happy about that!"

"Do you really care, as long as we find him?" I asked, rhetorically, I hoped.

She managed a weak smile. I thought, yes, you do care!

"Were you able to discover approximately when he was last seen?" I asked her.

"Sort of. I spoke with his receptionist, Miss LeMay. She was really not very helpful at first—seemed sort of insulted that I was trying to find him at all."

"What do you mean, insulted?"

"Well, she seemed to have the attitude that, if Colin didn't want anyone to know where he was, then I shouldn't be trying to find out. I reminded her that I was his wife, and that I had small children at home who were worried about their papa. That thawed her a little."

"And what did she say?"

"That the last he was in the office was Tuesday. That's the last day he was here, as well."

"Did she tell you anything else? I mean, was he feeling ill, or disturbed..."

"She hardly told me anything, Eben!" Evie snapped, then began to cry. "Oh, I am sorry! I just wish he'd just come home!"

I stubbed out my cigarette and moved to sit beside her on the sofa. She leaned heavily against my chest and I cradled her in my arms. Momentarily, she got hold of herself. She pushed away from me and sat upright. I handed her the handkerchief from my breast pocket.

"I'm sorry, Eben," she said again, "but it's been such a strain. The girls are worried, and I've been trying to put on a brave front for them..."

"It's good to let it out, Evie. You've nothing to apologize for. By the way, where are the girls?"

"At the park with Mrs. Riordan. It was such a nice day, I thought I'd send them off." She hesitated, then asked, "Well, what do you think we should do, now?"

That was a good question. "Have you looked around here to see if you can find anything to give a clue as to what might have happened to him?"

"Yes, and I had no luck. I'm not surprised. Even though this is his home, he kept most of his personal things at the office."

"I suppose that's the next step." I said.

Evie got a strange look on her face.

"What?" I asked.

"Eben, could you, I mean, would you look there?" I thought I detected a quaver in her voice.

"Very well. Do you have a key?"

"I'm sure there's one in the study, though I couldn't tell you which one it is. Let's go and look."

The study was on the second floor. Formally appointed with leather and mahogany, it was furnished with a massive desk that reposed in front of double windows overlooking the street, and had floor to ceiling bookshelves on the other walls. An expensive, comfortable-looking leather chair faced the door to the hallway. For all of its contrived elegance, the study was a sterile place; each piece of sculpture, the bric-à-brac on the desk, the enormous globe, all had been carefully placed to suggest that this was a working room, but all of those little imperfections that a man would create while doing his work were absent.

I tried the middle drawer of the desk. It slid out easily. The contents were very carefully arranged; some writing paper, envelopes, stamps and various other office supplies. Several keys were there, some that fit door locks and others that were obviously for a desk or a filing cabinet. I took them all. I also searched the fine wooden filing cabinet—only the top drawer contained files, all of which appeared to pertain to household affairs. The closet yielded a few castaways; a battered briefcase, a couple old coats, a man's hat now out of style. I searched the briefcase and the coats and discovered another door key.

Evie had stood silently, watching me ransack her husband's study.

"Anywhere else to look?" I asked her.

"We can check in the bedroom, but I don't think we'll find anything."

She was correct. The bureau that was Colin's was just as carefully arranged as the desk has been, all of the clothes and haberdashery aligned with military precision. Evie pointed out the small wooden box where Colin habitually deposited his money clip, keys and spare change before retiring—it was empty.

She was silent as she led the way back downstairs, then down the hallway to the front door. If I didn't know better, I would have thought she was anxious to get me out of the house. When we reached the exit, she turned to face me, and the tears ran down her cheeks like raindrops down a window. This was a different kind of crying than she'd done in the living room—it smacked more of grief than of uncertainty and frustration. I wanted out of there very badly, but I had a duty. I took her hands in mine.

"Promise you'll tell me what you find," she said. It was not a question.

"Yes, Evie." I hesitated. "I won't tell you not to worry, but you must have hope. It will help you make it through this, no matter what the outcome."

"I'll try Eben. I'll be waiting to hear from you."

As I left the townhouse, I reflected once again that this was a woman far too good for the likes of Colin McDowell.

Silas K. Henderson

CHAPTER 7

From the notebook of Sally Barton

Sunday, September 27, 1931, early morning

After leaving Charlie outside the speakeasy, I headed back for Times Square, where I was going to hop the el for the trip down 6th Avenue to my flat, but when I got there, I just kept walking instead. The evening was still real mild, and I wasn't looking forward to spending the night alone in my small, dark apartment; I knew what I was going to see when I closed my eyes. Besides, it was only a couple-mile walk to Chelsea; maybe the exercise on top of the hooch would make me tired enough to drop right off. I hoped so.

It was almost two o'clock when I unlocked my door. I didn't need the hall light to find the bedroom, but I flipped it on just the same. I knew it would be on all night, because the switches were at either end of the hall—I would have to leave the bedroom to turn it off. Not tonight! I looked at the little lamp on my nightstand, then turned on the overhead light in the bedroom; just as quickly, I turned it off again. I would never get to sleep with that glaring down on me. I turned on the bedside lamp, then sat down on the bed to undress.

After I had my nightie on I slid under the covers—it was warm in the flat and I really didn't need them, but like a little kid who covers her head to get away from the boogeyman, I took comfort in their weight, and in the barrier they made between me and the world. I looked at the lamp. I knew I wouldn't get to sleep with it on either, but I couldn't bring myself to turn it off, not yet. I wondered what Moscowicz was doing. Would he come if I called? I thought maybe he would. Annoyed, I reached over and yanked on the lamp chain. I would just have to rely on the light from the hallway to keep the boogeyman away.

Surprisingly, the combination of alcohol and a two-mile hike worked like magic. Morning sunshine washed out the light from the hallway. I stretched and sat up before swinging my legs to the floor, then I noticed the condition of the bed. One of the pillows was on the floor, and all of the covers hung over the side. My nightie was up to my waist. I had had a restless night, but thank goodness, no dreams I could remember.

I got up and pulled my red chenille bathrobe over my nightie, stepped into my slippers, and padded down the hallway to the kitchen, snapping off the light on the way. I got down the coffee tin from the cabinet. Damn! Nearly empty! Maybe just enough for a pot if I didn't use too much water. After I lit the stove and put the percolator on, I got a small piece of string from a drawer and tied it around my wrist. Wouldn't do to wake up with no coffee in the house tomorrow.

As I sat sipping the hot brew, I planned my day. From what Charlie had said last night, Simon Trulove was probably my best bet. He wasn't likely to welcome me with open arms if I called ahead; a rich bird like him probably had a flunkey guarding every door just to keep out the likes of me. The best plan was probably to just go and hang around, see if I could catch him coming in or out. Even then, I knew I needed an angle, or he would give me the bum's rush for sure.

Then there was Strangways. Maybe I could find out from Trulove if his wife had any connection with the good doctor. Gee, it would be great if I could track him down ahead of the cops, find out whether he was really the Ripper or just Henderson's fall guy. I wouldn't mind giving Henderson a black eye, I'll tell you that.

I got up and threw my coffee in the sink—it was cold, and too weak anyhow. If Trulove was a church-going man, my best chance of catching him out of his house was probably this morning. I went back to the bedroom to get changed. I reached for one of my standard skirt-and blouse outfits, then I thought better. Trulove was a swell and I needed to get his attention, grieving widower or not. I took down my slinky black nightclub dress and some stockings and heels. A while later, I looked at myself in the mirror after doing my eyes and lips. Not bad. A little doggy, no Merle Oberon for sure, but not bad. I grabbed my white turban, a purse to match and got the cultured pearl necklace from my jewelry box that ma and dad had given me for graduation. Look out, Mr. Trulove!

I locked up the flat and went down to 16th Street. It was a beautiful day, much warmer than usual for this time of year. Early Mass was just getting out across the street, and a crowd lingered in front of the church, people passing the time of day and enjoying the sunshine. I felt a pang of guilt—it was quite a while since I'd been to Mass—as a matter of fact, I'd missed my Easter duty, so I wasn't sure exactly what I'd have to do to get back into the Church, or if they'd even have me anymore. A figure in black stepped out of the double doors. It looked like Father Larkin. I turned my face away and hoofed it toward 6th Avenue; it wouldn't do to have him see me looking like a floozie on a Sunday morning.

I hopped the el to the newspaper office. I needed Trulove's address, and to find out what he looked like. There was no shortage of pictures—he'd made the news a few years back when he'd turned a little New York-Havana packet into a major shipping line, making himself a few million in the process. Like a lot of guys who were tops in their racket, there was nothing really special about his looks. He kept his hair real short and had sort of a round face with a big nose and heavy eyebrows. He was smiling in the morgue pic, probably because he'd just made a killing; he looked like somebody's jolly old uncle. I sure hoped he acted that way when I met him later. I turned up an address from the city directory—big surprise—The Ritz Tower Apartments on the corner of 57th and Park. I checked the time. I needed to really hoof it if I was going to catch him on the way home from church.

The Ritz Tower was a classy joint, decorated with lots of carved gargoyles and such, built about five years ago. That look was not exactly my cup of tea, but then again, I'd never have to worry about living there.

I checked my watch; I'd made good time from the office. I looked around for a coffee shop or someplace where I could wait sitting down, but I was out of luck. The only places were too far away for me to see my mark if he pulled up. Oh, well. I moved into the shade of a nearby building, hoping I didn't have too long to wait.

I didn't. A big gray roadster glided up to the curb and the driver hopped out and hurried around to open the rear door. Out popped my man, moving fast! I went for him quick, before the lackey could stop me.

"Hey, Mr. Trulove! Want to hear the latest scoop Henderson's got on the Ripper?" That got his attention in a hurry.

He turned and glared at me. He looked cheerful and friendly in the morgue shot, but he sure didn't look that way now. His cold eyes made my stomach drop and my tongue stick to the roof of my mouth. I stopped moving toward him.

C'mon, Barton! Don't blow it now!

"Ever hear of Addison Strangways, Mr. Trulove? He's the bird Henderson's got tabbed for killing your wife!" I forced myself to take another couple steps.

I could see his mind working. He wanted to tell me to blow, but he just couldn't. His mug was headed my way, though, and up to no good. This was my last chance!

"Let me come inside with you and I'll tell you all about it."

Trulove extended his arm. It didn't touch the mug, but it stopped him like he'd hit a brick wall.

"Who are you?" he grated.

"Sally Barton from the *Evening Graphic*." I smiled at him, hoping I wasn't looking like a hussy, or a whipped dog.

"A reporter." It was amazing, the amount of contempt he could cram into just two words. Then his curiosity got the better of him. "Strangways was my wife's doctor," he said. "Why does Henderson think he did it?"

"Let me come inside, and I'll tell you," I said again.

You could just see him fighting it. He was enough of a wise guy to know I'd run one over on him, but he just had to know what I had.

"Come on," he said.

Gotcha!

I followed him into the building. The doorman who held the door open for Trulove gave me a look as much to say, you sure don't belong in here, sister! I flashed him a real sweet smile. We rode the elevator upstairs, then went down a long hall with a plush rug running down the middle, and all sorts of fancy pictures of half-dressed women in gold frames hung along it. Trulove stopped at a heavy wooden door, unlocked it, and motioned me inside. He led the way to a big room with a high ceiling that smelled of leather and pipe tobacco. It was full of books, with a huge desk in front of the window. Trulove motioned me to a cushy leather armchair that faced the desk, then took the seat behind it.

He turned those snake-eyes of his on me again, saying nothing. He was probably hoping I'd look away. I wanted to, but I steeled myself and looked right back at him. God, I hoped he couldn't see how I scared I was!

I thought I saw a hint of a smile flicker across his face.

"Tell me about Strangways," he said. "What's Henderson got on him?"

"Not a lot. He knows that Strangways was involved in a sex scandal a while ago."

"What kind of sex scandal?" Those damned eyes of his never let up!

"He was accused of taking liberties with one of his patients. He beat the rap. I guess that's what got Henderson on to him."

"And what does Dr. Strangways have to say about this? I assume you've talked to him."

"No sir. Apparently, Strangways took a powder. Maybe that's more reason for Henderson to suspect him." Time to get the questions going the other way. "He was your wife's doctor?"

"Yes."

"She was pregnant?"

"Yes." *Bingo!* "We'd just found out a couple of weeks before she was killed." He looked annoyed. "What made you ask me that?"

I really struggled not to look away. "Strangways was an obstetrician," I said. I didn't think he believed me, but I wasn't about to tell him I'd seen the autopsy report. "What else can you tell me about her murder?" I didn't want to be on the receiving end of his questions again.

At first, I thought he wasn't going to answer me. He sort of swelled up, like he was going to explode, then he let out his breath with a hiss. Then he got control of himself.

"I found her," he said, "here, in the living room, in this apartment." He smiled wickedly. "Would you like to go and see her blood stains on the carpet? They're still there."

"That's all right," I shuddered.

"I'm going to leave them there until I get the bastard that did this." He was spitting me with that gaze again. "What do you think of that?"

He was trying to play me just like I was trying to play him. "It's your apartment, Mr. Trulove," I said. "And your carpet. I guess you can leave them there if that's what you want to do."

That wasn't the answer he expected—he looked angry again. I spoke up before he could compose himself enough to respond. "He was actually in the apartment? The killer, I mean."

"He was. It looked as if they'd had a drink together. My wife and him."

That was something nobody had yet, about the drink. I stayed quiet, hoping he'd go on.

"That was probably why Henderson thought I did it, at first," he said.

"I don't think so," I said. "The cops, they always suspect the husband first, in a wife's killing. Probably because most women are killed by their husbands. What made Henderson change his mind?"

"The other killings, I think. He couldn't come up with a reason that I'd killed the others."

"Did you know either of them?"

"Obliquely. Katherine Willoughby was the wife of one of the partners in my attorney's firm."

"Was she a patient of Strangways?"

"She was, now that you mention it. We asked around for an obstetrician when we suspected Eileen was pregnant, and Joe Wells, my attorney, mentioned that his partner's wife had just started seeing one."

"Did Strangways often come here to see your wife?"

"Never. She always went to his office."

"Can you think of any reason for him to come here?"

"No. He was her doctor for her pregnancy, but she didn't really know him personally." He paused, then continued, "Strangways came well recommended. Never heard anything about any sex scandal. You sure you got your facts straight?"

I was a little insulted. Would he have asked a man that question? "I can show you the newspaper articles," I said.

"I'll take you up on that, later." He got a funny look on his face. "How would you like to make ten thousand dollars?" he asked me.

I guess I was too surprised to be speechless. "I'd like that just fine," I told him.

"Here's the story you came to me to get." He was smiling even more wickedly, now. "I'll pay ten thousand dollars to you, or to anybody else who can tell me who killed Eileen, and give me the proof to send the son of a bitch to the chair! I'll even give it to Henderson, if he does that. Put that in your newspaper!"

Now I was speechless! What a story! Now they'd have to take me serious as a crime reporter at the *Graphic*! I struggled for a moment to

64

get control of myself before I answered him—wouldn't do to sound like a kid on her first date, or something.

"What do you think of that?" he asked.

"I think it's really going to shake things up, Mr. Trulove. Henderson won't like it a bit."

"Why not? He's in the running for it, same as anybody else. And that's what I want to do, shake things up. Maybe if the police get a little competition, they'll work a little harder so they won't look bad if somebody else finds him first."

"That's right," I said.

Trulove was really pleased with himself, now. You could tell it by the look on his face. "Well there's your story," he said. "Go ahead and print it."

I made no move to get up.

"You want something else?" he asked.

"Yeah. A lot. How will the money be paid? Is there anything up front, or does the person have to wait until the trial is over to get anything? What if more than one person comes up with the goods? Do they split it, or does each of them get ten grand?" I knew my editor would have a fit if I didn't give him details like that.

Trulove looked annoyed. He'd done his big number, and now he wanted to exit stage right, to grand applause. Tough.

He thought about it for a minute, then said, "Okay, write this down. My attorney is Joe Wells, of Wells, Harris and Willoughby, on Pearl Street. I'll deposit the money with him tomorrow morning, and we'll have a short meeting to work out some of the details you mentioned. You call him around noontime and he'll give you the dope. Meanwhile, you publish the offer in an extra, tonight. Details to follow. That ought to get things going."

"I can't promise you an extra, Mr. Trulove. That's my editor's call, not mine. But he might just go for it."

Simon Trulove sure didn't like anybody telling him no. He glared at me for a minute, then said, "Well, tell him I said it would be better that way. Got what you need, now?" His tone of voice said I'd better have.

"I think so. I'll call you if my editor wants anything else."

"Don't bother. Call Joe Wells tomorrow, like I told you to." He got up from behind the desk and opened the door to the hall outside. It was time to go.

I held it in until I got out on the street and out of sight of that doorman who thought I didn't belong there.

"Yes!" I hollered to the surrounding buildings. Then I just started running down Park Avenue, heels and all! People looked at me like I was nuts, but I didn't care. Wait till Charlie Killarney reads this one!

CHAPTER 8

The Statement of Dr. Ebeneezer Warman

It was but a short walk from the McDowells' townhouse to Colin's medical office on Park Avenue. The office occupied the second floor of a three-story, grey stone building, which Colin owned in addition to the townhouse. I stumbled slightly as I started up the steps; I was fumbling through the keys that I had gotten from Evie, looking for a likely candidate, so I did not notice the depression worn in the center of the stairs until I looked for whatever had caused me to trip. Apparently, the practices housed within were doing very well indeed. The first key I tried didn't work, but the next one did. I turned the well-worn brass knob and pushed the heavy door inward.

I entered a small vestibule, tastefully appointed with a red carpet, an ornate Roseville jardinière for umbrellas, a black rubber mat for boots, and a small armoire, presumably for hats and coats. I could see an interior room hazily through the glass in the far door; dark and apparently empty. The door stuck a little when I pushed and I found myself holding my breath; trying not to make any noise as I applied enough pressure to open it. Silly of me! I had every right to be here, but still, I felt a bit like a burglar.

The room beyond the vestibule was a hallway. A flight of stairs led upwards to Colin's offices. The portal to a large room adjacent to the stairs was blocked off with surveyor's tape. A sign dangling from the tape informed all concerned that the room beyond was restricted by order of the New York Police Department and that any who crossed the barricade without permission of same were guilty of a crime and would be justly prosecuted. Henderson had indeed "tossed" Strangways' digs, as Harvey put it. Fine. My business today did not lie there. I proceeded up the stairs.

The room at the top of the stairs was spacious, containing a large sofa, several overstuffed chairs and the obligatory magazines within easy reach. Typical doctor's waiting room, if a bit more richly appointed than my own. A waist-high, wooden gate, much like one in a bank, barred entry to a smaller room that contained a large desk and several filing cabinets—the receptionist's office. A flight of stairs led up to the top floor, and several doors gave access to other rooms on this floor. No sound breached the stillness.

Where to look? I opened a couple of the doors, confirming my suspicions that this floor contained the examining rooms and business offices. Colin's private sanctum was likely on the floor above.

I ascended the stairs. They ended at a closed door; a twist of the knob confirmed it was locked. I tried all of the keys I had gotten from Evie without success. Drat! I was sure that if I was to find anything useful it would be here in the private area, not in the business offices. Oh well, I could only hope to find a key in one of the rooms on the second floor. That door looked as if it would resist my best efforts to batter it down, even if I was so inclined.

I began a more careful survey of the medical offices. Colin had two consultation rooms—one done in maple and lace, scented with fresh flowers and the other in heavy wooden paneling and leather furniture, smelling of old wood and pipe tobacco. Another room housed a rather complete chemical and biological laboratory; no surprise, that, given Colin's scientific bent and expertise. There was an office adjacent, its walls lined with bookshelves and filing cabinets, and containing an ornately carved desk, a sofa and a comfortable leather armchair facing the desk. Several more straight-back chairs were pushed against a wall. Unlike the study at the Colin's townhouse, this room had an atmosphere of occupancy about it. I went straight for the desk, hoping to find what I needed there.

I sat in the large leather chair behind the desk and flipped though the keys I had, my fears growing. Not a desk key in the lot! I looked at the blotter; there was a pen and inkwell, a large book with a leather cover and, yes, a letter opener.

I will never be a good criminal. As I regarded the letter opener, guilt pangs born in my stomach traveled swiftly to my extremities, leaving them tingling with apprehension. Yes, I had Evie's permission to be here doing what I was doing, and yes, I was indeed acting in the service of Colin McDowell, who might just this minute be in a very bad way, but it wasn't an easy thing for me to break into a man's private desk, which he had deliberately locked. Nervously, I flipped open the book instead of reaching for the letter opener.

It was log of time spent each day with patients, probably kept for billing purposes. I flipped to the last page of entries; perhaps I could verify when Colin was most recently in the office. Strange. The last entry was made in early August—surely Colin had seen many patients after that. I examined some of the earlier entries. They were mostly names, but there were also numerous entries that read "clinic." Hmm. Probably the time that Colin had spent at the Settlement House—most of them seemed to be after business hours. There were also quite a few entries that read "Rockefeller," made on nights and weekends, probably a record of time spent conducting research in Alexis Carrell's laboratory at Rockefeller Institute. Hmph! Didn't leave much time for Evie and the girls, now did it?

I looked again at the last page. There was only one name listed for the entire last week—must have been a pretty sick patient if Colin had had to spend that much time in treatment. I noted the name down on one of the business cards I found in a container on the desk and slipped it into my wallet. Then I regarded the letter opener once again.

Dammitall! I *was* acting in Colin McDowell's best interests, whether he thought so or not. I took the letter opener and began to work on the lock on the top desk drawer. For a moment I wasn't sure which was going to give first, the lock or the letter opener; luckily, the latter was a sturdy piece of metal—the drawer suddenly popped open and the internal bar that locked the lower drawers dropped with a clank that almost brought me straight up out of the chair! Ruefully, I examined the drawer I'd pried open; it would never be the same. Well, dammitall, if I found Colin, I'd buy him a new desk!

Eureka! The top drawer contained a ring of keys. I snatched them up and pushed it closed again, eager to be away from the scene of the crime. As I moved to the door leading out of the room, I noticed a newspaper on the floor next to one of the chairs, and retrieved it. It was folded in thirds, as one will do to carry a newspaper in a jacket pocket. I unfolded it, thinking to check the date, which might give me a clue as to the last time Colin was in this room. To my surprise, I found that I was holding a copy of the *Boston Globe*, dated last Tuesday. Now, what on earth would Colin want with a Boston paper?

I slipped the paper in my jacket pocket, then went back to the main staircase, which led up to a locked door to the third-floor apartment. It was only a moment's work to find the proper key. I opened it and found myself looking into a comfortably furnished living room. A well- equipped bar graced one wall; several used tumblers and take-out food containers littered the top. I began to get a bad feeling about this. A number of doors led to other rooms. I tried one at random—it opened into a bedroom. The large tester bed was unmade and a woman's chemise lay on it. I could feel my features tense. Evie had suspected this—it was why she wanted me to come here without her.

"You'll tell me what you find," she had said to me. Suddenly, I wasn't looking forward to that.

I went inside. The room smelled strongly of flowery perfume, and other articles of feminine apparel were scattered about. Perhaps Colin's receptionist was just staying here until he turned up again, I rationalized. I slid open the door to a closet that occupied an entire wall of the room. It contained a rather complete female wardrobe, and a few articles of men's clothing besides.

I heard a rasping metallic click behind me.

"Put your hands up and turn around real slow," a woman said. "I've got a gun!"

My throat constricted and a loose feeling spread through my bowels and bladder. I did as instructed, while repeating mentally that I had a perfect right to be there.

Dana LeMay (for I was sure that it was she) did indeed have a gun. It was a very large gun, and it was pointed directly at me. She gripped it in both hands. Her finger was on the trigger as the enormous revolver trembled slightly, as if she was having trouble with its weight. She was only ten feet from me, standing in the door to the living room. I was certain she would not miss if she fired.

"What the hell do you think you're doing here?"

"Miss LeMay..."

"Put your hands up, I said! I will shoot you! I will!"

I jerked my arms, which I had unconsciously lowered a little, straight up again.

"Miss LeMay," I tried again, "My name is Dr. Warman..."

"What the hell are you doing in my room?" Her voice had an edge of hysteria to it that I didn't like at all.

"Mrs. McDowell sent me here, to find out what happened to Colin."

Her facial expression told me that was not what she wanted to hear. She bobbed the gun up and down.

"You get out of here! Get the hell out of here now!"

The revolver's hammer was cocked. I was unsure of how much pressure on the trigger was necessary to set it off, but her waving it around like that made me very nervous indeed. I would have been happy to comply with her request, but she still occupied the doorway, making that rather difficult.

I struggled to speak through parched lips. "You'll have to let me out of here, if you want me to go. You're blocking the doorway."

She looked at me stupidly while she processed that. At least she stopped waving the gun around. She backed slowly into the living room, bobbing it up and down yet again.

"Now get out!" she said, when there was enough room for me to pass through the door.

I lost no time doing as I was told.

It wasn't until I reached the street that the reaction set in. I simply stood there in the middle of Park Avenue, trembling like I had St. Vitus' Dance. I do not believe myself a coward, but that was the closest I had ever come to the business end of a revolver, and I found it to be a very humbling experience. I remembered that there was a little vest-pocket park with benches a few blocks away. I headed there to consider further action.

I found an unoccupied bench—a stroke of luck on such a fine day—and sank gratefully down on it, lighting a cigarette. As I drew the smoke into my lungs, I could feel the nicotine work its magic as the tenseness fled from my muscles and the knot in my abdomen relaxed. God, it was wonderful to be alive, for there was no finer place than Park Avenue on such a beautiful day. I shuddered again as I contemplated how near I had come to losing my life. Then I began to face some unpleasant considerations.

Evie had made me promise to tell her what I had found at Colin's office. But nearly thirty years of medical practice has taught me to sacrifice my honor where promises are concerned, for the good of my patients. Evie was waiting back at the town house to learn whether I'd made any headway at discovering her husband's whereabouts. She'd obviously had her suspicions as to Colin's infidelity, but she was the dutiful wife, excluded from the details of his professional life, keeping his house and raising his children because, I supposed, that was how she wanted it. It kept her from having to face some rather unpleasant facts. I dropped my cigarette and ground it out with my heel, lighted another and settled back to reflect a bit further.

What would be gained by telling her of her husband's peccadillo? Perhaps I could gain full access to Colin's office with her assistance, but to what end? I wasn't even sure there was anything there to give a clue to his whereabouts. I supposed I couldn't really blame Miss LeMay for bracing a strange man in her *boudoir* with a pistol, but I certainly didn't want Evie storming over there to have it out with the "other woman," knowing that the weapon was on the premises. Perhaps the best idea was to talk with some of Colin's other acquaintances, at Rockefeller and the Settlement. There would be time enough to readdress the issue of access to his office if those lines of inquiry proved fruitless.

I extinguished the second cigarette and contemplated lighting a third. It really was a fine day to enjoy the out of doors. However, I realized I was waffling. I didn't want to go and face Evie, but she was home, alone, anxiously awaiting any news I might bring her. I must confess that, in all my years as a doctor, I never became accustomed to delivering bad news, or to lying to someone who was hopelessly ill. The task I now faced was much the same. Reluctantly, I quitted the bench and began walking slowly downtown. I certainly did not have to hurry to carry out an unpleasant task.

She knew something was amiss the moment she opened the door.

"Eben," she said, "is something the matter?"

"No," I lied. "Let me in and I'll tell you about it."

She led me back to the living room and we took the same seats we had on my first visit that day, me in the armchair and she on the sofa.

"What did you find?" she asked.

"That's just the trouble," I said. "I really didn't find anything to tell where Colin has gone." That, at least, was the truth.

She looked as if I was going to hit her. "Did you look everywhere?" She emphasized that last word.

"As much as I could in a short time, Evie." I had a thought. "The only thing I found out of the ordinary was this." I handed her the Boston newspaper. "It was on the floor in his office."

"Why, he was in Boston last month," she said, "to see about a patient or something. Do you suppose he went back?"

"It's dated last Tuesday," I pointed out. "More likely that someone from Boston visited Colin at his office that day. Besides, why wouldn't he have told you if he was going back?"

"That's true," she admitted. "He made no secret of it the first time. He even left me a phone number where he could be contacted."

We looked at each other, then said simultaneously,

"Do you still have it?"

"I think I've still got it..."

She smiled in spite of herself, then said, "I think it's upstairs. Wait here, and I'll go and look."

She hurried out of the room.

I settled back in the chair and lighted a cigarette. This was going much better than I had hoped. I really didn't think Colin had gone to Boston; as Evie had pointed out, he had told her the first time, why not the second? Still, it couldn't hurt to check.

I had time to finish my cigarette and light another before she returned. She handed me a small scrap of paper with a phone number scrawled on it. I recognized Colin's cryptic hand, with which I had struggled many times in medical school.

"Well," I said, "let's see where this leads us."

I picked up the phone and dialed the operator. I told her I wanted her to put through a call to Boston for me and gave her the number.

"That's not a Boston exchange, sir," she informed after a moment.

I covered the mouthpiece with my hand. "She says it's not a Boston number," I told Evie.

"But..." She appeared perplexed, then a light came into her eyes. "Maybe it isn't. Colin called me the night after he left. He gave me that number and told me it was where he was staying."

"But it is in Massachusetts?"

"I don't know. I would think so. He did say he was taking the train to Boston."

I took my hand from the mouthpiece.

"Operator," I said, "it's possible this is a number from somewhere else in Massachusetts. Do you think you could determine where?"

"That could take a few moments, sir."

I gave her the McDowell's number. "Could you call back when you have it?"

"Yes, sir."

I rang off, then folded the paper containing the mysterious number in half, then placed it beneath the phone.

Evie and I looked at each other for a moment.

Evie said, "So, you found nothing amiss at Colin's office?"

I tried to look her in the eye as I said, "Not really." Why was it so difficult to lie to this woman? "Cigarette?" She nodded.

We sat and smoked for a few moments. The tension in the room was palpable; I felt sure Evie realized that I was keeping something from her, but I could think of nothing else to say to dissuade her of that. I willed the phone to ring, but it did not.

Finally I said, "Well, I really must be getting on."

"Yes. Mrs. Riordan and the girls will be returning soon. Are you sure you don't wish to stay for supper?"

"Yes." I was sure. "You'll call me if you find out about that number?"

"Of course."

Shortly, I found myself back out on the street, grateful to be out of there. Though evening had come, it was still mild, so I started uptown on foot. Harvey was in Pelham—I was on my own for dinner this evening, then back to the grindstone tomorrow. I ran through my mental catalog of nearby restaurants, then decided on the Hotel Ansonia. Red meat was what I wanted, to fortify my blood, which was almost spilled earlier, then maybe one *small* snifter of cognac before bed.

By ten p.m., I was in my pyjamas in my study, preparing to pour my brandy. The phone rang. Ah, I thought, Evie finally has news about that number. I picked up the receiver.

"Hello?"

"Dr. Warman?" It was a man's voice. "This is Dr. Strongman at Lenox Hill."

Why would he be calling me? I was supposed to be on vacation, and Prather was covering for me.

"Do you know an Evelyn McDowell?"

I was suddenly sick at my stomach.

"Yes, I surely do. What's the trouble?

"She's been shot. She's asked for you, Doctor. She's in a bit of a bad way."

"I'll be right over!"

The Legacy of the Unborn

I dropped the phone and rushed to the bedroom to dress.

CHAPTER 9

From the notebook of Sally Barton

Sunday, September 27, 1931, about 2 p.m.

I ran about a block before sanity set in—I couldn't run all the way to the office! I started to head for the el, then thought, 'To hell with it,' and began walking toward 5th Avenue, where I was sure to find a hack.

The ride down to Hudson Street was a quick one. Fifth Avenue traffic was light on Sunday afternoon and had the window open, enjoying the mild breeze. My hair would look like hell when I got there, but, for once, I really didn't care.

The office was humming as usual; when you work for a big city newspaper, Sunday is just another day. I hoped I wouldn't have to wait too long for a desk and a typewriter, and I was in luck; I spotted an empty chair over by the window. I pushed it open a few inches before I seriously set to writing.

After a couple of hours of furious typing, I filed two stories with the city editor; one on Colin McDowell, and the big one on Trulove's reward offer. I didn't file one on what I'd learned from the autopsy reports. I would call and try to confirm what Trulove told me about the women being pregnant with the coroner's office tomorrow. I knew damn well they wouldn't do that, but at least the call would be on the books if anybody looked. I kept my promise to Moscowicz.

I stood quietly watching while the city editor read the reward story.

"Holy cow, Barton! Is this the real McCoy?"

"I wouldn't have written it if it wasn't." I said. "Trulove wants you should put it out as an extra."

"I think he's gonna get what he wants!" He grabbed one of the phones on his desk. "Get me Grogin! We need a picture to go with this headline!" He covered the receiver with his hand and asked me, "You want to be Eileen Trulove for a while?" he asked me.

I shook my head. The *Graphic* had pioneered the use of composites in the early 20's. Composites were pictures created in the art department to illustrate stories for which real photographs couldn't be taken. This was generally done by putting faces from morgue pix onto bodies of models hired for that reason. They had a regular photography set downstairs too, which could be set up as anything from a prison cell to a hotel room in just a few minutes. Many newspapers considered this sort of thing bad journalism, but the *Graphic's* editors simply saw it as way to attract attention to a particular story—after all, if the facts in the story were true, then the manufactured photo really couldn't be considered unethical. It was only showing something that *could* have happened. I had an idea of what the editor had in mind for this one, though; something along the lines of Trulove standing over his wife's half-naked, dead body, vowing revenge. I didn't want to be a part of anything like that, especially after that story Charlie told me about Evans from the *News*. Besides, I felt like keeping my clothes on.

We argued for a while, with him crying about where he was gonna get a female model on a Sunday afternoon, but I didn't give in. He sure as hell wasn't gonna fire me after what I'd just handed him. He was still hollering as I closed the frosted glass door of the city room behind me.

Once on the street, I started walking toward Houston to catch the train. I wished I could walk home; it was only a couple of miles and it was so damn nice out, but there was no way that was gonna happen in these heels. It would be hard enough getting there on the train on a Sunday and probably take just as much time. I briefly considered another cab, but I'd calmed down a lot and realized I wasn't made of money. I would have to remember to leave a pair of flats at the office, though.

I was in the kitchen putting away the coffee I'd got at the market on my way in when the phone rang.

"Hello."

"Barton?" I felt a catch in my chest. "Waddaya know?"

"Oh hi..., Moscowicz!" I hesitated, wondering what to say next. "I guess I know a lot!"

"Yeah, I guess you do. I've got your extra here."

Damn, that was fast work! It sure didn't take 'em long to find that female model, now did it?

"Waddaya think?"

"You sure stirred things up. Henderson's mad as hell about the reward, but there's not a damn thing he can do about it!" He sounded kind of glad about that.

"Yeah, I figgered he would be."

The silence on the line was filled by a faint hiss.

"This is a big deal for you, huh?" he said at last.

"Yeah, I guess so."

"Well then, somebody oughta take you out for dinner, or something, to celebrate."

"You offering?" I asked. I shouldn't have. I should have just said I'd go.

More silence.

"Yeah, I'm offering," he said, finally. I felt that catch in my chest again.

"Well, when can you get here?"

"Fifteen, twenny minutes."

I considered. I was already dressed. I thought I could do something about my hair by then.

"Make it a half hour." I told him. "I'll meet you downstairs."

Of course, it took me nearly forty-five minutes, and I still wasn't satisfied—my hair really needed to be washed and set. I looked out the window to see if Moscowicz was out there. He was. It was getting dark, but there was no mistaking his bulk on the sidewalk, the soft orange glow of his cigarette moving rhythmically up and down. Jeez! Any other guy would've been up banging on my door by now. I really had to hurry.

He dropped his cigarette on the sidewalk and ground it underfoot when I came out on the porch.

"Geeze, Barton, you're a knockout!" he said.

"Thanks, Moscowicz." I hesitated. "I guess I really shouldn't be calling you Moscowicz tonight, should I? What do you go by, Moe?"

He looked at the sidewalk. "Actually, it's Morris," he said ruefully. "But hell, I don't care if you call me Moe, or Moscowicz, or whatever."

"No," I said. "Your name is Morris, so that's what I'll call you. And mine is Sally."

He smiled and that homely face of his seemed to light up the whole world.

"Okay, Sally!" he said. "Now, where would you like to eat?"

I thought about it a second. "I really don't care. Do you have a place you like to go, Morris?"

"Do you like German food?"

I nodded.

"Then Luchow's it is! C'mon, we'll walk. It's only a few blocks from here."

"Morris." I stopped him as he started to stride off. "If we're going to walk, I really have to go back upstairs and change these shoes." I had the heels on again.

"Oh!" He had that hangdog look of his on his face. "Well, we can take a cab. We'll get one on 5th Avenue."

80

I thought about what a policeman, even a detective, must make. "No," I said. "I'll lose the heels. It's a real nice night for a walk, anyway. I'll just be a minute."

When I came back down, we headed off east along 16th Street, toward Union Square. If Moscowicz had really stretched his long legs, I'd have had to run to keep up—as it was, I had to take his elbow to speed him along a little—I think he was deliberately slowing his pace for my comfort. We ended up strolling along hand in hand. Neither of us had much to say. I don't normally get all choked up around guys, but it was becoming obvious that I wasn't really sure how I felt about this one. Moscowicz just walked along without looking at me, but he sure had a great big grin on his face.

Union Square was crowded. It had clouded over some, but the weather was still pretty nice, and it looked like the commies from the Rand School were taking advantage—they were out in droves. There were at least four separate groups, each with a guy up on a box in the center; his audience waving their arms and shouting agreement and encouragement to the speaker. A couple of beggars approached us as we crossed the Square, but backed off when they got a load of Moscowicz. It seemed like beggars were everywhere these days. I heard another sound, first as a faint overtone to the buzz of the crowd which became more intelligible and distinct as we approached the source.

"Wuxtra, wuxtra! Ten thousand dollars offered for New York Ripper! Wuxtra!"

Moscowicz gave me an inquiring look. I nodded. He used his considerable bulk to force his way through the crowd surrounding the bootjack and returned in a moment with the paper. He handed it to me.

TYCOON OFFERS TEN THOUSAND FOR WIFE'S SLAYER! The headline screamed. Sure enough, the picture below showed a distraught Simon Trulove, shaking his fist at the heavens, standing above a female corpse, clad only in a scanty nightie, sprawled on a living room couch. Her face was conveniently turned into the cushions. I eagerly turned to the following page.

**Shipping Magnate Offers Ten Thousand
Simoleons for New York Ripper's Head!**

81

The Legacy of the Unborn

Vows "I'll leave my wife's blood on the carpet till he's fried!"

Exclusive to the *Evening Graphic* by Sally Barton

I jumped involuntarily as Simon Trulove's fist came crashing down on his pricey mahogany desk, scattering a picture of his dead wife and other knickknacks to the floor of his posh office on the forty-first floor of the Ritz Tower Apartments...

Exclusive! And with my byline! I folded it up and offered it to Moscowicz, who put it in his jacket pocket. He offered me his arm. We stepped out across the square, towards Klein's.

We were at Luchow's in just a couple of minutes. I tensed while the waiter led us through several rooms to our table, as other waiters balanced trays full of foamy pitchers of beer; this watery stuff was legal, but I was gonna have to find out how Moscowicz was about prohibition if we were gonna be together a lot. Many cops turned a blind eye and even drank a little themselves, but some felt obliged to uphold the law. I suspected that Moscowicz was that type.

I really didn't know that much about German food; I let Moscowicz do the ordering. He got sausages, sauerkraut, potatoes and rye bread, and yes...beer! Maybe I was wrong about him after all.

After the beer was poured and we had both taken a swig I said, "It's a shame. It's almost not beer."

"That's why they call it near beer. Have you ever had real German beer?"

"No. You?"

"Yeah, when I was in the army over there. It's really something, thick and rich, not at all like this swill."

"So, you were in the army? In the big war?"

"Yeah. I was lucky, I got in right near the end, so I didn't see a lot of the really bad stuff like some of the other guys."

"And you joined the police force right out of the army?"

"Uh huh." He took another swig of beer, draining the glass, then refilled it from the pitcher. "There was a lot of us lookin' for work in them days. One of my officers, a colonel, was a deputy chief on the force. I done him a good turn over there—he pulled some strings and got me on."

"Save his life?"

"Somethin' like that. What about you, Bar..., ah, Sally. Where you from?"

I smiled at him. "It's all right, Morris. You can call me Barton if you want. I don't mind." I fumbled in my purse for a cigarette and got it lit before I answered his question. "I grew up in a little town in New Jersey. Maplewood, near Newark."

"Come to the big city to seek your fortune?"

"Yeah, to go to school at Pace Institute. I was gonna get a job as a secretary." He grinned when I said that. "But I found a job on the paper instead, doing rewrites of human interest stories."

"Cat shows?"

"Not exactly. Answering lonely hearts letters, Charity Smythe. Stuff like that."

"Charity Smythe?"

"Yeah. Hard luck stories. People write letters to the paper about how tough they have it, and if they're really bad off, they'll send out a reporter to do a first-person story about it."

"Pretty boring, huh!"

"Sometimes. Sometimes it would just break your heart, and make you grateful for what you did have. And if their story's bad enough, people send in money for the folks. But the *Graphic's* really a great place to work. No matter what they got you doing, you bring them a great story, they'll print it. Give you a byline, too."

"So, this extra is a big break for you?"

"You bet!"

We were interrupted by the waiter bringing bread and butter and, of course, more beer. I thought, I could drink gallons of this stuff before I got blotto. Guess that's why it's legal.

Moscowicz was buttering a slice of brown bread. "So, how come a pretty dame like you ain't married, or somethin'," he said.

I hesitated, trying to stop my voice from catching as I answered him. "Oh, I dunno. Never met the right fella, I guess. Besides, bein' a reporter is a full-time job. I ain't got a lotta time for hangin' around with guys."

"That's what you're doin' now!" he grinned.

"Well, tonight's special. They'll have to take me serious after this, Moscowicz. It's what I've been working for."

"I know," he said. He paused and added, "Now don't take this wrong, Sally. I'm glad this story came your way and all, but I'm still a little worried about your diggin' around in all this Ripper stuff. Could be dangerous."

"Well, it's dangerous for you, too, you know."

"It's my job," he said.

"It's my job too!"

I couldn't figure out from the look he gave me, whether he was mad or not, but I quit trying when the waiter came back with a tray full of food. Moscowicz had ordered himself two dinners—guess it made sense for somebody as big as he was. As I began to eat, I suddenly realized I was starving; I hadn't had anything since breakfast! We stayed quiet for a while and just enjoyed the food. Finally, after I'd eaten everything on my plate (something I almost never do!), I pushed my chair back and lit the best cigarette of the day. Moscowicz was still eating, but he had slowed down a lot.

"Did you get anywhere with your John Doe?" I asked him.

"Uh-uh," he shook his head. "I spent some time in the neighborhood around Chatham Square today, askin' around, gettin' people to look at his pitcher. No luck. I think he ain't from around there. Too well dressed, for one thing." He paused, then continued, "I'm afraid I might have to wait for him to come to, or for somebody to come lookin' for him."

"He's still with us, then?" I asked, remembering what Eben had said last night.

"Uh-huh," he nodded.

"Heard any news on the Ripper stuff?"

He gave me that look again, the one I couldn't figure out before. I guessed it meant he was not real happy.

"Nope. I told you, that's Henderson's case. I could get in a lotta trouble for foolin' with it."

I don't know why I said it, but I did. "Wouldn't make a whole lotta difference how much trouble you got in if you had that ten thousand dollars, now would it? Trulove said he'd give it to a cop."

That shut him up for a minute. Then he said, "I guess it wouldn't, would it?"

"Maybe that's what Trulove was counting on."

"Maybe it was."

Another uncomfortable silence.

"So, you gonna do anything about it?" I asked.

"What did you have in mind?"

"Oh, I dunno." I thought a minute. "This Strangways, now. Seems he shared an office with this McDowell that Dr. Warman is looking for. Maybe we could find something there."

"Henderson's already tossed it."

"Yeah, and he didn't get anything, either, or he'd have the joker locked up! Maybe we could find something he missed."

It didn't get by him. "We?" he said.

"Yeah, we!" I wasn't sure where I was going with this, but I kept on going, anyhow. "If we find him, you can have the ten grand, if I can have the story about how we did it. I can really rate in this town if I can find the Ripper!"

"You're assuming it's him."

"Yep! Henderson is too, I'll bet. Wouldn't it be great if we could beat Henderson to him?"

He had that look of his on permanent now. He stayed quiet for a while, working on it. Then he gave me an even stranger look, one that gave me the shivers, and said, "Okay, Barton, you've convinced me. When do you want to do it?"

Now I was really sorry I started this, but I just couldn't back down. "What's wrong with right now?" I asked.

"Nuthin," he replied. "We'll have to go by Centre Street to pick up a set of skeleton keys to get into Strangways' office. I'd love to get a look at the case file too, but Henderson's probably got that locked up tight." He pushed back his chair and stood up. "You had all you want to eat?" he asked me.

"Yeah. You?"

"Naw!" He grinned that homely grin of his, the one I liked so much. "Tell you what, Barton. After we finish this damnfoolishness, maybe we can go out for a coffee and some pie. Deal?"

"Deal! Let's go!"

We got up, and he paid the cashier. We went out on 14th and he stepped right out in the street, looking both ways, then gave a piercing whistle and waved a meaty arm when he spotted a cab.

After we were inside, he said, "Ain't got time for the train, Barton! We'll get us a car when we get to HQ."

I smiled at him in the dark. Then I sidled over so I was up against his side. I felt him tense, then he relaxed as he draped a huge arm over my shoulders. I took his hand in mine and burrowed into his side a little deeper. Jeez, I thought, I sure hope I'm doing the right thing.

He made me wait outside when we got to headquarters while he went in, then came back and led the way to a car parked nearby. It wasn't a Black Maria, just a plain sedan. He unlocked the passenger's door and motioned me in, then went around and got in the driver's seat. The trip uptown didn't take long; the streets were pretty clear on a Sunday night. When we were in the East Sixties, he started paying attention to the house numbers, shining a powerful, hand-held searchlight on the buildings from the car. He pulled over into a parking place.

"Here," he said, "this is close enough. We can walk from here."

Compared to downtown, the streets up here were really quiet. There was a little traffic on Park Avenue, but no pedestrians. The big, stone townhouses looked down their noses at us in the dark and even the streetlights didn't seem as bright as downtown. Like this morning at the Ritz, I was impressed with the fact that here was a place I didn't, and wouldn't ever, belong.

I followed Moscowicz up the steps to one of the townhouses. I looked at his broad, strong back as he was working the skeleton keys in the lock on the front door, trying to find one that fit. I was beginning to get a little scared of what we were doing, not because it was wrong, but because I didn't want to get him in trouble, ten thousand dollars or no. I didn't want him mad at me, because, if he was, then I probably wouldn't see him anymore, and I sure didn't want that to happen. All the more reason to find this Strangways and to make a hero out of Moscowicz!

He turned the knob and grunted when the door didn't open.

"It must've been unlocked already," he muttered.

He fumbled with the key again, then opened the door.

He motioned me to go ahead of him, then pushed in behind me and shut the door. We were in a little room with two fancy glass doors on the other side. There was a wardrobe to hang coats in, and a tall, swanky vase for umbrellas. There wasn't a whole lot of room for the two of us, with one of us being Moscowicz. I felt him pressing up against me from behind, so I pressed back and felt him tense up again. This time he didn't relax.

"C'mon, Barton," he hissed, "open the goddamn door!"

I did, and stepped into the interior hallway. It was dark, and very little light came in through the front door. I jumped as a beam of light shot out from behind me; Moscowicz, the well-prepared copper, had a flashlight.

"Hit that light switch," he said, waggling the flashlight to show me where it was, next to the staircase going up to the second floor.

When the overhead light came on, I saw a closed door on the left side of the hall and another entrance leading to Strangways' office, or at least to his waiting room. It had no door, but the opening was blocked off by that yellow tape the cops use at a crime scene. Moscowicz pushed by me and just stepped over it. Me, I had to duck underneath.

It was a typical doctor's waiting room, if a bit swanky. There was a door on the opposite side, with a little window next to it that had a sliding glass panel, where the receptionist called the patients from, I supposed. Moscowicz went over and opened the door, then flipped the light on in the next room and went in. Made me nervous, turning on all those lights, but he was a police officer and had a perfect right to be here. Except if Henderson caught him. I followed him into the receptionist's office.

He already had the door open to the next room.

"We'll look here if we don't find anything anywhere else," he said. "I'm looking for his office. That's where we'll start."

Made sense to me.

It was an examining room, with one of those metal tables that had stirrups for your feet. I could feel myself turning red—this was not something you wanted to be looking at with your boyfriend around! Was Moscowicz my boyfriend?

The next room was an operating room, with a great big table that swiveled and a huge light above it. It had a mediciney smell, and the walls were covered with glass-doored cabinets that held all sorts of strange-looking stuff. Made me nervous; I never liked doctors all that much anyway. That got me thinking about those autopsy pictures again. Ugh!

We went through another examining room, then we finally found what we were looking for. The room was spacious with two windows overlooking Park Avenue—we had gone all the way around the first floor of the house and ended up at the front again. A large, dark wood table, with flashy carvings, sat in front of the windows, with several chairs around it. There was also a roll-top desk, with the top down, against a wall, and several filing cabinets. The usual framed stuff hung on the wall above the desk—a medical degree from Columbia, an honorable discharge from the Navy. Another wall was covered floor to ceiling with books.

"The desk is the place to start," said Moscowicz.

The key was in the lock; he turned it and I winced as the top rattled up. Why was I so nervous about being here?

"C'mon, Barton, this was your goddam idea," Moscowicz said. "Help me and let's go through this stuff."

Most of the papers were letters relating to running the office; ads for medical equipment, drugs and suchlike. There were a couple of fat file folders that held patient records; I flipped through them but really couldn't make head nor tail of anything. This had seemed like a really good idea when we were swilling beer at Luchow's, but now that we were here, I wasn't really sure what we were looking for. Besides, there was something about this desk that was bothering me. I sat back in the chair and let my eyes wander for a minute. The file cabinets probably wouldn't have much that would tell us about Strangways, and the books were probably all medical stuff. There were some pictures on top of the roll-top desk—one of a couple of older people and another of the same people with a younger guy—both looked like they were taken down the shore.

I stole a glance at Moscowicz. He was going through some papers in folders on the table. I didn't know why, but I took the picture of the couple and the young man and slid into my bag. He didn't see.

I looked back at the desk again, and something clicked in my head. I let out a yip!

"Jesus! Don't do that!" said Moscowicz. "Whatinhell's wrong?"

"Uncle Carl!" I said. "My Uncle Carl in Morristown had a desk like this!"

Moscowicz looked at me like I'd gone nuts.

"So what!"

"So, we'd go to see him when I was a little girl and I used to play with it! And if I remember right, it should be right about here..."

I reached inside the desk, up near the top, underneath what looked like a solid piece of wood until I felt the button. I pushed it, and the little secret drawer popped open! It was full of papers.

"Bingo!" I said.

Moscowicz came over to see what I'd found.

I pulled out a stack of them. They were pictures—no, postcards, and when I saw what they were, I wanted to cram them all back into the little drawer before Moscowicz could see them!

"Holy smoke!" said Moscowicz.

They were pictures of men and women, or just women, with little or no clothes on, doing all sorts of dirty things! Some of them were barely more than kids! I felt myself turning red as I looked at them and I was very aware of Moscowicz's bulk above me, the sweaty smell of him, and his breath on my neck.

"He is a sex fiend!" I gasped. "I'll bet Henderson didn't find this stuff!"

"I'll bet!" said Moscowicz. He whistled softly. "Ripper or no, this egg'll be washed up as a doctor when this stuff comes out!"

I tore my eyes away from the pictures to look at Moscowicz. He was red as a stop light, too!

"You still don't think it's him?" I said.

"Oh, it's him, all right," said Moscowicz, "but this don't *prove* he's the Ripper! It doesn't tell us where to find him, either."

"How do we do that?" I asked.

"Do what Henderson's probably done already. Talk to everybody who knows him, try to find out as much as we can, then make some educated guesses as to where to start looking. Police work ain't easy. Hey, what was that!"

A second sharp explosion echoed through the house.

"That's gunfire!" Moscowicz reached inside his jacket and produced a revolver. "Sally, you stay put!" He jerked open the door to the hallway and ran out.

Stay put? In a pig's eye! I thought, and followed him out.

He was bounding up the stairs, three at a time. I hurried after him and was about halfway up when I heard him bellow, "Lady, put the gun down now! I am a police officer!"

I reached the doorway at the top of the stairs and froze. Moscowicz was inside a waiting room, his gun leveled at a bleached blonde in a frilly bathrobe, who also had a gun pointed at him. Another blonde sprawled on the floor near the stairs. I could see two red stains rushing to meet each other on her lush pink dress.

Moscowicz said again, "Lady, I mean it! Put the gun down now! I will shoot you, so help me God!"

The thud as her pistol hit the floor made me jump, as the blonde bimbo collapsed in a heap, shrieking hysterically. Moscowicz didn't miss a beat. Reaching behind himself as he strode across the room, he had her cuffed in a jiffy. Then he turned on me.

"I told you to stay put!" he snarled. He looked at the woman bleeding on the floor. "Call an ambulance, then the cops, while I see to her."

I looked around for a phone. A wooden gate separated the room we were in from another where there was a desk, and yes, there was the phone! I picked up the receiver and jiggled the cradle to get the operator. She came on and I asked for the ambulance; I had to get the address from Moscowicz. Thank God he knew it! The dame on the floor was still squalling and would have been no help whatever.

The next few minutes were a blur. The ambulance guys took the victim away and uniformed bulls hauled off the shooter.

Finally, Moscowicz turned to me and said, "Well Barton, that makes two big stories for you in one day." His voice was bitter. "Now all I have to do is figger out how in hell I'm going to explain this to Henderson. C'mon. I'll take you home."

The look on his face made my stomach hurt. He was right. This *was* another big story for me. How come I wasn't happy about it?

CHAPTER 10

The Statement of Dr. Ebeneezer Warman

I dressed quickly and went downstairs, then walked over to Third Avenue, scanning the sparse traffic for a cab. No luck. I began walking briskly uptown on Third. It was sixteen blocks from my flat to the hospital; I should know, I'd walked it often enough. I would save no time waiting for a train.

As I walked, I ruminated. I knew exactly what had happened, of course. Evie had suspected that Colin was trysting with his receptionist and was relying on me to confirm or refute it. I didn't do that. After agonizing over the situation for some time after I departed, she went to Colin's office to see for herself, encountering the formidable Miss LeMay and her revolver. Accusations, then bullets, flew. No one had told me these things, but I knew them as surely as if I'd been witness to them. Was Evie's injury my fault? Most certainly not! Would I feel guilty about it for the rest of my life? Absolutely!

Upon arrival at Lenox Hill, I inquired for Dr. Strongman.

"He's in surgery, Doctor," said the nurse.

"Which theatre?"

She told me.

I went directly to prep, donned a gown and scrubbed. Then I went into surgery. It was a scene I had seen thousands of times; the great light glaring down on the doctors and nurses huddled together, surrounding the unfortunate on the cold metal table, oddly sexless in their white surgical gowns. The sharp tang of iodine hung heavily in the chilly air. No one looked up as I approached. Evie was difficult to recognize; she had a tight white cap on her head and a sheet covering her breasts, but she was bare from her diaphragm to below her navel and her stomach was laid open like a frog pinned on a dissection board. The surgeon's nimble fingers swooped and plucked, suturing broken blood vessels with a fine needle and thread. Nurses removed bloody sponges from her abdominal cavity and replaced them with fresh ones, keeping the blood from obscuring the doctor's view so he could work unhindered. How different this was, when one knew and had feelings for the patient! I felt curiously ashamed at seeing her thus, even moreso than if I had observed her in an intimate act. The pictures from the autopsy reports I viewed last evening kept insinuating themselves into my mind.

Before long, the surgeon muttered, "There, that's got it, I think." He looked up at me. "Want to close?"

"No, doctor. The patient is my friend. I'm Dr. Warman."

The eyes above the mask widened. "Sorry. I thought you were the intern."

He made short work of the closure. When he was finished, a nurse wheeled the gurney from the theatre. I followed Dr. Strongman through the door to the prep room.

"What's the prognosis, Doctor?" I asked as I removed my mask.

Strongman removed his mask as well. I was somewhat taken aback by his appearance—he looked to be no more than eighteen or twenty years old, although I knew he had to be older to have finished four years of medical school and a residency. I had seen his obvious skill as a surgeon in the operating room. I hoped he was as skilled in post-operative care.

"As well as can be expected, I think," Strongman said. "Both wounds were relatively clean. The bullets were jacketed and passed right through."

"Wounds?" I inquired.

"Yes. She had a collapsed lung also. Bullet missed the heart and major blood vessels, fortunately. You saw the abdominal wound. She's lost considerable blood, but she's a healthy young woman and should be all right if infection doesn't get her."

Hospital-acquired infection was every surgeon's nightmare in cases like this. Modern aseptic technique has greatly reduced its occurrence, but no surgeon, no matter how skilled, could rest easily during the first forty-eight hours after surgery.

"May I see her?"

"If you like. She'll be unconscious from the anesthesia for a while longer and I've prescribed opiates for the pain."

"Has anyone called her home? She has two young children."

"I don't think so. We were more concerned with saving her life when she arrived."

"I'll attend to it then."

I changed back into my street clothes, then went to the nurses' station in search of a phone. As I surmised, Evie had left Mrs. Riordan in charge of the girls before going to Colin's office. That poor woman was nearly beside herself with worry when I rang, and the news I had to deliver hardly helped matters. I was able to extract a promise from her to remain and care for the girls until Evie's release from the hospital.

I heard a familiar female voice as I hung up the phone. "Hey, Eben! How is Mrs. McDowell?"

Sally Barton and Detective Moscowicz stood in front of the counter at the nurse's station.

I passed on Dr. Strongman's comments. "How did you know she was here?" I asked.

"We were at McDowell's office when she got shot." Sally said. "Or rather, at Strangways'." Moscowicz looked distinctly uncomfortable at that remark. Sally went on, "Is there someplace we can talk?"

"I've an office here." I said. I had intended to go and look in on Evie, but it was really unnecessary; Lenox Hill had an excellent staff and they were doing all that anyone could. "Follow me."

"Barton, I have to go downtown and file a report on this before I go home." Moscowicz's voice was cold. "I'll see you later."

Now Sally had a look on her face as if she'd lost her best friend. What on earth was going on with these two?

After the detective departed, I led Sally to the floor where the physician's offices were. I unlocked the door to mine and motioned her inside.

The office was sparsely furnished with a desk and a couple of chairs. I didn't use it frequently, so I kept no personal items there. I sat in the chair behind the desk and Sally took one of the others.

"Cigarette?" I asked her as I took the case from my jacket pocket. She nodded. Her face still reflected some inner turmoil.

After the cigarettes were lighted, I said, "Now tell me how you happened to be at Colin's office when Evie was shot."

"It's sort of a long story," she answered. "You seen the *Graphic?* My story about the reward that Simon Trulove put out?"

I shook my head.

"He's offered ten thousand dollars to anybody who can find the guy who killed his wife. So I kinda talked Morris—I mean, Detective Moscowicz—into trying for it. He took me over to McDowell's office. We were tossing Strangways' place, looking for things that Henderson might have missed."

Morris? "Henderson wouldn't like that if he knew."

"I know. And of course, he'll find out now."

Things were becoming clearer. I surmised that I now knew the reason for Detective Moscowicz's attitude a little while ago.

"We didn't know that Mrs. McDowell was even there," Sally went on. "We were tossing Strangways' office when we heard the shots. Morris knew what it was right away and went charging upstairs with his gun out. He got the blonde to drop her gun, then told me to call an ambulance. I didn't even know it was Mrs. McDowell who was shot until after we got here."

An unpleasant thought occurred to me.

"I don't suppose you're going to print this?" I asked her.

"Why, sure!" she said. "It's news, ain't it? And it's a good follow up to the story about McDowell's disappearing act. That'll be in tomorrow's paper too."

"I don't suppose I could prevail upon you not to print it. It will be embarrassing to Evie. She does have small children, you know."

Her countenance was even sadder than before. "I'm sorry, Eben. I don't want to embarrass anybody, but it's news. It's my job to report it. And maybe the publicity will help to find your friend."

"Maybe. Maybe not. I do know that it won't do Evie any good at all to have her marital troubles broadcast all over the city." Knowing the *Graphic*, I had a good idea how the story would be slanted.

"I'm sorry, Eben," she said again, "But that's just the kind of thing the paper is looking for. Don't you see that this is my big chance to make it as a real reporter? Not a girl reporter, doing household hints and Charity Smythe! A real reporter, working on real news!"

"And, dammitall, you don't care who gets hurt along the way?" I was becoming angry.

"Sure I care!" Her brown eyes were blazing now. "But I think Mrs. McDowell's already been hurt! The bullets did that! Her husband did that too, shackin' up with that floozie at his office! And you know, there are probably a whole lotta other broads out there in the same situation. Maybe my story will let them know that they're not alone, that this kinda thing happens up on Park Avenue just like it does in the Alphabets! I don't make the goddamn news, Eben, I just report it!"

I was a little taken aback by the intensity of her response. I didn't necessarily agree with her concept of professional ethics, but I was oddly pleased to note that, at least, she *had* some ethics.

"Well, maybe you have a point at that." I allowed, grudgingly. "But I still hate to see a good woman's name dragged through the mud."

"I'm sorry, Eben. Husbands cheating on their wives isn't news, and I wouldn't print it if that's all there was. But when somebody gets shot over it, it is news. Especially when it's connected to something like the Ripper case. That's just the way things are."

Seeing that I wasn't going to move her, I changed the subject." Did you find anything at Strangways' office?"

"Did I! Enough to tell me that he's the Ripper for sure! He had some dirty pictures hidden away in his desk! And him a ladies' doctor! I also found out he's had trouble with the law—he was accused of taking advantage of some of his patients."

I frowned. That kind of thing is an occupational hazard for any doctor who works with women, which is why there is considerable emphasis in medical school about following proper procedures when examining them.

"What kind of pictures?" I asked her.

She blushed. "You know, French postcards, that kind of stuff."

Hardly the sort of thing a respectable physician would keep in his office. "And you're going to print that, too, I suppose."

She nodded. "That's news too, when it's a Park Avenue doctor with a past."

"I really wouldn't want your job, Sally."

"I wouldn't want yours either, Eben. But we both love what we do and try to do it the best we can. That's all anybody can do."

I had to give her that. I stubbed my cigarette out in the ashtray on my desk and stood up.

"Well, I've had a long evening, and I want to look in on Evie before I go home. And I imagine you've got a lot of writing to do before tomorrow's paper comes out."

"You bet," she said, as she put on her coat. "Got any plans for things to do to find McDowell?"

I thought about it for a minute. Did I really want to stay involved in this insanity? Then I thought about Evie, fighting for her life, and the girls.

"I'll probably go up to Rockefeller Institute tomorrow." I said. "Colin does some work there and they may have insight into his whereabouts."

She was suddenly standing right in front of me, looking up into my face with those big, melted chocolate eyes of hers.

"Let me know anything I can do to help, Eben. I really want to."

I felt the anger I had toward her ebbing away.

I took her hands in mine. "I will, Sally," I told her.

We boarded the elevator and rode down. I got off on Evie's floor, leaving Sally to ride down to the lobby. What a remarkable young woman she was! She had a furious drive to succeed, coupled with an engaging personality that would cause nearly anyone to like her. She was going to make one damned fine reporter one day. I only hoped she wouldn't get herself in serious trouble while she was learning her craft.

I looked in briefly on Evie. The clean, white sheets and the sanitized atmosphere of the room belied what I knew to be the seriousness of her condition. She seemed to be sleeping normally. She looked almost like a comely young man, lying there with her hair hidden under the hospital cap and the sheets pulled up to her chin. God knew she surely didn't deserve what she was going through right now. And she was in His hands for the next forty-eight hours, at least. I said a prayer that He would make everything better for her.

It was nearly four o'clock in the morning when I arrived back at my flat. As I crawled into bed, I reflected that I would get about three hours sleep tonight. I hoped that my appointment schedule was not a full one for tomorrow.

CHAPTER 11

From the Notebook of Sally Barton

Sunday, September 27, 1931, late evening

I slept really lousy the night after Mrs. Mc Dowell got shot. On the way to the hospital, I had a fight with Morris in the car and we both said some nasty things to each other. When it was over, he finally said he didn't really blame me for what happened, but I knew that he wouldn't be in the fix he was in if I hadn't egged him on. Some night! First date, first fight, all in one!

We ran into Eben at the hospital, and I had a fight with him, too, about my printing the story about Mrs. McDowell. I really hated that she was getting that kind of publicity, but news was news, and it was my job to report it. But when I was leaving Eben, I saw the same kind of hurt in his eyes that I saw earlier in Morris'. Oh, I was really batting a thousand with the men in my life!

After I left the hospital I went right to the office, wrote up the McDowell and Strangways stories, and gave them to the lobster editor. I stood there silently while he read them.

"Holy smoke!" he exclaimed when he finished. "Does anybody else have this?"

"Not that I know of. The boys in the shack probably got a bulletin about the shooting, and anybody who read our McDowell story should have no trouble putting two and two together. But I'm the only one with the goods on Strangways and the dirty pictures, for sure."

"Damn me, Barton!" He started singing, like a little kid playing ring-around-the-rosy! "We got the Ripper! We got the Ripper! Keep this up, and you'll be right up there with Winchell and Sullivan!" He waved the papers in the air and bellowed, "Copy!"

A thrill shot right to my toes! Walter Winchell and Ed Sullivan had gotten some of the *Graphic's* biggest scoops, like the arrest in the Hall-Mills murder, and Frank was talking about me in the same breath with them! I fairly danced out of the office to go home!

My good mood lasted till I got there, at nearly four in the morning. As I lay in bed, I got to thinking, about Morris, and what was going to happen to him when my story hit the streets in the morning (the *Graphic* was putting out another extra!), about Eben, and what he had said to me at the hospital, and even about poor Mrs. McDowell, lying in a sick bed hovering between life and death, and what it was going to be like for her if she did get better and found out the news about her husband's floozy was all over Manhattan. I tossed and turned for what seemed like hours. When I finally did go to sleep, the autopsy pictures started whirling through my head again.

Monday, September 28, 1931, 8 a.m.

I felt like hell when I woke up. I tried to go back to sleep after I saw what time it was, but I had a headache that wouldn't quit and truthfully, I was just too damn keyed up to sleep. I got up, put on a pot of strong coffee (yes, I remembered to buy some!) and took a sponge bath while it perked. I felt better as I sat sipping it and smoking a cigarette, thinking about my day.

The first order of business was to go downstairs, buy a copy of the *Graphic*, and gloat. Then I had to call Joe Wells to get the latest on Trulove's reward for the evening follow-up. Couldn't do that till after lunch, though. Was it really just yesterday morning that I had talked to

Trulove in that Park Avenue penthouse? I had to figure some angle to follow up on Strangways, too. And I needed to call Morris and apologize for last night. Suddenly, I felt the urge to pee, and I didn't think it was from the coffee.

Later on, in the office, everybody came up to me to say how great the stories were, how terrific it was that the *Graphic* was getting the news ahead of the big kids again. Ed Sullivan was there; he took my hand and said, "Good goin', kid! This is just like the old days!" as he looked at me with those sad eyes of his. I felt like I'd just been kissed by Gary Cooper!

I was really walking on air when I hit Hudson Street after leaving the office, so much so that I didn't even see the two bulls until they had me, one on each arm!

"Hey, what's the big idea!" I yowled.

They hustled me into a Black Maria waiting at the curb. I might as well have been fighting Sharkey for all the good my struggling did me. By the time I was jammed in the back between the two goons and heading downtown, I had a pretty good idea who had gotten me in this fix. Henderson!

They put me in handcuffs when we got to Centre Street. I thought they expected I was licked, because I was shaking and crying when they pulled me out of the car, but the tears were of rage, not fear. Just who in the hell did he think he was, anyway?

Sure enough, they hauled me to a pint-sized office upstairs where Henderson was waiting. One of the goons shoved me inside and sat me down, hard, in a wooden chair, that wobbled 'cause it had a short leg. He shut the door as he left.

I just glared at Henderson, way too mad to speak. The weaselly little runt stared at me with his beady eyes, a smug look on his face, puffing on his cigarette, elbows on the desk, his fingers interlaced. I knew we were in a war of nerves and I vowed silently that hell would freeze over before I spoke first.

It wasn't long before he knew it, too.

"You've been a busy girl, Sally." He fished a copy of this morning's extra out of the mess on his desk and held it so I could see my headline.

I didn't say a word.

"Enough right here, for the whole world to read, to indict you for obstruction. You got anything to say?"

"Take these goddam bracelets off if you want me to talk!"

"You're in no position to demand anything, Sally. I want to know how you got into a locked crime scene."

I stared at him. The sonuvabitch! He had to know how I got in, if he read his own goddam police reports! Then it hit me. He was going to use me to fink on Morris!

I thought fast. "It wasn't locked!" I said. "I knew you were investigating Strangways. I went up there just to snoop around, and found the door unlocked. So, I went in." That was God's truth!

"Uh-huh." he grunted, plainly disbelieving me. "You just waltzed in, right past the crime scene tape and tossed the dump? That's a felony, you know."

I didn't know. It was hot in here, and smoky, and my shoulders were starting to cramp awful bad because of my hands cuffed behind me. Through the pain, it dawned on me that the only way I was going to stay out of jail was to tell Henderson that Morris had given me permission to enter the crime scene. Well then, I guessed I was going to jail!

"I guess I wouldn't have had to do it if you'd done your own goddamn job right the first time!" I told him. That took the smile off his face!

A clatter arose from the hallway outside. I heard a few thumps and some muffled voices, getting louder, then a shout.

"Hen-der-son!"

Morris!

I jerked in my chair, and it damn near tipped over as the door behind me burst open. Cool air rushed over me. Morris was suddenly there, his huge hands gripping my shoulders from behind! I nearly cried out in agony as he raised me from the chair.

"You have her in handcuffs? Henderson, you schmuck!"

I felt his sausage-like fingers fumbling with the cuffs, then the pressure on my shoulders was abruptly relieved as they clattered to the floor.

"Detective Moscowicz! This woman is under arrest for the illegal entry of a crime scene and obstruction!"

"Henderson, you piece of shit, you know goddamn well she went in there with me! Any evidence she reported in her story, she did it with my blessing! You got what you want! Now charge me with obstruction, you prick!"

My stomach dropped into my shoes. Morris was hanging himself, and doing it for me!

"I think I'll do just that, Detective!" Henderson was actually grinning now, a disgusting sight.

Just one step in that miniscule office and Morris was at the desk. His huge arm swooped, plucking Henderson right out of his chair. Henderson's arm flailed under his jacket until Moscowicz's other hand grabbed it and a pistol clattered to the floor. Morris lifted him by the neck until his feet were kicking madly four feet off the floor, then shook him like he weighed nothing; I could see his tongue sticking out, his face turning purple!

"Don't you ever hurt her again, or use her to get at me! If you do, I will kill you, so help me God!"

I grabbed his arm and pulled. It was like trying to move a lamp post.

"Morris! Please! Don't kill him!"

Morris' arm twitched and Henderson catapulted into the wall; the thump literally shaking the tiny room. He lay in a heap in the corner and I nearly wet myself, thinking Morris *had* killed him! Then I saw him move, just barely.

"C'mon, Sally!" A hand the size of my purse grabbed mine. "Let's get you out of here!"

I followed him meekly from the office, awed by the display of raw strength I had just seen.

Other cops were coming down the hallway toward us, attracted by the commotion, but Morris just ignored them and took me to the elevator.

Neither of us spoke as we exited the building and headed east, toward Chinatown. My head was still in such a whirl that I hardly noticed where he was taking me. In what seemed like a minute we were in an alley off Mott Street and he was rapping on a plain metal door. A concealed window snapped open, closed again, and then we were in a room reeking of gin and crowded with tables and chairs! God, I could have kissed him right there!

Soon we were seated with drinks, a rye highball for me, a shot and a beer chaser for him. I thought vaguely that it didn't matter anymore anyway—because of me, Morris was washed up as a cop—it was okay that he should have a drink if he wanted one. Then I began to cry.

"Hey, Sally, c'mon, it's all right, don't do that!" He was trying awkwardly to embrace me while sitting bass-ackwards on a chair. It didn't work very well.

I cried a little while and got it out of my system. Then, while wiping my eyes, I caught a glimpse of the expression of pure misery on that homely phiz, and I just couldn't help it. I started to laugh! He looked at me strangely, then he started laughing, too!

"Oh, my dear God!" I said. "His face was purple, his tongue was sticking out and there was drool running down his chin!"

"I think he peed himself, he was so scared!" said Morris.

We dissolved into gales of laughter again.

The speak was filling up with the lunchtime crowd and we were starting to attract attention, so I swallowed hard to stifle my mirth. Then another thought came, and I wasn't laughing any more.

"Oh, Morris! What is he going to do to you? Are you going to lose your job? Go to jail?"

"Go to jail? For taking a poke at Henderson? I don't think so. It's not like I'm the first cop who's ever done it!"

"Really? Then what about your job?"

He picked up the shot glass and dropped it into the chaser, then drained the mug in one draught, the shot glass clinking against his teeth. He waved at the barman for another.

"Oh, I'll probably get suspended," he said. "Two weeks for sure, maybe a month at the outside. Henderson's got some clout, but not as much as he thinks he has. I've got some too."

"That deputy chief you saved?"

"Something like that."

He grinned and made me smile again.

"But can you afford it?" I asked. "They don't pay you while you're suspended, right?"

"Nope." he said, then took a swig of his second beer. "Guess I'll just have to earn that ten grand, then!" He grinned again.

I could hardly believe my ears! "You're really going to help me try and beat him to the Ripper, even after last night?"

"After what Henderson did to you today, I'm going to catch the goddamn Ripper and rub his nose in it!" His words made me tingle all over.

"Where do we start?"

"Like I said last night, we talk to everybody Strangways knows, see if we can't turn some leads. Then we chase 'em."

"You know," I said, "What you do and what I do, it ain't so different."

"Not really. Maybe I just have to follow a few more rules."

I couldn't tell if he was kidding or not.

"Where do we start?" I asked again.

He downed the second shot, then had some more beer. "I assume you've raided your morgues pretty good already?"

"Uh-huh. All I found was those old sex charges."

"Well, it's a cinch that Henderson's not going to leave anything laying around at Centre Street. Hall of Records then. See, we need to get more background on Strangways."

I remembered something. I rummaged in my purse until I found the picture I swiped from Strangways office.

"I pinched this from his office last night," I said, handing it to him. "Maybe it'll help."

"At least it'll give us an idea of what this Strangways bird looks like," he said as he examined it. "Don't know how old it is, though." He finished his beer, looked at his empty glass, then at mine. "You want another?"

"You trying to get me plastered so you can take advantage?" His face went red. I said, "Hey, I'm sorry! I mean, you know, I don't care if you take advantage." He turned even redder. "I mean... Shit! You know what I mean!"

"You want some lunch, Barton?" he asked. We both exploded in laughter, again.

After lunch at Port Arthur, we headed down the street to the Hall of Records. Both of us were quite familiar with the layout since we'd both been here to do research before. It was less than an hour before we had what we wanted.

"Son of a gun!" I whispered, looking over the papers we'd found. "I'd have never thought a guy like Strangways would have been married!"

"Well, he isn't any more," said Morris. "This certificate says he was divorced in '27."

"That's right around the time he beat the rap on those sex charges," I said. "Maybe his wife knew something the judge didn't."

"That's where we should start," said Morris. "Henderson's probably talked to her, but he didn't have everything we have now when he did."

"Think she still lives in the house on Staten Island?" I pointed to the deed we had found.

"Dunno," he said. "Stay put a minute and I'll call and find out."

He was back in no time.

"Feel like a boat ride?" he asked.

"I'd go anywhere with you," I said, and he blushed again. I was really going to have to stop making him do that, but it was kinda nice to be able to.

We decided to go back to Centre Street and get an unmarked radio car to take down to the ferry slip, so we would have a way to get out to Strangways' house after we arrived on the island. Morris seemed increasingly nervous the closer we got to Police Headquarters.

"What's wrong?" I asked him.

"I hope we can get away with this. I'm sure Henderson's been to the Chief by now, and suspended cops don't get to use radio cars whenever they want."

"You want to skip it?"

"Naw! I really don't want to rely on the borough of Richmond's public transportation system if we can help it."

Sure enough, when we approached the sergeant to get the keys for the radio car, he said to Morris, "Cap'n's lookin' fer you, Moe."

"C'mon, Murph, gimme a break! I'll see him soon as I get back, swear to God!"

Murphy tossed some keys to Morris. "All right, I was in the johnny when you took the keys and I never saw you." He smiled at Morris, "Oh boyo! I heard you handed Henderson what a lot of guys around here have been wantin' to for a long time. Congratulations!"

"Must be great when everybody loves you," I said to Morris as we walked back out on the street.

"Especially when it's the right person," he said, turning redder than ever. My burning cheeks told me that I was doing just the same.

The trip down to the ferry slip at Whitehall Street only took five minutes, which we spent in silence. It was like I didn't want to say anything to him because I didn't know what was going to come out of my mouth, or what he might say back. I now had a pretty good idea of what was happening, and I was scared to death over it!

The ferry was just pulling into the dock when we arrived. The steel ramp rumbled like the "A" train as we drove into the bowels of the boat and parked. The lower deck reeked of exhaust fumes. We got out of the car and picked our way among the vehicles along with the rest of the passengers to the stairs leading up. Even though it had been only a few minutes since we entered the dimness of the car deck, I squinted against the bright white sky as I came out onto the passenger deck. It was still a while till quitting time; there weren't that many passengers heading to Staten Island, and it was easy to get a good spot along the rail.

A chilly breeze sprang up when we cleared the dock, and Morris took off his jacket and wrapped it around me. For me, it was almost an overcoat! He left his hands on my shoulders after he'd finished adjusting the jacket and pulled me backwards till my back was against his chest. I went stiff for a minute, but he started to knead my neck muscles, ever so gently for such a big guy. I gave up and let my head fall back against his chest. The muted strains of the orchestra playing inside the cabin floated gently on the breeze, creating the perfect atmosphere for the moment.

This couldn't be happening to me again, I thought, as I watched the bulk of Ellis Island slowly coming into view between the ferry and the Jersey shore. I am not falling in love again, not after the last time, and especially not with a copper! Not Sally Barton, the tough lady reporter who was going to get the Ripper and take this town by storm! But as the colossal green figure of New York's great Lady came into view, surveying the harbor from her pedestal on Bedloe's Island, I realized that my freedom was slowly ebbing away, vanishing like the tension in my neck under the gentle kneading of those immense hands; hands that had nearly choked the life out of a man just a little while ago. For me!

This just couldn't be happening to me again!

The two of us just stayed like that, not saying a word, all the way to Staten Island.

Silas K. Henderson

The Legacy of the Unborn

CHAPTER 12

The Statement of Dr. Ebeneezer Warman

I arose at seven and made a quick breakfast of bread and coffee, then hiked back to Lenox Hill. The weather was cloudy and a bit cool. I couldn't have borne the thought of going to work, had today been as fine as yesterday was.

Upon reaching the hospital, I quickly made my rounds—both of my patients had improved greatly over the weekend, one so much so that I wrote an order for her release. Then I checked on Evie—not surprisingly, there was no change. I watched her for about five minutes, gazing upon her beautiful, serene face and once again beseeched the Almighty to see to her recovery, then I went down to the street for a brisk walk to my office.

As was my custom, I arrived before Sarah did and checked the appointment book. The morning was full, but I had only one after lunch—an old biddy who really didn't have anything the matter with her, but who had to check in monthly for reassurance on that point. The bread and butter of my practice! I left a note for Sarah to reschedule that one.

Once settled, I placed a call to Alexis Carrel at Rockefeller Institute to see if he could meet with me that afternoon. Would I care to join him for lunch, he asked? Certainly!

The morning passed quickly. As usual, none of the patients I saw had any serious medical problems—such are the rewards of affluence! One young lady in particular was delighted to discover that she was pregnant. I was somewhat dismayed that current events made an announcement I normally took much pleasure in delivering into a cause for gloomy reflection; I imagined this sweet young girl lying in an alley, her innards strewn about like so much rubbish, with the cats licking at her life's blood as it mingled with the filth in the gutters. Ugh! Maybe Sally's profession was a noble one at that, if she could hasten the capture of that fiend!

Finally, the last patient was gone. In a spontaneous gesture of benevolence, I gave Sarah the afternoon off. I made a quick phone call to Harvey at his office to see if he was free for dinner. He was, so we made a date to meet at his club at seven. He threatened me with all manner of exotic tortures should I be late or absent, and I assured him that all the fiends of hell arrayed against me would not keep me from his side before ringing off. My chores complete, I took up my hat and stick and set off for the Rockefeller Institute of Medical Research.

The Institute, not far from my office, was founded at the turn of the century by the great American philanthropist John D. Rockefeller. He had a great desire to see a medical research institute of European quality on American soil. He invested millions of dollars to build an imposing edifice on a promontory overlooking the East River, furnished it with the best and most modern scientific equipment, in the hope of attracting the greatest minds in the world to come and work there. One of these men, Alexis Carrel, a Frenchman by birth, had won the Nobel prize in medicine several years ago for his contributions to vascular surgery, and had doubtless pioneered some of the techniques that Dr. Strongman used to save Evie's life last night. Colin and Carrel had met in scientific circles and discovered mutual interests, which had led to an invitation to Colin to use Carrel's facilities for his own research.

I asked at the guard post for the location of the dining room where I was to meet Carrel. True to his word, he was waiting outside for me—he'd said I'd have difficulty finding him among the myriad of tables inside if he did not.

Carrel was the archetypical Frenchman—a short, balding man with a broad Gallic face, a nose like Cyrano's and a smile that made you feel warm all over. That day he was still wearing his white laboratory coat buttoned to the top, the knot of his tie peeping over the collar.

"Dr. Warman?" he said as I approached him. He had a very subtle French accent.

"Dr. Carrel." He took my extended hand loosely in his and shook it gently in the French manner. "We met several years ago, at a party at Colin's home," I reminded him.

"I remember," he said graciously. "And now you say that our good friend Colin may be in some trouble? This is too bad."

"I hope not, but I fear he is. I hope you might give me some idea of his whereabouts."

"I do not think so, but we shall talk nevertheless. Come, let us go inside." He directed me to the door of the Institute's dining room.

The room was richly paneled and furnished with many long tables covered in white cloths, reminding me of somewhat of a military mess hall, except for its relative opulence. It was crowded at the lunch hour and the smell of food made my mouth water. Carrel led me around the perimeter, then across to one of the tables near the rear.

"This is where I usually sit," he said, raising his voice slightly to be audible over the buzz of conversation and the clink of silverware against china. "There is another who will be joining us for lunch. I hope you will not mind. He and Colin are acquainted as well, and he may have something to contribute to our discussion. We will wait for him before we get our food."

Carrel took a seat at the foot of the table, his back to the wall.

"Here I can see what everyone is doing!" he smiled, his soft, cocoa eyes gleaming behind his wire-rimmed glasses.

After taking one of the adjacent seats, I withdrew my cigarette case and offered him one, which he refused. I lighted up, then I asked him, "When did you see Colin last?"

"I knew you would ask me that question, so I thought about it before meeting you and I consulted my journal. I think it has been several months, maybe near the beginning of August."

I was crestfallen. "That long!"

"Yes, Dr. Warman. But you must realize that this is normal for Colin and me. He comes to work in the laboratory late in the evenings, after everyone has left. Rarely, he likes to consult with me about some problems he may be having with his research."

"And what is the nature of that research?"

"A problem which has intrigued me and many others for quite some time. Organ transplantation."

"Organ transplantation?"

"Yes, Dr. Warman. Colin and me, we would like to know how it is possible to take an organ from one animal and transplant it to another, so that it retains its full function."

I felt a catch in my chest as I considered what Carrel was saying.

"Of course, I am aware of the concept, Dr. Carrel. But I must confess I have little idea of the state of the field at the present time."

"It is as it has been for centuries, Dr Warman." He struck the table with his fist and I could hear the frustration in his voice. "Men have tried to do this thing since before the time of Christ. As you would surmise, the greatest difficulty has been with infection, although there are reports of the successful reattachment of human limbs dating back to the Middle Ages."

"Then one would think we should make great strides now, with our modern methods of asepsis."

"That is true, except for one thing," Carrel replied. "The success rate for the transplantation of an organ to the individual from which it came, like the reattachment of a severed limb, is orders of magnitude greater than that for transplantation from one individual to another, even within the same species. There is a process beyond simple infection occurring here, one that we know very little about. This phenomenon has been recognized from at least the sixteenth century. This is the problem that Colin has found so fascinating."

"As a general practitioner, I must confess I also know very little about it." My cheeks burned a bit. This was usually how I felt when I engaged in medical discussions with Colin. Inadequate.

"Do not apologize for your ignorance, Dr Warman," Carrel said graciously. "It is an arcane field of study. Many of its practitioners are reviled by the anti-vivisectionists and the medical community both. Some of them are outright charlatans. Me, I have done some small experiments with transplantation, enough to convince myself that the differences in the success rate between homologous and heterologous transplants are real, and due to an unknown cause. I am also fairly well convinced that we do not yet have the necessary data to understand the reasons for it, though the work of my colleague Dr. Landsteiner seems to be relevant. That is why I have turned my own research in other directions."

"And those are..."

"I am very interested in the maintenance of tissues and organs outside of the body. This has some relevance to organ transplantation, but it also has much importance as regards any number of surgical procedures. For instance, it might be possible for one to remove diseased tissue from the body, treat it *in vitro* and transplant the now healthy tissue back into the patient."

"You can actually maintain living tissue autonomously? Fascinating!"

"Yes, it is. I have in my laboratory tissue from the heart of a chicken, which has been growing in a jar for nearly twenty years. The chicken himself would not have lasted so long, *n'est-ce pas*? Ah! But here is someone who can tell you much more about this, because of the work he has been doing."

I saw that Carrel was looking at someone approaching from behind me. I turned and started to rise to greet the newcomer. When I saw who it was, my knees turned to jelly—I could not help but flop back into my chair. I have frequently thought since that I must have looked like quite the idiot, sprawled in that chair with my mouth agape!

"Dr. Ebeneezer Warman," said Carrel, "Meet Colonel Charles Lindbergh."

I never thought I was one for hero worship, but I had seen that boyish face beaming a thousand times from the front pages of as many newspapers over the past decade, and meeting him there in the flesh left me totally nonplussed. If there was one person I never expected to actually meet and have lunch with, much less that day, it was Charles Augustus Lindbergh, the hero of the Atlantic! My breath seemed to be literally sucked from my chest as the handsome aviator stood there in front of me, his hand extended. Somehow, I recovered some self-control and rose to take it, nearly toppling my chair as I did so.

I stammered something like, "Why Colonel Lindbergh, this is a great honor, to meet you, I mean, I'm sorry, I didn't expect..." I must have sounded like an addlepated schoolgirl!

Lindbergh took my hand and clasped it solidly in both of his. "Pleased to meet you too, Dr. Warman," he said courteously.

Carrel had also risen from his chair. "Now that we are all here," he said, "Let us go and get some food! I am hungry as a wolf!"

The line for food had shortened considerably since Carrel and I entered the dining room, so it was not long before we were back to the table with our trays. I hoped I had used the time to get my emotions under control so I could converse with these men on an educated level. I couldn't wait to tell Harvey with whom I had lunched, though. He would be green, positively green!

"Colonel Lindbergh, how is it that you are associated with Dr. Carrel?" I began.

"Oh, he is a valued member of my team!" the Frenchman answered for Lindbergh. "He has made great strides in organ perfusion."

"Organ perfusion?" Among these giants, I was becoming like a broken record!

"Yes, Doctor." Lindbergh spoke for himself. "One of the great problems in keeping an organ alive outside of the body involves getting enough oxygen to every single cell. Now, when the organ is inside the body, that's no problem, as you know, because we have the heart and the circulatory system to take care of it. But if it's outside, we have to use something else. An artificial heart, if you will."

An artificial heart! That was something straight out of the pulp magazines!

"But Colonel," I said, "Forgive me for asking, but how did you get involved in such fantastic things? I know only of your exploits as an aviator."

"I got interested in biology a couple of years ago," Lindbergh told me. "I never did go to college. I just bought a couple of textbooks and started reading them on my own."

And now you're in a collegial relationship with a Nobel laureate, I said to myself. I was beginning to get a glimpse into the greatness of this man!

"My wife's sister has heart trouble," Lindbergh went on. "One day, I asked one of her doctors why they couldn't do some surgery to fix the damage. She's a young woman, and healthy except for her heart; she should have many good years ahead of her. But the doctor told me that to do that kind of surgery her heart would have to be stopped for a long time. Now I'm a simple man, Doctor. It seemed to me that the heart's just a pump and what a biological pump could do, a mechanical one could do just as well. But when I asked the doctor about that, he told me that he didn't know. But he knew of someone who might." Lindbergh nodded toward Carrel.

Carrel took up the tale. "Charles did not know it, but I had been working on that problem in my laboratory for several years. But the problems!" His darting hands punctuated each word. "Blood clots instantly on contact with glass or metal, mechanical pistons cause erythrocytes to rupture, rendering them useless to carry oxygen. We have to use a nutritional medium instead of blood, which means that the organ must be maintained outside of the body. Then there is always the problem of bacterial contamination. Such an apparatus as Charles envisioned would have to be completely autoclavable and maintained aseptically all during its operation, so infection would not be introduced."

117

"Dr. Carrel showed me a pump he had been working on," said Lindbergh, "and I saw at once where I could make several improvements to make it more workable. I could eliminate the pistons, use a peristaltic flow mechanism to provide a constant, steady pressure and build it entirely of Pyrex, making it autoclavable. When I mentioned these things to Dr. Carrel, he took it as a challenge and invited me to come and work in his lab to make it happen. So, here I am."

Such is the power of genius! No one had told either Carrel or Lindbergh that such things were impossible. They just naturally assumed that they weren't and proceeded to try and accomplish them! I felt like an ugly duckling among swans!

"You have an apparatus that is workable, then?" I asked.

"I think so." said Lindbergh. "It's pretty big and clunky, not suitable for fine work at all. But we can keep an excised liver or kidney from a monkey or a dog alive for several days, as long as we provide enough nutrient medium and observe rigorous aseptic technique. Would you like to see it? We're running an experiment right now to test ways of replacing the nutrient medium aseptically and going for a new duration record in maintaining a kidney alive."

"I would love to see it, Colonel!" I said. Then my primary reason for this visit came back to mind. "Colonel, are you acquainted with Colin McDowell?"

He took a long pull from his glass before responding. "I am. Brilliant man, Colin. I wish I had a tenth of his intellect and drive."

"When did you last see him? He's gone missing, and his wife and family are very worried."

He considered a moment before responding. "It's been several weeks at least," he said finally. "Sometime in late July or early August, I think. I have missed him of late—we were often in the lab together late at night."

"Had you noticed any change in his demeanor prior to the time he stopped coming in?" I persisted.

"Not really. He and I didn't talk much. Oh sure, I may have explained the workings of my pump to him once and he'd occasionally inquire as to how things were progressing, but mostly, we just worked in the same lab. I didn't realize how much of a comfort it was to have someone else working when I was, in the wee hours, until he stopped coming in." He paused, then said, "Do you think something has happened to him?"

"It's beginning to look that way." I said. "He didn't talk to you about his work?"

"Oh, he may have tried, once or twice, but what he was doing was way over my head. I'm more of a technician than a real biologist and the stuff he was working on was really deep."

"Besides," Carrel broke in, "what could his work have to do with his disappearance?"

"Most likely, nothing." I admitted, frustrated. "I just wish I could find someone who's spoken to him in the last little while, to get a possible inkling of what may have happened to him."

"Colin is an intensely private man." Carrel said. "He said little to anyone, unless he was looking for information, or had something momentous to report."

"That I know," I said ruefully.

We finished our lunch, then Lindbergh and Carrel took me on a tour of the lab. Lindbergh proudly exhibited his perfusion pump, a Rube Goldberg contraption of shiny metal and gleaming glass, with tubes feeding into an excised dog kidney, floating in the center of a transparent jar. While the apparatus was definitely scientifically impressive, it lent a macabre air to the room, reminding me of a Hollywood set for a bad horror film. I also examined the area where Colin habitually worked, but that was not helpful. The laboratory was so small that everyone was required to clean up after an experiment, and Colin had left no notes or journals there.

Lindbergh and Carrel were gracious enough to walk with me to the gate when my visit was over. I must confess that a thrill went through me when I grasped the aviator's hand to bid him farewell.

"I hope you can find out what happened to Dr. McDowell quickly, Dr. Warman," Lindbergh said. "His would be a great loss to the world of science, as well as to his friends and family." Ashamedly, I agreed with only the first part of that statement.

Once on the street, I reached to my vest for my watch fob. Just before three o'clock; still plenty of time before my evening rounds to do a little more investigating. I crossed 68th Street and wandered toward the river, fumbling in my jacket for my cigarette case. I regarded the impressive new hospital complex adjacent to the Institute, still under construction, which was touted to be the most technologically advanced facility in the city. Reaching the river, I stood smoking awhile, contemplating the broad expanse of Welfare Island that lay halfway to Brooklyn; its profusion of hospitals, asylums and sanitaria spewing clouds of dark smoke into the milky sky. Impressive it was that the collective wealth of this great city had been committed to erect such a plethora of scientific palaces, all dedicated to healing the sick and to the relief of pain and suffering. Yes, impressive and sobering as well, for despite our vaunted modern medicine, despite the millions of dollars and as many hours spent in its pursuit, despite this imposing array of edifices, mankind has made pitifully little headway against disease and human suffering since we crawled about in caves, hiding from the wolves. Indeed, what piddling progress we have made has come only in the last century. My conversation with Lindbergh and Carrel made me realize how very much we still do not understand, about ourselves and our origins, about how our bodies function, or how they malfunction, as the case may be. Standing there, I re-experienced that common frustration of doctors—that all too often, despite our best efforts, we lose too many patients that we so desperately want to save. It is that frustration, above all, that drives men like Lindbergh, Carrel and Colin McDowell to the Herculean efforts they expend on behalf of the rest of us, who are condemned to await their successes to mitigate our frustrations. If Evie survived, I would have to pay Carrel another visit and thank him personally!

I pitched the remains of my cigarette to the ground and crushed it out with my shoe. Where to go next?

Colin's office was nearby. How could I forget that my search of it had been interrupted by the formidable Miss LeMay and her pistol?

However, since the assault on Evie, it was a *bona fide* crime scene, and I was not as certain of my right to be there as I was when Evie first asked me to go. It seemed good sense to contact the police before returning.

Besides his office and Rockefeller Institute, Colin McDowell was known to frequent the College Settlement House, where he performed medical procedures *pro bono*. True, Evie had called the settlement from my office the day she'd told me of Colin's disappearance and had been told that Colin hadn't been there for some time, but, I reasoned, it couldn't hurt to talk to some more people who had known him, to try to get some clue as to what had happened to him.

My decision made, I set off at a lope for the elevated station at 65th. Soon I was rattling along above 2nd Avenue, headed for the Lower East Side.

I disembarked from the train at the Rivington Street station and was shortly knocking at the door of the College Settlement House, housed in a fine brick, Greek revival rowhouse that looked to date from the last century, just west of the intersection of Rivington and Ludlow. The door was opened by a rather plain-looking young lady with sandy hair, dressed in a striped jumper that came to her ankles. She didn't seem glad to see me. I handed her my card, explained to her what I was about, and asked to see the person in charge.

"That would be Annabelle. I'll see if she can see you. Please follow me." She trudged off, shuffling her feet with head bowed. She installed me in a parlor overlooking Rivington Street, then disappeared in search of Annabelle.

Momentarily, a large, matronly lady of perhaps thirty-five came bustling into the room. She too, wore the long jumper; it seemed a sort of uniform here. Dark curly hair peeked out from under a lacy cap, worn after the fashion of the Mennonite women, and a pair of pince-nez dangled from a chain round her neck. She approached me, her hand extended.

"My dear Dr. Warman, Annabelle Akers, head resident, so good to meet you! And what, you still have your hat and coat? Christine! Come here this minute and take the gentleman's things! That's no way to treat such a distinguished visitor!"

I disrobed and handed my garments to the dour Christine, who seemed oddly apathetic about the chiding she'd just gotten from her mistress. She shuffled from the room, leaving me to the imposing Miss Akers.

"You will take tea, won't you doctor? Come into the parlor, we can talk there. It's ever so pleasant at this time of day."

When we were settled, I broached the subject that had brought me there as Miss Akers poured tea and hot water into my cup.

"As I told his wife on the phone the other day, Doctor, we haven't seen Dr. McDowell here for several weeks. I do hope nothing has happened to him! He's been our guardian angel here; I don't know how we'll get on without him!"

I wielded the silver tongs to drop two lumps of sugar in my tea, then stirred it gently. "He had a regular schedule here, then?" I asked. I took a sip; it was strong, astringent, and very good.

"Yes, he held a clinic every Tuesday evening. He's been doing it for nearly a couple of years, now. For many of our clients, it was their only opportunity to receive medical care."

"And when did he stop coming?"

Miss Akers sipped her tea as she considered the question. "I think it was around the second week of August. I could check my house log and give you an exact date." She put her cup and saucer down on the low table between us and began to rise.

"That's really not necessary, Miss Akers..."

"Oh, do call me Annabelle, Dr. Warman. Everyone around here does, you know." She smiled at me most ingratiatingly as she settled back into her seat. Then the smile faded as her face turned serious. "Without Dr. McDowell, I have no idea what we're going to do. He was monitoring some of our clients continually, for conditions that could prove serious. Since he's stopped coming, their care has been cut off completely."

"What kinds of conditions?" I could not help but ask.

"The scourges of poverty, Dr. Warman, the scourges of poverty!" Her voice rang with the timbre of the zealot. "Consumption, malnutrition, venereal disease, illnesses of the mind as well as the body! Dr. McDowell was also treating some infants, and counseling several expectant mothers." She paused and looked at me with a plea in her eyes. "There was a horrible tenement fire up on 7th Street just yesterday, Dr. Warman. Three were killed, fifty more burned to some degree or another. Had we our clinic here, some of them might have come to us for aid. But now, what are these unfortunates to do?"

Suddenly, I had a very good idea where this conversation was going. I started to fumble for my cigarette case, then stopped as I realized I hadn't asked permission.

"Miss Akers..."

"Annabelle, Doctor."

"Yes, Annabelle, may I smoke?"

"But of course, Doctor. I'll get you an ashtray." Her tone could not have been any more accommodating. She rose and left the room.

Dammitall! I should have seen this coming! With my regular patients, hospital rounds, and now, this search for Colin, I absolutely did not have the time or energy to take on any more! Then the guilt set in. I considered Colin, who also had regular patients, hospital rounds, and an ongoing research program in the laboratory of a Nobel laureate, who still found the time to come here once a week to minister to those who could not afford to pay for their medical care! Because of his deception of Evie and his lack of attention to his children, my opinion of Colin had been rather low of late, but now, I was forced to realize he had some very exemplary character traits as well as some reprehensible ones. If the latter made him such a despicable man, then what was I, who made an excellent living treating the phantom ailments of rich old biddies?

Miss Akers returned, struggling with a heavy bronze smoking stand in both hands. I rose hurriedly to assist her. We both took our seats again. As I extracted a cigarette from my case and lighted it, the question occurred to me—was I going to make her beg, or was I just going to volunteer? I inhaled the cigarette deeply, filling my lungs with smoke, and my muscles relaxed under the effects of the nicotine. I made my decision.

"Miss, ah, Annabelle, perhaps I could fill in for Dr. McDowell just for a while, either till he turns up or we can find someone else..."

"Oh, Doctor!" Her smile was now positively effusive. "Would you! That's positively noble of you! Could you start tomorrow night? That was Dr. McDowell's regular night, you know, and I'm sure I can have the word spread by then."

"That may be a bit fast..." The smile vanished and her face fell. "But, if you can get me a list of who is coming and I can find Dr. McDowell's records..." The smile was back again. "I don't suppose he kept any records here, did he?"

She pursed her lips. "No, I don't believe so. He took notes in a black book that he carried with him in his bag. I suppose he kept it in his office."

Wonderful! Now, I had an excuse to revisit Colin's office and good ammunition to get the local constabulary to grant me permission to do it. I was almost certain I had already seen that book, but I was under no obligation to let the police know that—even if I had an escort, I could now search the office with impunity.

I stubbed out my cigarette. Now that I had been properly hoodwinked, I thought again of the reason I'd come here in the first place.

"Annabelle. Would it be possible to talk with some of the others here who knew Dr. McDowell, to see if anyone can give me a clue to what may have happened to him?"

"Of course, Doctor, you may talk to anyone you wish. But I'm afraid you will be disappointed. Dr. McDowell had very little interaction with any of the residents, including myself. He simply came, tended to his patients and left. A charitable and generous man he may be, but he is certainly not a gregarious one."

Dammitall! Colin was nothing if not predictable—it was beginning to seem that he had met with some sort of foul play, which had wrenched him from his customary routine. Still, I had to try.

"When would be a good time to interview the residents?"

"It's approaching the dinner hour, most everyone should be here. I can gather them, if you wish."

I consulted my watch. Just after five. If I could interview the residents as a group, it should go quickly—I could still meet Harvey for dinner at seven, then do my rounds afterwards. Dammitall! I'd had visions of spending a leisurely evening with Harvey, to atone for my recent lack of attention, but some things were just not to be.

Unfortunately, Miss Akers' somber prediction came to pass. After she had assembled the dozen or so women who lived at the settlement in the parlor, I asked the group to tell me anything they could, which would help me to ascertain Colin's current whereabouts. To a woman, they asserted that they had no congress with him except to fulfill his requests as pertaining to the care of his patients. I saw no reason to doubt the veracity of any one of them.

It was just before six when I donned my hat and coat, bade Miss Akers farewell with a promise to return tomorrow evening and stepped into the gathering dusk. I had not gone but half a block when I heard a voice from behind.

"Oh Doctor! Please wait a moment!"

I turned to see one of the residents hurrying towards me, her arms wrapped around her middle to hold her sweater closed. Obviously, she'd thrown it on in some haste.

She stopped a pace or two from me, breathing a bit heavily. She was a pretty girl, barely twenty, I surmised, and made even more attractive by her shoulder length blonde hair, tousled by her recent celerity. She looked confused, and a bit frightened.

"How can I help you, Miss..." I had of course been introduced to all of the residents, but this one's name escaped me.

"Hannah Slater, Doctor." She hesitated, then continued cautiously, "Do you mind if we walk a bit? I'd rather that none of the others know I've been talking with you."

She looked about warily, then took my hand and led me into the doorway of the synagogue adjacent to the Settlement, where we could not be seen from the house, and placed her back against the double doors, facing me.

"Come, Miss Slater," I said, somewhat amused by her antics. "Surely it is no disgrace to be seen talking with the Settlement's new physician."

"Of course not, Doctor." She sounded offended. "It's just that, well, I didn't want to say what I have to say to you in front of the others."

Now I was curious. "And what might that be, Miss Slater?"

"I saw Dr. McDowell the other day." She cast her eyes downward, as if she was ashamed.

Silas K. Henderson

CHAPTER 13

From the notebook of Sally Barton

Monday, September 28, 1931, 2:30 p.m.

As the ferry eased into the dock at St. George, an overhead canopy blocked the sun and a shadow fell over the deck as the comforting weight of Morris' hands disappeared from my shoulders, leaving me with an unsettling sense of loss. Peeling off his coat, I turned toward him, looking into his eyes as I handed it back to him, and I shivered inside because of what I saw there. We didn't say anything to each other as we followed the other passengers back down the stairs into the bowels of the ferry.

We were both still quiet as we rumbled down the ramp onto the dock and out into the daylight once again. It was Morris who spoke first.

"Sally...," he began.

"Yes, Morris?"

"We need to find out where we're going."

"I think so, too," I agreed. I was not looking forward to this conversation!

"Dig in that glove compartment. There should be a city map in there. It has Staten Island on it."

"Oh!" I cocked my head to glare at him; he sat ramrod-stiff at the wheel, his eyes focused resolutely ahead. His words caused an icy ball to grow in my belly—that's not what I thought you meant, you big palooka! I wanted to sass him but I couldn't find the words, then it dawned on me. He didn't know what to say any more than I did! A little ashamed of myself, I leaned forward to do what he had asked.

After consulting the map, I looked in my notebook for Mrs. Strangways' address. It didn't take me long to find her street.

"It's not far," I told Morris. "It's just off Richmond. That should be it, up there on the left."

Though I'd lived in the city for quite a few years, this was my first trip to Staten Island. The area around the ferry terminal was pretty citified with some good-sized government buildings and big new apartment houses, but as we got further from the slip there were more factories, with lots of little one room houses crammed among them, most of them the worse for wear. The air stank of smoke and salt water. I knew what it was like inside those little houses; I had been in a few like that doing my Charity Smythe stuff. There were some nice houses too, up in the hills, their turrets sticking up above the trees; no doubt this was where the fat cats who ran the factories lived, looking down on the little people whose sweat and toil had got them up there in the first place.

Once we took the turn off Richmond, it was hard to believe we were still in New York City. The houses thinned out real fast—now most were two- or three-story clapboard affairs with big, fenced back yards, and lots of trees—it made me a little homesick for Maplewood. I glanced at Morris, who was still staring straight ahead, and wondered if he'd want to live in a little house like these someday. Whoa, Sally! Ain't you getting a bit ahead of things?

Mrs. Strangways lived in one of those clapboard houses in a place called Dongan Hills, at the end of a tree-lined street with a row of homes on one side and a vacant lot on the other. A sign said the lot was for sale and great for development. Morris parked the car at the curb in front of her house and said the first words to me since he'd asked for the map.

"Well, she's expecting us." He hesitated, then said, "Better let me do the talking first. You can ask her some questions later if you want to, but don't let on you're a reporter."

That just hit me wrong. "Why? It ain't nothing to be ashamed of!"

"No, it isn't," he said in a reasonable tone, "But she might open up a little more if she doesn't think everything she tells us is going to wind up in the bulldog edition."

He had a point, but what he'd said still rubbed me the wrong way.

"Don't worry," I said, "I won't crab your act."

He got that hurt look on his face again and I was sorry I said it. He looked like he was going to say something else, then he thought better and got out of the car.

I followed him up to gate, which he opened for me. We proceeded into the front yard, along a flower-lined, red brick path leading to a front porch complete with rocking chairs and a swing. As we went up the short flight of steps, I could see that the front door was open—a screen door in front of it kept out the flies and allowed a warm, yeasty aroma to reach us. I looked for a doorbell but didn't see one. Morris stepped up and rapped on the wooden door frame, then started backwards as an outbreak of furious yapping erupted. A little white-furred bullet struck the screen, and the door lurched in its frame, but it didn't open.

"Basil!" A voice shouted from inside the house.

A woman came hurrying down the hall, snatched the little terrier out of the air in mid-leap, and said through the screen, "I'll be with you in a moment." She carried the struggling dog back into the house, and we heard a door slam. Then she was back, unhooking the screen door.

Louella Strangways wasn't at all what I expected. Middle-aged, she had dark black hair cut short, showing a little gray. She had a square face, not homely by any means, but certainly not pretty either. She was wearing a house dress like you could get at Klein's, and a pair of slippers. She just looked like somebody's mom. After what I'd found in Strangways' office, I guess I'd expected his wife to be a real dish.

"You must be Detective Moscowicz," she said, then looked at me quizzically.

"This is my, ...err, associate, Sally Barton." Morris said.

We went inside and followed her down a hallway into a living room, furnished with heavy, dark furniture, smelling of years of cooking. I could still hear the terrier's muffled yaps somewhere else in the house. Mrs. Strangways invited us to sit on a plush, flowery sofa and asked if we would have tea. To my surprise, Morris accepted.

We sat quietly while we waited for her to come back with the tea. I wanted to slide over to touch Morris on the sofa, but I knew this was not the place for that. He must've had the same idea, because he turned and smiled at me—that warm smile of his that filled up his homely face and made me tingle all over—then he squeezed my shoulder. I heard the clank of china from the hallway; Morris removed his hand and his face became all business again.

Mrs. Strangways came in with the tray and we went through the one-lump-or-two routine. I took some tea even though I really don't like the stuff; it occurred to me that a nice, stiff highball would be just fine right about now.

Finally, after sipping the tea and saying how good it was, we were ready to get down to business.

"Your call this afternoon surprised me a little, Detective Moscowicz," Mrs. Strangways began. "I've already told your Inspector Henderson what little I know about Addison's doings." She paused, then continued, "Even though we're not married anymore, I do hope he's not in any trouble."

"Well, ma'am, that's the problem," Morris said. "We don't know if your husband's in any trouble, because he's gone missing. We were hoping you could help us locate him."

"Addison is my *ex*-husband, Detective," she said, stressing the ex. "I haven't seen or talked with him in months." She hesitated again, then said, "Inspector Henderson didn't say anything about him being missing."

"Well, it's just been in the last few days. That's why we decided we'd better talk to you again."

Smooth, Morris, real smooth. I was wondering how he was going to explain why he was sticking his nose in on Henderson's case. My professional opinion of him went up a notch.

Morris went on, "Can you think of any reason that Dr. Strangways would take a powder?"

"Like I said, Detective, I haven't seen Addison for months. As far as I know, everything is just ducky for him these days."

There was something fishy about the way she said that.

"So, you two have been apart, how long?" asked Morris.

"Almost five years, Detective." She sounded a little irritated.

"Did your marriage trouble start because of that, ...err, problem that Dr. Strangways had about that time?"

"You mean those charges filed by that patient of his," she answered matter-of-factly. She took a sip of tea. "Oddly enough, Detective, I think Addison was actually innocent, that time. No, our problems had been going on for a while before that. And afterwards."

Morris didn't say anything, waiting for her to go on.

"It's hard, being married to someone in Addison's line of work," she said. "He saw hundreds of women, all the time, a lot of them awfully young and pretty."

"He was steppin' out on you?" I asked.

"I thought so," she said. "I still do, though he always said he wasn't."

"What finally caused you two to break up?" Morris asked.

She didn't answer and I could see her turning red. "Is all this really necessary, Detective? Addison's and my marriage troubles are ancient history. I don't see how discussing them is going to help you find him."

Suddenly, I knew. "It was the pictures!" I blurted. "You found his postcards, didn't you?"

She looked daggers at me for a second, then the fight went out of her.

"How...how did you know about that?" Obviously, she hadn't seen my story in the *Graphic*.

I looked at Morris, to see how he was taking this. I really didn't want to crab his act. The look he gave me told me it was okay.

"We were going through his office the other night," I told her, "looking for clues about what might have happened to him. We found some dirty pictures in his desk."

"You're right, Miss Barton," she said, "I found some of those filthy things in his den one day when I was cleaning. That was the last straw."

I thought about what she had said before, about everything going swell for Strangways right now. I asked her, "Is Addison, you know, seeing anybody else these days?"

She gave me another dirty look; apparently, I'd hit the bull's-eye again. I could tell she really didn't want to answer this question, either.

"I think so," she said, finally. "If you must know, I think he was playing around with that floozie upstairs!"

"You mean Dr. McDowell's secretary?" Morris asked.

"If that's what she is!" Mrs. Strangways spat. "She doesn't impress me as having enough brains to make a living any way other than on her back!"

"It sounds to me like you have seen your husband a lot more recently than you told us, Mrs. Strangways," Morris said with an edge in his voice. "Why'd you lie about that?"

"I... I don't really know, Detective." She leaned forward and fished a cigarette out of an enameled box on the table in front of us. Her hands shook as she lit it. She took a deep drag and exhaled forcefully. She continued, "When Inspector Henderson was here, he asked a lot of questions about Addison and me and... and our relations..., when we were married, that is." Her face was so red she could have stopped traffic. "When I asked him why he needed to know these things, he wouldn't tell me. But I'm not stupid, Detective. I know what's been going on the last few months in that neighborhood where Addison's office is. If Addison had anything to do with what happened to those women... well, I'd really rather not get involved, you know?"

"Do you think Addison could be responsible for what happened to those women?" Morris asked her.

She sucked furiously on the cigarette again, then stabbed out the two-inch butt in the ashtray. "Oh, I don't know, Detective! I don't think so, but I don't know! Those pictures of his, some of the... things... he asked me to do for him..., look. Addison is far from a perfect man, but he was never mean to me, never cruel, like he'd have to be to hurt those women. He's a doctor, for Christ's sake! He helps people!" She was almost crying now.

Morris gave me a look that said, don't say anything right now. He let her calm down a little before he asked, quietly, "When did you see him last?"

"It was about three weeks ago," she said. "He was late with the alimony again. I'm supposed to go through the lawyer when that happens, but, well, sometimes Addison just forgets, you know? I don't need to make trouble for him when he just forgets."

You could have called him, I thought, you didn't have to go, but I didn't say it.

"How was he when you saw him?" Morris asked.

She took another cigarette from the box. She looked at me and said, "I'm trying to stop, you know?" She lit it, and Morris and me lit up, too.

"He seemed preoccupied," she said to Morris, "More so than usual. He said he was sorry about the check."

Again, I knew there was something she wasn't telling us. "And?" I said.

"Well, he was sitting there at his desk, you know, writing the check. Then she comes waltzing in, just like she belongs there, or something!"

"You mean Miss Le May," I said.

"Yes, I mean Miss Le May," she gritted her teeth when she said her name. "'Oh, sorry, Addison', she goes, 'I thought you were through with your last patient.'" She looked at her cigarette like she didn't know what it was doing there, then stabbed it out again. "Addison, she calls him. Not Doctor Strangways. Addison!"

"What happened then?" asked Morris.

"Addison just sits there, with a dumb look on his face, then he goes, 'Oh. Dana. I forgot. Be right with you.' She looks at me like I'm some kind of dirt or something, then she just flounces out."

She lifted the lid of the box to take another cigarette, then let it drop with a Crack! when she realized what she was doing.

"What did Addison do then?" I prompted.

"Hands me the check, tells me he has an 'appointment' with Miss LeMay and that he'd see me later. So, I left."

She doesn't read the papers, I thought. She doesn't know about LeMay and Mrs. McDowell. Should I tell her?

"Did you tell all of this to Inspector Henderson?" Morris asked.

She gave him a funny 'Don't you know?' look and said, "No. He didn't ask. Well, maybe he did, but I didn't like some of the things he was asking me, and I wanted to get rid of him."

I could sympathize.

"Do you think something has happened to Addison?" she asked. "Something bad?"

"We don't know," Morris admitted. "He hasn't been seen for a few days. Seems like his upstairs neighbor, Dr. McDowell, has also disappeared. Can you tell me anything about him?"

"Not really. I mean, he was Addison's landlord, but I only remember meeting him once or twice. Funny duck. He didn't say much. I got the impression he thought he was better than everybody else."

"Why?" asked Morris.

"I don't know. Maybe it was just the way he looked at you -- or through you really, like you weren't even there."

"So, as far as you know, he and Addison weren't friends. Didn't talk shop, or anything like that?" Morris prodded.

"If they did, I sure didn't know about it."

I decided not to say anything to her about LeMay and Mrs. McDowell. She seemed genuinely worried about her ex-husband and I didn't want to pour any oil on that fire.

Apparently, Morris felt the same way. He said, "Well, Mrs. Strangways, is there anything else you can tell us that you think might help us to find Dr. Strangways?"

She shook her head.

"Well then, I guess we won't be taking up any more of your time." He reached in his jacket for his card case. "You can give me a call at that number if you think of anything else."

As we were getting up to go, I suddenly remembered something. I dug in my purse for the picture I filched from Strangways' desk the other night, and handed it to her.

"What can you tell me about that?" I asked her.

She just barely glanced at it. "Oh that," she said. "It's the picture from his desk in the office."

"We thought it might help us recognize him," I told her, not wanting her to think I was a common thief or something. "When was it taken?"

"Oh, it's pretty old. It was taken when Addison's parents were still alive, fifteen, twenty years ago. That's them in the picture. Addison really doesn't look like that anymore."

"You wouldn't have a more recent picture of him we could have?" Morris asked her.

"I gave one to that Inspector Henderson."

"I know," said Morris, "but we'll need one too, if we're going to be helping him look for Addison."

She didn't say anything for a minute, thinking it over. "Well, if it's going to help you find him. I'll be right back."

She got up and left the room. I could hear her footsteps going up the stairs. A couple minutes later, she was back, holding a picture in a frame.

"That was taken a little over five years ago, just before me and Addison split up," she said.

I looked at the picture. It showed her and Strangways standing on a beach in bathing suits, with a large L-shaped building in the background, its roof supported by many tall pillars.

"Where was this taken?" I asked her.

"Same as the one you just showed me," she said. "Cape May, New Jersey. That's Congress Hall, one of the biggest hotels down there. We stayed there for a couple of weeks every summer. Addison and his parents had done that all of his life." She added, "I'll want that back. It's the last one I have. You better keep it in the frame so it doesn't get ruined."

It was times like this I was glad I carried a really big purse. I slid the picture inside, along with the one I'd taken from Strangways' office.

We got up and went through the "we're going now..." routine. I didn't say anything to Morris until we were out in the car.

"She still loves him, you know," I said after he slid behind the wheel.

"Yeah, I caught that," he said. "Think she knows where he's lammed?"

I didn't really have to think about it. "Nope," I said. "She's worried about him, and not because she thinks he's the Ripper." I paused, then asked him, "Do you still think it's him?"

"Yep," said Morris. "I'll bet money on it. Ten thousand smackeroos! And I'll bet LeMay found out it was him. That's why she was so nervous with that gun of hers."

"Maybe Dr. McDowell found out, too," I said, following his line of thought. "And maybe Strangways did him in to keep him quiet. I'll bet LeMay was waiting for him to show up and getting scareder by the minute. By the time Mrs. McDowell walked in, she was probably fit to be tied."

"It all fits," said Morris. "The pictures, the fact that all the victims were Strangways' patients. No wonder he was 'preoccupied' when Mrs. Strangways talked to him last."

"But why do something like this? Like she said, he's a doctor. He's supposed to help people!"

"He's a pervert!" spat Morris. "You saw them pitchers! Whips, cuffs, girls young enough to be his daughter…"

I could feel myself turning red again. This was not a conversation I wanted to be having with Morris! I changed the subject. "What's next?" I asked him.

"Well, I need to return this radio car, and go take my medicine for what happened with Henderson. Then I'll have some time on my hands." He turned and grinned at me. "Feel like a trip to the beach?"

"Cape May?"

"Where else?"

"I'd go anywhere with you," I said, then he turned bright red again. I was really going to have to stop doing that!

On the trip back across New York Bay, Morris and I discussed the trip to Cape May some more and he brought up the very good point that we didn't really know whether Strangways had gone there or not.

"It's an awful long way to go on a wild goose chase," he said. "Clear down the end of the Jersey shore. We'll have to catch a train outta Philly. Take the whole damn day to get there."

"You got a better idea?"

"Maybe," he said. "Maybe we oughta toss old Strangways' digs first. Might find something there to tell us where to look."

"I'm sure Henderson's probably tossed that dump, too," I said. I turned and looked at Morris and grinned. "But I guess he ain't had too much luck with things like that, huh?" A bad thought came into my head. "How can you talk about tossing Strangways' joint when you're about to get the bum's rush from the force for a while? Ain't they got rules about that?"

"Heck, sweetie," he said, "if I played by the rules all the time, I wouldn't be getting the bum's rush."

I thought that "sweetie" sounded a whole lot better than "Barton"!

I looked out over the water, towards Jersey. The sun was sinking low in the sky, behind the clouds, causing them to take on a strange, deep yellow glow, sorta like a preview to sunset. The buildings beyond the Battery were still so far away that it was hard to see them as separate; they looked like giant gray kid's blocks tossed one on top of the other, with nothing at all to show that they were teeming with people. An ocean liner crossed in front of us, heading out to sea. I wondered where it was going. England? Africa? The folks on board sure knew, which was more than I could say for myself. I really had no idea where I was going.

When we reached the Battery, we decided to split up; I offered to wait at Police Headquarters until Morris found out what was going to happen, but he nixed that idea. "The Chief may have already gone for the day, or he could have me there half the night," he said. "Just go home, and I'll call you when I know something."

"I need to go by the paper," I said, "find out what's happening."

"You're not going to write about what we did today, are you?"

I gave him my best dirty look. "Do I look stupid or was that just a guess on your part?" He had the courtesy to look at his shoes. "I don't want old Strangways knowing that we're coming for him anymore than you do!"

"Well, they'll probably be pushing you for something, you go in."

He was right about that.

"Okay," I said, "We'll play it your way. I'll go straight home, but don't you dare toss Strangways' place without me. And I don't want to wait until tomorrow to find out what happened with the Chief. Call me, no matter how late it gets."

He promised. I scooted over, put my hands on his shoulders (I could barely reach!), and kissed him. He sure did kiss me back! When we came up for air, I noticed that his face wasn't red this time.

"Want me to drive you home while I've still got the radio car?" he asked.

"No," I said. "You go do what you need to do. I'll take the train."

He kissed me once more, then I got out of the radio car and crossed the street, heading for the subway. I turned and saw that he was still there, watching me out the driver's window. When he saw me turn, he raised a hand to the window and drove away.

"Remember, you big palooka," I called after him. "Call me!

The Legacy of the Unborn

CHAPTER 14

The Statement of Dr. Ebeneezer Warman

"I saw Dr. McDowell the other day," Hannah Slater said. She cast her eyes downward, as if ashamed.

"Which day?"

"Last Wednesday." That was the day after Evie saw him last!

"At the Settlement?" *Not another paramour, Colin,* I thought!

"No. Coming out of Miss Lucy's."

"Miss Lucy's? And what..." Looking at her face, I knew the answer as soon as the question came out of my mouth. "Ah!"

"A brothel, Doctor. On Allen Street."

Dammitall! Surely Colin, of all people, had more sense than that! Deceiving Evie with his secretary was one thing, but this, consorting with whores, the diseases... I was speechless!

She must have seen the reaction on my face. "I'm sorry, Doctor," she said. "I thought you'd want to know.

"You're quite right," I said. "I do." I paused for a moment, gathering my thoughts. "Did you speak to him?"

"No. I was a little ways away when I saw him come out. I started to call to him, then I realized where he'd come from. I, ... I didn't know what to do."

"He didn't see you?"

"No. He was walking away from me. Toward Rivington Street. I thought he was coming here."

"But he wasn't."

"No. He turned on Rivington, but on the other side. From the Settlement, I mean. I followed, watching him from across the street until I got here. He kept on heading east."

"You don't know where he was going?"

"No. I was returning home for the evening. If he wasn't coming here, I didn't think his destination was any of my business."

"And you didn't say anything to anyone? That you'd seen him?"

"No. I knew that Annabelle was worried about him, because he hadn't come for clinic for so long. But if I said anything, I was afraid she'd ask questions. I didn't want to say where I'd seen him."

That was understandable. I spent a moment digesting what she had told me, then, I had a thought.

"I don't suppose he was treating someone at Miss Lucy's?" I said.

She gave me a disbelieving gaze. "Why would he do that, after deserting us? Besides, those...ladies... are welcome to come to the Settlement for clinic like anyone else from the neighborhood."

A point well taken.

"Did any ever come?" I asked her.

"What do you think?" she responded.

She shivered a little and pulled her sweater more closely about her. "Well, I'd best be getting in," she said. She pushed past me, going out of the doorway to the sidewalk, then she turned her head, looking at me over her shoulder. "I'm sorry if what I said about Dr. McDowell has hurt you, Doctor. I just thought you'd want to know. Maybe you'd want to talk with him about what he's doing there."

She waited a moment as if expecting an answer, then hurried back to the Settlement House.

I took advantage of the shelter of the doorway to light a cigarette. Was it my imagination, or did Miss Slater have an ulterior motive for telling me about Colin's peccadillos? I fished my watch out of my vest. Nearly six thirty. I was going to have to hurry if I was going to make my dinner date with Harvey. I inhaled deeply on the cigarette, filling my lungs with smoke, then pitched the long stub into the street. I set off for Broadway at a brisk pace, thinking furiously.

I'd good luck with the train; one was just leaving as I arrived on the platform. I'd come to no firm conclusions about Colin and Miss Slater during the ride. Given his behavior with his receptionist, I supposed Colin could have been conducting an affair with Miss Slater as well. But it still strained my credulity to believe that he would avail himself of a prostitute's services, given the medical risks.

It was nearly quarter after when I spied the red awning of the Harvard Club on 44th Street. I knew I was going to hear from Harvey about being late. He was waiting for me in the lounge, scowling at his watch, when I came in.

"You really have developed some dreadful habits of late, y'know," were his first words to me.

"I'm sorry, Harvey, I really am. I spent much too much time talking with Colonel Lindbergh at our lunch date, and it threw off my schedule for the whole rest of the day."

His eyes widened. "You had a lunch date with whom? D'you expect me to believe…"

I knew I had him. We adjourned to the main dining room while I told him about meeting the famous aviator. By the time we were seated and perusing menus, my tardiness was forgiven.

Over dinner, I related the events that occurred after I left him on Sunday afternoon. A concerned look flashed across his face as I told him about Miss LeMay and the revolver.

"I should have gone with you!" His fist crashed onto the table, causing the glasses and silverware to jump. "You were damned lucky, Eben. She sounds like a very unstable person. You could have been killed!"

"You've no idea how unstable." I told him about Evie's encounter with her.

"Will she live?"

"I hope so," I said. "I'll check on her again when I make rounds tonight."

"I never thought I'd hear myself say this," said Harvey, "but I suppose I'll have to take up reading the *Evening Graphic* if I want to keep up with your activities. I never expect to find any real news in that rag."

I continued my narrative, telling Harvey about my lunch with Lindbergh and Carrel and of my subsequent meetings with Annabelle Akers and Hannah Slater. By the time I was through, the waiter was clearing away the remains of dinner. We retired to the smoking lounge for cigars and brandy.

Harvey had a contemplative look as he swirled his snifter of cognac. "It looks as if the trail of the elusive McDowell leads to the Lower East Side." He cocked an eyebrow. "Do you intend to follow it?"

I never hesitated with my answer. "I have to, Harvey. It seems that all Henderson is interested in is this Ripper business; there will be little help from the police. Evie and Colin have two little girls, you know. They're being looked after by their nanny, for now, but I don't know how long that situation can continue, with both parents gone." I took a sip of brandy. "At least, as of now, it seems that Colin hasn't come to any harm."

"What makes you say that, Eben?"

"Well, he was seen the day after he went missing..." I began.

"Which! Means! Nothing!" Harvey barked, in his best courtroom manner. "He could be lying dead in an alley on the Lower East Side, or he could have returned to his office to be done in by his doxy, or Strangways, or the Ripper, or any combination thereof." He took a long drag on his corona and let the fragrant smoke dribble from his nostrils. "The trouble with you, Eben, is that you're too damned ingenuous. Always were. Sterling quality for a doctor, don't y'know, but a definite liability in an affair such as this one. If you are going to pursue this, I think you need a partner with some experience with the seamier side of the city."

"That would be you, I suppose?" I was affronted and pleased at the same time.

He put on that little sardonic smirk of his. "Tell me again about your chat with Evie McDowell, and what you found at McDowell's office."

I did so as he listened, wreathed in smoke, with his hands peaked together on his chest, as if praying.

"You never followed up on the phone number that Evie gave you?" he asked when I was finished.

"We called the operator and asked her to find out who it belongs to. She never called back, at least not while I was there."

"Did it ever occur to you to just call the number and ask for Colin?"

I felt like a dolt. Harvey had a way of doing that to me.

"The number's still at the McDowells," I said. "I was going there tonight, after my rounds, to check on the children..."

"You can try it then," said Harvey. He finished his brandy. "Now, about McDowell's office. Did it seem like it had seen a normal amount of activity recently?"

"I don't think so," I told him. "I didn't really have a chance to look around much; I thought the answers I was seeking would be in the suite upstairs rather than the office. But I did check his appointment schedule and it was curiously sparse—just one name for the entire last week listed."

"And you never checked his files to see if you could find a dossier for that patient?"

"No. As I said, I was looking for a way to get upstairs when Miss LeMay braced me with her revolver. I did write down the name, though." I fumbled for my wallet, extracted the card I used to note the name, and handed it to him."

"W. Danforth," he read. "Well, if we can locate Mr. or Miss Danforth, p'haps we can glean some indication of how McDowell spent his last normal hours."

I was suddenly very glad that Harvey had decided to become involved in this affair. I felt like a ship that had been drifting, which now had a firm, steady hand on the tiller.

"What are your plans for tomorrow?" Harvey asked me.

"Well, I have rounds and appointments; I expect I can reschedule some of those. I really need to make a more thorough examination of Colin's office, I suppose, and take a look at his files. And I have to make some arrangements for Evie's children. Oh, and I've promised to do a clinic at the College Settlement tomorrow evening. Then there's Miss Lucy's..."

"Which you will not go near without me at your side!" he said emphatically. "I will call the police in the morning and clear the way for a search of McDowell's office. Give me a call after you know when you can get loose."

The grandfather clock began to chime.

"Great Scott!" I exclaimed. "Ten already! Harvey, I really must make my rounds, check on Evie and the children, then get to bed."

"Go," he said. "Just remember, stay away from McDowell's office and that bordello until you've heard from me."

As I rose to gather my things, I assured him that I would.

I knew that trains would be infrequent at this hour. I hailed a cab on Sixth Avenue. Traffic was relatively sparse on the East Side, so the trip uptown did not take long.

The news at the hospital was not good. Evie had begun running a fever about mid-morning, which had inched steadily higher during the course of the day; a sure sign that infection had set in. The fever became high enough that the nurses began alcohol rubs to bring it down. When I looked in on her, superficially, she looked much the same as she had last evening, but a closer look revealed that her skin had taken on an unhealthy pallor and was glazed with a thin sheen of sweat, doubtless due to the fever.

The situation at the McDowell townhouse was not good, either. With both parents gone, the children had become concerned, and the concern had progressed toward hysteria during the course of the day. The nanny, Mrs. Riordan, had been hired to work only during the day;

now, that she was required to spend the nights with the children as well, stresses on her own family life were escalating.

"I don't know how much longer I can look after the poor darlin's," she told me. "Me old one is ailin' as well, and needs me home in the evenin' to look after him."

I extracted a promise from her to watch over the girls for least one more day while I tried to find someone else who could fill in until Evie became well again. If she became well again... My list of responsibilities was becoming ever longer. I was nearly certain that Colin had no family other than Evie and the girls, and I didn't think that Evie did, either.

Indeed, I was so addled by the situation that it wasn't until I was heading down the front steps to 67th Street that I realized I had forgotten once again about the phone number that Colin had given Evie prior to his trip to Boston.

Mrs. Riordan looked vaguely exasperated with me as she let me in the second time. I muttered some absentminded drivel about having forgotten something, all the while thinking furiously. Now where was I the last time I had seen that number?

It came to me as I was walking down the hall to the living room. I kept going, right to the phone. My heart sank when I saw no paper underneath; I was sure that was where I'd left it! The end table that the phone rested on had a single drawer; I grasped the center handle and eased it open; my heart leapt as I saw the paper within! Now I would not be forced to humble myself to Harvey tomorrow!

I unfolded it, and there was the number, scrawled in Colin's careless hand. Written in Evie's fine script beneath was:

Miskatonic Arms, Arkham, Mass.

CHAPTER 15

From the notebook of Sally Barton

Tuesday, September 29, 1931, morning

My flat seemed really empty when I got home last night. I'd done a lot of thinking during the train ride. I sure hadn't intended to get dizzy about a guy when I got up yesterday morning, especially not a copper, but that was what happened. In just one day! Or maybe I had loved him all along, ever since I met him, and just didn't know it. I was really antsy about getting involved again after the last time. Thinking about that really opened a can of worms—I knew I was gonna have to tell Morris what happened, and I didn't know how he was gonna take it. I briefly considered not telling him at all, but I knew that I just couldn't do it. It would always be hanging there between us, and I couldn't live like that.

I guess the flat seemed empty because I just wasn't very good company for myself. I thought about going up to the fly beat to pull Charlie loose for a couple of drinks, but I was stuck, waiting for Morris to call. An hour passed, then two, and still nothing. I knew I wouldn't sleep all night if he didn't call, and I swore that I would kill him if he did that to me.

It was after ten when the phone finally rang.

"Morris?"

"Yeah, it's me," he said. "Just like I figgered. Two weeks."

"The Chief gave you two weeks suspension for beating up Henderson?"

"Yeah, and he didn't even want to give me that much. I told you, a lot of people here don't like Henderson, and the Chief is one. But he said that he had to give me that much, or it would look like he was playing favorites. I guess we can go to the beach if we want to."

"Can you afford it with no pay for two weeks?" I still felt pretty bad that all this happened over me.

"Sure! I've got a little bit put up. But we really need to toss Strangways' digs first."

"When do you want to get started?"

"Eight too early?"

"Nope. You want to come by?"

"Yep. But there won't be no radio car this time. We'll have to ride the train like everybody else."

"That's fine with me. I'll see you in the morning." I hesitated, then thought, what the hell!

"Love you, Morris."

"Love you too, Sally. See you in the morning."

I didn't sleep too well that night anyway, but for a different reason.

True to his word, Morris rang my bell right at eight and I buzzed him in. A moment later there was a knock at my door, then we were in each others' arms at the threshold.

"God!" I said to him when we disengaged, "Was the night as long for you as it was for me?"

He didn't answer, he just picked me up bodily and kissed me again.

Addison Strangways had his office on Park Avenue, but he lived in the much more modest neighborhood of University Heights in the Bronx. His apartment was on the Grand Concourse, which was not by any means an address affordable by just anybody, but it was much less spiffy than the Manhattan neighborhood where his office was. It was a long ride on the East Side subway from Chelsea, and we spent it holding hands. I was glad that the squealing and clanking of the train made conversation awkward, so I could just enjoy the closeness.

The sun shone brightly as we came up from the subway at 176th Street, but the chill wind cut right through my coat. We turned crosstown, and the buildings lent us some protection from the gusts, but after we reached the Concourse and turned north, we were again walking into the teeth of the wind.

I saw Strangways' building up ahead. Built of sandy-colored stone, it occupied an entire block on the east side of the street. There were several entrances, each recessed in its own little courtyard opening off the sidewalk. I tugged on Morris' sleeve to get him to hurry so we could get out of that biting wind.

As we approached the massive, ornate door, I wondered how we were going to get in; I assumed that Morris would just ring several apartments until someone buzzed us in, but he reached into his overcoat pocket and came up with a key.

I raised an eyebrow at him. "You swiped that from Police Headquarters?"

"Yep." He grinned. "Right after the Chief told me not to show my face for two weeks. Figgered I was in trouble anyway—what'd I have to lose?"

Strangways' apartment was on the eighth floor. The elevator operator gave us a look as we got on, but he didn't say anything; I figured he pretty much knew everybody in the building and recognized us as out of place. I hoped Henderson wouldn't talk to him any time soon. After we got out, Morris waited for the elevator to leave, then withdrew another key and led the way to a door at the end of the hall. The door opened into a vestibule spacious enough for a bench along one wall, and a good-sized wardrobe on the other. From there we walked into a large, airy living room with windows on two sides. I was immediately jealous; I would kill for cross-ventilation like that in my little flat in the summertime.

A stack of dirty dishes in the kitchen sink, unemptied ash trays, and a trash can filled the place with an evil odor; it was obvious that no one had lived here for several days, at least. The bed was unmade; a quick check of the closets and some dresser drawers revealed missing clothing. It didn't take us long to find another stash of dirty pictures either, this time in the nightstand drawer. Apparently Strangways didn't feel he had to hide them as well in his home as he did in his office.

"Well, this bird's flown the coop, for sure." Morris said. "Question is, did he go to Cape May?"

"I'll bet anything he did," I said. I pointed to an ashtray on the nightstand. "Look at this. Congress Hall Hotel, Cape May. And it ain't the only one he has from there, either."

"Looks like we're on for that beach trip, then. Don't forget to pack your bathing suit."

I shivered, thinking of that chilly wind outside.

On the ride back to Manhattan, we decided to catch the five o'clock train to Philly. We would take the first one in the morning to Cape May. We agreed to meet at Penn Station at four. I got off at 15th Street, leaving Morris for his ride out to Brooklyn.

It was after twelve when I got back to the flat. I was hungry, but I had to skip lunch; I didn't have a lot of time to get packed and I had no idea what I was going to take.

The next few hours were a blur. By three thirty, I had three big suitcases and four hatboxes ready to go. No way I was going to the station by subway.

It was just a little after four when my cab pulled up in front of Penn Station. Morris was right there; big as he was, he wasn't hard to spot in a crowd.

"Holy smokes, Barton!" he said, as the cabbie unloaded my stuff. "We ain't goin' on safari, you know! We're just gonna spend a few days at the beach!"

I just glared at him. "Morris Moscowicz, I don't even know how long we're going to be gone! I figured I'd better pack for at least a week, and this is the bare minimum!"

He shook his head, then moved his suitcase next to my stuff. "I'll call a porter," he sighed.

It was rush hour and people were everywhere. Morris went off to get the tickets while I grabbed a sandwich; I felt like I was going to pass out from hunger while I waited for it. We met at the train and Morris shouldered his way on board while I followed. Finally in our seats, I was able to relax for the first time in hours.

The train lurched, then smoothed out as we slowly pulled out of the darkened station into the fading daylight, before plunging back into darkness as we entered the long tunnel that ran under the Hudson River. I smiled up at Morris and said, "We've got some time. Tell me the story of your life."

Surprisingly, he complied.

"Well, I was born and raised in Brooklyn," he began. "Even though my folks came here from the old country with a lot of nothing, we weren't too badly off, because my father had a trade. He was a butcher. Never had no brothers or sisters. I guess I was pretty spoiled."

He went on to talk about what it was like growing up in Brooklyn thirty years ago —not much different than growing up in Maplewood, really. I guess I always knew he was Jewish, but he really brought it home when he talked about his mom keeping kosher. It didn't make any difference to me if it didn't to him, I decided.

"I guess I had a pretty ordinary childhood..." he hesitated, "except that I was always, y'know, big. Took a lotta ribbing because of that."

I smiled up at him. "Seems like ribbing you would have been dangerous, considering how you handled Henderson."

He reddened "Hey, I'm not usually like that, you know. I don't like pushing people around. But when I saw you handcuffed like that, something just snapped!"

"I know you're no bully, Morris," I said, "I'm sorry if I hurt your feelings."

He grinned. "You don't need to apologize. Anyway, the ribbing stopped when I got to high school, 'cause there was football."

"So, you were a big football hero"

"Nah! I was the center. That's the guy who gives the ball to the quarterback. He was the hero! But just being on the team carried some weight."

"I'll bet it did. Especially with the girls, huh?"

I'd apparently said the wrong thing again, because I saw a frown cross his face.

"Sally," he began, "If we're going to do this, there's something you need to know..."

"That's alright, Morris," I tried to cut him off, "You don't need to tell me anything you don't want to..."

"I been married!" he said. That shut me up.

"It was right outta high school," he said, "before the war. Lots of guys did it, you know. Never knew if we were gonna see each other again, so we got married before we got shipped over there."

I asked what I really didn't want to. "Where is she now?"

"Dunno." He paused for a minute, then continued, "She waited for me, though. Lotsa of war brides didn't. I guess she thought with me back in one piece, I'd get a reg'lar job and be home every night. Then I joined the force. She put up with it for a while, but then she told me that it was just like me bein' over there again. When I left in the mornin', she never knew when, or if, I'd come home. Guess she didn't wanna live like that forever."

"She left you!"

"Yep, sure did. Came home one night after I'd been gone a couple days, and found her note. Couldn't call her, we didn't have a phone then. Her note said not to look for her, so I didn't."

Another thought I didn't want pushed itself into my head. I had to ask him, "You ever get the marriage annulled?"

"Yeah. Took me a couple of years to get around to it, though." He actually smiled at me. "Are we OK?"

I forced a smile in return. "Sure, you big palooka, we're OK."

His face lit up with that homely smile of his.

I sure hoped we were OK, now that he told me his biggest secret, but I didn't have the guts to tell him mine.

The Legacy of the Unborn

Silas K. Henderson

CHAPTER 16

The Statement of Dr. Ebeneezer Warman

When the jangling alarm wrenched me back to consciousness, it seemed that I had just closed my eyes. I sat up in bed, temples throbbing. My sleep had been troubled by dreams of crying children and eviscerated women, suffused with an overwhelming sense of powerlessness to stop it all.

I felt little better after several cigarettes and cups of strong coffee, but it made no difference, for I knew I had much ahead of me that day.

My first stop was the hospital. I found Evie no better nor worse, merely hovering in no-man's land between life and death. An accurate prognosis was simply impossible. I also visited my patient there and found her little improved as well—her illness had progressed to seizures. I scribbled a prescription for some medication on her chart before departing for the office.

Once there, I scanned my list of appointments and checked off those I knew I simply had to see that day, then directed Sarah to call the rest of them and reschedule.

The morning seemed interminable. Thoughts of Evie's condition, Colin's disappearance, and the Ripper murders continually insinuated themselves into my awareness—it took a great, conscious effort to force them out and get my mind back on my patients, where it properly belonged.

About mid-morning, as I was having a discussion with Mrs. Van Beck about her incipient goiter, there was a knock on the door. Sarah opened it and said, "Sorry for the interruption, Dr. Warman, but Lenox Hill Hospital is on the line. They say it's urgent,

Evie!

Stammering an apology to Dame Van Beck, I rushed to take the call in my office.

"Dr. Warman, this is Nurse Thompson. Did you mean to prescribe 500 milligrams of phenobarbital for Mrs. Jacobs for her seizures?"

Five hundred milligrams! "Of course not! That could be a lethal dose! One hundred milligrams is what I prescribed!"

"I thought so, Doctor," Nurse Thompson said, "But it did read 500 milligrams on the chart."

An overwhelming temptation to contradict and upbraid her arose in me, but I bit my tongue. Nurse Thompson would not have called me unless the chart did indeed read 500 milligrams.

"I'm sorry, Nurse Thompson. My mind must have drifted when I was writing. Thank you for noticing the error and for following up."

"It's no trouble, Doctor. That's what I'm here for. We all make mistakes." She rang off.

This was inexcusable! Had the nurse followed my careless instructions, there would have been at least a medical emergency, if not a fatality! Recent events had taken more of a toll on me than I realized!

When I returned to Mrs. Van Beck, I found myself much more solicitous of her condition than previously. I wrote her a referral for the best thyroid doctor in the city, and asked her to follow up with me again as well, after she had seen him. When she had gone, I reviewed the rest of the prescriptions I had written that morning to ensure they were accurate. They were.

There were only two more patients to see, and I was irritated that, even after the incident with Mrs. Jacobs, I had to struggle not to give them short shrift. However, I felt that I succeeded, and finally, my duties were over. I retired to my office to take care of one more chore before contacting Harvey.

I called the Miskatonic Arms in Arkham, Massachusetts, and asked for Dr. Colin McDowell. After checking, the receptionist informed me that no one with that name was currently a guest at the hotel.

"Can you tell me if he stayed with you recently?" I asked her, "Say, within the last six weeks?"

"That could take some time to look up, sir," she told me. "Could you be more specific about the date?"

I knew Colin had been in the city for approximately the last three weeks. I remembered that the appointments in his book had tapered off the last week in August or thereabouts. "Try mid-August," I suggested.

"This will take a few minutes," she said.

I heard the bump as she laid the phone on the desk. I tried to be patient as I waited for her to page through the register, but I found myself becoming irritated. Dammitall! Why couldn't she hurry?

Finally, she came back on the line. "Your Dr. McDowell was a guest here from August 11 through the 14th," she said.

"I don't suppose you know why he was in town, do you?"

"No sir. We don't inquire about the business of our guests. But I would assume it had something to do with the University, him being a doctor and all."

"Which University?"

I could hear the contempt in her voice. "Why, Miskatonic University, of course!"

"I'm sorry," I said reluctantly. "I've never been in that area of Massachusetts. Are you near to Boston?" I was thinking of the newspaper I had found in Colin's office.

"About three quarters of an hour by train. Is there anything else?"

I wanted to say, don't you take that snippy tone with me, you hussy! But instead, I replied, "No. Thanks for your time." And I hung up abruptly.

So, Colin had traveled to Arkham last month to meet with someone at a second-rate university! Perhaps the explanation for the Boston paper was that that someone had returned the visit more recently. I made a mental note to find out more about this Miskatonic University.

I thought about calling Lenox Hill to check on Evie's condition, but, unless I talked to Dr. Strongman himself, I was likely to get only a cursory report. Better to just check myself later, when I made my rounds.

Unable to wait any longer, I picked up the receiver again and dialed up Harvey. His receptionist answered, and when I gave my name, she patched me right through.

"Eben, old dear! I was anxiously awaiting your call!"

I came right to the point. "Did you talk to the police about getting us permission to go through Colin's office?"

"It pains me that you would ask, Eben. Did I not say I would?"

"Yes, you did, Harvey. But I have met the fearsome Inspector Henderson, and it occurred to me that he might have some objections on that score."

"He might have had, was he there," said Harvey, "But the Inspector seems to be ailin' right now. His Chief was much more accommodatin' than Henderson would have been, I'm sure."

"That's wonderful, Harvey! Can you meet me right away? I can walk down directly."

"There is a little matter of lunch, Eben,"

What was the matter with me? I suddenly realized that I had had nothing at all to eat that day—that was probably the reason that I had been forgetful, not to mention irritable, all morning. How could a doctor who didn't care for himself take care of others?

"Where shall we meet?"

"Buchler's is fairly close by McDowell's office. Its luncheon fare is inexpensive, but good."

"I really don't care what I eat, right now, Harvey." I could hear his quick intake of breath at that incredible statement. "I'll see you there in twenty minutes." I rang off.

Lunch seemed interminable. Harvey disliked discussing business during meals—claimed it interfered with his savoring of his food—and apparently, this search for Colin had attained the category of business. All I could get out of him was that he had secured keys to Colin's office, and that the notorious Miss LeMay would be out of the picture for a considerable time, as she was now a guest of the City.

It was about twoish when we found ourselves at the door to Colin's practice. We went straight up the red-carpeted stairs to the receptionist's office, stepping over the surveyors' tape that blocked the gate. There we paused to work out a strategy for our search. I had already informed Harvey about the things I had found during my earlier, abortive foray.

"The first thing to do is to see if we can trace the elusive Danforth," said Harvey, gesturing towards the filing cabinets that housed the patients' records.

Colin kept a well-run office—apparently Miss LeMay had abilities other than those of the amatory variety—we had Danforth's billing record in hand in seconds. His first name was Wesley, and his address was given as Arkham, Massachusetts. His current residence was apparently the Manhattan Psychiatric Hospital on Ward's Island. His guardian was a Doctor William Dyer, also of Arkham, who was paying his bills. The record also showed that Colin had tended to Danforth almost exclusively during the first week of September. Unfortunately, there was no description of the treatment he received in the file. That record might be somewhere else in the office.

So, Mr. Danforth's unspecified malady was likely the reason for Colin's trip to Arkham in August.

The next stop was Colin's private office, which I had already searched, but Harvey insisted on seeing it. I experienced a flash of guilt on seeing the damaged desk drawer again. I withdrew the keys I had removed from it from my pocket, in which I had dropped them before proceeding to my encounter with Miss LeMay, and turned to the filing cabinets in this room, which I was sure would contain the patients' medical records. Those records were indeed present, but Wesley Danforth's was not among them.

"Show me where you found the newspaper, exactly," Harvey ordered.

I complied.

He considered a moment, then turned the cushion out of the leather armchair facing the desk. A guttural, "Aha!" escaped his lips, and he turned towards me, waving the piece of paper he had found.

It was the return portion of a train ticket, from New York City to Arkham, Massachusetts, made out to one William Dyer, with a purchase date of September 21, 1931! Monday last!

"Apparently the good Doctor Dyer had to use his return on the 23rd," said Harvey. "Its presence here indicates that he did not. He is likely still in New York."

"Unless he bought another ticket," I replied.

"Possible, but unlikely," said Harvey. "That ticket was expensive enough that I'm sure he would have made some effort to look for it, had he missed it." He turned towards the door to the hall. "What else is on this floor?"

"Examining rooms, and a lab," I said, following him out.

We gave those areas a quick survey, but found nothing of interest.

"I never did get to thoroughly search upstairs," I told Harvey. "Miss LeMay's revolver interrupted that."

"Then let us go and see what secrets Dr. McDowell is hiding in his *sanctum sanctorum*," said Harvey.

We went back to the main staircase and proceeded up to the room where Miss LeMay had held me at gunpoint. A cold shiver went through me as we entered that chamber. The doors leading into the other rooms were all closed.

"That one's a bedroom," I told Harvey, gesturing towards the appropriate door. "I didn't get a chance to search it last time."

"Men seldom keep interesting items in their bedrooms," said Harvey. He opened an adjacent door. "But in their offices, on the other hand..."

The room revealed was indeed another office, and this one projected an aura of well-used intimacy. It was dominated by an enormous ebony desk, carved in an oriental style depicting serpents

161

and dragons. A window overlooking the rear yard was concealed by a heavy curtain, embroidered in a similar motif. An overstuffed sofa faced the desk, and more bookshelves lined the walls.

But by far, the most singular feature of the room was the painting hung behind the desk. I moved into the room to get a closer look at it.

It portrayed two men, heavily enrobed, with halos round their heads, standing by the bedside of a third man. The occupant of the bed, a white man, was regarding his right leg, which was black, and being held by one of the haloed men. A turbaned Negro, apparently dead, and with one white leg, was lying on the floor next to the bed in the foreground.

"Hmpf! Your Doctor McDowell is apparently quite the devotee of obscure medieval paintings," said Harvey. "This is a rather fine reproduction of Fernando Rincon's Cosmas and Damian. The original was done circa 1560, if I am not mistaken. It hangs in the Prado in Madrid, where I was fortunate enough to see it some years ago."

I have ceased to be amazed at Harvey's encyclopedic knowledge of art and music. It had earned him a place on the board of the prestigious Metropolitan Museum of Art, where he was instrumental in the acquisition of an exemplary collection of French impressionist paintings a couple of years ago.

"Apparently the holy men were involved in the replacement of the injured leg of a sexton with that of a recently deceased Moor." Harvey said. "Of course, the story is apocryphal. It is curiously convenient, don'tcha think, that the donor was of another race, for it allows us to easily observe the results of the operation."

"Dr. Carrel told me the other day that Colin's principal research interest was organ transplantation," I informed Harvey. "It doesn't surprise me, given his characteristic thoroughness, that he has delved into the history of the subject."

Harvey shuddered visibly. "Promise me, Eben," he said, "that should I ever lose a part of myself, you will let me go peacefully into the hereafter, unencumbered by spare parts from another human being."

I moved to examine the desk, which was, of course, locked, but once again I was able to find the requisite key on the ring I had found downstairs. The main drawer contained the usual, hugger-mugger conglomeration of effluvia found in such places—scraps of paper, pencils, paper clips, rubber bands and the like—nothing immediately interesting, so I progressed to the lower drawers. Harvey, however, elbowed me aside and removed the entire drawer, placing it on the desk.

"For a doctor," he said to me, as he began sifting through the contents, "You seem awfully prone to snap judgments."

Somewhat offended, I turned toward the filing cabinet, hoping to find the treatment record for Mr. Danforth. I was not disappointed, for I had it in my hands in a moment. I sat on the sofa to peruse it while Harvey continued to busy himself at the desk.

The file made for very interesting reading. While participating in an expedition to Antarctica, sponsored by Miskatonic University, Danforth experienced a nervous breakdown, apparently precipitated by an unknown psychic trauma. Colin suspected that Dr. Dyer, who had brought Danforth to Colin's attention, was aware of the nature of that trauma, but unwilling to give Colin any specific information concerning it. Danforth's initial symptoms consisted of catatonia, periodically interspersed with incoherent muttering. Colin began treatment by subjecting Danforth to electrical shocks, followed by dosing him with a drug of his own manufacture, which he characterized as a derivative of lysergic acid. Disturbingly, Colin indicated that he had also tested the drug on himself in order to establish the proper dosage for Danforth. This curious regimen apparently worked well enough: The catatonia was relieved, and Colin was able to initiate interviews with his patient, attempting to define the event that had triggered the disorder. Detailed notes on those interviews were referred to but not contained in the file: they were likely entered in a notebook that Colin kept on his person. There were no entries after August 14. Had Colin abruptly terminated treatment, or simply not bothered to enter any more notes in the file?

Harvey had finished with the top drawer and replaced it, and was opening the side drawers, inspecting their contents. I hoped that he would find Colin's notebook within, but my wishes on that score were not to be gratified. However, he did remove a rather large wooden box from the bottom drawer.

As he opened it, he exclaimed, "Well, wadda y'know!"

As I approached the desk, he removed nearly a ream of paper from the box, which he placed on the blotter.

"This appears to be McDowell's *magnum opus*," he said.

I examined the title page:

A Short History of Organ Transplantation and Skin Grafting
By
Colin Parlan McDowell, M.D., Ph.D.

"Much more under your purview, than mine, Eben," Harvey said.

"I claim to be a fairly good doctor, Harvey, when it comes to treating the ills of my patients, but I freely admit that I don't remotely approach Colin McDowell, when it comes to knowledge about the scientific basis of organ transplantation."

"Well, here is your chance to catch up a little," said Harvey, handing me the manuscript.

"What possible information could this contain that would indicate Colin's present whereabouts?"

"You won't know until you read it, now will you, old dear," said Harvey, infuriatingly.

I gave up and took the manuscript. We'd see whether I'd read it or not!

"Did you find anything else of interest?" I asked.

"Only this." Harvey proffered a slip of paper. "It's dated August 19th of this year."

He handed me a call slip from the New York public library.

I read it, and quickly handed it back to Harvey.

"This makes no sense," I said. "Colin, wouldn't have the time to be bothered with that sort of stuff."

The slip was for a volume titled *Notes on the Necronomicon*, apparently written in the last century, and another, *Necr.*—1540 ed.

"He must have been bothered, or we wouldn't have found the slip here," Harvey said reasonably. "And he appears to have an abiding interest in the medieval, given the Rincon painting and the date on that last book. That is his handwriting?"

"I'm not that familiar with his handwriting, but it's easy enough to ascertain, since we are standing in his office," I replied, somewhat peevishly.

"Then let's do so." Harvey offered the slip back to me.

It only took a few minutes to show that Harvey was, as usual, correct.

I sat down on the sofa again, considering all that we had found, and how little it informed us about Colin's present whereabouts. I said as much to Harvey.

"Not so!" He had taken a position in the center of the room and stood facing me, as if he was declaiming to a jury. "We have gotten much forrader, methinks. We have discovered the identity of the mysterious patient who consumed most of McDowell's time in the weeks before his disappearance. And I have a distinct feeling that the good doctor's visit to the library will ultimately prove much more crucial to understanding his fate than you currently seem to think. I suggest that these two things are appropriate for you to follow up."

"And what will you be doing, pray tell, whilst I am thus engaged?" I asked, sarcastically.

"I will be investigating the infamous Miss Lucy's," he said with an evil grin on his face. "You are much too much the innocent for that endeavor."

I started to frame a petulant retort, then stifled it. He was right, again.

Harvey consulted a large gold watch from his waistcoat. "The day is rapidly fading," he said. "We will have to postpone further investigation for the nonce. Are you available for dinner?"

"I don't think so. I must make my rounds at Lennox Hill, and I've promised to conduct Colin's clinic at the Settlement, this evening. I shall have to grab something on the run."

"Pity. That's a good reason to have chosen law over medicine."

We tidied the office a bit—little of our plundering was evident. I hoped again that Colin would forgive me for these intrusions into his privacy, should he resurface.

Harvey and I took our leave of each other on the street in front of Colin's office.

"I'm very grateful to you for your assistance with this, Harvey," I began.

He interrupted, "Nonsense, old dear. It seems that helping you clear this matter up is the only way I'll ever get our dinner and concert schedule back on track. Call me some time tomorrow and let me know of your progress."

I embraced him briefly, then departed.

The situation at the hospital was not good. Evie had been running a fever all day She had been given several blood transfusions to replace the blood she had lost due to her injuries and surgery, and intravenous fluids to prevent dehydration. There was little that could be done for an infection, however. I said a silent prayer at her bedside, then departed for the Settlement.

Miss Annabel was all over me the moment I entered the house. Apparently, she had recruited numerous patients for the clinic from the Settlement's client list whilst simultaneously doing her utmost to convince herself that I would not show up at the appointed time; hence her overly effusive display when I did, in fact, appear.

"Thank God for you, Dr. Warman!" she said for perhaps the thirtieth time, as she led me into the commodious drawing room, where perhaps two dozen patients—most of them women and children—waited. I mentally rolled my eyes. I would not be out of there until nearly midnight.

"Annabel, we will have to discuss the number of patients you can allow to come to these clinics—it is not fair to any of them if I don't have sufficient time for examination and treatment."

166

"I know it, Dr. Warman, I know it! But many have been waiting for weeks to see Dr. McDowell! It will not be as bad next time, I assure you! Thank God for you!"

But I suspected it would be as bad, if not worse.

However, as it always did, the time passed swiftly when I was working. I could do nothing but prescribe palliatives for approximately a third of the patients, who had relatively advanced cases of tuberculosis or venereal disease. There was a fair amount of malnutrition as well—again I could only suggest that these people use their limited resources to pursue a proper diet to make the best of what they had. The rest had nonspecific fevers or respiratory diseases for which I prescribed bed rest and supportive care. However, I could tell that many would be unable to follow even that simple advice.

I looked at my watch as the last unfortunate exited the sitting room that Annabel had assigned to me as an examination and consulting room. One-thirty in the morning! And I had to go by the McDowell house to check on Mrs. Riordan and the children, before I could go home to bed! Then, inspiration struck!

I sought out Annabel, whom I found still awake, in the kitchen supervising the preparation of tomorrow's (or was it today's?) breakfast.

She embraced me in a bear hug while pouring out her thanks. I disengaged as soon as I was able, then said, "Now, Annabel, how would you like to do something for me?"

"Anything, Dr. Warman, if it is in my power to do it!"

I told her Evie's sad story, and about the children who had no one to care for them.

"Say no more, Dr. Warman! I would be a poor humanitarian indeed if I did not realize that tragedy can strike as easily on Park Avenue as on the Bowery! There will be a place for the little darlings here until their mother recovers."

We made arrangements for the transfer of the McDowell children later in the day, then I left to go back uptown. It was a long trip—trains are far between at that hour.

The Legacy of the Unborn

It was nearly four o'clock as I lay my head on the pillow. By rights, I should have passed out immediately, but sleep was elusive. An overpowering feeling of dread intruded on my slumbers.

CHAPTER 17

From the notebook of Sally Barton

Tuesday, September 29, 1931, evening

The train ride to Philly seemed to last forever, in a good way mostly. The train did a lot of stopping and standing, to let other trains clear off the tracks, I guessed. Morris and I shared stories of our childhood and found out we really weren't all that different, though he had it rougher than I did. His parents came here from Germany, and he grew up in the tenements in Williamsburg. It was a few years before his dad's butcher shop became successful, and Morris talked of many happy days working there. Me, I never had to work. My dad was a travelling salesman, so he wasn't around a lot, but he always sent home enough money that me and mom never wanted for anything. Maplewood in those days was just a perfect little town, all green lawns and white picket fences, with the occasional farm so we could get everything fresh. Reading between the lines, I guessed that it wasn't always that way for Morris. As much as I enjoyed getting to know this man that I was now sure I loved, my damned secret cast a shadow over everything. I knew I was gonna have to tell him, sooner rather than later, but a crowded train car was definitely not the place.

Finally, we pulled into the Philly station, the big one downtown on Broad Street. Morris had only brought a small suitcase that he had carried with him on the train, but since I had so much luggage, we had to pick it up downstairs after they got it off the baggage car. While I waited, Morris went to check on the train to Cape May. After I had gotten my things and loaded them on a cart, I met him coming back to the baggage room.

He looked blue. "Well, we're not gonna get to Cape May tonight," he said. "The last train left twenny minutes ago."

"We'll have to go to a hotel," I said. "I hope we can afford rooms around here."

"You can always find a cheap room near a train station," Morris said, confidently. "Let's go see what's around."

It didn't take long to find out that the two closest hotels were the Ritz Carlton and the Bellevue Stratford.

"I don't think the Ritz is gonna be in my budget for this trip," I said.

"Well, if we catch old Strangways and get that ten thousand..." Morris said.

"We ain't got it yet," I replied. "Let's try the Bellevue."

The Bellevue was a short walk from the station. We couldn't take the luggage cart out of the station, and didn't want to pay a cab for only four blocks. Morris asked me if I thought I could get by with one bag for the night. I thought that I could, so we checked the others.

As we approached the Bellevue, I began to reconsider. It was about twenty stories tall and looked like it belonged in London or Paris. Sure, we had hotels just as fancy in New York, but I didn't stay in those, either. The lobby was enormous, with ceilings two or three stories high decorated with carvings and swanky light fixtures, and a grand staircase to the upper floors that was wide enough for five or six people. The bellhops had snazzy uniforms and sported little pillbox hats, and the men behind the reception desk were dressed in suits that would fit in any boardroom.

Morris approached the reception desk while I stood back watching our bags. In a few minutes, he approached carrying two room keys.

We're on the fifteenth floor," he said.

"How much do I owe you?" I really didn't want to know.

"Fugeddaboudit," he said.

There was no way I was going to let that stand, and we argued about it all the way to the fifteenth floor. The elevator operator was greatly amused. Finally, Morris told me to give him five bucks, just to shut me up.

Five bucks? For one room for one night? Omigod!

I found out a few days later that he paid ten dollars each!

He had gotten us adjoining rooms. They were swell. Mine had a nice double bed, a day bed and a dresser, with a sink in one corner. His was pretty much the same. There was a connecting door that could be locked or unlocked from inside the room.

After I had gotten settled in, I heard a knock on the connecting door. I unlocked and opened it to let him in.

Since neither of us really knew Philly, we decided just to have dinner at the hotel. I put up a weak argument about the expense, but I was beginning to fall in with Morris' idea of treating this as a vacation. After all, when does a working girl really get a chance to splurge?

The dining room on the first floor next to the lobby was huge—the tables were all decked out in white linen and the china and glassware sparkled like diamonds under huge crystal chandeliers. The guy charged with seating us led us over to a small table against the wall, but Morris said that wouldn't do. At first the guy looked as if he was going to insist, but Morris straightened up to his full height, squared his shoulders and put a scowl on his homely face, and all of a sudden we were shown to a nice table right in the center of everything. The guy was going to hold my chair for me, but Morris gently eased him out of the way and did it himself.

The multi-page menu contained appetizers, entrees, side dishes, deserts, and even cigars. I guess confusion showed on my face, because Morris just reached across the table and took the menu. "Let me take care of this," he said.

When the waiter came, Morris ordered three shrimp cocktails, Chateaubriand for four, and two orders of Lyonnaise potatoes and asparagus with Hollandaise, just like he'd been doing it all his life. "And bring us a big basket of dinner rolls, please," he finished.

The rolls came out quickly, along with pats of butter on ice in a silver bowl.

"I don't know how I'm gonna pay for all this," I said.

"You're not," he replied. "It's my treat. It's not every day that a beautiful girl tells me she loves me."

That shut me up.

He pulled a schedule for the Pennsylvania-Reading Seashore Lines from an inside pocket of his jacket and gave it the once over.

"We can sleep in a little tomorrow," he said. "The first train doesn't leave until eight fifty-five."

"What's the plan when we get to Cape May?" I asked.

"Check into Congress Hall, I guess," Morris said. "The season is mostly over—it oughtn't to be too expensive. Then we can surreptitiously show that photo of Strangways around and see if we can get a line on him."

"Can you arrest him if we see him?"

"I don't have jurisdiction." He paused, then, "I can likely get the local cops to do it, if I tell them what we got on him."

"But would that mess up us getting the reward?" I asked.

He pursed his lips. "Maybe," he said. "Maybe I should try to arrest him—he might not know about the jurisdiction. I could just cuff him and carry him off."

"What could he do about it?"

"Not much... He could holler for a cop, but I can't see somebody who killed all them women doing that. And even if he did, like I said before, we got enough on him to get the local cops to arrest him. And if I've already got him cuffed, it's pretty damn obvious who got to him first."

The shrimp came—a half a dozen in each cocktail, all sitting on crushed ice in a silver cup, decorated with lemons, parsley and a small bowl of red sauce in the center. The pungent aroma of horseradish made my eyes tear.

"You expect me to eat steak and potatoes after a dozen shrimp?" I asked him.

"Just eat as many as you want to," he grinned. "I'll take care of the rest!"

The shrimp were luscious, and I did eat a couple more than I really should have. "Get those away from me!" I pushed my bowl toward Morris.

He was already on his second cocktail. He reached across and scooped up my bowl. "Thanks," he said.

The waiter rolled a silver cart filled with covered silver dishes next to the table. He uncovered the largest one with a flourish. "Voila!" he said.

Steam rose from a positively enormous hunk of beef. The aroma was divine! Its mahogany surface glistened with droplets of red juice intermingled with fat. Suddenly, I was hungry again! The waiter brandished a carving knife and sharpening steel, and the sound of ringing metal filled the air.

"Would Madame prefer rare or medium rare?" he asked.

"I'll have the piece from the end," I said. "It's the best part!"

He served me a hunk about two inches thick. It looked as if there was a couple of pounds left on the tray.

"I hope you're going to eat all that," I said.

He just smiled.

Conversation stopped while I enjoyed one of the best meals I ever had in my life. Even Morris couldn't eat all of that steak, but he sure gave it a good try.

Finally, I pushed my plate away. "I don't ever want to see food again!" I said.

Morris grinned. "I'll bet you'll eat a big breakfast tomorrow," he replied.

"I better not. I'll get so fat you won't even want to look at me."

He reached over and took my hand, and looked me straight in the eyes. "Sally," he said. "There will never be a day that I don't want to look at you. I promise."

I started to tear up, then the secret I hadn't told him yet just jumped into my head. That would make him not want to look at me, I thought! I really started to cry, then.

"Hey, hey..." he said, suddenly letting go of my hand. "I didn't mean to get you all upset."

I really wanted to tell him right there, but it just wasn't the time or place. Somehow, I managed to get control of myself to turn off the waterworks. I blotted my eyes with my napkin. I shuddered at the thought of what this was doing to my makeup!

"I must look terrible," I said. "Let me go and fix my face."

When I returned to the table, Morris was busily demolishing a large slab of chocolate cake. He poured me a cup of coffee from a silver pot as I sat.

"Maybe I better not," I said. "Coffee too late in the evening keeps me up."

"We can get a drink in a while to counteract it." Morris suggested.

"You know where the speaks are in Philly?"

"No, but I bet the concierge does!"

The concierge sure did, and a little later we found ourselves in a third-floor apartment a couple of blocks from the hotel. All of the rooms but the bathroom and the kitchen, whose doorway had been blocked with a table turned crosswise to form a makeshift bar, were filled with tables and chairs. The place was only half full, since it was a weeknight, I guessed. We didn't have a problem finding a little privacy. Morris was jovial, just like any working stiff enjoying himself on a rare vacation. I tried to join in, but the thought that I hadn't told him everything about me that he needed to know kept nagging at me. Again, I figured that this just wasn't the time or the place. But was there a good one?

Maybe another drink would help.

I'm not sure what time it was when we left. I'm ashamed to say I was downright tipsy, which almost never happens, and that I had to lean heavily on Morris during the walk back to the hotel. It seemed to me that the elevator operator frowned disapprovingly as we entered. When we got to my room, I had some trouble with the key. He took it from me and opened the door.

"You're coming in," I said. It was not a question.

As soon as the door closed behind us, I was all over him. I think he may have tried to push me away at first, but that sure didn't last long! He picked me up bodily to kiss me—I'm sure it was uncomfortable for him to bend down to reach my lips. I wrapped my legs around his torso as far as they would go. He carried me over to the bed and put me down gently. I pulled him down on top of me.

Afterwards, I lay halfway on top of him, playing with the hairs on his chest as he snored gently. It was only a double bed—there wasn't really anyplace else for me to be with him in it. The single sheet was barely enough to cover both of us. I thought that we'd definitely have to get an oversized bed made when we moved in together... if we moved in together.

I knew I had to tell him tomorrow. I just had to!

CHAPTER 18

The Statement of Dr. Ebeneezer Warman

I was wooly-headed when I arose Wednesday morning—by my reckoning, I had gotten only three hours of sleep. In the kitchen, I mechanically performed the process of making coffee. While it brewed, I went to retrieve my paper from the front door. A glance at the front page woke me rather quickly!

September 30, 1931—New York Times

Vandals destroy Rockefeller laboratory

The laboratory at Rockefeller University administered by Dr. Alexis Carrel, winner of the Nobel Prize for medicine in 1913, was broken into and vandalized in the early hours Wednesday morning.

A security guard, injured in the course of the burglary, lies in critical condition in the University hospital.

Dr. Carrel and the police are currently conducting an inventory of the laboratory to determine what, if anything, may have been stolen.

The famed aviator Colonel Charles Lindbergh is
a colleague of Carrel's. It is not known at this time
how Lindbergh has been affected by the incident.

The story continued, but it was just a rehash of Carrel's and
Lindbergh's accomplishments; filler, I suspected, to justify the first
page publication.

I retrieved my address book and placed a call to Carrel. I was
mildly surprised when he answered.

"Dr. Carrel, it's Dr. Warman. We met the other day. I just read
about the incident at your laboratory last night. I wanted to let you
know how sorry I am, and to ask if there's anything I can do to help?"

Carrel sounded remarkably composed. "Thank you for your
concern, Dr. Warman. We are still in the process of sorting through the
mess. I don't think there's too much you can do."

"Have you any idea who has done this terrible thing?" I asked.

"The police think it was someone looking for drugs," Carrel
replied. "That would account for the wanton destruction, but I am not
sure. The only thing we have found missing so far is Colonel
Lindbergh's perfusion pump."

"That makes no sense!" I said. "Who would want that?"

"I'm sure I don't know," Carrel said. "Perhaps the thief thought
he could get something for it. He went to considerable trouble to
disassemble it and cart it away."

"How is the security guard?"

"Not well, I'm afraid. He has a fractured skull. Now, Dr. Warman, I
am sorry that I must ring off. I have a great deal to do."

"I don't suppose you've heard anything from Colin?"

"No, I have not." Carrel said. "Goodbye, Doctor."

I poured a cup of coffee and drank it while I dressed, mentally
planning my day.

I did not remember any non-routine appointments today. I called
Sarah to check, then asked her to reschedule them. She assented, of
course, but I thought I detected a note of disapproval.

My next call was to Manhattan State Hospital, inquiring about
Wesley Danforth. Familiar with the bureaucracy of a large hospital, I
immediately informed them that I was a doctor, to cut through the red

tape that a layman would surely have become entangled in. Very soon, I found myself speaking with a Dr. Oglethorpe.

"Hello, Dr. Warman! You inquired about Wesley Danforth? We were worried—his treatments seem to have stopped inexplicably, and we've been unable to contact anyone for an update on his status."

"His doctor, Colin McDowell, is my friend," I said, "but Dr. McDowell seems to have disappeared. I would be happy to stand in for him as best I can while we are attempting to find out what has happened. To that end, I would like to review any files you may have on Mr. Danforth, and perhaps visit with him today if I could."

"I'll have to check with the hospital administration about the files. They would be Dr. McDowell's property, and I would need a release from him to let you see them. Patient confidentiality, you know. However, I have no problem sharing with you what I know about Mr. Danforth and his treatment, and arranging for you to meet him. He is much improved since his sessions with Dr. McDowell."

I pointed out the obvious. "It will be difficult to get a release from Dr. McDowell, since he is currently missing. However, it might be possible to get a statement from the police that he is indeed unavailable, and that an investigation is in progress. Would that help?"

"I'll talk to the administrator before you arrive, Dr. Warman, and let you know when we meet. Will that do?"

I assured him it would have to, and arranged to meet him at the hospital later that day.

I called police headquarters to see if Henderson was there, would give me something I could show Dr. Oglethorpe, and let me know if there were any updates on Colin's whereabouts. Unfortunately, I was told that he was not in, and that no one knew where he was or when he would be in. I explained my problem to the lady I was speaking with, and she transferred me to a sergeant, whom surprisingly, proved helpful.

"All I want you to do is to inform Dr. Oglethorpe at Manhattan State Hospital that you have missing person's report on Dr. Colin McDowell." I told him.

"I guess I can do that, Doctor. Can you give me this Oglethorpe's number?"

I did so, and the sergeant told me that he'd call just as soon as he'd verified that a missing person's report was indeed on file.

My last call was to Dr. Strongman at Lenox Hill Hospital, to check on Evie. The news was not good—I could hear the concern in his voice. She was definitely suffering from an infection. Her condition hadn't worsened since yesterday, but it hadn't improved, either. The next twenty-four hours were going to be crucial.

I had to consult a street directory for directions to Manhattan State Hospital. It was located on Ward's Island, which was north of Welfare Island in the East River. There was no road access—the city had started the construction of the Triborough Bridge a few years ago, which was supposed to unite the boroughs of Manhattan, the Bronx and Queens, and provide access to Randall's and Ward's Islands as well, but the project had run into financial difficulties and work had ceased. The directory informed me that a little-known ferry at the base of 116th Street on the East River served the island. I also discovered that I didn't have very much time if I wanted to catch the morning run, because the next trip did not leave until late afternoon.

Luckily, it was short walk to the Second Avenue elevated line from my flat, and the local was just pulling into the station as I deposited my nickel in the turnstile. There were half a dozen stops before 117th Street—it seemed as if the train spent more time standing than moving, as the distance between the stations was so short. The ferry slip was only a couple of blocks east of the train station. If you weren't looking for it, you would have missed it—a squat, nondescript shed, with peeling paint and cracked window panes that served a dual purpose as ticket outlet and waiting area. A morbidly obese man who sat outside on a bench gave me a disinterested glance as I approached. I entered the shed, which was entirely bare inside. I saw no kiosk where I could purchase passage. As I exited, I asked him where I could buy a ticket. He jammed a hand in his jacket pocket and withdrew a filthy roll.

"Five cents," he grunted.

He waved his other hand towards a small, flat-bottomed boat at the nearby dock. A cabin on the deck featured an overly tall smokestack, belching black smoke, sprouting from the middle of the roof. The vessel lay low in the water—I fervently hoped it would remain afloat for the trip. I joined perhaps a dozen other passengers on deck. It wasn't long before a crewman cast off and the ferry pulled out into the river.

It was a clear, somewhat warmish day, and I could see the bulk of Manhattan State Hospital perched on the island about three hundred yards across the black river. It was an imposing, multistoried brownstone structure, steepled and dormered, rambling across several acres. It was one of the largest, if not the largest insane asylum in the world.

It has always been the preference of the sane majority to ostracize their insane brethren to out-of-the-way places. Ward's Island was the location chosen by New York City as its Coventry—it had been used to house the mentally afflicted for half a century or more in its various institutions, and contained a Potter's Field—not even death released the outcasts from their exile. Even with the advent of modern psychotherapy and electroshock treatment, the prognosis for patients afflicted with disorders of the mind remains grim. It's natural, I suppose—out of sight, out of mind—people would rather not see unfortunate things about which little can be done. A sad testament to our so-called enlightened society. A man is no better than the manner in which he treats the meanest of his fellows.

The trip across the river was surprisingly long, because the little boat had to fight the Hell Gate current most of the way. The facilities at the dock on Ward's Island were no better than those on the Manhattan side. I climbed a rickety ladder to a dilapidated pier, then followed the crowd up to the hospital, thinking to ask one of my fellow travelers when the last ferry for Manhattan departed. He informed me that if I was not on the six o'clock ferry, I would be spending the night.

I caught my breath as I entered the main doorway. The stench was appalling. Even copious amounts of disinfectant could not mask the fetor of the unwashed humanity housed here. As I approached the reception desk to ask about the whereabouts of Dr. Oglethorpe, I noticed several patients wearing open-backed hospital gowns simply wandering about in the lobby.

The receptionist moved some plugs in her switchboard and spoke into the microphone on her headset, then informed me that Dr. Oglethorpe would be down momentarily. I felt a pluck at my sleeve, and I turned to see an emaciated young man in a dirty, white gown. He spoke through cracked, dry lips. "Papa?" he asked plaintively.

"No, no," I responded as gently as I could.

"Go away Albert, he's not your Papa," the receptionist said mechanically. Her statement had no effect whatsoever on Albert, who, by this time, clutched my hand tightly in both of his. Even though I was somewhat disconcerted by the uninvited personal contact, I squeezed his hands reassuringly.

His rheumy eyes brightened. The light of madness gleamed within. "Papa," he said with certainty.

"His father hasn't been to see him for twenty years," the receptionist said. "It calms him to be down here during the day to watch the people come and go. He thinks every middle-aged gentleman he sees is his Papa."

One of the first things you learn in medical school is that you cannot save everyone, but that doesn't make it any easier to encounter someone like Albert. I simply let him hold on to me for a few moments until a tall, young man in an immaculate white coat walked up me.

"Dr. Warman?" he smiled. "Dr. Hiram Oglethorpe. I see you've met Albert."

It took a few moments to become disengaged from Albert, who apparently would have clung to me for the balance of the day if allowed. He was dragged off, blubbering, by a large male attendant summoned for the purpose.

"Don't worry about Albert," Dr. Oglethorpe told me. "He'll forget about you five minutes after you're out of sight. Then they'll let him back into the lobby."

I accompanied Dr. Oglethorpe up a large staircase to the wards.

"I'm so glad someone's here to see Wesley," Dr. Oglethorpe said. "He was in pretty bad shape when he first arrived. As you'll see, Dr. McDowell has done wonders with him. But he still has a ways to go."

We ascended several floors, stopping before a locked metal door that had a small pane of wired glass in the center. I could see several cracks in the glass. Dr. Oglethorpe produced a key ring and unlocked it, motioning me to precede him.

I was totally unprepared for the shock that awaited me. The odor that I had noticed downstairs seemed magnified a hundredfold as the door opened, and was accompanied by a cacophony of voices—muttering, squealing, shouting. The corridor inside was broad, with high vaulted ceilings, and it teemed with humanity, mostly patients in the ubiquitous open-backed gowns, with a few scrub-clad attendants and white-coated hospital personnel intermingled. Many bed-ridden patients also occupied the periphery of the corridor—one every few feet, it seemed. Never in my life had I encountered such a place. It truly fit the definition of Bedlam!

Oglethorpe, seeming not to notice the surrounding chaos, pushed in behind me and secured the door. He took my arm and leaned close to my ear to be heard over the hubbub and said, "Follow me," then led the way down the hall.

As a doctor, I am accustomed to seeing people at less than their best, but the crowd in this place made me truly uncomfortable. While no one was overly violent or obscene, it was obvious that most of the patients were mentally disturbed, and even more obvious that they were under no supervision whatsoever. Some conversed, some argued, some wandered, some just sat against the walls with their legs splayed out in front of them. For the most part, the doctors and attendants simply ignored them unless their progress was impeded—to them, the corridor was merely a route between two points and the patients simply obstructions in their path. Again, while no one was overly violent when moving a patient aside, the hospital personnel treated them more like obstacles than people. Oglethorpe was no exception. For my part, I stayed as close to him as I could, so I would not have to clear my own path through the rabble.

Finally, we came to another locked door, which Oglethorpe quickly negotiated. When he pushed it closed after we had entered, cutting off the din, my relief was palpable.

We were in a tiny office that contained a desk and two chairs, a couple of filing cabinets, a daybed along one wall, and a small sink on another. Oglethorpe took the chair behind the desk, motioning me to the other one. He struggled a bit to get his legs into the kneehole, because the desk was too close to the wall.

I began to protest the appalling things I had just witnessed, but Oglethorpe cut me off. "I apologize for the conditions you just experienced, Dr. Warman," said Oglethorpe. "This facility was built to house 4,000 patients. It now holds nearly twice that many. Unless a patient is physically ill, there is simply no bed in a ward for him. Some actually sleep in that corridor with only a blanket and no mattress. And since the madhouse is not at the top of anyone's list for the allocation of public monies, our funding is pitifully inadequate." He hesitated, then continued, "We even had a suicide in a ward last week. A disturbed patient stripped off her hospital gown, tied one end around her neck and the other to a steam pipe, then used the weight of her body to shut off her airway. The other patients just stood and watched."

The young doctor was clearly distressed. A wave of shame crept over me when I considered my own elegant uptown practice. There was so much more I could do to relieve human suffering!

"How do you stand it, Doctor?" I asked.

"We do what we can. Doing something is always better than doing nothing, Doctor Warman. We don't help many of those poor wretches out there, but we do help some. That is what allows me to sleep at night. And speaking of those we have helped, let us discuss Danforth."

He was clearly happy to change the subject. "What was the initial diagnosis?" I asked.

"Catatonia, probably brought on by shock. The only sounds he would utter periodically were nonsensical."

"How did Dr. McDowell get involved with this case?"

"He contacted us several months ago, looking for a patient with symptoms like Danforth's, for a test of an experimental drug he was working on. Dr. Dyer told me that traditional approaches had been tried with Danforth and had proven ineffective. He was happy to hear that Dr. McDowell had a new approach, and authorized it immediately."

"Who is this Dr. Dyer?" I asked.

"Dr. William Dyer was Danforth's graduate advisor at Miskatonic University. It was while he and Danforth were on an expedition sponsored by the school that the shock occurred. Feeling responsible for the young man, Dyer had himself appointed as Danforth's guardian so he could see to his care."

"Has Dyer arranged for alternative care for Danforth in Dr. McDowell's absence?"

"No, Doctor," Oglethorpe replied. "It's strange. We haven't seen Dr. Dyer in weeks, either. I tried to get in touch with him at the university after Dr. McDowell's visits stopped, but I was told he was still out of town."

Now that was troubling news. Could Colin and this Dyer have been together when some calamity struck, accounting for the disappearance of both men at once? That could account for the Boston paper that I found in Colin's office, and Colin's visit to Arkham, as well. And how did the Ripper fit in to all of this? Did he attack Colin and Dyer when they were together?

"Did the police call you and verify that Dr. McDowell is missing?" I asked Oglethorpe.

"Yes, but it makes no difference. I can't release Dr. McDowell's notes to you without authorization."

I told Oglethorpe of the burglary at Carrel's lab last night, and of Colin's involvement with him.

"Well, it is a mystery, to be sure, Dr. Warman," said Oglethorpe. "And I hope that the police are actively investigating it. But our immediate problem seems to be Wesley Danforth. Would you like to meet him, and see if you feel up to continuing his care?"

"I am certainly no psychiatrist, and do not know how much help I could be to him, but I would like to talk with him to see if he could provide some indication of what happened to Dr. McDowell." I continued, cutting off Oglethorpe, who began to speak, "And don't worry, I am going to take it easy with Danforth. I'll get to know him before making any demands of him. But again, access to Dr. McDowell's notes would help greatly."

"Good," said Oglethorpe. "It may be easier to get the authorization I need if you agree to become his doctor."

"Have you read the notes, Doctor?"

"No. They're rather extensive, and I've enough patients of my own that I can't take on any more, and do them justice. And please realize that it may not sit well with Danforth to be told that his doctor is missing."

"I realize that, but there is another reason that I would like to locate Dr. McDowell as quickly as possible." I told him about Evie and the children.

"I understand your concern, Dr. Warman," said Oglethorpe.

"When and where can I see him?"

"How about right here and right now?" said Oglethorpe. "Please remember that Wesley is still very ill, even though he may not look it. Because of the seriousness of his condition, we were keeping him isolated in a cell until quite recently. After working with Dr. McDowell for a few weeks, we were able to move him to a ward."

"Not well enough to graduate to the corridor, yet?" I regretted that immediately as I said it.

Oglethorpe looked pained. "As I said, doctor, we do what we can. Anyway, the ward is not conducive to interviews. I will bring Danforth here. I have other patients to attend to; you'll have some privacy."

"That will be fine, doctor."

Oglethorpe extricated himself from behind the desk and left, closing the door behind him. I briefly considered taking his place, but then I decided, for our first interview it would probably be wise not to assume an authoritarian position behind the desk. Danforth could use the daybed, and I would stay where I was. About ten minutes had passed when the clamor and the stink from the hallway announced Oglethorpe and Danforth.

Wesley Danforth was a young man in his early twenties and must have formerly been a fine specimen of manhood. He was over six feet in height, with broad shoulders evident beneath the hospital gown he now wore, and there was still a suggestion of well-developed musculature in his exposed forearms. However, one glance at his face revealed that he had been very ill. His features were well chiseled; one could see that there used to be a rugged handsomeness there. But now he had the drawn, wizened look of long convalescence. His head had been shaved not too long ago, probably as a treatment for lice, and his overall carriage was stooped. He moved with a shuffle rather than a stride.

I stood as the two of them entered and motioned Danforth toward the daybed. Oglethorpe waited at the door until his patient was comfortably settled.

"I have enough work to occupy me for the rest of the morning Take all of the time you need, Dr. Warman," Oglethorpe said. "I have already informed Wesley about you and your relationship with Dr. McDowell. If you need me, just use the phone on the desk. The receptionist will have someone track me down."

Oglethorpe left, closing the door behind him. I regarded Danforth, who was perched on the edge of the daybed. His gaze was focused on the door through which Oglethorpe had departed —he would not look at me—a bad sign. If I could but win his confidence today, I would count it a victory.

"So, Mr. Danforth—may I call you Wesley?" Good, a nod, but he was still focused on the doorway. "As Dr. Oglethorpe told you, I am Dr. Ebeneezer Warman, and I am a friend of Dr. McDowell's." Danforth made no response, so I carried on. "I understand that Dr. McDowell has not been to see you recently. That is because he has gone away for a little while. If it is acceptable to you, I would like to get an idea of what the two of you have been discussing. Perhaps then I can help you move along with your recovery."

Another nod, but still no eye contact. Then Danforth said, "I don't care if I see Dr. McDowell again or not. I didn't like the shocks he ordered for me, nor the medicine he gave me. It made me see things, horrible things..."

There was an edge to his voice that I didn't like. I quickly interrupted, "No, Wesley, I am not going to order any more shocks for you. I just want to talk with you, to find out what you and Dr. McDowell have been talking about. Is that all right with you?"

I thought I saw a furtive glance in my direction, then he returned to his scrutiny of the doorway again. "I guess so," he said. "Dr. McDowell wanted to know about our Antarctic expedition. I didn't want to tell him—Professor Dyer said I should tell no one what we found there. But Dr. McDowell said that the shocks would have to continue until I did tell him. I didn't want that."

"So, you told him?" A nod. "Can you tell me?" Silence. "It's all right if you don't, Wesley. I told you I wouldn't order any more shocks, and I won't. But it was Professor Dyer who sent you here to get better. Dr. McDowell thought that you had to be able to talk about what was troubling you to do that. Even though you didn't like them, the shocks and the medicine were given to you to help you."

I saw no point in pushing him to discuss things he was obviously still uneasy about, and I was also keenly aware that not only did I not have Colin's expertise in this field, but I also had absolutely no background concerning this patient. What I really needed was access to Colin's case notes. Since we could not find them in his office, they were most likely in this hospital, and Oglethorpe had already made it clear that he wasn't going to release them. I was going to have to get Harvey involved. I channeled our conversation away from the expedition and the electroshock treatment, and simply tried to get Danforth to open up about who he was. I asked him about his childhood and his studies, and tried to get him to tell me about some of his happier days. It was slow going at first, but after about forty-five minutes, he was actually giving me a lecture on the Precambrian and Cambrian fossil collection at Miskatonic University! Apparently, this tiny institution boasted one of the larger collections of these extremely rare microliths. There was even some intermittent eye contact during his discourse.

When he finally wound down about the fossils, I determined we'd done enough for the day. I wanted to end our conversation on a high note. I picked up the desk phone and told the receptionist to tell Oglethorpe we were finished.

"Wesley, I have greatly enjoyed our conversation. May I come back and see you again tomorrow?" I extended my hand to him as I finished speaking.

He seemed not to see it for a moment, then he surprised me by giving me full eye contact as he took my hand.

"I'd like that, Dr. Warman, I really would."

Oglethorpe arrived shortly thereafter with an attendant to escort Danforth back to his ward. We had a brief discussion about the session we'd just completed, and arranged for my return tomorrow. Then Oglethorpe conveyed me back through Bedlam to the lobby, where he bade me good bye.

As I stood on the dock waiting for the ferry to depart, I reflected on the progress I'd made. While I was no closer to finding out what happened to Colin than I was when I got up this morning, I felt like I had done some good today—a feeling that I had experienced rarely in my medical practice of late. I savored it. I resolved to spend the balance of the day and evening at the library reading up on the Miskatonic Antarctic expedition; I remembered there was some press coverage at the time. I also had to get in touch with Harvey about his investigations and to determine how to get access to Colin's notes. He needed to know about Dyer, and the Boston paper. And, oh yes, I had to visit Evie in the hospital as well. It looked as if I wouldn't be getting to my bed until the wee hours for another evening.

CHAPTER 19

From the notebook of Sally Barton

Wednesday, September 30, 1931, morning

I was alone in bed when I awoke. I had a tight band around my forehead, and I knew what that meant. Might as well get it over with!

I struggled to sit upright. The band tightened, then pain lanced through my forehead, followed by a wave of nausea. I wondered if we hadn't gotten into some bad hooch at that speak last night—I knew I'd drank too damn much, but I didn't think I'd had that much! Another wave of nausea rolled in.

I gritted my teeth and swallowed, then jumped out of bed and headed for the sink. I just made it! When I finished, I vowed that there would be no more rich food and drink for me this trip!

A little while later as I was brushing my teeth, there was a knock on the connecting door. Despite my discomfort, I had to smile. He still was gentleman enough to knock, even after what we had shared last night! "Come in," I said.

"Good morning!" He said in a cheery voice. He had a tray balanced on one huge hand like a waiter, with a coffee pot, three domed plates and a bread basket on top.

He must have seen me wince, because he immediately became solicitous. He helped me back to the bed, sat me down and poured me a cup of coffee that he set on the nightstand. He poured another for himself, then went and sat on the daybed.

"I'm sorry I left you last night, Sally," Morris said, "but I thought that you would sleep better if you had the bed to yourself."

"You're sweet!" I said. "But believe me, I had no trouble sleeping. How do you feel?"

"A little rocky," he admitted, "but I've been worse. Come on, you'll feel better if you eat something."

The coffee had worked some magic, because at least I felt that I could try to eat. He set one of the plates beside me on the bed and removed the cover to reveal eggs, bacon, fried potatoes, and grilled tomatoes. The odor hit me and I almost lost it again! I turned my head away and said, "How 'bout just some toast?"

The toast helped, and after a second cup of coffee and a couple cigarettes, I felt almost human. Morris had no problem putting away three breakfasts instead of two.

He told me we would have to hustle to make the morning train to Cape May, then left me to get packed to go. That didn't take long, since I hadn't really unpacked all that much. Soon, we found ourselves boarding the train. I'd even had time to get a tin of aspirin in the station, thank God!

We were quiet as the train pulled out of the station. Morris obviously knew I didn't feel well and was giving me my space, and I certainly didn't feel like talking because I was dreading the conversation that I knew we were going to have to have later today. I wasn't about to broach the subject on the train, but I would have to after we got settled in Cape May. This was just going to get worse until I cleared the air! I sighed inwardly, then leaned my head against his shoulder and closed my eyes. Might as well enjoy it while I could.

I woke to Morris' gentle shaking.

"We're almost in," he said. "How are you feeling?"

I took inventory. The headache had subsided to a dull throb, and I had a burning sensation in my stomach, probably because of the aspirin. Other than that, I felt fine.

I looked out of the window. It was a sunny midmorning. The view was unattractive; the landscape flat and grassy with a few stunted shrubs and trees scattered here and there. A small, single-story house came into view, and then another, then we were coming into town and the houses got bigger, finally becoming mostly two- and three-storied, with dormers, gables and turrets. They were painted in all combinations of colors, each one distinctive. There was certainly money here!

The train slowed, the brakes squealing as we approached the railway station. If the houses were classy and posh, the station was just the opposite. It was brick, and only two stories, with a single flattened dormer in front on a gabled roof. After train ground to a halt we disembarked, jumping down to the ground next to the tracks from the last step, as there was no platform. The smell of salt air and coal smoke washed over us as we lined up outside the baggage car to collect our luggage; thankfully, since it was off-season, there was only a handful of travelers for whom Cape May was the final destination, so it didn't take very long to get our things.

Morris asked for directions to Congress Hall and found out that it was within walking distance. The poor guy took the bulk of my luggage and we started walking.

We turned down what looked like the town's main street. It was unpaved and lined with two and three story flat-roofed buildings, mostly with storefronts. The stuff in the windows seemed to be mostly gift shop junk, which I guess was normal for a tourist town. Even though it was midmorning, many of the shops were closed and there were only a few people on the street. Since I was used to Manhattan, the loneliness gave me the creeps.

The street was only a couple of short blocks long. We turned right the end of it, and I recognized Congress Hall from Strangways' picture. The place was huge—an L-shaped, canary yellow brick building with a front lawn as big as the Polo Grounds! The numerous windows sparkling in the morning sun told me that it probably had a hundred rooms or more. The top story was a giant dormer that ran the length of the building, with regularly-spaced double windows along the entire front. A slanting roof shading the front porch was supported by dozens of gleaming white pillars that reached up to the third floor. Those fourth-floor dormer rooms were probably hot as hell in the summer, but they would likely be delightful now, way up there in the sea air.

We walked along a long sidewalk that cut through the center of the lawn. The rocking chairs that lined the front porch, overlooking the lawn and the beach beyond, looked comfortable and inviting. There were balconies on some of the second-floor rooms. Now I was torn; did I want a balcony, or one of those cozy top floor dormer rooms? Crossly, I reminded myself that we were not here on vacation—we had work to do! Maybe if we got Trulove's ten grand for catching the Ripper we could come back here for a honeymoon.

The front doors were located in the crook of the L. Since Morris' hands were occupied with my luggage, I opened the door for him. The odors of old wood and food came out to greet us weary travelers, and they sure smelled fine! The lobby was elegant, but in a different way from the Bellevue. Bright and sunny, it was furnished with wicker chairs and sofas scattered about to create many welcoming nooks where you could have privacy but still be in the middle of things. The walls were painted white, emerald, and the ever-present yellow, which seemed to be the main theme of the place. Even though it was off-season, a good number of seats were occupied by mainly older people who had a look of wealth about them.

We approached the front desk, where a well-dressed man waited. I knew it wasn't so, but his smiling face seemed to say to me, what are YOU doing here? A uniformed bellhop in a pillbox hat rushed up to Morris to relieve him of the bags.

"Good morning, sir!" The clerk addressed Morris. "I assume you would like a room—we have many available. What's your pleasure?"

Morris cocked an eye at me. I was on the spot!

"I guess I'd like one of those top floor rooms, if..."

Morris cut me off before I could say, "... if it isn't too much!" He said, "We'll take a top floor room, if you have one open."

One room, I thought. My, how things had changed!

"Of course, sir, those are some of our best!"

I glanced around the spacious lobby looking for Addison Strangways while Morris took care of the paperwork. Strangways had never laid eyes on us, so I wasn't worried about spooking him, but he didn't seem to be around. We'd have to make a plan of action for finding him after we got settled.

The clerk hit a bell on the desk and summoned three bellhops — one to take Morris' bag and two for mine. The upper floors were reached by a grand staircase. It was quite a hike up to the fourth floor, and I sure didn't envy those guys who were carrying my bags.

Finally we arrived at the room and the bellhop unlocked and opened the door. The room was as bright and airy as I thought it would be. It had two huge, white wrought iron beds, several comfortable chairs, a bureau and a vanity. Best of all, the dormer had a cushioned window seat where you could lay and look out over the beach and the ocean!

Morris tipped the bellhops a buck apiece. Man, he was really throwing it around — not to impress me, I hoped. He should know he didn't have to do that. I thought we were sure gonna have to take old Strangways back with us now, if we were ever gonna pay for this trip! Morris shooed the bellhops out, then shut the door behind them. He turned to me, his face all lit up with his sappy smile and said, "Wow! Now ain't this just somethin'?"

I ran over to him and he enfolded me in his huge arms. I snuggled against his chest. Damn it! I had to tell him!

"Morris...," I began.

"It's gonna be hard to find Strangways here," he said. "It's off-season, the hotel ain't full, but it's really big! If we're lucky, maybe we'll see him when he comes in for meals. On the other hand, if he's really spooked, he may be holed up in his room, and having all his meals sent up. Got any bright ideas about how we can get a look at the front desk ledger to see if he's even checked in?"

194

Oh, the big palooka! He'd effectively destroyed the moment, so I went along.

"I dunno," I said. "Maybe the best thing to do is just ask."

"Yeah, but if he finds out somebody's lookin' for him when there ain't supposed to be nobody knows he's here, he might just take a powder. He does that, we'll never find him! Let's leave asking till last."

"You could tell the clerk you're a bull, get him to tell you what he knows and tell him not to alert Strangways," I offered.

"Yes, and I'll do that if we can't find him some other way." He looked at his watch. "This room comes with meals. Why don't we do some unpacking, then head down to the dining room and see if old Addison shows up? Besides, I'm starved!"

I guessed I'd have to put off that talk till later...

About twenty minutes later, we were walking into the hotel dining room off the lobby. I tried not to gape like a schoolgirl! It was a gigantic room with a checkerboard floor, pastel blue walls and glossy white accents. Waiters in formal white shirts with black trousers and bow ties scurried about, serving the diners. The place was about half full—probably about a hundred people. I looked around as we were waiting to be seated, trying to spot a single guy. No luck.

The waiter brought menus on a card. There were appetizers, salads, fish and meat dishes and desserts, with no prices, but Morris had said that the food came with the room. I was feeling a lot better than I was at breakfast, so I got some soup and a salad. Morris ordered his usual gargantuan meal.

We just made small talk at lunch, and it was hard. I had something I needed to get off my chest, and I didn't know how he was gonna take it, so I certainly wasn't gonna do it here. I waited until we were done eating and having coffee, then I said, "Morris, there something I really need to talk to you about. How about we take a walk on the beach when we're through here?"

He got a puzzled look on his face. "We can't talk about it here?" he asked.

I shook my head. "I'd rather not."

"Ok," he said. He drained his coffee. "Let's go."

As we stepped outside, the cold breeze off the ocean hit me. I really needed a sweater or something, but I was afraid if I went upstairs to get one, I'd chicken out of the whole thing. I walked ahead of him down the long walkway toward the beach, past a few diehards out there in front of the hotel. I turned and headed for a deserted section of sand. I felt Morris' hand on my shoulder, gently stopping me. I turned to face him.

The look on his face told me that he knew something was up. I started to speak, but he shushed me with a finger on my lips.

"Look, Sal, I know you have something to say, but so do I. I didn't expect what happened last night to happen, but I'm happy it did. I want to make an honest woman out of you. Marry me, Sally!"

My heart sank. Oh my God...

"Morris, I need to tell you something. If you still want to marry me after I tell you, I'll marry you. But I need to tell you."

"What is it?"

"Morris, I had another boyfriend a few years ago. We were gonna get married, or so I thought. Then, I got pregnant."

He didn't say anything, just looked at me.

"He said that he wasn't ready to be a father, that he needed more time. I thought he was gonna skedaddle and leave me with a baby, and I just couldn't deal with that. So, I got rid of it."

"What do you mean, you got rid of it?" There was an edge to his voice I didn't like.

"I went to this doctor a friend of mine told me about, and I got rid of it."

"You mean that you had your baby killed," he said.

I thought about that for a second. "Yeah, I guess that's what I did."

He didn't say anything.

"Worst part was," I continued, "after I'd done it and told my boyfriend, he said he'd thought more about us, and he really didn't want to get married after all, baby or no baby."

"You really killed it?" There was almost a plaintive tone in his voice.

Suddenly all of the emotion in me exploded! "Yes, goddamn it, that's what I did! I killed my baby! What the hell else was I supposed to do? For God's sakes, I didn't know that even my parents would have wanted me, pregnant with no husband and no prospects! And I couldn't disgrace them like that! I just got rid of it!"

He looked like somebody had hit him in the gut. "But that's against the law," he muttered. "I'm a cop, Sally. I'm supposed to uphold the law! I gotta think about this..."

What the hell did I expect? I was drained!

"Look," I said. "You go think about it. Meanwhile, I think I'm just gonna go back to the City. You don't need me to get Strangways."

"Ok," he said. He still looked stunned.

"Ok," I replied. I headed back to the hotel to arrange to have my bags sent to the train station. I looked back once, and he was still standing there like a post, staring out to sea.

The Legacy of the Unborn

CHAPTER 20

The Statement of Dr. Ebeneezer Warman

I was running with leaden feet from some nameless horror pursuing me. The blackness all around deadened any sound, even the sound of my own breathing. Then the jangling began. It emanated from everywhere—it seemed to fill the world! It acted to provide cover for the thing behind me—I couldn't tell where it was, when I would feel its sharp fangs in my back...

I woke to the sound of my telephone shrilling on my bedside stand. I groped for the receiver, nearly knocking the phone to the floor. I pulled it to my ear.

"Yes?" I croaked.

"Dr. Warman?"

"Yes."

"This is Dr. Strongman at Lennox Hill. You asked to be kept informed of Mrs. McDowell's condition. Well, she isn't doing very well at all. Perhaps you'd better come, if you want to see her..."

Alive. He didn't say it, but I heard it.

"Yes, Doctor. I'll be there as soon as I can."

I hung up the receiver and looked at my bedside clock. Four-thirty! I'd had a tot of brandy last night to help me off to sleep. My head was swimming. I lay back for a moment, then struggled to sit upright. I had to get to Evie!

I dressed quickly, trying manfully to stay out of the lavatory as my stomach churned. My posh Eastside practice had made me unused to an early morning summons such as this one. Once dressed, I grabbed a jacket and my Fedora against the morning chill and hurried down to the street.

There were no people or vehicles on East 66th Street at that early hour. I walked quickly over to Third Avenue, and while there were a few vehicles out as I expected, no taxi was in sight. There was nothing for it but to walk. I continued westward to Lexington Avenue, turned north and hiked the eleven blocks to the hospital as quickly as I could.

On arrival, I went straight to Evie's room. She was not there! The bed was still tousled, indicating that she had not been gone long, but worse, her chart was absent from the receptacle on the end of the bed. Was I too late?

I went immediately to the nurse's station to inquire.

"Doctor, she developed pneumonia over the course of the day yesterday," the head nurse said in reply to my question regarding Evie's whereabouts. "Dr. Strongman has had her moved into the Drinker respirator room. I'll get someone to take you."

"No need," I said. "I am affiliated with this hospital—I know where it is."

The Drinker respirator, known colloquially as the "iron lung", was housed in the basement. It had seen much use during last summer's poliomyelitis epidemic. That terrible disease sometimes had the effect of paralyzing the muscles that control the diaphragm, making it impossible for an afflicted patient to breathe on his own. The iron lung operated on the basis of negative pressure. It was placed around the patient's torso and hermetically sealed, then a powerful electric motor caused a vacuum inside the chamber, which caused the patient's chest to expand, filling his lungs with air. The pump then reversed, pressurizing the chamber and forcing the air back out the lungs. The cycle repeated endlessly as long as the power remained on. An iron lung patient was virtually a prisoner; the device was so large and heavy that the patient's movement was extremely limited when encased in it. However, it could keep a paralyzed patient alive indefinitely. The hospital had chosen to locate the device in a relatively isolated area in the basement because of the continuous drone of the electric motor and the hissing sounds it made as air was forced in and out of the chamber.

Strongman's use of the iron lung for a pneumonia patient was puzzling, however. The reason a pneumonia patient has difficulty breathing is different than with polio. Pneumonia is an infection of the lungs, caused by a bacterium or a virus. The infection causes inflammation, and the body responds by producing fluid and mucus to soothe the inflamed tissue, which has the unfortunate side effect of filling the lungs with fluid, blocking the breathing passages. A pneumonia patient could literally drown in his own body fluids, and no amount of chest manipulation would prevent it. Sometimes it is effective to roll the patient on his side to let some of the obstructing fluid drain away, clearing the lungs for a bit. Of course, that would be impossible in an iron lung. To me, Strongman's action smacked of desperation, possibly due to inexperience. I hoped I was wrong.

I arrived at the iron lung room, which was entered through a stout metal door with a tiny wired glass window at eye height. I didn't bother looking inside, I just grabbed the handle and open the door.

A cacophony of the electric motors and the pumps assaulted my ears as I entered. The place stank of carbolic and was unbearably hot, likely due to its proximity to the hospital furnace room. The relatively large chamber was lit by a fixture that overhung the gurney in the center. Half of the incandescent bulbs it contained were out—the remainder provided a dim, yellowish aura that suffused the room and doubtless added to the oppressive heat. I could see legs protruding from the gray cylinder on top. The iron lung blocked my view of the patient's features—I could not tell whether this was Evie.

I moved around so I could see her head protruding from the other end of the device, which was still swathed in the tight-fitting white hospital cap, making it difficult to discern her features. I moved closer and saw that it was, indeed, Evie. She looked dreadful! Her face was terribly gaunt and she was definitely cyanotic—a very bad sign. I bent over her face to listen to her breathing—a task made difficult by the clanking and wheezing of the iron lung—but I was able to hear the characteristic rustling of pneumonia coming from deep inside of her. My heart sank.

I placed my hand on her neck to gauge her fever. She was burning up! Then, her eyes snapped open!

At first all I saw in her eyes was fear. She didn't know me! Then, recognition dawned. She mouthed my name. I could barely hear her croaking voice over the din of the equipment. "Eben..."

"I'm here, Evie. I'm here."

"My girls..."

"They are fine, Evie. They are being cared for until you get well and get out of here."

"My girls, Eben! Promise you'll take care of my girls..."

"Evie, you'll do it yourself..."

"Promise!" She had a wild, hunted look in her eyes!

"I promise, Evie..."

She exploded into a fit of coughing. Phlegm mixed with blood erupted from her mouth! She was trying to inhale on her own and not succeeding, as the iron lung cycle was probably preventing it. Damn Strongman for an idiot, putting her in that contraption! I took a corner of the sheet to wipe the blood and mucus out of her mouth to see if I could give her breathing room, then set about trying to release her from that infernal device!

It was anything but easy. I knew I had to shut down the pump before I did anything else, and I had to do it when the chamber was charging rather than evacuating, or I'd never get it open to get her out. I found the pressure gauge and maddeningly, I saw that the needle was dropping—I had to wait until the cycle finished and it started pressurizing again. Meanwhile, I thought I had identified the switch to kill the pump. All the while, Evie was coughing and retching in a way I had only seen in patients suffering from severe smoke inhalation!

The needle of the pressure gauge reached normal and I cut the switch. Now, to get her out! The two halves of the iron lung were held together by bolts dogged tight with nuts—I tried loosening one by hand with no luck—this was going to require a wrench!

I looked at Evie's face again and my stomach shrank against my backbone! The fluid had stopped gushing from her mouth, but now she was simply trying to breathe but couldn't—I could see her throat constricting, but the breath neither went in nor out!

I frantically cast about for a wrench. If I could but get her out of that iron prison, I could roll her on her side or her belly and get that damnable fluid out of her chest! I didn't see the wrench, but I did see a button of the side of the bed to summon a nurse. I hit it.

The iron lung room obviously wasn't wired into the regular hospital intercom system, because a rather strident bell started jangling outside in the hall!

I looked again and saw the toolbox half hidden under a table on the other side of the room. I tore it open. I could have cried! I grabbed up the wrench and started undoing the bolts on the side of the iron lung.

By the time I had it open, Evie wasn't breathing anymore. I had to pull her off the gurney and put her on the floor to get her on her stomach, because that God-damned iron monstrosity was in the way! I was sitting astride her back with my hands on her shoulder blades, pumping away like a madman when the white-coated people started filling the room. Somebody pulled me off her, and a nurse flipped her face up. I could see she still wasn't breathing. The nurse began raising Evie's arms above her head, then bringing them back down to her chest in an effort to get her breathing restarted.

Suddenly Evie inhaled, but when she exhaled, I heard the dreaded "death rattle" and I knew it was over. I looked away from her, towards the doorway to the hall.

Dr. Strongman came into the room and stopped in his tracks. He looked at Evie lying on the floor in her own blood, horror writ large on his boyish features, then he looked at me apologetically, as if unsure where to go or what to do next. I made it easy for him. I hit him in the face as hard as I could!

The Legacy of the Unborn

CHAPTER 21

From the notebook of Sally Barton

Wednesday, September 30, 1931, late afternoon

The wind off the ocean blew cold and damp, and the streets of the town funneled it into the depot where I sat on my stacked luggage. The sun had vanished behind the buildings, and the sky was reddening. I was chilled to the bone, but I didn't care. The frost in my heart was a thousand times worse.

The train we'd arrived on was still on the tracks. It was scheduled to leave in a couple of hours. I already had my ticket, but it would be a while before we boarded. I just sat there in the cold, waiting.

Waiting—the story of my life! When I was a little girl, I waited to grow up. All grown up, I waited for Prince Charming, and when he came along, the louse knocked me up and dumped me. After I took care of that problem, I got a job, and now I was waiting to be accepted in my profession like a man. I thought this Ripper case was really my ticket. Guess not. Dumped again!

I had no idea what I was gonna do when I got back to the city. This case was effectively over for me, and my romance too! I didn't think I could face going back to writing obits and Charity Smythe. Hey, maybe I should write up my own hard luck story! Maybe there was somebody out there who could give me some advice. I sure needed some!

I was so caught up in my own misery that I never even heard him, big as he was.

"Hey, Sally."

I whirled around and he was standing there, looking down at me. His shamefaced expression was worse than ever. His eyes were red. He'd been crying?

"Look," he said, "I was way out of line. I had no right to say what I did, after you just told me the worst secret you had. You caught me off guard, is all. I'm sorry. I love you, no matter what. And I still want to marry you, if you'll even have me after what I just did."

Did he just say he still loved me?

"C'mon, get off those damn bags and let's go back to the hotel."

He picked me up off the luggage. He tried to set me down on the platform, but I wrapped my arms around his neck, buried my face in his chest and bawled like a little girl! He tightened his own arms around me and held on, rocking me back and forth, until I'd cried myself out. Then I loosened my grip so he could set me down.

He looked straight into my eyes.

"I'll never hurt you like that again as long as I live, Sally Barton. I promise! I'll blow my brains out if I do!"

I just hugged him to me again.

He picked up most of the bags and we headed back to Congress Hall. I walked quickly, both because I was cold and because I didn't know how long it would be before the reaction set in, and my legs gave out.

I was beat and thoroughly chilled by the time we made it back to the room. I really thought he was gonna have to carry me up that last flight of stairs, but somehow, I made it. I collapsed on the bed when we got inside. I must have passed out.

Next thing I knew, he was undressing me! I struggled feebly, but he picked me up like a doll, carried me into the warm, steamy bathroom and gently placed me in the tub. The water was a little too hot at first, but then it wasn't, and the warmth began to penetrate my frigid bones.

"You relax and get warm," he said. "Stay awake—don't drown! I'm going down for a pot of coffee."

I tried to follow his advice and stay awake, but it was hard! I was about to get out of the tub so I wouldn't pass out again, when I heard him come back into the room. In another minute, he was back in the bathroom, with a glass in his hand.

"I took a chance and asked a bellhop if he could get us a drink," he said. "Would you believe he turned up a bottle of Canadian! Here!" He offered me a glass half full of amber ambrosia. After this, I would die for him!

There isn't much to say about the rest of the night. He helped me out of the tub and got me dried off and tucked into bed. I think I was gone before he even pulled the covers over me.

The Legacy of the Unborn

CHAPTER 22

The Statement of Dr. Ebeneezer Warman

That was the first time in my life that I had ever hit someone.

I must say, I thoroughly enjoyed it!

The scene in the iron lung room was chaos for a while. The nurses had to tear me away from Strongman, or I'd have pounded his face to a pulp. They tried to assist Evie, but it became quickly apparent that she was gone. Then a couple of burly male attendants arrived to hustle me out of the room. They were going to call the police until they realized who I was—a resident at the hospital. By that time, I had calmed down somewhat. I asked if I could go to my office, and they assented. It was obvious they were glad to be rid of me.

"We're going to have to report this to the director, you know," one of the attendants told me.

I didn't answer him. I knew they would. I would just have to deal with the consequences when they came.

When I got to my office, I closed and locked the door, then retrieved the bottle of Scotch that I kept in the desk for emergencies. I thought this situation qualified. I splashed a couple of fingers into a coffee cup, then sat on the divan and drank it off. The whisky burned its way into my stomach, forming a little hot ball that began to send tendrils out into my limbs. I could feel the tension draining out of me. I reached for the bottle on the desk and poured another dollop into the cup. I would have to be careful not to get soused, I thought. It's early, I've had no breakfast, and I've got a long day ahead of me.

I settled back on the divan and lighted a cigarette to think. Was it only last Friday that Evie had shown up at my office, to entreat me to find her wayward husband? I wasn't at all sure that I could help her find Colin, but it never entered my mind that I might be burying her before the week was out. I remembered how vivacious and alive she was when I knew her in college. We had met at a social to which the Wellesley women had been invited. I made it my business to attend such events in those days, for obvious reasons. For some reason I couldn't fathom, she took quite a shine to me, and in the ensuing weeks, she began a quiet but determined pursuit. I did my best to discourage her without being disagreeable, but she took my standoffishness for shyness and redoubled her efforts to make me her beau. I even introduced her to Colin, who had let me know that he was keen on her as well, but to no avail. Finally, at my wits end, I decided that if I couldn't trust Evelyn Porter, I couldn't trust anyone. I steeled myself, and I told her the truth about why we could never be together.

Naturally, she was taken aback—who wouldn't be? But then, she showed me exactly the kind of person she was. She told me she was immensely flattered that I would choose to share such a thing with her. She assured me that my secret was safe, that she would cease all advances towards me, and that she would always be my friend, if I would have her as one. Of course, I would! Until this terrible day, Evie had remained true to her word. She hadn't even told Colin, her husband, about me, although I was sure he suspected. Now she was gone, and I couldn't help but feel it was my fault. I missed my beautiful and loyal friend badly, and I wept.

A growing heat on my fingers warned me that my cigarette had burned down to a stub. I ground it out in an ashtray on the desk. I would arrange for the disposition of Evie's remains before I left the hospital, then I would go home and call Harvey. I needed some time with him badly, and I was sure he would realize that. But first, I would have to go and see Wesley Danforth again. I had promised him that I would, and he'd told me that he'd like that. And I felt that I owed it to Evie's memory to find Colin, or at least to find out what had become of him. Someone would have to break all this to the girls, as well, and I was just selfish enough that I did not want it to be me.

A couple of hours later, I was in my flat, calling Harvey's office. His direct line didn't answer, so I rang his secretary, who told me he wouldn't be in today.

"Did he say why?" I asked.

"No, Doctor," she replied. "He was all very mysterious. He told me he might be out for a couple of days. Do you know where he might be?"

I was vaguely bothered by the idea that Harvey's private secretary thought that I might know his whereabouts when she didn't.

"No, I don't," I said. "If he comes in or calls, tell him I'll call him back there and at home this evening."

The next call was one I didn't want to make—Annabel at the Settlement. When she answered, I told her about Evie, and that I would leave it to her to break the news to girls.

"What a tragedy!" she said. "Is there any other family?"

"I don't think so," I said, "But I'll try to find out. And I still haven't given up on finding their father."

Annabel assured me that she could keep the girls indefinitely, and if the worst came to pass, she knew people who would see to it that they had a loving home to grow up in. It was all that I could have asked for.

My last call was to Sarah, to cancel my appointments for the day.

"A couple of your patients have told me they're going to go elsewhere," she said.

I could tell that she disapproved of my actions of late, but dammitall, it was my practice, not hers! And I had promised Wesley I'd see him today.

"Then that's what they'll have to do," I told her. "There are more old biddies where they came from."

I heard her snort before she rang off.

I made the ferry to Ward's Island with only a few minutes to spare. This trip, I recognized many of the passengers, and it was evident that a few of them recognized me as well, given their nods in my direction.

Unfortunately, I had failed in my resolve to read up on the Miskatonic Antarctic Expedition before my meeting with Danforth today, at which it was supposed to be the topic of conversation. Very well, I would just have to let Danforth inform me—he would be a much better *raconteur* than a newspaper article anyway, having been a participant. I would simply have to keep a close eye on him to apprise me when I might be straying onto ground that he was uncomfortable traversing.

My journey from the pier on Ward's Island to the little office where I had met with Danforth was much the same as it had been yesterday, with the notable absence of Albert.

"He got much worse yesterday afternoon," Dr. Oglethorpe told me when I inquired. "We thought that a few days cooling off in solitary after an electroshock treatment would set him right again."

Poor Albert! I knew in my heart that I hadn't done anything to hurt him, but I could not help but wonder if his present situation was somehow my fault as well. Dammitall, I was accumulating a load of misery to be responsible for!

As we had done yesterday, Oglethorpe and I exchanged a few pleasantries, then he left me in the office while he went to fetch Danforth.

Unlike yesterday, Danforth was not clad in a hospital gown. He was wearing a pair of green OR scrubs and looked as if he'd made an effort to shave and comb his hair. It was obvious that he'd anticipated my visit and had attempted to be ready for company. Now I was glad indeed that I had kept our appointment and had not disappointed him.

As said to Sarah, those old crones who were upset that I could not attend to their imaginary ills today would just have to find someone else to put up with them!

"How are we today, Wesley?" I asked him.

"Just fine, Doctor. I hope you are as well."

"Well, I'll just leave you two alone," said Doctor Oglethorpe. "Take as much time as you need, Doctor Warman." I winced at the noise as he opened the door to leave, but I noticed that it didn't seem to bother Danforth. Then Oglethorpe was gone and it was quiet again.

I began with some general questions to put the young man at his ease. We had a bad moment when he told me that he had no family—his father had been killed in the war and his mother and sister followed in the Spanish flu epidemic.

"But I actually credit my time in the orphanage with sparking my interest in science," Danforth told me. "I started collecting all sorts of things—rocks, leaves, bugs, and of course I had to know what everything was. I had a fair understanding of taxonomy and geology by the time I finished high school."

"You've been at Miskatonic for your entire college career?"

"Yes, Doctor. I grew up in Arkham. Miskatonic had a program where each year, they'd give one bright high school senior in foster care a shot at college. They assigned you a mentor when you started, and in my case, it was Professor Dyer. That was all I needed. I finished my baccalaureate, then stayed on with the professor for my Master's and Ph.D. I was supposed to be finished the year after the expedition returned."

I smiled. Danforth had been kind enough to provide me with the *segue* I needed to begin a discussion of the expedition. "I assume it was a very exciting opportunity for you to take a trip to the Antarctic."

"It was something I'd dreamed about ever since I got into geology. It's the last great unexplored territory, you know." He warmed to his subject. "Most people don't even know that Antarctica once had a temperate climate, maybe even tropical. The fauna and flora were diverse and prolific—seed ferns, ginko trees and there were even coniferous forests during the Cretaceous. And dinosaurs too! Now all you can find there are lichens, fish, arachnids and the penguins, of course. And it's a geologist's dream! But because of that thick ice sheet, we know almost nothing about its geology."

"When did you go?"

Danforth looked puzzled. "What's the date?" he asked.

"It's Friday, October second."

"What year?"

I suddenly remembered the immense impact that a long hospitalization can have on a patient. "1931," I told him.

He looked relieved. "Then it wasn't really that long ago. We left Boston on September second, last year and arrived at Ross Island in November."

I decided that a few more factual questions were in order before I tried to get him talking about any specific events that might prove traumatic. "Was it a large expedition?"

"I guess. I don't really have anything to compare it to. There were four professors. Professor Dyer, the geologist, was nominally in charge. There was Pabodie, from engineering, Atwood the physicist, and Lake..." he stopped speaking and a look of sadness suffused his countenance. I could see him gather himself before he continued. "There were seven of us grad students. Then we had about twenty-five technicians and mechanics. You don't want to run out of mechanics in Antarctica."

It seemed there was just a hint of panic in that last statement. I started to speak, to reassure him, but he went right on.

"We had two ships to carry all our gear. Of course, part of that was the five Dornier aeroplanes, which served as our principal means of transportation after we got there. And we also had the dog sleds if the planes failed."

Again the panicked tone.

"Listen, Wesley, if you're uncomfortable discussing the expedition, we can talk about something else. Whatever you want to."

He went on like he hadn't even heard me. "The plan was to spend one Antarctic summer on the work, mostly in the mountains and on the plateau south of the Ross Sea. We were following in the footsteps of Shackleton, Amundsen, Scott and Byrd. I felt just like Arthur Gordon Pym!"

Now he sounded proud.

"The first four gentlemen you've mentioned I've heard of, of course, but who is Arthur Gordon Pym?"

"Oh, he's not real," was his surprising answer. "He's from the story by Poe."

"I've not read that one."

"I'm not surprised. Many people haven't. The *Narrative of Arthur Gordon Pym of Nantucket* was Poe's only novel, you know."

This interview was going much better that I could have hoped for. Aside from a few minor abnormalities, Danforth seemed completely at ease and his demeanor was becoming ever more exhilarated and engaging. He was looking me right in the eye, a huge difference from our first meeting only yesterday. I returned his gaze expectantly, silently encouraging him to go on.

He launched into a detailed synopsis of Poe's tale. It was a story about a young Nantucket lad, who stowed away on a whaler and found himself embroiled in a maritime adventure that became increasingly bizarre. It seemed to be a compendium of all of the seafaring yarns of the time, involving a shipwreck, a mutiny and even an attack by cannibals. Eventually Pym and his companion, a doughty wight named Dirk Peters, wound up in the Antarctic Ocean, where they made some fantastic discoveries.

"After they escaped from the cannibals," Danforth was saying, "Pym and Peters hid in the mountains. They were seeking shelter, and they discovered a labyrinth of passages with strange marks on the walls..." Suddenly, like a switch had flipped inside of him, Danforth's eyes glazed over. He was no longer looking at me, but through me, it seemed. A pool of saliva welled up in the corner of his open mouth and turned to drool as it ran down his chin.

Oglethorpe said that Danforth had initially presented with catatonia, and this was indeed catatonia if I had ever seen it! But what had triggered it? Oglethorpe had also said that Danforth had gotten much better after Colin's treatments.

As quickly as he had lapsed into his trance, Danforth came back. "...we had to restrict our work to exposed or nearly exposed land surfaces because of the thickness of the ice—that's why we chose the mountains for our surveys," he said.

"What surveys do you mean, Wesley?" I tried to go along with him as if nothing had happened, to find out where he was.

"Taking soil and rock cores, and analyzing them to elucidate the geological and natural history of Antarctica."

"An ambitious project indeed!" I exclaimed. "And difficult too, I imagine, with the ground permanently frozen, and the ice sheet." It seemed as if he'd completely blanked out that he had been discussing Poe's story—now he was back on the particulars of the expedition. I saw no reason to steer him away from that.

"That's where Doctor Pabodie's drill came in," Danforth continued. "Nothing like it had ever been seen before. He made it out of an aluminum alloy that he'd created. The drill was unbelievably light, portable and durable, and it had a whole new way of working. It combined the functionality of an artesian drill with the principle of the small circular rock drill. It could drill evenly through strata of varying hardnesses, which was absolutely essential if we were to recover intact cores, especially from the pre-Cambrian strata."

Now he had warmed to his subject again. He spoke eloquently of the expedition's early endeavors on Ross Island and their heroic ascent of Mount Erebus. Danforth was a pilot, and his skill was pivotal in the expedition's nerve-wracking, four-hour, non-stop flight to Beardmore Glacier to establish its southern base. I was absolutely spellbound by his description of those frantic hours, during which they flew blindly over the uncharted wasteland with the wildly gyrating compass as their only guide, and the thick cottony clouds hugging the ship so tightly that they could barely hear the drone of their own engines. They had to use the altimeter to land because they couldn't see the ground! As harrowing as the story was, Danforth evidenced no more episodes of panic or distress, nor any lapses in his electrifying account.

A glance at my watch confirmed that we'd been talking for nearly two hours. I had no wish to tire him or cause him further stress. I somewhat reluctantly called a halt to our discourse.

"You'll come back tomorrow, Dr. Warman?" His plaintive tone was like a little boy's. It couldn't help but remind me of poor Albert.

"Yes, Wesley. And I'll want you to continue telling me of your adventures. I find them absolutely fascinating!"

I caught the mid-afternoon ferry and was back in Manhattan in short order. As I stepped on to the quay, I realized I was in an unfamiliar situation. I had no appointments this afternoon, no patients at the hospital, no rounds to make later this evening. I wasn't accustomed to being footloose, and I had to grapple with my leisure for a few moments before I could decide what to do. Finally, I opted to go to the library and read up on the Miskatonic Expedition before I had any more discussions with Danforth.

The unseasonably warm weather was still with us, and the sky was positively cerulean with nary a cloud. I remembered the seemingly interminable ride on the Second Avenue line up here from 65th Street, so I opted to walk the eight blocks to 125th Street to see if I could catch an express instead of the local that I would have to board at the 116th Street station. My skin was damp under my worsted suit by the time I arrived at 125th Street.

I was in luck! As I surmounted the metal stairs to the train platform, I saw the downtown express standing on the track, its doors open and beckoning. I boarded, and soon we were rattling along through the city at third story height. The windows in the car were open because of the warmish day, and the effluvium of the metropolis wafted in with the breeze—mingled scents of automobile exhaust, the hot metal smell of the train, aromas of the foods of all nations, and the lot of it topped off with a soupçon of unwashed humanity. I would recognize the fragrance of my city even if I were a blind man.

The train stopped once at 86th Street, then after another short jaunt, the doors slid open at 42nd Street, where I disembarked. I walked west from 2nd Avenue towards the Hudson, under the Park Avenue bridge and past the massive bulk of Grand Central Terminal, with its assemblage of Greek gods looking down disapprovingly from their Olympian perch at the mortals who scurried by. I was heading for the city's main library on 5th Avenue, where I was sure I could find the information I required about the Miskatonic expedition.

The main library of the City of New York was a huge, neoclassical edifice, constructed entirely of white marble, which occupied an entire city block on the southwest side of the intersection of 42nd Street and 5th Avenue. The three flights of steps at the 5th Avenue entrance were guarded by colossal, crouching marble lions and separated by broad walkways. The steps and the walkways had become a meeting place for all of the denizens of the city —working girls, businessmen, tourists and spooning lovers alike, with the ubiquitous pigeons annoying all equally. A broad portico at the top of the steps was pierced by three doorways, which gave ingress to a cavernous, two-story vestibule. The newspaper room was only a few steps away. I entered the mahogany paneled room and was immediately comforted by the smells of old wood and paper—that fragrance had been part of the happiest times in my life when I was immersed in my studies at Harvard.

Since Danforth had given me the dates of the expedition earlier today, it did not take me long to acquire an armload of the appropriate dailies and to find a seat next to a window. I had chosen the old Gray Lady herself. the venerable *New York Times*, which I surmised would provide me with the most accurate and complete account. However, I found that I was in error on that point, as the expedition had submitted their original reports to a local paper, *The Arkham Advertiser*, and to the Associated Press, a wire service. However, the *Times* had reproduced all of the material faithfully. I started reading the accounts from the beginning. At first, I learned not much more than I already knew from my colloquy with Danforth—indeed, he had provided a more complete narrative than the paper did. However, it became quickly apparent that we had not progressed to the heartbreaking news. Here is the article that I found:

March 4, 1931—Boston Globe

Silas K. Henderson

Dr. Percy Lake and Ten Others Lost Under Mysterious Circumstances

Miskatonic Antarctic expedition ends in tragedy—exclusive from the Arkham Advertiser (Arkham, MA)

The brig *Arkham* and the barque *Miskatonic*, bearing the remnants of the ill-fated Miskatonic University Antarctic expedition, docked at Boston Harbor late this afternoon. The ships were met by grieving family members, friends and co-workers who sadly awaited the unloading of the bodies of their loved ones, only to find that the remains had been interred at the bottom of the world. They had to resign themselves to the fact that they would never get the opportunity to say goodbye, or to lay their dearly departed to rest.

The expedition was financed largely by the Nathaniel Derby Pickman Foundation, and it left Boston on September 2nd of last year. It was to remain in the Antarctic for two years. Dr. William Dyer of the M.U. Anthropology department was the head of the expedition, and he had little comment about its failure. The expedition was organized for a general exploration of the little-known continent, as well as to procure cores from deep in the ice using a revolutionary new drilling apparatus invented by Dr. Frank Pabodie of M.U., who also accompanied the expedition.

Dyer said, "Our hearts are heavy with grief over the passing of our colleagues. We felt that, given the magnitude of the disaster, that we simply could not go on. Thus, I determined to end the expedition at this time. Their deaths were not in vain, however, for we did gather much new rock and ice samples that should lead us to a much better understanding of this dark continent at the bottom of the world."

Dyer, as leader of the expedition, authorized a group led by the biologist Geoffery Lake of the M.U. Biology department to take three of the expedition's four planes to explore a newly discovered mountain range in the vicinity of Beardmore Glacier. Lake decided to form a sub-expedition and strike out to the northwest. For a time, the group sent out periodic wireless reports on their progress, which were relayed worldwide through the transmitter on the *Arkham*. Their foray culminated in the discovery of some hitherto unknown fossils, which caused great excitement in the scientific community. The reports abruptly ceased during a freak storm which allegedly cost the lives of all of the members of Lake's expedition. Shortly after discovering the carnage at Lake's camp—eleven men dead and one missing—Dyer made the decision to terminate the entire expedition. Dyer said, "The bodies were so mangled by the violence of the storm that the decision was taken not even to pack them out." In addition to the remains of the scientists, the fossils were left behind as well. The remaining members of the expedition also had little comment, but their great disappointment, and even resentment in a few cases, was evident.

Dr. Hugo Starkweather of Columbia University was on hand to meet the returning expedition. "We are not done with the Antarctic," he said. "It was criminal to leave those fossils behind, considering the cost that was paid to procure them. Under the auspices of Columbia, Dr. Reginald Moore and I will be organizing a new expedition to accomplish what the group from Miskatonic University could not. Columbia will not fail!"

Dyer's statement that the bodies were so mangled by the storm that he decided not to pack them out bothered me for several reasons, beyond the obvious. As a young doctor, I had seen bodies mangled by a tornado in the Midwest, but it was the debris carried by the wind that did all of the damage, not the wind itself. Such debris was generally composed of the remnants of trees, structures, dirt and stones, and other vegetation, none of which would be present a storm in the barren Antarctic wasteland. There was also no mention of the disposition of the bodies. It would seem rather callous to simply leave them exposed on the ice, but a proper burial would have been out of the question in that permanently ice-covered landscape. Perhaps Pabodie's drilling apparatus had been utilized somehow to inter them?

The subsequent transmissions were terse, lacking the detail of the previous bulletins. The rescue party remained at the ill-fated camp for only a day before flying back to the coast where the ships were anchored, and packed up for home. I understood why such a catastrophe could take the heart out of the explorers, but the fact was that they had at least a few weeks of summer remaining, during which further work could have been accomplished. Regardless, the decision was taken to terminate the expedition and return to Arkham.

When I finished my reading, I sat back and lighted a cigarette. The final dispatches left me with the distinct impression that information about the true nature of the tragedy was being withheld, although I could not imagine why. Might this have something to do with Danforth's subsequent nervous breakdown? This information had given me an area to explore with him at tomorrow's session, but I realized that I would have to tread lightly indeed, to avoid causing him further mental anguish.

A glance out of the window informed me that darkness had fallen. I considered calling Harvey for a late dinner, but I surmised that if he had returned at all from his mysterious investigation, he would have likely eaten already. I decided to simply stop by Otto's for a sandwich to take home.

I was on my way to the front door when I suddenly remembered the call slip that Harvey and I had found in Colin's office. I was chagrined that it had slipped my mind, but grateful that I'd remembered it. If Harvey knew that I had come here and not followed up, I'd never hear the end of it. I plucked my watch from my vest. Nearly eight o'clock—the library was open for another couple of hours yet. Plenty of time to investigate Colin's reading material.

The library is so vast that a delivery system for any book housed there has been set up—a user did not have to navigate its seemingly endless reaches on his own. One simply identified the desired tome from the card catalog in the Public Catalogue Room and filled out a call slip, which was handed to a runner who delivered the material to the requester in the Main Reading Room. Fortunately, because I already had the call slip that Colin had filled out, I was able to skip the first step. After I had handed it off to a flunky, I proceeded to the Main Reading Room to await delivery.

The North and South Reading Rooms were adjoined; they were actually a single immense chamber that ran the entire width of the library at the back of the building. The ceiling soared some fifty feet overhead and was adorned with painted panels of open skies and cottony clouds. Huge arched windows in both the left and right walls would have let in ample light were it daytime, but at night the light was provided by concentric rings of small bulbs that encircled the single, massive tiered chandelier that dominated the center of the room. It was flanked on both sides by smaller versions of itself that illuminated the columns of reading tables that ran along both walls. Because the overhead lights afforded insufficient lighting for close reading at the tables, each table also contained a half dozen cone-shaded brass lamps that glowed softly like so many Christmas lights. I took a seat at one of the reading tables to await the arrival of my books.

It was less than ten minutes when the flunky returned. He looked around in an attempt to find me, and I made it easy for him by waving.

As he approached, I noticed that he was carrying a single book, when I had requested two.

"I'm sorry sir," he said as he handed me the tome. "The other volume you requested is one of our rare books, and it's temporarily unavailable. However, if you will come back in the morning and meet with our director in Room 303 upstairs, I'm sure an accommodation can be made for you."

I frowned at him, and he obsequiously regarded the floor. I was not happy about this development, as I was anxious to get back to Danforth. The morning ferry for Ward's Island left at eight-thirty, and I would not catch it if I was here with the Director of Rare Books. The next trip did not go until after lunch, which would afford me much less time with my patient. Well, there wasn't much to be done about it if I wanted to see that book.

"You can tell the director that I will be here at eight to meet with him," I said. "And tell him I have no wish to be kept waiting—I am a physician, and I have patients to see."

"Yes, doctor, I will tell him."

I turned to the book he had brought. It was in *duodecimo* format and approximately half an inch in thickness. The cover was a soft brown suede of the kind used in the last century for bibles and other important works. The title was embossed on the spine in gold, and a clue to the age of the volume could be gleaned from the fact that a goodly part of the metal had flaked and fallen out of the impressions of the letters. However, I could still make out the enigmatic title, *Notes on the Necronomicon.* The cover bore the bust of some fantastic creature with a tentacled visage.

I set the book on its spine and opened it, and it fell open as a book will do when the spine has been broken. I clucked my tongue—that was no way to handle an old book! I hoped Colin hadn't done it.

The type was standard for the period, and the book was in a two-column format. The column headings read *Shoggoth... Shub-Niggurath.*

The text was continued from the previous page. "*...servants of an Ancient non-terrestrial Race. They were constructs, made of the nascent tissues of their Masters, and were therefore formless, or rather able to assume any form as their masters would deem suitable for an assigned task. The Shoggoth was immensely powerful, able to lift many times its own weight by simple tissue expansion, so they were used to erect all manner of buildings and other structures. The creatures were also possessed of an evil intelligence, able to work independently but aware of their enslavement and bitterly resentful towards it, hence rigorous control and the utmost caution exercised by the Master was obligatory lest the Shoggoth turn on its tormentor and destroy it...*

There was more in a similar vein, but I stopped reading. Why on earth would Colin, consummate scientist that he was, be reading dreck like this? I closed the book.

On my way out of the library, I debated about keeping my promise to meet with the Rare Book Director in the morning. I was anxious to get back to Danforth—I wanted to know if any information about what happened to Lake and his men had been held back, and if it had anything to do with Danforth's condition. Then Harvey's face popped into my head, wiggling his wicked finger in my face.

"You didn't think it was important? Or maybe you just didn't think!"

I decided to keep the appointment.

Silas K. Henderson

CHAPTER 23

From the notebook of Sally Barton

Thursday morning, October 1, 1931

I awoke to bright sunshine streaming into the room through the double window. Morris had pushed the other bed over next to mine so we could sleep together. He was still out like a light and snoring gently. He had me cuddled in both arms—one behind my head and the other draped over my chest. There was no way I was getting out of that bed without moving them, which would probably wake him. I decided just to settle back and enjoy it.

I thought about what he had said yesterday—about me killing my baby. It hurt me when he said it, but I had to admit, he had it right. I had taken its life to make my own manageable again, to avoid the shame of being an unmarried mother, and to get on with my career. I had no defense other than weakness and selfishness. Morris had proven he was a big man in more ways than one—he had obviously forgiven me for what I had done. Now all I had to do was to forgive myself!

I must have had fallen back to sleep, because I woke up when Morris groaned. He relaxed his embrace enough so I could wiggle free. I started to get out of bed, but his massive hand fell on my shoulder.

"Don't leave so fast," he said.

"I've got to pee," I told him. He had that hangdog look again. "I'll come right back."

He had put me straight to bed out of the tub. I wasn't wearing a nightie, and I was self-conscious as hell as I came back to bed. Would he like what he saw? His big grin answered that question.

About an hour later as we lay in each other's arms, he said, "As wonderful as this is, maybe we'd better have a plan for finding Addison Strangways, if you want to have that ten grand as a wedding present."

Our personal troubles had kept us from nosing around yesterday. Now it was time to go to work.

"We need to get a look at the front desk register," I said.

"Do you think he'd be dumb enough to register under his own name?" he asked.

"Stranger things have happened. But I think the odds are against it. He might have stuck with the same initials, though, or used a name similar to his own."

"When would he have arrived?" Morris asked. "If we can pin that down, we'll have to check fewer pages."

"Strangways hasn't been at his office since Eben started looking into his friends' disappearance. That was a week ago."

"Let's start with last Thursday and work backwards. Now how do we get a look at the book?"

I thought for a minute. "How about we steal it? For just a little while, I mean."

Now it was Morris' turn to think. "I guess," he said finally. "All we're really concerned with is that the clerk doesn't get wind of what we're up to. But that's a pretty big book."

"You're a pretty big joe. You've got a lotta room under your jacket."

"And what are you gonna do?"

"That's easy. I'll distract him and you can get the book."

"And how are you gonna do that?"

I shook my bosom at him. "I'll think of something."

It was nearly noon before we were finally out of bed.

We decided to have lunch before making a run at the front desk. Maybe Strangways would show up in the dining room after all. No such luck. There were a few single male diners, but none was our man.

"He's got to be keeping to his room," I told Morris after we had gotten a table.

"If he's even here."

"He's here. I can feel it."

The ploy at the reception desk was absurdly easy. Who expects somebody to steal a hotel register? I had selected a tight blouse to wear to lunch, and I unbuttoned a couple of buttons before I went to talk to the clerk. I made like I was looking for a certain kind of gift shop in town, and made some eyes at the clerk. I knew I had him when his eyes went to my chest. I just kept inching along the reception desk till his back was to the register, drawing him along like you draw a cat with a string. Morris appeared from nowhere, dropped a copy of the *Cape May Star and Wave* on top of the register, picked it up and vanished upstairs. It was amazing how inconspicuous he could be for such a big guy. Guess that's part of what made him such a good cop.

I joined him up in our room a few minutes later, leaving a frustrated and disappointed desk clerk behind. We spread the register out on the joined beds and went through all of the entries for September, but there was no joy in Mudville. No Addison Strangways, no single men with the initials A.S., not even a sawbones. There were some entries for the number in the party, but by no means for every name. We made a list of eight single joes with their room numbers, but that was going to be difficult to check out discreetly. We didn't want the house dick getting wind of what we were up to. I was pretty sure Trulove's offer had made the news down here, too.

"I hate to say it," Morris said, "but maybe it would be worth our time to stake out the lobby and just see if he turns up. He's going to go stir-crazy if he just camps in his room all the time."

"Leave it to a flattie to suggest a stakeout," I said. The hurt look on his face made me wish I hadn't. I continued, "Oh, all right! There are enough people in that lobby that it won't be hard to be inconspicuous. I'll take the first shift if you want me to."

"Naw, I'll do it," he said. "I gotta return this register, anyhow. I'll just leave it on a table under the newspaper where somebody will be sure to find it." That was my Morris, honest to a fault. That was also part of what made him a good cop.

We talked about it some more and agreed that there was no reason we both couldn't be down there. We spent the afternoon sitting in the lobby reading the plentiful books, newspapers and magazines they had. It was a popular hangout, so we had plenty of company, but Addison Strangways wasn't part of it.

We had a gloomy dinner, and of course there was no sign of our quarry in the dining room. We spent another couple of hours in the lobby after dinner, again with no luck. Do you know how hard it is to convince a copper to give up on a stakeout? It's like they have a mental problem!

Finally, we were back in our room.

"Barton," he said dejectedly, lapsing back into his old way of addressing me, "we've got to come up with another bright idea. Unless you want to go banging on those eight doors tomorrow."

"Ixnay on that!" I thought for a minute. "Hey, I know! Who could we talk to, to find out who's getting all their meals sent up to the room?"

"Maybe the bell captain," he said. "That's the guy who's responsible for managing the bellhops."

"Any chance he'd report something like that to the house peeper?"

"Maybe. But maybe we can slip him a fin so that doesn't happen."

"Well, it's too late now," I said. "Let's do it first thing in the morning. Make it a sawbuck, and we can even get him to let us know when the fella orders down. We can show up at his door pretending we have his food. That'll be sure to get him to open up."

"I can see why you're such a good reporter," he said.

I gave him a great big kiss for that.

We turned in early, and were asleep by at least midnight..., I think!

We went down to breakfast early the next morning. We kept an eye out for Strangways and it was no surprise he didn't show. Morris left me at the table with my coffee while he went to chin with the bell captain—I reluctantly agreed that he was the better one for that job if we wanted to maintain a low profile.

He was back in a jiffy, with a big grin on his ugly mug.

"Got 'em!" he said. "And he's gonna call us when Strangways orders up lunch. We'll go in then."

We had some time to kill. We went back upstairs to figure out what we were gonna do after we gave old Addison the buzz.

"I say just barge in and pinch him," Morris said. "It's not like he's gonna call the cops."

"We could." I agreed "He won't be expecting a grab. But I was kinda hoping we could talk to him before putting the collar on him."

Morris looked at me quizzically. "What for? You're not trying to find a Chinese angle on this, are you?"

"Not at all. But what if he won't cop to it? A lot of these guys swear that the worst thing they've ever done is love their mother."

He gave me a sour look. "In case you haven't noticed, I'm a cop, Barton. I hear that hooey all the time. Doesn't stop me from pinching them, though. I'm getting the bracelets on him the minute we're through that door."

"It would be great if we could get him to open up about the killings. Make it easier for you pin the rap on him, and get copy for me. Maybe even get us that ten grand quicker."

His expression got worse, if anything. I pushed on. "Look, wouldn't it be great if we could just get him to come back to the city with us on the train. No cuffs, no rough stuff. We could take him to the Graphic office, get his story, some pictures, turn him in from there."

Now his face plainly said I was dingy. "You're lookin' for another extra," he accused.

He had that right. If I could pull this off, I'd be right up there with Winchell and Sullivan! "Yeah, so what if I am?' I said "Look, we tell him we think he's getting a raw deal, offer to help him beat the rap, and he comes along quiet, what's the harm in that?"

"Plenty, if he decides to take the heel and toe on the way. We might never find him again!"

"Yeah, but you're gonna be right there, Morris, stickin' to him like horseshit. He'll never get away from you."

I could tell he really didn't like it. "There's plenty of reasons we cops do things like we do," he said. "If this bird has killed three women, he's dangerous as hell! It's stupid to give him any shot at all at getting away, or hurting us."

I let a tear well up and run down my cheek. Now he looked like somebody just hit him in the gut.

"Okay, Barton. We'll try it your way. But if he as much as looks at us cross-eyed, I'm slapping him in irons."

I felt like a louse, but I smiled at him and hugged him.

The call from the bell captain came a little before noon.

"Don't send the order up," Morris told him. "We'll tell you when."

In a matter of a few minutes, we were in front of what we hoped was Strangways' door on the second floor. Morris knocked, and announced, "Room service."

"Just leave it there on the floor," said the muffled voice from within.

Oh shit! What do we do now?

Morris didn't miss a beat. He stomped his big foot lightly on the floor to mimic a tray being put down, then said, "Okay, sir. Enjoy your lunch."

He pressed his back against the wall, then motioned for me to do the same on the other side of the door.

A minute passed, then two, with no activity from inside the room. Shit! Did he smell a rat? Was he in there tying bedsheets together to go out the window? I started to move away from the wall.

Morris put his finger to his lips. I moved back.

I heard a metallic rattle as the lock was disengaged from inside the room. We were gonna have to move fast before he noticed there was no tray on the floor.

The door opened just the slightest crack, and Morris slammed it hard with a fist the size of a small watermelon. The chain broke with a SNAP! and the door flew fully open. Morris pivoted and rushed in first, me right behind him.

Addison Strangways lay sprawled on the floor with blood running from his nose where the door hit him. He looked at us like a puppy who'd been kicked.

"Oh, dear," he said. "I've been expecting this."

Silas K. Henderson

CHAPTER 24

The Statement of Dr. Ebeneezer Warman

I arrived at the library punctually at 8 a.m. on Saturday for my meeting with the Director of Rare Books. I had briefly considered not keeping the appointment, but then I noticed the peculiarity that the appointment was on a Saturday morning—surely that wasn't a regular work day for a library employee as high up as director. I thought I'd better go and see what was so urgent that that worthy would get up early on a Saturday to meet with me.

I found myself standing in front of a solid wooden door. I was unsure whether to knock or simply go in—I finally decided to do the latter because the door looked solid enough that a knock would not be heard. I pushed the heavy door open and the smell of paper and leather, ubiquitous in this place, became almost overwhelming. I entered a very large room, whose ceiling nearly thirty feet above allowed space for the two tiers of bookshelves that encircled the room's perimeter. A staircase in the rear led up to a balcony that allowed access to the upper tier. The omnipresent reading lamps studded long tables on either side that ran the length of the room. A lone man occupied the chamber, standing at one of the tables near the rear. A very large folio lay on the table in front of him. He looked up as I came in, but he neither greeted nor approached me. He seemed to be glaring at me as I neared, and an almost palpable chill emanated from him.

I extended my hand from a few feet away. "Good morning," I said. "I assume you are the Director. I am Doctor Warman."

He made no move to take my hand. His glare was undoubtedly apparent now, as he replied, "I am Director Leland."

The hostility in his tone was obvious. What had I done to this man? Surely this could not be because he had to come into work on Saturday to meet me. The meeting wasn't even my idea!

He indicated the book on the table.

"This is one of less than a half-dozen extant copies of the Latin translation of the al-Azif, from the 16th century." He was so angry his voice was quivering. "You are a colleague of this McDowell person," he said accusingly. "Perhaps you can explain this?"

The front cover of the book hit the top of the table with a startling BANG! as he savagely flipped it open. I could see now that this was an ancient book—the pages were thick, yellow parchment with umber print, interspersed with elaborate wood cut engravings. My breath caught as I saw the protruding remnant of parchment near the bottom of the page. The book had been torn!

I adopted a firm tone. "No sir, I don't think I can. And I take umbrage at your blatant insinuation that Doctor McDowell was responsible." I deliberately emphasized the *Doctor*. "He is a Harvard man and a scholar. He would not treat such an obviously valuable tome in this fashion."

"Well, somebody has," the Director growled. "And McDowell was the last one with the book."

"Surely that's not true," I told him. "Wouldn't it have been brought to him by one of your employees? And returned by the same person?"

"That's who reported this obscenity to me."

"Then I think it much more likely that your man tore the book. When he realized what he'd done, he removed the page and attempted to lay the blame on Doctor McDowell, to save his job."

"We screen our employees and hire only those of the highest character," he replied.

Another scathing rejoinder hung on the tip of my tongue, but I reconsidered. I would gain nothing by engaging in a war of words with this man. I took a more conciliatory tone. "Even if Doctor McDowell has done this, there is very little I can do for you." I told him. "Doctor McDowell has gone missing, and I am looking for him so he can take charge of his children after the untimely death of their mother."

I could see that last cracked his angry *façade* a bit. "Perhaps he decamped after he'd done this," he said.

I waited a moment to see if he would recognize the pure absurdity of that statement, then said, "That's preposterous! If Doctor McDowell had done this, he would have simply come to you and offered to pay to have the book restored."

"Restored? It can't be restored, not without the missing material! I haven't told you that two other pages have also been torn out. He wouldn't have come to us, if he was facing jail for vandalism. This was deliberate!"

Now I was taken aback. I just couldn't imagine the Colin I knew despoiling such a valuable book.

"What is the book about?" I asked.

"I know very little about the content," Director Leland replied. "It deals with an unorthodox mythology, that is to say, one that is unconventional in terms of its Arab origins. It discusses none of the traditional Arabian mythological themes or figures, and it is very important in that regard."

"And you say this is a translation?"

"From the original Arabic, done in manuscript form sometime in the 13th century."

"I thought you said it was 16th century?"

"This book is. The manuscript was produced in a monastery much earlier. Apparently, several copies were made. The work was banned by the Vatican and most of the copies were destroyed, but one of them ended up in the hands of a German printer. This book is the result."

"This is all very interesting, but I cannot imagine what my friend Colin McDowell would be doing with such a work."

"That's none of my affair," the Director said. "All I know is that he requested it by name and number, signed for it, and left it on the table in the reading room in this condition."

"What do you mean, he left it on the table?"

Now it was Director Leland's turn to look discomfited. "We don't allow just anybody access to books such as this. As you pointed out, your friend was a doctor and a Harvard man, and he indicated as much when challenged as to why he wanted the book. And he wasn't allowed to use it unsupervised, either. However, the employee who was supervising him had to answer nature's call, and rather than lock the book away, he allowed McDowell to continue his work while he was absent. He returned to find McDowell gone and the book in this condition. Or so he said."

"And you have no idea what was on the missing pages."

"As I said, I'm no expert on the content. I have a little general knowledge, is all."

"Well, I'm sorry this happened." I said. "The best I can do is tell you that I'll ask Dr. McDowell about it, if and when I find him."

"I'd appreciate it if you'd let us know if you do find him."

"We'll see," I said. "I tell you again, Dr. McDowell would not do such a thing unless something was very wrong with him. Nor would he desert his family. I'll not help you persecute him if he is ill."

He bristled again at that, but then apparently thought better about what he was going to say. "Very well," he said finally. "You can tell him that we will bring charges, and maybe a civil suit as well. We'll let the courts sort it out."

I saw no point in continuing the conversation. I left.

Several hours later. I was in the interview room at Manhattan State Hospital, waiting for Danforth. Oglethorpe had been called away to the telephone and said he'd bring Danforth when he finished his call.

The door opened, and Dr. Oglethorpe came in, but no Danforth. I looked at him quizzically, and then I saw that he carried something in one hand.

"I still haven't received authorization to release Dr. McDowell's records to you," Oglethorpe said, "But I expect that will come very soon. However, this was in Dr. McDowell's things. It's medicine that he was using to treat Wesley, and apparently, he had good results with it."

He offered me a small, amber glass jar with a screw cap. I read the handwritten label:

> **(6aR,9R)-N,N-diethyl-7-methyl-6,6a,8,9-tetrahydro-4H-indolo[4,3-fg]** **quinoline-9-carboxamide** Give 1 sq. per os, 30 min. before needed, or for catatonia. Place on tongue 1 min, then remove. May be used every 12 hr. Maximum 2 sq, in 24 hr. period.

I unscrewed the cap and was surprised to see that the jar contained small circles of thick white paper.

"Thanks Doctor," I said. "This may be quite helpful." I meant it, as I was much more comfortable with pharmaceuticals than with verbal therapy.

"I'll go and get Wesley now." Oglethorpe said.

A few minutes later, he returned with Danforth in tow. We took our customary positions as the doctor departed.

I began by inquiring about Danforth's sleep and how his day had been. Even though I was keen to get him back to Antarctica, we chatted about his meals and the latest book he was reading, all to get him relaxed and ready for the meat of the session.

"So, Wesley", I began, "I'd like to discuss more about what you found after you arrived at Beardmore Glacier, and what happened to Lake and his men."

The color immediately drained from his face, and he stammered, "I-, I-, I don't know that I can do that, Doctor."

I decided to take a bit more of an authoritarian tone. "Wesley, if you want to get better, you must confront your demons. You do want to get better, don't you?"

He was looking at me stupidly, his mouth agape. "No, I mean, yes, I mean..." His eyes glazed over and he was suddenly no longer there. Again, a rivulet of drool began to make the journey from his mouth to his chin.

Dammitall! I didn't have time for this! Then it occurred to me that I might have the means to combat it.

I went to the sink and thoroughly washed my hands. I undid the cap on the amber jar and shook out one of the paper circles on my palm. I picked it up between my thumb and forefinger, placed it on his protruding tongue. After a minute, I removed it and dropped it in the wastebasket. The label said to use it 30 minutes before it was needed, so I settled back to wait.

I was still puzzled over my latest discovery. Harvey had always told me that when you were trying to solve a complex problem, the key was to simplify it as much as possible. Write down the facts you were sure of, without embellishment or interpretation, then see where they led you. I took my notebook from an inner pocket, and a pencil.

Fact: Colin McDowell had disappeared last week without notifying his wife, his mistress or his colleagues.

Fact: Prior to his disappearance, Colin had made a trip to Arkham, Massachusetts.

Fact: Colin had been retained by Dr. William Dyer of Miskatonic University in Arkham, to treat Dyer's student, Wesley Danforth, who had suffered emotional trauma on a university-sponsored expedition to Antarctica.

Fact: Colin had decided to devote himself full time to Danforth's treatment, eschewing his regular practice, his research at Rockefeller University and his volunteer work at the College Settlement House.

Fact: Colin had developed an inexplicable interest in arcane Arabian mythology.

Fact: Colin had been seen the day after Evie missed him, exiting a brothel on the lower East Side.

The Legacy of the Unborn

Fact: A murderer has been terrorizing the Upper East Side. The evidence is strong that the murderer is Dr. Addison Strangways, Colin's tenant.

What inferences about Colin's present whereabouts could be made from these facts?

One possibility was that Colin was alive and well, and living somewhere on the Lower East Side. But why would he do that?

The other possibility was more troubling. Colin found out what Strangways was doing, and Strangways killed him and disposed of his body. This theory neatly explained Colin's apparent desertion of his family, his paramour, his practice, and his research. And why he left Danforth in the lurch, as well.

What was I going to tell Colin's daughters?

I regarded Danforth to see if there were any changes due to the medication. The color had come back into his face, and his forehead glistened with a thin sheen of perspiration. I went to him and tilted his head back so I could see his pupils in the overhead light. They were completely dilated. Unexpectedly, he jerked his head aside.

"Stop it! That hurts!" He abruptly jerked his head aside, causing me to release him in the process.

"I'm sorry, Wesley, I didn't realize that you were awake."

He was looking at the floor, obviously discomfited by the glaring overhead light. I turned on the banker's lamp on the desk, then clicked off the ceiling light with the wall switch. I turned the glass shade on the lamp towards Danforth so the white light was cast back toward me, and his side of the room was suffused with a muted green glow.

Given his present condition, I saw no reason not to take the bull by the horns.

"Do you feel up to telling me what you found at Dr. Lake's camp, Wesley?"

He had a haunted look. "I'd rather not talk about it," he said.

"But it's only by talking about it that you will free yourself from the memory of it that haunts you. I know that you found all of Lake's crew dead. Your dispatches said that they died in a windstorm. Is that what happened? It's terrible, but you surely must have realized that your expedition was dangerous, and that you might lose some members."

He looked at the floor and muttered something into his chest.

"What's that, Wesley? I didn't hear you."

"I said that they didn't die in a storm."

"Then how did they die?"

"Something killed them."

Of course! This was the only explanation for the falsified dispatches. Dyer was attempting to protect loved ones at home from the knowledge that an expedition member was a murderer.

"They'd all been hacked, or torn to pieces. It was horrible! Didn't look like a person could do that. At first we thought it was the dogs, but we found them all tore up too. Then we thought it was Gedney, because we couldn't find him."

"Why did you change your mind about Gedney?"

"Because we did find him."

It was obvious from his demeanor that there was more that he didn't want to tell me.

"Alive? Where?"

"No, he was dead, all right." Danforth began laughing. "Oh yes, he was dead. So was the dog!"

"You found him in the medical tent?"

"No, not him."

"Then whom?"

"Lake! It was Lake that we found in the medical tent. All cut up and sorted into nice little piles!"

"You don't mean that someone dissected him?"

"It was them!" he said. "It had to be! They were gone, too!'

Colin's medicine had obviously relieved his catatonia, but it had done nothing for his underlying mental disorder.

"Whom do you mean, Wesley? Who was gone?"

"Them! Those things that Lake found! The ones who built the city."

Did he mean the fossils?

"City? What city?"

"The city in the mountains. Dr. Dyer and I explored it."

There was nothing about a city in the dispatches. Was this a delusion, or did Dyer avoid mentioning it for some reason?

"Tell me about the city, Wesley."

"We saw it when we were flying in," said Danforth. "The mountains were incredible, higher than the Himalayas. We saw cubes of stone set into the mountainsides. They were so regular that we knew they had to have been fabricated! There was a low pass—twenty-three, twenty-four thousand feet—that was wide enough for a plane and it enclosed a flat area where we could land on skis. Of course Dr. Dyer, always a geologist, had to go up there to investigate the blocks. He wanted me to take him. I didn't want to, but he said that I was the best pilot they had. He was like my father. I just couldn't say no."

He began to assume that thousand-yard stare, so I prompted him before he fell into the catatonic state again. "And what did you find up there, Wesley."

His eyes widened, and I fancied that I could see his dilated pupils from across the room, gaping at me like ebon pits. Surely it was my imagination?

"It was fantastic! It was like the plateau of Leng, or the Giant's Causeway on the Irish coast, but on a truly Cyclopean scale! Not basalt though, but quartzite from the Archean, or even the Hadean! Heaps of huge stones of regular geometric shapes—cubes, hexahedrons, octahedrons, and others that natural law says shouldn't even be—strewn about like the toys of some hideous, gargantuan toddler, as far as the eye could see! And there were ramparts, arches and buttresses that just had to have been intelligently contrived. But that's codswallop of course, because intelligence wouldn't even exist on this Earth for many millions of years after those shapes had been formed. And then there were the cave mouths that told us that this blasphemous city was subterranean as well as on the surface. When we saw this, we just knew that we just had to go down there and look."

Danforth's description was so riveting that I actually fancied myself there with him for a moment. I shook my head, and the disturbing vision went away.

"So, we went down into the underground city. It seemed impossibly far away at first—we wondered if would even have time to get there before darkness fell. But the distances were deceiving. It seemed to actually rush up to meet us! I can't describe the feelings I had as I walked amongst those enormous structures."

Danforth went on to describe his and Dyer's peregrinations at length. His voice became monotonous, rhythmic, and ultimately hypnotic—suddenly I found myself in that Hyperborean world along with Dyer and Danforth. I meandered among the massive cavalcade of immense blocks, mighty towers pierced by star-shaped windows and doors, and reconnoitered the stellate courtyards they surrounded, caressing Mezozoic shutters of petrified wood that hung from those windows, marveling at the sculpted monuments of their makers who had sprung from beneath Earth's seas, with their barrel-shaped torsos, membranous wings and echinodermal heads. I stared awestruck at the complex bas-reliefs they had hewn, which depicted the erection of this fantastic metropolis—the mind-boggling energies that these creatures had harnessed and employed to carve these edifices from the living rock, and the mighty amoebic shoggoths who placed them where their masters willed, all by the dint of the expansion of their infinitely malleable bodies.

The bas-reliefs depicted the other denizens of the primordial Earth who inhabited it along with the Old Ones, and with whom they waged constant war—the prodigious Lizard folk, who predated even the Old Ones, the Cthulhu spawn, who reside under our seas to this day, the mind-rending Lloigor, and the abominable Mi-go, who emigrated to Earth from beyond the stars, and who scholars think to be the modern-day sasquatches and yeti. The Old Ones were able to resist these fearsome enemies only because of their slaves, the shoggoths, whom they forced to fight for them, and who hated them for it. The headless corpses these monsters left behind spoke to their prowess in battle, and hinted at what they longed to do their masters.

243

"All of this is impossible." Danforth said. "It flies in the face of everything I thought science had taught me, but here it is, etched in stone!"

I simply stared at Danforth and his companion. Dyer? I knew him! I had seen him before! But where? Then suddenly I knew.

The man in the bed at Bellevue!

"I've read of these things," Danforth was saying. "In the library at school! The cities, the Old Ones that created them, our kinfolk the shoggoths, and all the rest." His expression changed to one of sheer terror "Abd al Azrad didn't write mythology! *He wrote history!*"

We made our way into the underworld, inexorably drawn to that primal, feral realm by our suicidal thirst for knowledge. It was not long before we encountered something wholly unexpected. The pungent, fruity odor of gasoline!

We knew it had to have come from the camp. But how? We decided to try and locate the source of the odor. We turned off our torches to conserve the batteries and followed the scent, intermittently turning them on so we would not meet our doom by tumbling into a hidden pit. We proceeded through an infinity of corridors and arches, and even squeezed through cracks in the wall. We knew intuitively that we could not retrace our path, but the scent grew ever stronger, and we had to follow it, like some obscene pheromone that lured us into the grasp of a nameless predator. Then we found the campsite.

It was in a cavernous, cubical room. Danforth's sharp eyes picked it out because he noticed an irregularity in the debris on the floor, which turned out to be items from Lake's camp, scattered about and abandoned. One of those was a gasoline can that had been spilled in a corner of the room. We also found some curious sketches that depicted a map of the city above and some singular glyphs, which Dyer and Danforth surmised that Gedney had made. We thought we recognized some of the tunnels we had traversed to get to this place, and we noticed that a route had been laid out to a remarkable, vast circular chamber even deeper in the Earth. Having nowhere else to aim for, we followed the map.

After several hours travel through that glaciated warren, we arrived at the circular room. It was immense—easily a hundred yards in all dimensions. It was also freezing, because of a strong icy wind that rushed down from above. We saw that a ramp spiraled around the chamber wall. We looked up and saw the light of the gloaming through an aperture in the top. We realized we had found a way out of this horrible abyss, and we made for the place where the ramp met the floor of the chamber.

It was there that we found young Gedney, and the missing dog.

They were laid out together, the dog on its side and Gedney on his back, with his hand clasped on his belly, as if for a viewing in a mortuary. The dog's head had been removed and set upright on the stump of his neck. Gedney's mutilation was more creative—his head had been placed on his chest, just above his clasped hands. A thin layer of translucent, greyish ooze slathered his remains.

Sane men would have fled that horrible place forthwith, leaving Gedney and his canine companion as an ice-rimed memorial to the folly of so-called scientists who had the temerity to think they could ever understand the universe. But another sound became apparent, one that attracted us deeper into the bowels of this place—a sound with which we'd become very familiar since crossing the Antarctic circle. It was familiar, but terrifyingly out of place here—the raucous squawking of penguins!

The penguin is a wholly aquatic beast, as much so as any fish or pinniped. They are never found far from a body of water, as they will die without periodic immersion. Yet here they were, nearly as far from the ocean as one could get on this frigid continent, despite their fightless habit. We just had to go and see!

The rest of our journey was a blur. We found the penguins all right—huge, albino, sightless things seven feet tall, who seemed terrified of us. Later on, we also found the remains of the creatures from Lake's camp, leaving no doubt that they had been responsible for the carnage there, probably in retribution for Lake's treatment of them as fossils for dissection, instead of as intelligent life forms. We were so addled from the continuous assault on our senses and our reason in this hellish place that I doubt we'd realized the import of what we found.

There were but four of Lake's eight creatures, and they were all dead—dead, decapitated, and covered with the same evil grey slime we found on poor Gedney's remains. When we saw it, we instantly knew what had done the killing, and then we heard the eerie piping sound which indicated its proximity. "*Tekeli-li! Tekeli-li!*"

A mist rose in the corridor, obscuring the Old Ones, and the eerie piping intensified as a cloud of mist roiled towards us. We needed no one to tell us it was time to run, and to make for the chamber with the ramp that would take us out of this hellhole!

Our mad dash through the bowels of the earth seemed interminable. The frenetic wailing ever-present behind us seemed to become softer as we ran, indicating that we had gained ground on the horror. I mention this to emphasize that we had no reason to look back to see if the creature was nipping at our heels—all we had to do was keep running.

But look back we did, like Lot's wife, as if some irresistible force froze us in our tracks and turned us round. I saw it then—a mountain of iridescent slime oozing toward us, filling the entire twenty-foot corridor with its mass. The white mist swirled up around it, doubtless due to the heat of its body in this frigid environment. I swear that I could see human faces as well as the stellate heads of the Old Ones appearing and vanishing from its forefront, like a seething, cannibalistic stew. The creature bore down on us as fast as a subway train, and now the hideous piping—"*Tekeli-li! Tekeli-li!*"—that mingled with the shrieks from the innumerable mouths rippling across its skin...

Abruptly I found myself at the desk, facing Danforth, who gazed at me in the emerald light like an imbecile, babbling meaningless drivel, "South Station Under—Washington Under—Park Street Under—Kendell—Central—Harvard..."

I was horrified at the thought that Oglethorpe might come in and find his patient in this state while under my care. Almost without thinking, I grabbed the bottle of Colin's medicine from the desk, extracted another of the paper circles, and popped in into his open mouth. He spat it out again almost immediately. There was no way I was going to give him another dose—I had no idea what this drug was, or knowledge about its mode of action or side effects.

The drug must have been potent though, because Danforth's rhythmic chanting ceased abruptly. He simply sat there for a while, regarding me stupidly, and I was praying as fervently as I could that he would come back from where ever he had escaped to. Finally, sanity crept back into his eyes, and he said, "No, Dr. Warman, I'm afraid I'm just not up to discussing that today. Can we try again tomorrow?"

Now it was me who regarded him stupidly. Was it possible that he had no memory of our shared delusion? I reached for the desk phone to summon Oglethorpe. I had to get out of here! However, before I could pick up the receiver from the cradle, the door opened and Oglethorpe entered. My God! I shuddered at the thought of how close he'd come to discovering our mutual lunacy.

"I had a call from your Mr. Harrigan during your session," Oglethorpe said. "He told me he expected to have a court order on Monday that would direct me to release Dr. McDowell's notes to you. I told the hospital director about it, and I also told him that you had consented to take over Danforth's case. He agreed that, under those circumstances, there was no further reason to withhold these from you."

He handed me a brown leather briefcase of the Messenger style that was closed by a broad belt and buckle on the center of the flap, flanked by two narrower belts. It took me sometime to undo the buckles, and I ardently hoped that Oglethorpe didn't see my hands trembling as I did. The bag contained two items

One was a large black leather notebook with brass corners on the front and rear covers. It was about eight by ten inches and half an inch thick. I flipped it open to see that was roughly three-quarters full of Colin's precise copperplate script. There was no way I could read all of this now—that would have to wait until this evening.

The other item was a manila envelope of the kind that was held closed by a thread that could be wrapped around a button, which was big enough to have held the notebook. I undid the thread and opened the flap, dreading what I was going to find.

The missing pages from the library book!

I knew then that I had to get to the bottom of this affair, no matter what it took.

I really don't remember the lame excuses I must have made to get out of there and back down to the ferry slip.

CHAPTER 25

From the notebook of Sally Barton

Friday afternoon, October 2, 1931

Morris had his revolver out, covering Strangways as he cowered on the floor with his hands in front of his face. As if that would stop a bullet!

"Please, don't shoot! I'll go quietly." The doctor was clearly terrified. It was hard to believe that this sad little man had butchered three women.

"Get up and turn your back to me!" Morris ordered.

Strangways struggled to his feet, then turned to face the French doors. The curtains billowed out into the room, driven by the fresh ocean breeze. Even though it was afternoon, the doctor was wearing a faded plaid bathrobe. I could see his pyjama bottoms peeping out below his knees, and he had on bedroom slippers.

Still holding the pistol, Morris frisked him with the other hand. Apparently satisfied that Strangways was not armed, he said. "You can turn around." He gestured with the pistol towards a chair near the window. "Go sit in that chair. Cross your arms and keep both feet flat on the floor."

The doctor again followed orders. When he was seated, Morris holstered his piece. "We're here to take you back to face the music, Strangways," Morris said. "But before we do, I want to know one thing. Why'd you kill them women?"

The little doctor looked at us gloomily. "I know you won't believe me, officer, but I didn't kill them."

Morris' disbelief was plain on his face.

"Then why'd you take a powder," I asked him.

"Because the women who were killed were all my patients. I knew the police would consider me a suspect because of my past. I knew that they would keep digging until they found something incriminating. I knew I didn't have a chance."

This meeting wasn't going as planned. I thought I was going to be interviewing the Ripper and getting the details of all his sordid crimes from his own lips. That would be worth an extra for sure! Instead I found myself talking to a depressed little man who claimed he was innocent, and dammit, I was close to believing him!

"How was it that all of the Ripper's victims were your patients, if it wasn't you that done it?" asked Morris.

"I'd be a pretty sorry excuse for a murderer if I killed my patients so you'd come right to me," the doctor said in a querulous tone. "It would be pretty bad for business, too." Apparently, Strangways had regained some spunk when Morris put his gun away.

"Well how do you explain it?" asked Morris.

"I can't explain it." Strangways said. "I just know it wasn't me."

"They were all your current patients," I said. "I mean, they were all pregnant."

"Yes," said Strangways. "All in the early stages. Eileen Trulove was the furthest along, almost 12 weeks. The others were a couple of weeks behind."

"When did you realize that someone was killing your patients?" I asked.

"Not until Mrs. Willoughby was murdered. She was the last one killed. I didn't even realize that someone had murdered Mary Courtney until Eileen Trulove was killed. I don't read the papers very much—it was Maggie, my receptionist, who told me what had happened to the two of them. I thought it was just some kind of bizarre coincidence, but when Katherine Willoughby was murdered, I knew that someone was targeting my patients. That's when I did the stupidest thing I'd ever done in my life."

"Run away?" said Morris.

Strangways gave him a sour look. "No, officer. The stupid thing that I did was actually to call the police and tell them that somebody was murdering my patients. That's when I got a visit from your Inspector Henderson."

Henderson had talked to Strangways! That was news. We didn't know it before because we'd never seen Henderson's case file.

"He as much as told me that he was going to lock me up for the murders," the doctor went on. "He didn't have any evidence that I had done it, but he said he'd get some. I knew that as soon as he'd found out that one of my patients had accused me of assaulting her a few years ago, he'd be back to lock me up. So, I ran."

"That's not the only reason you ran," Morris said. The little doctor looked at him quizzically. "We found those pictures of yours. Why'n't you get rid of 'em?"

Strangways turned bright red, and looked truly defeated. "I didn't get rid of them because it wouldn't have made any difference if I did. Louella knew about them. It's why she divorced me. I knew Henderson would give her the third degree and make her tell. Once that happened, I was sunk. No jury in the world would believe me."

"You got that right," Morris told him unkindly.

Strangways looked like he was about to cry. Damn me, but I just couldn't picture this little mouse carving up those women the way I had seen in that autopsy file!

"Look," I said. "If you didn't do it, then the guy that did had access to your records. It can't be a coincidence that all three were your patients. Who else could have gotten to your records?"

"No one," he said. "Maggie and me are the only staff in the office."

A sudden shiver ran through me. Could it be? "How about Doctor McDowell?"

"Preposterous!" Strangways exploded. "Dr. McDowell is a learned man and a fine gentleman. He's a Harvard man! Why would he want to kill my patients?"

I didn't know why he would, but I pressed on anyway. "But he had access to your records, didn't he?"

"I guess so," Strangways said. "If you were in my office, you saw that there's no door to lock it off from the rest of the brownstone. That didn't bother me, because the street door has a lock, and I have private rooms to see my patients in. The only people with keys to the brownstone are myself, Maggie, Doctor McDowell and his receptionist, Miss LeMay."

"And where did you keep the victims' records?" I asked him.

"Normally, in the filing cabinet."

"Was that locked?"

"No. I never saw any need to lock it. It would just make it difficult to get into."

"Courtney, Trulove, Willoughby," I listed the victims' names. "Their files would all be in different drawers, right?"

"Normally, yes," Strangways replied, "But they were all coming in for an examination every month, because they were pregnant. They would all be in the active file."

"And where was the active file kept?"

"On Maggie's desk. If I was working on a particular case, that folder would be on my desk."

"What's in these files?" asked Morris.

"Everything," said Strangways. "Name, address, appointment dates, and case notes."

"In chronological order?"

"Of course, Detective. How else?"

"How many patients are usually in the active file?" I asked him.

Silas K. Henderson

"Oh, anywhere from a dozen to about thirty, depending on how busy we are."

"Then why'd he pick those three?" I asked no one in particular.

"Goddam it!" Morris barked, making me jump. "We gotta check those files pronto! The name of the Ripper's next vic is in there!"

"And howinhell are we gonna do that from out here in the Jersey sticks?" I said.

Morris looked almost sick. "I gotta call headquarters," he said. "Talk to Henderson. Get him to do it."

A sick feeling welled up in my stomach. Morris was right—it was the only thing to do. But then Henderson would know that Morris was working on the Ripper case.

Morris picked up the phone of the bedside table, got in touch with the hotel switchboard, and told them to place the call.

After he hung up, he said. "It will take them a little while to get through. They'll call back when Henderson's on the line."

"So, I take it you believe that I'm not your Ripper after all," Strangways said to Morris.

"Let's just say I'm keeping an open mind at this point," Morris replied. "C'mon. Let's get you packed up. I'm still taking you in. If you're innocent, you've got nothing to worry about."

Strangways looked at Morris as if he didn't believe that last statement. He reluctantly arose and went to the wardrobe for a suitcase, and began to pack his things under Morris' vigilant gaze.

After a little while, the phone rang and Morris answered it. "Put them on, please," he said. After a moment, he continued, "This is Detective Moscowicz. Badge number 835. Give me Inspector Henderson please."

My heart was breaking for Morris. I knew he was doing what he had to do despite the personal cost, but I was the one who got him into this. And for what? Because I wanted to see my name up in lights. Anything bad that happened to him was all my fault!

"Well, do you know where he is?" Morris said after a minute of silence. "Better give me the Deputy Chief, then. This can't wait."

253

Morris apparently got the Chief, and they talked for a while. He hung up and looked at me with a grim expression.

"Henderson's not there," he said. "Nobody knows where he is. And the Deputy Chief says that they can't check the files because Henderson's taken every last damn one of them with him! They checked his office." He glared at Strangways. "Mister, you don't know how much I wish you were the Ripper right now!"

"I'm sorry, officer. I'm not him, and I'm not responsible if your department is inefficiently run. I don't want any more of my patients murdered, either!"

Morris looked like he was going to haul off and paste him one, so I talked fast. "C'mon, youse guys! The best thing we can do right now is pack up and get back to the city on the double." I addressed Strangways. "Doc, is there any way you can remember who else was in that batch of files with the ladies that got the shiv?"

He looked distressed. "Some, maybe, but surely not all." He brightened a little. "But maybe Maggie can help. She's got a pretty good memory."

I turned to Morris. "I wonder if there's a quicker way back to the city than the train. We really don't have a day and a half to waste."

"Maybe we can hire a car somewhere, or get somebody to drive us." Morris said. "Sally, I have to stick with this mug whether he's guilty or innocent. Why don't you go downstairs and ask the concierge?"

"Ok." I grabbed my purse and went to the door, turned the knob and pulled it open. That's when I found myself staring straight into the barrel of a police positive!

"Just step back inside slowly, Miss Barton," said Inspector Henderson. He had two local cops behind him in the hallway.

Things happened real fast after that. I backed into the room, my eyes riveted on Henderson's gun, with him following me in. As soon as we got far enough inside that he could see Strangways, he pointed the gun at the doctor and said, "Addison Strangways! Put your hands in the air! You're under arrest for the Ripper murders!"

I don't know what the hell Strangways was thinking. Maybe he thought that he'd never get a fair deal from Henderson. Maybe he just didn't want to sit in a court room while his dirty pictures got passed around by the jury members, then read about it in the papers the next day along with the rest of New York City. Instead of following Henderson's orders, he turned and made a mad dash for the French doors. Henderson's pistol barked twice, and a crimson flower blossomed on Strangways' back. But he kept on going! Out on to the balcony, then he disappeared over the low railing!

We all stood there speechless for a moment, then rushed out on to the veranda. Strangways was sprawled out on the pavement twenty feet below, his arms and legs at odd angles. As we watched, a dark pool began to form by his head.

"Well, shit," said Henderson. "I wonder if Trulove will still pay up if he's dead."

CHAPTER 26

The Statement of Dr. Ebeneezer Warman

The ferry ride back to Manhattan was a ghastly nightmare. The weather was still mild, yet I shivered as if I was in the frigid Antarctic. Even though Manhattan was only about three hundred yards from Ward's Island, the East River currents could be quite strong at spring tide. The trip across took longer than one would expect, because the little ship had to fight its way back upstream as well as accomplish the east-west passage. Eddies and waves created by the swirling current pirouetted on the water's surface but I had to turn my eyes away—their undulations recalled the horror that had pursued us through the icy caverns. I regarded the sky instead, streaked with orange from the setting sun, which eerily evoked the Aurora Australis.

At last, we docked. I trudged along the sidewalk to the elevated station on 117th Street. The train rattled overhead. My legs were icy weights that I struggled to move up the stairs—I had no wish to loiter on the local platform waiting for another train to arrive I knew not when. The car doors were closing when I reached the apex of the stairs, but the conductor must have seen me, because they popped open again. I dashed inside and threw myself into one of the hard rattan seats.

The train clattered out of the station, squealing and swaying precariously. It was mostly empty on Saturday, this far uptown—a workman in a steel helmet and an older woman with a handled cloth bag on the floor in front of her were my traveling companions. As a true New Yorker, I tried not to look at them, casting my gaze out of the window into the city instead. The buildings flashed by ever more rapidly, then suddenly morphed into the immense, monolithic stone masses of the Antarctic plateau! The squealing of the train transformed into an insidious, incessant piping—Tekeli-li! Tekeli-li! A glance at my fellow travelers revealed that they had assumed an alien form, with great avian heads and enormous flippers!

The train lurched to a halt and the doors slid open. I sprang from my seat, neither knowing nor caring where I was, dashed out onto the platform, and stumbled down the stairs onto the city streets. I don't know how long I ran—I stopped only when my aching chest would let me run no more. I realized that I was back in Manhattan again. A bizarre, inexplicable homing instinct had brought me within a couple of blocks from my flat.

A shudder went through me when my door closed behind me. I was immensely grateful to be home, but I was suddenly freezing. Somehow, I had managed to keep with me the briefcase that Dr. Oglethorpe had given me; the one with Colin's notes. I dropped it on the floor in the foyer, then made for the bathroom, shedding clothes as I went. I filled the tub with water as hot as I could stand and immersed myself. The heat began to seep into my bones. I must have passed out.

I was still in the bathtub when I awoke. Sunlight was streaming through the window, and I was freezing again, immersed in ice-cold water. An iceberg grew in the pit of my stomach as I realized that only the grace of a merciful God that had prevented me from drowning in my sleep! I struggled to free myself from the frigid tub only to discover that every bone in my body throbbed with a cold ache induced by the long immersion, and the pressure of my soft torso on that unyielding porcelain surface. I managed to struggle halfway out of the water, only to fall back as my hands slid along the slippery porcelain. Lights flashed as the back of my head bounced on the hard lip of the tub and frigid water splattered all over the bathroom floor. I lay still for a moment until the panic subsided, then made another effort—this time I was able to struggle to my feet and to grab the rail on the wall to prevent another fall. My teeth were chattering and I literally groaned in pain as I stepped out of the tub. I wrapped myself in my Turkish cotton bathrobe and staggered to the study for a glass of brandy to stop that damned shivering. I rummaged in a sideboard drawer and found the bottle of Dicodid, shook one tablet out onto my hand and washed it down with the brandy.

I was still shivering slightly as I lay back in my chair to allow the alcohol and the opiate to take hold. I took another big swallow of brandy, but it stuck halfway down my gullet, then came back up to explode into the room. I struggled out of the chair to get back to the bathroom but I couldn't because I couldn't stop coughing! The liquor seared my trachea and nasal passages like liquid fire, and I thought I would pass out from inhaling the vitriolic alcohol fumes. Finally, the coughing subsided. I couldn't tell if the lightness in my head was from the effects of the alcohol and the drug, or a lack of oxygen. I fell back into my chair, spent.

I awoke again, wooly-headed, and still in the chair. The tambour clock was chiming—that must have been what awakened me. Counting the chimes would tell me nothing. I writhed out of the chair so I could see the dial. Oh my God! Eleven thirty! I had been due at church with Harvey half an hour ago! I staggered into the bedroom and started pulling clothes out of the closet to dress.

I must have passed out yet again. This time when I roused, I was sprawled across the bed. I was freezing again because my robe had apparently come undone, exposing my nakedness. My bedside clock and the daylight outside informed me that it was 4:15 p.m.

I got up and closed my robe. My skin was dry and tight after a long exposure to the air. I still hurt all over and had a raging hangover from the Dicodid and booze, but I dared not take any more medicine. I lurched into the kitchen. The thought of food sickened me, but I endeavored to put on a pot of double strength coffee.

My head began to clear a little as the heat from the gas burner warmed me a little and the sharp, acrid aroma of the coffee suffused the room. I watched as the black liquid welled up into the glass bulb of the percolator, but it nauseated me again—I had to avert my gaze.

I tried to think clearly, analyze what had happened. I shuddered as I realized that even though my mind told me that I had never left that hospital room, I was also with Danforth and Dyer, exploring the icy plateau. I remembered that I had hallucinated once before as a child, when I had a high fever. But that incident was like a waking dream. My experience in Danforth's room was much more vivid—I was actually on the slopes with the adventurers, the glaring Antarctic sun burning my eyes and the icy wind flaying my skin. I realized that I must have gone into some kind of a fugue state on the train as well. I had to ask myself what I was avoiding—was I going mad?

The coffee had been brewing for a while. I poured some into the thick, restaurant-style mug I used for my breakfast coffee. I eschewed my usual cream and sugar and blew across the steaming black surface to cool it, then slurped some of the scorching liquid onto my tongue. It was hellishly strong and bitter, and it burned! I swallowed it quickly, then forced myself to take more. This was medicinal, not for pleasure.

By the time I finished the cup, I felt better. I poured another and returned to my ruminations. No, I thought, I wasn't mad, although I had no explanation for what had happened.

I needed to know what day it was. I turned on the kitchen table radio and found myself listening to Reverend Coughlin on WOR. So, it was still Sunday. I thought that I had best call Harvey—he would surely be as mad as fire that I had missed church. And it boded ill that he had not been banging on my door this afternoon. Or had he? Was I too drugged to even notice? No, he'd have used his key to let himself in in that case.

I went back to the study with my coffee and dialed him up. I let it ring a dozen times. No answer.

My nerves tingled from the caffeine. Because of all of the sleep that I'd had, I knew that any more was a pipe dream. I went back to the foyer and retrieved the briefcase containing Colin's notes, then brought the coffee pot from the kitchen to the den. I topped up my cup and settled back in my chair to read.

CHAPTER 27

Excerpts from the Casebook of Dr. Colin Parham McDowell
July 30, 1931

    Patient Name: Danforth Wesley Charles
    Referred by: William V. Dyer, Ph.D
    Age: 22   Race: Caucasian
    Address: Saltonstall Hall, Miskatonic University, Arkham, Mass.
    Chief Complaint: Catatonia

Telephone consultation with Dr. Dyer (D hereafter) of the Geology Dept. at M.U. Danforth (i.e., the patient), is a graduate student who suffered an apparent psychotic break during a recent university expedition to Antarctica. D seems reluctant to discuss the source of the trauma that induced the patient's present state, although it seems likely that he knows or suspects what it was—possibly it affected D as well? No matter. He is bringing the patient to Manhattan State in a few days. After the patient settles in, I will make my initial assessment...

August 4, 1931

    Patient is a Ph.D. candidate in Geology at M.U., an accomplished pilot and a veteran of several previous expeditions with the University, although none were as ambitious or dangerous as the recent Antarctic expedition. Patient presents with acute stupefaction, characterized by infantile gurgling noises. Also presents with mild anthrophobia, severe mycophobia and severe myxophobia. No coherent speech evident, but sporadic utterance of nonsense syllables occurs (i.e., tekkaleelee). D, who has known the patient for ten years or more, attests that no obvious symptoms of mental illness were apparent prior to the Antarctic trip. I have made several unsuccessful attempts to establish communication with the patient. I am prescribing a course of electroshock, and a dosage regimen with a new drug of my own design—a derivative of lysergic acid that has shown some psychotropic properties. The drug is also a hallucinogen, so any information obtained from the patient must be independently validated.

Must have discussion with D and get him to tell me of the nature of the trauma responsible for the patient's present condition...

August 5, 1931

My discussion with D was unproductive. I am sure he knows what the incident that triggered the patient's psychotic break was, but he is unwilling to discuss it. Perhaps I should be treating him as well, though I doubt he would consent. He did suggest I ask the patient about Lake's demise.

Later—Made a trip to the library to read up on the M.U. expedition. What a balls-up! Apparently, dissension within the group led to a sub-expedition flying hundreds of miles away from the main body. Fantastic finds by the sub-group were alluded to in the reports, but never documented, because the entire party was wiped out in a freak storm. This was discovered by D, the patient and others who flew to their rescue, and quite possibly could be part of the reason for the patient's condition. But why would D simply not say so? I'm sure he is still holding something back, and I think he wants me to get it from the patient instead of telling me himself...

August 6, 1931

The opposing effects of the two therapies I am employing seem to be efficacious. Patient was somewhat lucid and I coaxed him to tell me his name and a bit about his life at school. However, anything that remotely approached the expedition led to a relapse of the catatonia and the nonsense syllables. He uttered another word, 'shogoth' or something similar, along with 'tekkaleelee". I will avoid the sensitive topics for the present and allow the electricity and the drug to do their work.

August 8, 1931

More library research has unearthed the genesis of the word, "Tekeli-li!" It was an utterance by fictional savages in the "Narrative of A. Gordon Pym," the only novel written by Edgar Allan Poe, which also involved an ill-fated Antarctic expedition. D. confirmed that Poe was one of the patient's favorite authors, along with Sheridan Le Fanu, Tod Robbins and others. Indeed, the patient showed D. the copy of Poe's novel that he brought with him on the expedition. This is interesting because it speaks to a predisposition to flights of fancy, in contrast to the committed scientist that I thought the patient to be...

August 8, 1931

Placed patient into deep trance after drug treatment, then broached the sensitive topics, with good results. Patient described a lengthy delusion concerning the expedition to Lake's camp and a long trek with D to the top of an impossibly high mountain range during which alien creatures, who were the antecedents and creators of humans on Earth, were discovered. patient was able to describe these creatures in great detail, undoubtedly due to the mind-opening effects of the drug. His concept of the 'shogoth' certainly accounts for his present aversion to egg whites and mushrooms. I shall apprise D of these revelations to see what light he can shed on the actual occurrences during this time period...

Later—D. was enigmatic, to say the least. He suggested that before he discussed these matters with me, I should read the relevant parts of a book entitled *Notes on the Necronomicon.* I don't understand why such research should be useful, but I will do it this evening and bring the matter up with D. again...

August 14, 1931

It is the most incredible thing! I consulted the volume that D recommended and another, far older, of which it was merely an annotation. Apparently, the patient's delusions have a basis in historical fact! Dyer hinted that he and the patient did actually discover the things that the patient discussed in his delusion, which I attributed to the drug. However, D was never treated with the drug. It's possibly a shared delusion (such things have been previously documented), but I think not. The description of the shoggoth particularly intrigues me—if it's in any way factual, it could have very important ramifications concerning my work at Rockefeller. Dyer tells me that much more material on these subjects is to be found in the library at Miskatonic, and seemed amenable to my making a trip there to research the subject...

September 2, 1931

Have just returned from Arkham. It is staggering! What I have learned could provide the answers to all I have worked for and more—the secret of the very origin of humankind and eternal life! I found a protocol for the creation of a shoggoth. Could undifferentiated human tissue be substituted for the material used by the Old Ones? I know a ready source! I've secured a place near the Settlement where I can work undisturbed, away from prying eyes. I can get the specialized equipment I need from the lab at the office, or from Rockefeller—L's pump should be just the thing. I shall get D. to help me, whether he wants to or not—his petty desires cannot be allowed to stand in the way of such a momentous discovery. A few days of sensory deprivation should do the trick nicely. As for the patient, I shall leave the pitiable wretch where he lies. He's not insane, he's just not enough of a man to embrace the earth-shattering discovery he has made. Let him wallow in his misery!

Silas K. Henderson

CHAPTER 28

From the notebook of Sally Barton

Monday, October 5, 1931

I'm back in the City, but I sure wish I wasn't. We blew in from Cape May late last night on the last train from Philly.

Things are bleak. Strangways ain't the Ripper, and he's dead. Morris is still suspended, and Henderson is trying to get him fired for interfering with an active investigation that he was not part of. Morris said he wasn't sure if his rabbi could protect him or not.

Our working theory now is that Eben's friend Colin McDowell is the Ripper, but we don't have a shred of evidence for it, and even the *Graphic* won't publish an unsubstantiated accusation like that without something to back it up. I wish we had searched McDowell's office when we were there tossing Strangways', but we had no reason to suspect him then.

Morris was understandably upset about Strangways. We were so sure he was our guy! He told me he needed a couple of days by himself to think about things, and that he'd call me. I've heard that before. I wonder if he blames me for this whole thing—after all, I was the one who egged him on into interfering with Henderson's investigation. I guess we're still engaged; I sure want to be, and Morris hasn't said he doesn't want to be. I really don't want to think about how I'll take it if he drops me. I thought I was in love with that guy who knocked me up, but after spending time with Morris, I know better. I slept with the first guy because I thought he'd marry me if I did. Not that I really wanted to get married, but I sure did want somebody to ask me, if that makes any sense.

It's different with Morris. Sure, I was a little pie-eyed the first time I slept with him in Philly, but after he came to get me at the train station and said what he did, I slept with him because it was how I could give him all that I had to give. I'm ashamed that I pushed him so hard about Strangways—he kept telling me that it was a bad idea, but I was sure that Strangways was the Ripper. I wanted to get the story and be like Winchell and Sullivan, I wanted Morris to get the ten grand and rub Henderson's nose in it, and I wanted us to have enough money to get a little house in Staten Island or Jersey free and clear. But most of all, I want to be with Morris. Forever. And now I wonder if that ain't gonna happen.

I brushed the tears off my cheek. Goddammit, Barton!

Work was always a good cure for the blues. I grabbed my copy of Donnelley's and looked up Eben. There were numbers for both his home and office. Since it was after 9 a.m., I tried to get him at the office, but his receptionist, who sounded like she was mad at the world, said he wasn't in yet. I tried his home number, but it rang and rang with no answer. Maybe he was on his way to the office. I could wait and try again in a while, but I knew if I hung around my flat, I'd just worry. I decided to go on over to Eben's office and see if I could catch him in. If not, I'd have to figure another angle.

It was after ten when I arrived. Eben's office was in Lenox Hill near McDowell's, but closer to the river in an area that was a little less ritzy, East 66th between Second and Third. His digs were on the first floor of a grey stone building that also contained a lawyer's office and an interior decorator, or so the embossed, bronze sign on the front gate informed me. The wrought iron gate was part of a fence that

267

surrounded a little garden that you had to pass through to get to the front steps. It was full of knee high, light purple, fall-blooming asters interspersed with yellow goldenrod and vivid green ornamental grasses, all arranged around a golden gazing globe that brought a little bit of the country into the heart of the City. It probably served to calm the patients before they entered the doctor's office. I know it had that effect on me.

I entered the building through the vestibule and stopped in front of a door made up of many small glass panes. The doctor's waiting room beyond looked like a jigsaw puzzle picturing three rather large, older women—the kind who wear a sweater over a floor-length dress regardless of the weather just because it's fall, along with half a dozen necklaces and other dangling bangles. I could see another grey-haired lady in a white dress and a nurse's cap at a desk at the end of the room, whom I assumed was Eben's gate-keeper. I decided that I didn't want to get involved with any of that bunch. I turned and followed the corridor around a corner toward the rear of the building. I passed a solid wooden door, which I assumed was to an examining room, and stopped at another at the far end of the hall. I thought this was likely the door to Eben's office.

I rapped loudly.

After a few seconds, the door swung inwards, and Eben was there. He looked like a ragamuffin—his hair was mussed, he was unshaven and his suit looked like he had slept in it. He wasn't even wearing a white coat. That's not how a doctor receiving patients should look.

"Finally!" he burst out. "Where the hell have you..." He did a double take. "Oh! Miss Barton, it's you!"

He was obviously expecting someone else.

"What do you want?" he said. He made no motion to move out of the doorway to let me come in.

"I wanted to talk with you about your pal McDowell. Find out if you've gotten anywhere hunting for him."

"No, I still haven't found him."

I stepped forward as if to come in, but he still didn't budge.

"Miss Barton, I have patients waiting. I can't talk to you now."

Sometimes my big mouth gets me in trouble, but I just can't help it. "Was it a patient that you thought was banging on your door just now?"

Anger flashed in his eyes. "No it wasn't," he said. "Good day, Miss Barton." He shut the door in my face.

Great. You sure aced that one, Barton. Now what?

I headed back outside. Almost all of the early morning fog had burned off and it looked like another mild fall day was in the cards. I needed a place to sit and think. I walked over to Second Avenue and turned downtown, spotted a newsstand under the el and picked up an armload of papers, including last Friday's *Graphic*. I spotted one of Manhattan's ubiquitous coffee shops, went in, got a table, and ordered a regular coffee and an egg sandwich. While I was waiting for it, I pulled my notebook out of my purse and flipped to the notes I made when I first talked to Eben about McDowell. I was sure that this joker was the Ripper, and if I was gonna track him down, I needed a plan.

Breakfast came and I lit a smoke, then started with the papers. Two articles caught my eye.

October 4, 1931—New York Evening Graphic

Young Woman Missing from East Side Settlement House

The head resident of the College Settlement House on Rivington Street has reported to police that a settler has been missing since last Thursday. Hannah Slater failed to come home that evening and has not been seen since. Foul play remains a possibility, according to Inspector William Henderson of the NYPD. Inspector Henderson is the chief investigating officer of the so-called "Manhattan Ripper" murders—he declined to speculate as to whether Miss Slater had become the latest victim of that fiend. His presence on this case is certainly suggestive, however.

The College Settlement House was opened in 1889 at No. 9 Rivington Street to allow educated young ladies the opportunity to interact with the underprivileged class. The Settlement residents have matriculated from some of the finest colleges in the Northeast including Smith, Vassar and Miskatonic University. The Settlement movement provides many services to the Lower East Side neighborhood, including classes in English and practical skills, a kindergarten, a medical clinic and a circulating library. The College Settlement House has been so successful that other such houses have opened in Philadelphia, Boston and Baltimore.

October 5, 1931—New York Evening Post

Child Disappears from Tompkins Square Park

A nine-year old boy has been reported missing from Tompkins Square Park on the Lower East Side of Manhattan. The boy, Bennie Goldblum, was playing Ringolevio with a group of friends and was in hiding. His playmates became concerned when he could not be found after the game was over and he did not return home. A search of the park did not locate the youngster.

Police advise that parents inform all of their children to be extremely circumspect with strangers and to report any suspicious individuals immediately. It is also highly advisable that all children be kept inside after dark.

Tompkins Square—wasn't that where Morris' Bellevue guy was found? I checked my notebook. Yep. Sure was. And I remembered that Eben gave me a lecture about a Settlement House. I flipped more pages in the notebook. Bingo! McDowell ran a clinic at the College Settlement at 95 Rivington Street. Looked to me like the Lower East Side was the place to start looking for him.

I walked over to the 65th Street el station, the quickest way to the Lower East Side. I only had a few minutes to wait, and the train wasn't crowded in midmorning. It was loud though, because many of the windows were open on this mild day. The ride seemed long—both 65th and Rivington were local stations, and there were plenty more between them, not far apart, so we stopped every couple of minutes.

Silas K. Henderson

I tried to use the time to plan a strategy. I didn't want the folks at the Settlement to think that I was trying to tighten the screws on their beloved doctor. I needed an angle to justify digging around. I thought following up on the disappearance of that Hannah dame might fill the bill. Besides, if McDowell was the Ripper, maybe he got her too.

The doors finally popped open at Rivington Street. I had done a feature for the *Graphic* a year ago on the Lower East Side, one of the City's most infamous neighborhoods. For many immigrants seeking freedom from oppression in the old country, it was the gateway to a better life. For many others. it became a living hell, with its street gangs and dark, poisonous backstreet tenements. Jacob Riis, a Danish immigrant and photojournalist, shocked the world with his 1890 expose of the neighborhood, *How the Other Half Lives*, in which he showed in pictures the filthy buildings that the masses had to occupy, as well as exposing the sweatshops that employed women and children in awful conditions for only pennies a day. His work led to the regulation of tenements by city law, which included such things as increased room space and better ventilation, shorter buildings, and improved fire codes. It was guys like Riis that inspired me to become a journalist, so I could make people's lives better too.

Number 95 was two blocks east. Rivington Street teemed with life in the late morning sun. The smell of auto exhaust mingled with cooking aromas from neighborhood eateries and pushcarts. The air hummed with the hubbub of a thousand voices, speaking hundreds of languages, from peddlers hawking their wares to skylarking kids and yentas arguing with passers-by while hanging out a window above the street. The avenue teemed with people going here and there, and with pushcarts that seemed to sell just about everything—food, tea, coffee and spices, all manner of clothing and costume jewelry, books and records, even varnish, paint and furniture. I had to fix my gaze resolutely forward so as not to stop and browse. I knew that I'd never do what I came for if I got hooked on shopping.

I passed the orange façade of the synagogue of the First Roumanian-American Convention. The College Settlement occupied a three-story brownstone next door. A knock at the door brought a youngish, homely woman in a frowsy, striped ankle-length jumper over a white blouse that was way too big for her. She also wore a white cotton bonnet from the 1800s. I wouldn't be caught dead on the street in a rig like that!

"Can I help you, Ma'am?" she asked

Do I look like a Ma'am to you, lady? I thought but didn't say.

"I'm Sally Barton," I said, extracting my card from my purse. The usual cascade of other items fell to the porch. "I'm a reporter with the *Evening Graphic.*"

The Jane didn't even look at the card, but her eyes got big when I said "reporter." "I don't think we're supposed to talk to reporters," she said.

The way I was feeling today, this dumb Dora didn't know how close she was to getting pasted. I gritted my teeth. "Can I at least talk to somebody in charge?" I asked her.

"That would be Annabelle. I'll get her." She shut the door in my face, leaving me standing there. I used the time to pick up the stuff from my purse.

After a few minutes, during which I wondered if I was getting the cold shoulder, the door opened again. A big stout broad in the same rig as dumb Dora looked me up and down as if I was something she didn't want to see.

"Christine tells me you're a reporter." She said *reporter* like a bad word. I have never figured out why some people, especially women, disrespect us so much.

"That's right, for the *Evening Graphic.*" I offered my card again, and it was refused again. "I wanted to follow up on Hannah Slater's disappearance." I wanted to get a foot in the door so I wouldn't get it shut in my face again, but Big Bertha made that impossible.

"We have a policy of not discussing the affairs of our residents." Really? Getting kidnapped is an affair now, is it? She stepped back, and the door was beginning to swing closed.

"I was wondering if it had anything to do with the disappearance of Dr. McDowell."

The door stooped swinging. "You are acquainted with Dr. McDowell?"

"Not really," I said. "But I've been helping a friend of his look into his disappearance."

"Which friend?" She asked me.

"Dr. Eben Warman."

The door swung open all the way. "You can come in," she said.

As I followed her down the hallway, I was grateful that I got in, but I was insulted that I had to use Eben's name to do it.

We went into a parlor with two tall windows that looked out on to Rivington Street full of swanky furniture—a couple of crushed velvet wingback armchairs and a matching sofa, with a low, glass-topped cocktail table in front. No way I wanted to sit on a sofa with that dame! I took an armchair. She looked vaguely disappointed, but then sat in the other armchair.

She introduced herself as Annabelle Akers and offered me tea, which I accepted only because I thought a warm drink might improve the chilly atmosphere in here. She called in Christine, the broad who had first opened the door for me, and ordered it, earning me a dirty look from Christine. If these Settlement women were here to minister to the downtrodden, I thought they ought to cop a better attitude.

We chitchatted about the weather, and how did I ever get to be a lady reporter while waiting for the tea to arrive. Christine finally brought it in in a silver pot on a silver tray, along with a couple of china cups and a plate of cookies.

"I was curious about Hannah Slater," I began as Annabelle poured the tea. "Was she the kind to take a powder, or do you think something happened to her?" I noticed that Christine, who was on her way out of the room, suddenly looked back at us.

Annabelle frowned. "She was most certainly not the kind to take a powder, as you put it, none of our ladies are. She was committed to our work here." She noticed that Christine was still in the room and said to her, "Christine, don't you have work in the kitchen?"

"Yes, ma'am." Christine left.

I had my notebook out now. "Tell me about the day Miss Slater went missing," I said.

"There really isn't anything to tell. Hannah went out to the market and didn't return. When I noticed she was missing at dinnertime, I made some inquires, then I phoned the police."

"What day was that?"

"Last Thursday, the second."

"And Inspector Henderson showed up?"

"Not at first. It was a uniformed constable that took the report. The Inspector dropped by on Saturday."

Of course. Henderson was busy shooting Strangways in Cape May on Friday. That little copper sure got around.

"Did Henderson say anything about why he caught the case?"

She gave me a strange look. "Why do you ask that? I assumed they sent an inspector because our case was important. Because of the work we do here."

If she was clueless about the Ripper, I sure wasn't going to bring him up. "That must be why," I said. I hesitated, not sure how to ask what I wanted to, then I just spit it out. "Did Miss Slater have anything to do with Dr. McDowell?"

The frown became a glare. "What are you insinuating?"

"I'm not insinuating anything. It's just that two people connected with this place have gone missing in a short period of time. I'm wondering if there could be a connection."

"What connection could there be?" said Annabelle. "Doctor McDowell is a fine gentleman who was helping us with our mission, by caring for our residents and the people of the neighborhood. I don't know that he and Hannah ever even conversed." She paused, and then said, "I hope you're not going to imply something tawdry, just to sell newspapers."

I wanted to say, *Screw you, lady!* but what came out was, "I wouldn't do that ma'am. The *Graphic* just wants to help find them, is all."

Her expression was plainly disbelieving. "I really don't think I can help you, Miss Barton. I told the Inspector everything I know about this unfortunate incident, and I think that we'll just have to leave it in his capable hands." She arose from her chair. "I think you can find your own way to the door," she said. Then she was gone.

Oh, brother! I surely struck out today! I gathered my things and went into the corridor, heading for the front door. Before I had taken two steps, I heard "Hssst!" from behind me. When I looked back, I saw Christine leaning out of a door at the end of the hallway. She motioned for me to come that way. I quickly scurried down the hallway and went through the door.

Yeasty food smells overwhelmed me. I found myself in a gleaming white kitchen worthy of a restaurant. Pots and pans dangled from overhead fixtures, and large vessels steamed on an oversized stove. Other than me, Christine was the only one in the room.

"I couldn't help overhearing your conversation with Annabelle," she said, looking at the floor. She seemed reluctant to say anymore.

"Do you know something about Miss Slater's disappearance?"

She looked up to meet my gaze. "Mebbe," she said. "Mebbe you got it right that Hannah was a little sweet on the Doc."

"What do you mean?"

"The Doc is a swell-lookin' gent. A lot of the girls here got a thing for him. Mostly he don't notice, but he mighta made an exception for Hannah."

"You think they had something going?"

"Like I said, mebbe. I know that sometimes the Doc held clinic during the daytime, and sometimes Hannah would go out a few minutes after he left. She'd come back a couple of hours later, lookin' like somethin' the cat dragged in."

"How do you mean?"

"You know, hair all tousled, clothes wrinkled... She'd run straight up to her room before anybody noticed."

"But you noticed." That made her smile.

"Well, nothin' much around here gets past Christine."

I waited a beat, then asked, "I don't suppose I could get a look at Hannah's room?"

The smile vanished. "I dunno," she said. "I don't think Annabelle would like that..."

"I won't tell her if you don't."

"Well, she has a roommate." My spirits fell. "But she's out now."

I smiled encouragingly at Christine. "Could you show me where her room is, and which are her things? I'll just take a quick look, then I'll go. Annabelle will never have to know."

She remained silent.

"Please," I added, trying to keep the desperation out of my voice.

"Okay," she said.

Thank Christ!

Christine opened the hallway door and peered outside, then said, "C'mon! It's clear."

I followed her out into the hallway and to the front of the house, where a broad, carpeted staircase led to the upper stories. We ascended to the second floor, then turned a corner and went up another flight of stairs to the top floor. Turning another corner put us in a long hallway with a window at the far end. Christine led me to a door halfway down the hall.

"This is Hannah's room," she announced. She opened the door and ushered me inside, closing it behind us.

The room was cramped, about ten feet on a side, and had that musty. mildewy stink common to older buildings, partly masked by the scent of femininity. Daylight streamed in through a window on the far wall illuminating the hideous wallpaper, white with multicolored stripes. Two wrought iron single beds, with an army blanket and a single pillow on each, ran along the right and left walls, with matching three-drawer bureaus on the wall at their feet that flanked the door. It reminded me of a jail cell, not a place where somebody lived. That is, except for the doll.

She stood on top of the bureau on the left, a display doll about two feet tall on a stand in a glass showcase. A stunning representation of a modern flapper, she had the classic short haircut, and a beaded gold lamé turban held in place by a rhinestoned black satin headband. A honey-blonde mink stole was draped over her shoulders. She wore a gold and black fringed knee-length dress in a diamonded deco pattern over black seamed stockings and gold shoes. She held a graceful black cigarette holder in her right hand. She was absolutely one of the most gorgeous things I had ever seen in my life. I would kill for clothes like that!

Christine indicated the doll, which she didn't even appear to see. "That's Hannah's side," she said. She opened the door again and stepped outside. "Do what you need to, then go," she said. "Anybody asks, I never saw you come up here." The door clicked shut.

Shit! I was going to ask her about the doll, and to keep a lookout while I nosed around, but that was out now.

I looked at the doll more closely. Her head and arms appeared to be made of flesh-toned porcelain. The hair on her head and her eyebrows looked real. Her eyes were a pale blue and her lips bright pink. It was obvious that she had been handcrafted, and was likely very pricey. How could a woman who chose to live in a place like this afford such an expensive ornament?

I attacked the bureau. The top drawer contained socks and underthings, and there were a couple of the billowy white blouses in the middle drawer. The bottom drawer contained a heavy green sweater and a wool skirt.

I nudged the sweater aside and found a maroon faux leather box with gold trim around the perimeter, which placed on top of the bureau. It was latched, with a button next to the latch that obviously released it. I pushed the button but it didn't move. Locked! I reached into my hair and extracted a bobby pin, removed the plastic tit on the tip with my teeth, and had the box open quick as you could say "Jack Robinson."

An unsightly necklace of green and yellow glass beads and a matching pair of earrings that probably came from a street cart lay on top of a sheaf of folded papers. I took out both, and the Indian headdress on a five-dollar gold piece on the bottom caught my eye. Her entire worldly wealth, except for that doll! A business card slid face down out of the sheaf of papers as I set them down on the bureau, and almost skittered on to the floor.

The Legacy of the Unborn

The papers were a baptismal certificate for Hannah Slater and a diploma from St. Leo's school in Irvington, New Jersey, the town next to Maplewood. That made me smile. Hannah and I were neighbors.

There was writing on the back of the business card, in a fine, angular script that was halfway between printing and cursive. It read:

To a fine and beautiful lady—CM

CM? Colin McDowell!

What kind of guy writes a love note to a girl on the back of a business card?

I turned the card over. On the front was:

S. Jupiter

Fine Follies Dollies

146 Ridge Street, New York City

Just a few blocks from here!

OK, it looked like I'd gotten all there was to get here. Time to get out. I cracked the door to the hallway and peered out. The hall was empty. I stepped out and closed the door softly behind me, then quickly hurried down to the street.

Once outside, I lit a fag and stopped to consider. Did I really want to visit the doll shop? What could I get there that I didn't already have? Charlie McCarthy's voice echoed inside my head. "*A good newshound runs every lead, Barton, no matter how thin.*" OK. This lead was so thin that I could about see through it, but I'll run it down.

Ridge crossed Rivington about five blocks down. Once there, I turned north, and was soon standing in front of the doll shop. No. 146 was actually a double storefront, with a pigeon shop on one side and Jupiter's Fine Follies Dollies on the other. I wrinkled my nose at the sharp odor of the bird waste, but I had to endure it to take a look at the window display in the doll shop, which was truly amazing. Jupiter specialized in contemporary display dolls, all female. McDowell had bought Hannah one of the smaller dolls; a couple of life-sized flappers occupied seats at a glass-topped table in the window. You could mistake this place for a café at first glance. Other dolls lined shelves that flanked the table—everything from can-can dancers to recognizable screen stars like Lillian Gish and Gloria Swanson. I pushed the door open, and a little bell tinkled as I entered.

Jupiter (at least I assumed that's who he was) was a short, balding man impeccably dressed in a light gray suit with a dark blue polka-dotted cravat. He was surprisingly young—no more than 40. He was behind a glass showcase filled with dolls, and many more sat on shelves or stood on pedestals behind him. Another lay in pieces on the counter in front of him, on a green velvet cloth. It was disturbing—a dismembered woman in miniature. My face began to tighten.

He noticed my distress and flipped a cloth over the pieces. "Good morning, Miss," he said. "How may I help you?"

I showed him my press card, and bless him, he took it from me and examined it critically.

Handing it back, he said again, "How may I help you today?"

"I wonder if you remember a doll you sold some time ago."

"I remember all of my dollys. They're like my children." He placed his hand of the cloth covering his disarticulated child. Suddenly, I wanted out of there!

I forced myself to speak. "This one was a flapper in a black and gold deco outfit, about..." I spread my hands apart to indicate the size.

"Charlie." He pronounced it with an sh. "She was one of my favorites. I hated to see her go."

"I wonder if you have any information about the buyer."

"May I ask why you would like to know?"

"If he's who I think, he's been missing. We'd like to find out what happened to him."

He clicked his tongue against his palate. "That's terrible. The doctor is a fine gentleman."

"You do know him!"

"Of course. He's a neighborhood icon —he helps a lot of people. Missing you say? That's odd. I saw him just the other day."

I could feel a rush starting in my belly. My earlier discomfort vanished. "When?" I asked him.

"Day before yesterday, I think. Or was it the day before that? I was going home, and I saw him going into his place."

His place! "And where would that be?"

"On Rivington, between Suffolk and Clinton."

"Got an address?"

"No, but you can't miss it. It's on the south side, about halfway down the block. It's a two story, boarded-up building, with an alley down one side. The Rudingers used to live there, but Rolf made it big and moved the family uptown. I've been wondering when the doctor's going to take the boards off, now that he's living there."

"How long has he lived there?"

"A few weeks, I think. He probably moved to be closer to his work down here."

With a wife and kids uptown? I didn't think so.

I thanked Jupiter and left the shop. Oh boy, I hit pay dirt again!

I thought about my next move as I headed back to Rivington. Maybe I should call Morris and tell him what I've got. He now thinks McDowell is the Ripper, and I'm pretty sure he's right.

But what would cause a respected uptown doctor to start murdering and cutting up women? According to Eben, this McDowell was an odd duck, but he wasn't crazy like you'd have to be to do such a thing. There was sure still a lot of mystery to be figured out.

What I'd really like to do is to find McDowell and convince him to turn himself in, from the *Graphic* office, of course. If he says he innocent, I could tell him that the paper will stand behind him to make sure he gets a fair hearing.

I thought about Morris again. When I saw him last, he gave me the distinct impression that he didn't want to hear from me for a while. And I sure didn't want to drag him down here just to find an empty building. Maybe the thing to do was to go down there and see if I could find out if McDowell was even there. If he was, then I'd decide whether to call Morris.

In five minutes, I was across the street from the place that Jupiter had described. It was a flat-roofed, two-story brick building with boarded-up windows fronting on Rivington, and other windows above the alley that Jupiter had mentioned. A drainpipe on the second story hung askew. It was hard to see from this angle, but it looked like the boards were off the window next to where the pipe used to be attached. There was fair bit of traffic on Rivington in front of the place, but I couldn't see anyone moving inside. It seemed safe enough to go over and check it out.

I was right! Some of the boards on the second story window next to the pipe were missing. The alley was strewn with all sorts of junk, but it looked like the boards had fallen next to the building. I noticed basement windows running along the foundation a few inches above the ground, but they were boarded up too.

The alley led to a back yard. I inspected the black hole beyond the upper story window and didn't see anything. All the rest of the windows were concealed behind lumber— a walk down the alley should be safe enough, as long as I was mindful of the scattered trash.

The back yard used to have a garden with an arbor, but everything was overgrown now. Boards covered all of the windows back here too. Rickety steps on a covered wooden porch led up to a back door. It looked safe enough, though. I went up and put my ear to the door.

Not a sound.

I expected the door to be locked, but I tried the knob anyway.

It turned, and the door swung open a crack.

Somebody was using this place!

Alarm bells blaring in my head warned me that going inside was a really bad idea. I should go find a pay phone and call Morris, and tell him that I found McDowell.

But what if the doctor wasn't in there?

I carry an oversized purse for a reason. I rummaged around inside it and came up with a small flashlight that had come in handy before. As usual, a few items fell while I was digging around, and I scooped them up and put them back inside, trying to leave behind most of the dirt and other litter on the porch.

I thought it would be safe to just go inside and make sure each room was empty before entering it. The first hint that I had that anyone besides me was in there, I could go get Morris.

I listened carefully once more. The place was a quiet as a tomb. I pushed the door open slightly and peeked in—a kitchen that had seen better days. Nobody was there.

I eased the door open and slipped inside...

CHAPTER 29

The Statement of Dr. Ebeneezer Warman

I spent the bulk of Monday morning in my inner office waiting to hear from Harvey. I was convinced that his silence and absence was payback for my behavior during the past weeks.

A little before ten, there were a couple of loud knocks on the door to the hallway. Harvey! I leapt up from the chair and snatched open the door.

"Finally!" I said. "Where the hell have you..."

It wasn't Harvey!

"Oh! Miss Barton, it's you!" I was beyond annoyed. "What do you want?"

"I wanted to talk with you about your pal McDowell. Find out if you've gotten anywhere hunting for him."

"No, I still haven't found him." I told her, glaring, so she'd get the hint that I was in no mood for company. But of course, she didn't. The hussy started to push forward, as if she would move me out of my own doorway!

"Miss Barton, I have patients waiting, I can't talk to you now." I said. It was a lie. I had told Sarah to send them all away when I got in this morning.

"Was it a patient that you thought was banging on your door just now?" she asked.

The nerve! "No it wasn't," I told her. "Good day, Miss Barton."

I slammed the door in her face.

I called Harvey's home and office half a dozen times after she left, always with the same result—no answer at home, or a polite "He's not in as yet" at work. I began fantasizing about precisely how and where I was going to hit him.

Finally, at about eleven-thirty, there was a light rap on the hallway door, followed by the scratching sound of the key in the lock. This had to be Harvey!

The door opened and he was there. All thoughts of doing him harm vanished in my joy to see him. I jumped up and went to him, enfolded him in an embrace and kissed him as if I could never let him go!

"Oy, Eben, easy!" he pushed me away and I reluctantly released him. "What's gotten into you, old man?"

Suddenly my eyes were filled with tears. "I..., I thought something terrible had happened," I said. "It's been days since I heard from you."

He looked at me skeptically, and then his expression changed to one of apprehension. "I thought I'd told you that I'd be *incognito* for a few days. It consumed that much time for me to infiltrate that damned bordello. Are you sure you're all right, old dear?"

"I am now," I said. "Just never go away like that again, Harvey!"

His frown of concern deepened. "P'haps you better prescribe yourself something for those nerves."

"I'm fine now, Harvey," I repeated, and I meant it. "Did you find out anything about Colin?"

He tossed himself into the leather wing back, dropping the canvas valise that he carried on the floor beside it. Atypically for a warmish Monday morning, he was wearing a blue fisherman's sweater with a high collar, tight black dungarees, and a pair of Wellingtons. It was obvious that he hadn't been to the office. He pointed at the gasogene.

284

"It's not too early for a whisky-soda," he said. "Make one for yourself, too."

"What about Colin?" I asked again.

"Drinks first," he said in his adamant voice. "You'll need one when you hear what I have to say."

I did as he bade me. After I handed him his drink, I took mine and sat behind my desk, facing him. He'd already emptied his glass by half.

"Dammitall, Harvey..."

"I've discovered what McDowell was doing in that brothel. And it wasn't fornication." He leaned forward and lowered his voice. "Eben, he was doing abortions!"

I was speechless!

"As one might expect, pregnancy is an occupational hazard of the oldest profession. The ladies have some dubious means of taking care of that themselves, but such practices all too often lead to more serious medical problems. The good doctor apparently volunteered his services to remediate that difficulty."

"That's scandalous!" I said. "Some doctors will do the procedure for a friend or a trusted patient, but even that is risky. It could lead to the loss of one's license to practice, even to prison time."

"Oh, and it gets worse," Harvey said. "Not only was McDowell servicin' Miss Lucy's girls, but the word about his availability had also gone out on the street. He was treatin' half the whores in Lower Manhattan!"

It was unbelievable to me that a respected physician like Colin McDowell could have sunk to such depths! "He's living in the whorehouse?"

"No." Harvey said.

Thank God for that!

"He has a place nearby, however. It took me until this mornin' to ascertain precisely where that was."

"You found him!"

"I think so. What do you want to do about it?"

I started to say, 'Go and get him!' but then I thought about it. I wondered if Colin even knew about Evie. He had apparently deserted

Danforth, as well as his practice, in order to consort with harlots. Reading his unholy journal left me with the distinct impression that Colin's mental state had undergone a drastic deterioration. I pondered whether he was even capable of caring for his girls anymore. Then I realized that there was only one way to know for sure. Talk to him.

But if Colin had really gone crackers, confronting him could be extremely dangerous. His journal implied that he might have had something to do with the current state of the unfortunate Dr. Dyer.

That was when the impact of the missing uteri hit me.

God in heaven! Was Colin McDowell the Ripper?

I said as much to Harvey.

"I thought of that, too," he replied. "But I could conceive of no earthly reason why he would do such a thing. Any crime must have a motive, y'know."

"Maybe the motive is locked into a deranged mind," I said. "Surely no sane person would commit such horrible crimes."

"Actually, that's not the case," said Harvey. "But now is not the time to expound on the finer points of criminal psychology. I think we must quickly decide what to do about the errant Doctor McDowell. We have two choices—inform the police, or confront him ourselves. While the former course has some merits, it is true that, as far as the law is concerned, Colin McDowell has committed no crimes as yet—he has simply gone missing."

"Abortion is against the law," I reminded Harvey.

"True enough, and p'haps we should report it, along with the elusive physician's whereabouts."

I took up the argument. "But Colin is, or was, a friend. Perhaps I at least owe him a chance to explain himself. Some doctors believe it is wrong that a medical procedure is criminalized. And I just can't imagine that Colin McDowell is guilty of the Ripper's crimes."

"Do you want to confront him?" Harvey asked.

"Yes, I think so. But it could be dangerous."

"Indubitably," said Harvey. He reached into his front pants pocket and produced a little pistol, no bigger than his hand, with two heavily engraved barrels one above the other, and an ivory handle. "I can be a bit dangerous too, don't y'know."

"Then let's go find Colin," I said. This was not the first time that Harvey helped me come to grips with a difficult decision. That was one of the reasons that I loved him.

Another thought intruded. "I find that I might have some other information for the police," I told Harvey. "Last week, Detective Moscowicz took me to see an unidentified man in a bad way at Bellevue, who had been found wandering the streets. At the time I couldn't identify him, but now I think I know who he is."

"Who is he?"

"Dr. William Dyer of Miskatonic University at Arkham, Massachusetts."

"Are you sure it's him?"

I hesitated. I had never actually met Dyer. If the police asked how I knew him, could I tell him that I identified him while in some kind of fugue state in a mental hospital?

Harvey recognized my indecision. "If you aren't sure, it might be better to say nothing until you are."

"You're right, of course," I said. "Let's go see about Colin. We may be talking to the police after we do."

"I suggest we visit your digs first; you can change into clothes resembling mine." Harvey said. "Then we can call on McDowell's at his new residence, which is not nearly as pristine as his old one, and see if we can resolve this distasteful affair."

It was mid-afternoon before we found ourselves on Rivington Street on the Lower East side. If I didn't know that we were in Manhattan, I would have assumed that it was an exotic foreign metropolis from the variety of humanity present on that thoroughfare. European workingmen in flat caps and overalls, mingled with orthodox Jews with their tall hats, black overcoats and long beards, dark-skinned, turbaned folk in brightly colored raiments, and Chinese coolies in billowing coats and knickers. They didn't confine themselves to the sidewalks either, but meandered in the roadway along with the cars, lorries and horse-drawn wagons, probably because the going was easier away from the innumerable pushcarts in the former location. It was hard to believe that Colin, who had always been fond of his creature comforts, had chosen this place as a refuge.

I had asked Harvey where Colin was, but the only answer he would give me was an enigmatic "You'll see!" After we disembarked from the train, he led us down Rivington past the College Settlement, then a few blocks further on. We stopped in front of a two story, boarded-up building on the same side of the street as the Settlement, which was somewhat dilapidated and looked as if no one had lived here for a while. An alley ran down the east side.

I looked at Harvey and asked, "Here?" somewhat disbelievingly.

He nodded. "So my source informed me."

I realized that we really didn't have plan, or at least I didn't. "What do we do?' I asked Harvey. "Go bang on the front door?"

"We could, but I don't think it would be helpful." He pointed to the front porch. A large, wide board nailed to the wall on either side covered the front door, so this was obviously not a means of ingress or egress. All of the windows facing the street were similarly shrouded with stout wood.

"Let's reconnoiter a bit, then decide." Always the careful man, Harvey.

We proceeded to the alley. It ran down the east side of the building and was littered with urban effluvium—loose stones, broken glass and boards, and shredded paper. We picked our way carefully among the debris into the back yard.

A ramshackle wooden porch hung from the back of the house, overlooking what used to be a garden, as evidenced by a grape arbor that was now overgrown with grass and vines. We ascended the stairs carefully. Harvey preceded me, testing each step before putting his weight on it to ensure that he wouldn't break through. When we were both standing before the back door, Harvey tried the knob, then looked at me with tight lips. Locked!

The rear door was the type with multiple small rectangular panes of glass in the upper half. I looked to the floor of the porch to find something with which we could break a pane and reach in to turn the latch from the inside. I saw a flash of white, and reached down to retrieve a laminated card.

NEW YORK EVENING GRAPHIC

REPORTER

<u>Sally Barton</u>

Sally! She was here? I showed Harvey the card.

I found a piece of wood about six inches long and used it to break the glass, and knock all of the little jagged pieces out of the window frame. Harvey reached through, then pulled his hand back out and looked at me with a frustrated expression.

"It takes a key on both sides!" he said.

"Let's break it down!" I answered. "Sally may be in there!"

He sidled over to make room for me beside him, then said, "Put your shoulder to it on three. One, two, ..."

Crunch! The door remained closed.

"Again! One, two, ..."

Crunch! I felt it give that time, but we were still locked out.

"This one should do it," Harvey said. One, two, ..."

I went stumbling across the kitchen floor after the doorframe splintered at the lock and the door sprang open, nearly sprawling headlong because my shoes caught on the broken floor tiles. Harvey came in on my heels.

The kitchen smelled vaguely of wood smoke with the underlying reek of sewage—a most unpleasant combination. A sink full of old pots and dishes was under a boarded-up rear window, and a wood stove occupied another wall, the doors to the oven and the firebox open. It was very warm in the house. The central heat must have been on.

289

"Sally!" I shouted. "It's Eben!"

"Well now, everyone knows we're here," said Harvey. "Sally!"

No answer. We could faintly hear the street noises from Rivington coming in through the shattered rear door, but the house itself was silent.

"We must find her quickly!" I said, and moved quickly into the hallway outside the kitchen. To my left, stairs went up to the second floor. I surmised that the adjacent door opened on the stairs down to the basement. The darkened hallway, black as a blind man's sight, stretched to the front of the house to my left. A bolt of white light stabbed out from the kitchen, transforming the corridor and the heap of clothing that lay in the center of it, just in front of the front door, into a macabre carnival haunted house. The light picked out a woman's shoe.

"Sally! No!"

I rushed down the hallway. Harvey hurried behind with the light. A dark-haired woman's body was lying face down on the filthy floor. The light illuminated the shiny, dark red pool that extended beneath her.

Gritting my teeth, I knelt beside her and took her head gently in my hands. "Shine the light on her face," I told Harvey. He did so.

"It's not Sally!" I exclaimed in relief. But I knew that face. It was Hannah Slater, the girl from the Settlement!

"Is she..." asked Harvey.

"She's not breathing," I said. "Help me turn her over."

Harvey laid the flashlight on the floor, shining on the body and knelt next to me in the pool of blood.

"Get your hands under her hips," I told him. I took the shoulders. "On three. One, two, ..."

The body rolled over and the light revealed a gruesome sight. Her white blouse glistened crimson and was stuck to her torso by all of the blood. Her skirt fell open, slit down the middle, and the protruding intestines made it obvious that the gaping cleft continued into the body beneath the clothes.

The Ripper!

I stood carefully to avoid slipping in the blood that now soaked my shoes, then offered a hand to Harvey. "There's nothing I can do for her. She's gone. We need to find Sally, if she's here."

"And McDowell!" Harvey grated.

"Yes," I said. "We need to find Colin, too."

"We'll check all of the rooms," Harvey said. "There's another of these lights for you in the bag."

I went back to the kitchen and retrieved the light from the bag, then brought them to where poor Hannah lay. Meanwhile, Harvey had checked the two front rooms. No Sally.

I opened a door further up the hall, and the sewage fetor that rolled out nearly overwhelmed me. As I hurriedly closed the door, I saw that the room was a water closet that had apparently not been operational for quite some time. That hadn't prevented someone from using it, however.

Harvey opened the door to the remaining room on the other side of the hall and shined his light inside. After a minute he said, "She's not in here, either, but y'should see this."

The scene in the room was appalling. The beam of Harvey's flashlight played over the ruins of a once-elegant bed, with shreds of the tattered canopy dangling over the mattress like obscene, otherworldly epiphytes. As the light played on the bed, a small dark shape leapt out and loudly scurried to escape the beam. The roaming light exposed greasy take-out bags and wrapping paper strewn about on the putrid carpet, then stopped on a decaying chair, its springs poking up through the seat cushion like misshapen fungi sucking life from a dung heap. An adjacent table contained a decaying meal, and this time the rat squatting there did not flee the light, but hissed his defiance at the interlopers who would deprive him of a hard-won feast. The stink of human and animal waste intermingled with decomposing food washed over me, and my knees became weak.

"My God!" I said. "He's been living like this?"

Harvey silently pushed me back, and pulled the door shut.

That was the last room on this floor. We retreated back to the double staircase next to the kitchen.

"Up or down?" asked Harvey.

The thought of going into that basement begot a primal terror in my breast. I wasn't going down there if I didn't have to!

"Up," I said.

He inched up the deteriorating staircase, again testing each step. I let him get halfway up, then followed just as carefully.

The second floor was much like the first, with the same moldy, fecal miasma as downstairs. A series of closed doors flanked the hallway from the rear to the front of the house. The latches on all of them had been destroyed long ago, but someone had installed a hasp on a doorframe and a u-bolt on the door itself so it could be padlocked, I supposed. No padlock was there now though. This was the room from which the boards on the window had fallen in the alley outside. The room showed signs of occupancy as well, evidenced by a filthy mattress in the corner and food wrappers scattered about. Surely it was my imagination that the mattress surface seethed like a simmering cauldron.

We found no evidence of Sally in any of the upstairs rooms.

She had to be in the basement then. Why did it always have to be the basement?

We went back down to the ground floor, and Harvey pulled open the basement door, which made a grinding sound. No use trying to disguise our presence here. "Sally!" I shouted down the stairs. "Colin! Are you here?"

Harvey started down the cement steps, with me following. We were about halfway down when we heard it.

An infant crying.

An infant, here?

The cry had that particular, high-pitched note that engenders anxiety in adults, making it more likely that the hearerer will serve the child's needs just to shut him up.

At the bottom of the stairs, we found ourselves in a small entry chamber barely large enough for the two of us. It was beastly hot, and a pervasive yeasty redolence hung heavily in the air. A pair of metal doors stood ajar on the side of the room opposite the stairs, and a draught of hot air appeared to be blowing in from there.

The yowling was louder and appeared to be coming from beyond the doors.

Harvey yanked the door wide and went inside. Following, I saw that yellow light was streaming into the room at the far end, bringing the heaps of broken furniture and other trash into stark relief. The infantile wailing became ever louder, and appeared to be emanating from the lighted room.

We approached an opening in the cement wall of the basement that led to an adjacent chamber. I glanced towards the floor, then grabbed Harvey by the shoulder to stop him from taking another step.

"Take care," I hissed.

A black hole about eighteen inches in diameter opened in the floor in the entry. As we approached it, I could smell the reek of sewage that came out. Someone had placed a six-inch wide board across it to use a bridge, but it would be very easy to miss it and step into the cavity. One could break a hip that way. The hole was in front of another metal door that was halfway open. The yellow light was coming from behind that door, as was the now nearly continuous bawling of the infant. Harvey pulled the door wide and we stepped inside.

This is the thing that I must forget, if I am to join the world of men again. Something so wrong, so irrational, so vile, that to allow it to occupy my consciousness is to admit that all I ever learned or believed until now was a sham. If a merciful God who made man in his own image existed, surely he would not, he could not allow the existence of such a horror!

The stifling heat was emanating from the Brobdingnagian bulk of a furnace that squatted in the far corner of the chamber. Flanking it was a long table, probably from the upstairs dining room. The head of Colin McDowell surveyed us from inside a large glass vessel that stood in the center of the table, its mouth agape in the rictus of a silent scream! Translucent tubes penetrated the cranial orifices—eyes, ears, and mouth—and were connected to bulbous glass vessels sitting on ring stands on either side, which gave the entire tableau a ghastly, cephalopodan aspect. But, horrible as it was, the head in the vessel was not that which I must banish from my memory. That thing was in the bathtub next to the table. Where the crying originated.

There was no baby here! A white, cast iron, clawfoot bath tub clearly showed rivulets of blood running down the sides, coming from the naked, headless body sitting erect in the tub. The corpse did not sit in water, but in what absurdly appeared to be vanilla pudding, which came nearly to the rim of the tub. As I watched it, I saw that the infantile cries arose from a myriad of tiny mouths that appeared and vanished in turn on its surface.

A spherical lump began to bulge from the surface of the pudding. In a few seconds, it was about the size of a human head. A pair of eyes opened, stark white and sightless at first, then they became brown, and roved about the room until they fixed on us. The skin of the head undulated and assumed features—a nose, a mouth, ears appeared. They took on a distinctly feminine aspect.

The mouth opened and it spoke.

"Morris." It said. "Morris, are you there?"

God in heaven, no!

"Morris, I'm sorry. I shouldn't have come in here. Forgive me, Morris!

It began screaming now! "Morris! Help me, Morris! Oh God, it hurts, it hurts! Morris!" The shrieking intermingled with the baby's howling from a thousand other orifices that suddenly rippled along the oily, pinkish surface of the horror.

"This must not be!" Harvey,standing next to me, spat out. I saw that he had drawn his derringer. It looked pitifully small in his hand.

The creature fluxed, then flowed over the rim of the tub towards us with unearthly speed. Harvey thrust me back with his free hand and interposed himself between me and it. The boom of the little gun was impossibly loud in those close quarters, and the screeching voice and the baby's cries were suddenly blotted out by a continuous ringing in my ears. A flame erupting from the muzzle told me that Harvey had fired the second barrel, but I hardly heard it.

The thing swirled round Harvey's legs, snaked up to his torso. His elegant features were distorted by a soundless cry for mercy. A tentacle yanked him forward into the bulk of the thing, and he was engulfed.

God help me, I ran. I ran away like a whipped cur and left him there. Left the only one on this earth whom I loved in the embrace of that obscenity!

CHAPTER 30
October 6, 1931—New York Morning Telegraph

Many Deaths in Rivington Street Fire

A fire in an abandoned building on Rivington Street between Suffolk and Clinton Streets on the Lower East Side claimed the lives of an as yet undetermined number of neighborhood residents last night. Fire officials confirm that the fire started at 145 Rivington Street after midnight and spread to adjacent buildings. Two people, whose bodies were burned beyond recognition, have been confirmed dead. An anonymous source told this reporter that the death toll could go as high as ten. Further details about the particulars of any of the bodies were unavailable from the coroner's office, by the orders of Inspector William Henderson of the NYPD.

A local realtor told the *Telegraph* that the building had been rented to Dr. Colin McDowell, an eminent psychiatrist with a home and office in Manhattan's fashionable Lenox Hill section. No one was available at the McDowell home or office for comment, but a police source revealed that Mrs. McDowell had died under mysterious circumstances last Thursday at Lenox Hill

296

Silas K. Henderson

Hospital. Mrs. McDowell had previously reported her husband as a missing person, the police source revealed, but further information concerning his alleged disappearance were not forthcoming.

October 7, 1931—New York Morning Telegraph

Headless Corpse Found on Lower East Side

The decapitated body of a man was found early this morning on Pitt Street, between Broome and Grande Streets, by a policeman walking his beat. The constable also reported that the corpse was covered with a nondescript slimy substance. The unfortunate's head was not located, even after an extensive search of the area. The victim remains unidentified. Anyone with knowledge of who the victim might be is encouraged to call police headquarters at SPring-3100.

October 21, 1931—New York Evening Graphic

Lower East Side Headhunter Strikes Again!

Two more slaughtered—Previous victims identified

Lower East Side residents were horrified to learn that another "Headhunter" murder took place in this district late last night or early this morning. The mutilated bodies of a man and a woman were found in an 8th Street alley between 1st Avenue and Avenue A. Both victims were beheaded in the style of the earlier killings and both were covered with the slimy substance that has been the hallmark of the Headhunter murders, and which police have not identified as yet. As for the previous murders, a search of the area in which the bodies were found failed to locate the missing heads.

Inspector William Henderson, the detective in charge of the investigation, had little to say to the press except that he believed that an arrest would be made in the next few days. He had no comment about the possibility of a link between these killings and the recent cessation of the "New York

297

The Legacy of the Unborn

Ripper" murders that occurred uptown, which also remains unsolved by New York's finest.

The first two Headhunter victims have been identified. Lazlo Strzelczyvsky, unemployed, was apparently scavenging when he was attacked on Pitt Street. His body was found two weeks ago on Wednesday morning. Late last Saturday evening, two workers returning home from their jobs at the Singer Sewing Machine factory on Delancey Street found the body of Michael O'Connor, a co-worker, in an alley near the plant. All of the bodies were covered with a similar slimy substance. Additionally, a nine-year-old boy named Bennie Goldblum disappeared near Tompkins Square Park on October 5. It is unknown if this incident is connected to the subsequent murders.

November 2, 1931—The New York Times

More Headless Bodies Discovered on the Lower East Side

Death toll now at least nine—Mayor orders increased police presence

At least five more headless bodies have been discovered on the Lower East Side over the last two weeks. Police have declined to provide specifics. "There is no cover-up!" said Inspector William Henderson, who is in charge of the investigation. "We just don't want to contribute to a general panic." Henderson would only confirm that bodies have been found, and that circumstances strongly suggested that the same unknown person was responsible for all of the murders. With the four previous victims included, this murderer's body count is now at least nine. A nine-year-old boy who vanished from Tompkins Square Park on October 5, who could also be a victim of this fiend, has yet to be found. It has also been speculated that other recent disappearances in the city, including that of Dr. Colin McDowell, a noted Lenox Hill psychiatrist, Dr. Ebeneezer Warman, a resident at Lenox Hill Hospital and friend of McDowell, the famous criminal defense attorney Mr. Harvey Harrigan, Esq., and a

298

reporter for the New York Evening Graphic might be linked to these murders.

Mayor Walker has said that the police presence on the streets of the Lower East side from Houston Street south will be dramatically increased, starting today. He cautioned all residents to remain inside, especially during darkness, unless it is absolutely essential to be abroad. "The situation is well in hand, and we expect an arrest momentarily," the Mayor said.

CHAPTER 31

The Statement of Dr. Ebeneezer Warman

It's dark. I'm cold and wet, and hungry.

There were a lot of people in the street earlier, but they're mostly gone now, and the ones who are left look at me strangely. They shy away from me, as if I had some deadly disease.

I'm starving. I don't know when I last ate —maybe a few days ago, some food from a trash can in an alley. I had to grab it quick before the thing that follows me came. That taught me to check the cans, but I haven't found any more food. The others must have eaten it all.

My hands and arms hurt. I look at them in the glow of a streetlamp and see that they are red and blistered. Burned? I burned myself? I don't remember.

The buildings are mostly dark and locked. I know because I've been trying the doors. A man in a blue suit with brass buttons caught me at it a while ago. "Hey you bum!" he yelled, shaking a club at me. "Get away from there, unless you want a wood shampoo!" I don't know why he wanted to hurt me. I'm cold and wet, and just wanted to go inside. There are buildings with lights, too, but they also have people there to chase me away.

Harvey... no!

I'm starving! I smell wood smoke, and food! It's coming from up ahead. From that alley!

Shanties made of packing crates and cardboard occupy one wall of the alley. The door of one of them stands open, and a pale-yellow light streams out. That's where the food is!

I hurry to the door. It's so smoky in the shack that I can hardly see the woman inside. She's got a little fire going on the floor, and a paint can hangs over it from a hook on a tripod. I look closer—two urchins squat on the dirt floor, further away from the fire. They're staring hard at the can—they don't even notice me. The woman does, though, and fear leaps in to her eyes. She fumbles inside her sweater and comes out with a short knife. Her mouth twists into a snarl, and she brandishes the weapon at me.

I'm not afraid. I think I can get it away from her, then get the food! I start forward.

Suddenly, something grips my shoulder and yanks me backwards, throwing me on the ground! The thing! It followed me! It's towering over me! It's speaking?

"I'll teach you to steal food from women and kids!"

A heavy boot hits me in the side and I hear something crack. The foot draws back and launches forward again, but somehow my hands rise to grab it. I heave, and the man sails over backwards, cursing. I scramble to my feet, almost passing out from a sharp pain lancing through my side. My assailant is getting up too. I must get away from here before he makes it to his feet! I tear out of the alley, back to the street. I dare not look to see if he's chasing me. I run until I'm panting, the pain in my side like a thousand knives piercing me. I have to stop!

My breathing slows. Fear and the pain have dulled my hunger, but now I'm really cold. A word I used to know pops into my head—hypothermia. Hypothermia will kill me! Suddenly I'm back in the caves at the end of the earth, embraced in icy terror!

I wrap my arms around my middle and stagger up the street, headed I know not where. A yellow light on a pole glares on a railing through the mist, and I see a flight of stairs, leading down. Down? I can't go down! It lurks there! But I have to go down. Hypothermia! I must go!

I hold on to the railing with both hands as I navigate the stairs. It hurts! I make it to the bottom. It's warmer. A row of turnstiles is up ahead, and a little booth with bars on the windows. I'm too weak to jump a turnstile, but perhaps I can slide under. I start to, and I hear someone shout "Hey!" from the booth.

I ignore the voice and force my body through. The pain in my side erupts again, taking my breath away, but I'm suddenly on the other side.

"Hey you bum! You can't do that! You got to pay the fare!"

He's fishing in his pocket for a nickel so he can get through the turnstile. I must get away before he finds one! I scramble to my feet and run into the station. I glance over my shoulder and see him following. My god, he's big! He'll get me and drag me upstairs, throw me out into the cold rain! Hypothermia! I'll die!

I'm running along the platform beside the track. There's a blank wall at the end. There's nowhere to run to! Unless...

I leap off the platform! My knees buckle and I fall face first into the filthy water running between the rails. The vomit rises in my throat.

"Hey, idjit! You trine to kill yourself or what? Get outta there!"

Somehow I struggle to my feet and drag myself into the tunnel.

"I ain't comin' down there! A train comes, that's it for you!"

I don't care. It's warm here, and I've stopped shivering. I move into the tunnel, and the shouts behind me are smothered in the inky blackness.

It had to happen. Ahead in the dark, a pair of milky lights winks on. A vague thrumming begins, then escalates into a rumbling. The train is coming!

Where to go? There's no light but that from the rapidly approaching train, but I know that this is a single tunnel, with only about a foot between the track and the side of the tunnel. Not enough space to be safe, even with my back against the wall. There's also the deadly third rail on the left of the track, covered by a wooden housing. Man-shaped hollows line the wall at intervals, but it will be difficult to locate one without a light. I must try!

I move to the left wall and run my hands along it. It's rough but even, with no sign of a hollow.

I'm going to die here! Well, what of it? If the religionists are right, Jesus, Harvey and Sally will all be there to greet me.

I face the onrushing train, extending my arms like Moses on the rock above the Red Sea, singing, "Bringing in the sheaves, bringing..."

Something grabs my ankles. No! It found me! I fall flat on my face for the second time. Now I'm roughly hauled backwards out of the tunnel. My extended arms hit the tunnel wall, stopping my backward progress. The train is roaring now, the tunnel is as bright as daylight. I extend my arms over my head and I'm jerked backwards through a hole low down on the wall. The light goes out as the train rushes by in a haze of noise.

A match scratches, flares to life. It illuminates a female face. I know those features!

"Sally?"

She applies the match to a lantern and the cavity is bathed in crimson light.

"I'm Marnie, mister, not Sally. That's Enoch."

I become aware of the man who grabbed my ankles. He's black and huge, with long snaky hair and a beard nearly to his waist. He's let go of me, and is squatting on his haunches at my feet.

"Why did you help me?" I asked.

"Because if we don't take care of each other down here, who will?" said Marnie. She went on, "You're new in the cattycombs, ain'tcha?"

Enoch stands. He can't straighten all the way up because the space we're in is cramped, but he's easily as large as Moscowicz. He reaches out a hand and I take it, and he hauls me to my feet.

Moscowicz! Does he know about Sally? I begin to cry.

"Let's get out of here," Marnie says. She picks up her red lantern by a handle on top, leading the way. Enoch gives me a rough shove in the middle of the back to indicate that I should follow.

Marnie and Enoch live down here in the tunnels. It is a wild trek to their lair, through the darkness in the eerie glow of the red lantern. We traverse tunnels, wade through waist-deep water, clamber over piles of rubble and force our aching bodies through jagged holes. Finally, we arrive at a wrought-iron ladder embedded in the concrete. Marnie leaves the lantern with Enoch and me, and ascends into the darkness. After a moment, Enoch gestures that I should go up. I balk—these people did save me from being killed by the train, but I have no idea where they are taking me or what they might want of me. Enoch becomes impatient and gives me a shove towards the ladder. I know I can't fight him, weak as I am. I grab a rung and climb. After mounting a few rungs, I notice a soft glow above, brightening as I approach. I reach the top rung and find a rectangular opening. Marnie is inside. She has lighted candles in a cozy, furnished cement chamber. The furnishings all look as if they have been scavenged from the trash—there are cushions on the floor for sitting, a couple of low tables, some mismatched short cabinets and a mattress along the back wall. A tattered carpet covers the floor. I can barely lever myself inside from the top of the ladder. Marnie comes to help me.

I attempt to stand and get a painful bump on the head from the low ceiling. Falling back to my knees, I crawl over to one of the cushions. Enoch pops into view at the entrance and crawls inside. I wonder what it's like not to be able to stand up straight for most of one's life.

I address Marnie. "Do you have anything to eat? I'm starving!

"Enoch will get something."

The big man dutifully crawls back to the ladder, and disappears.

While he's gone, Marnie busies herself kindling a fire in a can near the opening from scraps of paper and wood left there for that purpose. The draft that blows by the entrance acts as a natural flue and draws most of the smoke outside.

"What's your name?" she asks me.

"Eben." I hesitate, then ask her the question that's been on my mind since we met. How did you come to live in this place?"

"My Pa lost his job in the crash," she says. "When we couldn't pay the rent, we were put out on the street. Ma and Pa died that first winter, and I thought I would too. But Enoch found me and took me here."

"How do you stand it?" I asked her.

"Oh, it's way better than living on the street," she said. "It's warm and dry here, and there's plenty of food. And I don't have to worry about somebody stealing my stuff or raping me." She says it like those two problems are equivalent. "What about you? What happened?"

I start to speak, but my throat closes up and the tears begin to flow. I can't talk about it! It's insane!

"Hey, that's okay, you don't have to say if you don't want to. A lot of us have done things we're ashamed of." She pauses, then says, "You can stay here for a while till you get on your feet. Me and Enoch will show you the ropes and help you get a place of your own."

I cry all the harder. Such kindness in the bowels of the Earth!

Enoch returns in a little while. He's carrying three rats by their tails, the size of small dogs!

Horrified, I watch as Marnie produces a little knife and neatly dresses them out. I start to sing: "Three blind mice. Three blind mice. See how they run. See how they run. They all ran after the farmer's wife, she cut off their tails with a carving knife, did you ever see such a sight in your life, as three blind mice?"

Marnie smiles. "Haven't heard that since I was a little girl." She deftly skewers each naked rodent on a piece of rebar and sets them over the fire. God help me, the aroma that arises nearly drives me crazy! I want to rip them from those spits and devour them right now!

Marnie expertly rotates the spits until the rats are done to a turn. She hands me one, and I burn my fingers and my tongue as I wolf it down. It was one of the best meals of my life!

True to her word, Marnie helps me settle into underground life over the new few weeks. She and Enoch show me a recess in the wall near to theirs that is close to the ground that does not require a ladder for access. It is less secure than their den, but easier for me to get into in my weakened state. We make periodic forays to the outside so I can gather furniture for my new abode. It's disgustingly easy. So many are being evicted from their homes because they can't pay their rent. I obtain a mattress, an easy chair with a back but no legs perfect for my low-ceilinged cave and an erstwhile cocktail table to go in front of it. I know I should feel guilty about taking others' things, but I rationalize that the owners can't use them anymore and they'll just end up in a landfill. We also find plenty of food. Grocery stores and restaurants throw away perfectly usable food, cooked and uncooked, every day. Once in a while we have to join a breadline, but it's not often.

There's a larger community of Trogs nearby, which Marnie and Enoch have declined to join. "Too many rules," Marnie says. But the couple does have a loose relationship with them, and Marnie introduces me to a few of them. They share information with us—which restaurants throw out the best stuff at what time, or when a particular bonanza of discarded belongings hits the street. One day while I'm visiting, I hear that a man had fallen in the tunnels and broken his arm. I examine it—it's not a compound fracture, thank God. Somebody produces a bottle of whisky and he drinks until he passes out, then I set the bone and splint it with boards and pieces of cloth. Now that they know I have medical skill, the Trogs literally can't do too much for me! They bring me many things they've scavenged. Some are worthless patent medicines, others are from drugstores and a few were probably stolen from hospital stores. They begin to come to my cubicle when they are ill. I lightheartedly wonder if I should post office hours!

As the time passes, I try to blot the Rivington Street horror from my mind. Some days it's easy—it's as if it's just a scary story that someone told me long ago. Other days, it all comes rushing back. Poor Sally! Harvey, my lost love! That hideous creature! On those days, I resort to a bottle of Dicodid that someone brought to me, and as much whisky as it takes for a black, dreamless sleep.

Marnie arrives at my cavern in tears. Enoch didn't come home last night.

"He never stays away a whole day without telling me!" she says. "I'm sure something has happened."

We go to the community and get them to organize search parties. I have a bad feeling about this!

Marnie and I are at the Trogs' community with nearly a hundred other tunnel dwellers, next to a roaring bonfire that brings an unaccustomed clarity to this place. The community is in a large cavern that was apparently excavated during subway construction, and now contains about three dozen shanties. The fire illuminates the ceiling nearly thirty feet overhead and I can see that the plume of black smoke rising from it bends sideways about twenty feet up and rushes into a side tunnel presumably connecting to the surface.

A stage of packing crates has been constructed. Willie, a fiftyish white man, the elected leader of the community, is helped to mount it by two other Trogs. He raises his arms for silence, and when the crowd quiets, he begins to speak.

"I know that most of you don't give a tinker's damn about what goes on up in the world, but there's something you should know. Bodies with no heads have been turnin' up, and the cops think they've got a crazy killer on their hands. Well, whoever it is has started killin' down here. We found Enoch's body last night, and it had no head."

Next to me, Marnie gives out a piteous wail and crumples to the ground.

Jesus have mercy! It's come, and it's after me!

I'm back in my lair, packing my few meager possessions into a decrepit duffle. I have no idea where to go. I don't know what has become of my flat and my office, and anyway, the creature, with its sinister intelligence, could likely find me there. My bank accounts are surely extant, perhaps I can get enough money to flee to Europe, or Asia. Certainly it couldn't pursue me across the sea!

A voice hails from the darkness outside.

"Doctor Ebeneezer Warman! Eben! Are you in there?"

Moscowicz?

His great bulk rears up in the opening to my den, vaguely spectral in the glow of the flashlight he carries.

"Moscowicz! How did you ever find me?"

"I'm a detective, ain't I?" he says. "Besides, I had help."

There's another figure standing with him. I recognize him from my time with Danforth. Dyer! He's got a yellow sailor's oilskin buttoned up to his throat, and a tight-fitting miner's helmet, with a light on the front. A pair of goggles around his neck faces backwards. He's wearing a curious amulet on a heavy metal chain around his neck as well, made from a single metal rod bent into the shape of a five-pointed star, with a metal eye welded into the center. It reminds me of the many star shapes I saw in my shared dream with Danforth. There's also a curious contraption on his back—a couple of gas tanks and a long, thin rod.

Rather than make the big detective come into my cramped quarters, I come outside.

"You need to tell me what you know about Sally," Moscowicz says to me.

I can't! I just can't! But I know he won't take no for an answer. "I'm not sure," I tell him. "I haven't seen her since the morning she came to my office. I'm afraid I wasn't very pleasant to her."

"Dr. Dyer here has told me about the thing. I ain't sure it's for real. Is it?"

There's no point in lying to him about that. "It's real, detective. I've seen it."

"You've seen it?" says Dyer. "At the house on Rivington Street?"

I nod soberly.

"Did it get her?" Moscowicz asks. When I don't answer, he says "Goddammit, Eben! I deserve to know! We were gonna get married!"

I simply cannot, will not tell him of the terrible sight I saw in that house! But the man does deserve an answer. "I..., I think it might have gotten her. I didn't see it. But Harvey and I found her press card on the back porch." I rummage in the duffle bag, find the card and hand it to him. "You should have this."

His expression now is one of stupefaction. He simply stares at the card, holding it in his huge hand, caressing the face of it with his thumb. Finally, he grates, "I'm gonna kill that fucking thing."

I have a vague recollection of moving through the upstairs rooms of the house, liberally pouring kerosene on the floors, walls and furnishings, before dropping a match and watching the flames spread. I couldn't bring myself to go back downstairs, where it was. Perhaps my cowardice is responsible for its presence here in the underworld.

"That may not be easy," I say.

He reaches down for a two-handled bag, unzips it, takes out a boxy black gun about three feet long, and snaps a disc-like magazine to the underside. "I came prepared," he says.

I'm not sure that mere bullets would be of any use against the thing, but I don't say so.

"I don't know where it is," I say, "but I think it followed me down here."

"I can find it," says Dyer.

"How?" I ask.

"You wouldn't believe me if I told you." He produces a canvas-wrapped package from a pocket. "Take this," he says. "It might protect you when we find the Shoggoth."

Shoggoth! I know the word from Colin's books.

I unwrap the package and find an amulet identical to the one that Dyer's wearing.

I hold mine out to Moscowicz and ask, "Where's yours?"

He pats his gun. "This is all I need," he says.

I hope he's right.

That last foray into the echoing blackness of the Underworld with Dyer and Moscowicz will be forever etched into my memory. Dyer leads the way. Some of the tunnels are lit by electric fixtures on the walls, but many are not. The large hand-held searchlight that Dyer carries bounces crazily, alternately illuminating sections of the tunnel ahead as bright as daylight, then allowing them to plunge into darkness again. He's given me one just like it. The walls seem in constant motion with crawling things, and rats as large as cats grudgingly make way for us. Dyer has no map, compass or other means of navigation, but some strange sense seems to direct him precisely.

The Manhattan subway tunnels and the sewers are intertwined, and we pass freely from one to the other through breaks in the tunnel walls and deliberately constructed connections. A fecal reek tells me that sometimes we're in the sewers, traversing slippery brick walkways flanking squalid streams of raw sewage, which run in a concrete channel in the center of the tunnel. Other times we follow the subway tracks, and I'm nervous about the approach of another train. We (even Moscowicz) can walk upright in most of the tunnels, but some require us to stoop over. Dyer halts in front of a six-foot-wide, semicircular side tunnel at the base of a wall, indicating that it is the way we must go. We drop to our knees to crawl inside. Dyer lets Moscowicz go first in case the way becomes too constricted for the big detective—I hate the thought of having to back out of there if that happens. Dyer slides his searchlight into a pocket in his oilskin and switches on his helmet light. My pants are soaked with the putrid water and my gorge rises, but Harvey's face pops into my head, and I'm suddenly all right again.

The passage we are in is inclined slightly downward, which makes crawling on the slimy, wet floor all the more difficult. A murmuring sound arises up ahead, becoming louder as we crawl forward. Soon it's obvious that the sound is running water.

"Holy shit!" Moscowicz says.

I'm last in line, so I can't see what prompted the big detective's expletive. Dyer is stopped in front of me, but he begins crawling again and I follow. Suddenly, the light in front of me winks out and I'm encased in Stygian blackness. I start to panic, but the light reappears, shining upward into the tunnel.

"Come forward slowly, Doctor," says Dyer. There's a drop here."

I do as he says and soon find myself on the lip of a precipice.

"It's only about five feet," says Dyer. "You can slide out on to the floor if you're careful."

I do so, but I guess I'm not careful enough, because I stumble and plop face first into the nasty pool of water below. I arise, sputtering, then my breath is taken away by the sight I behold.

We are in a vast chamber in the bowels of the city. The domed ceiling of this immense hemispherical space arching nearly a hundred feet overhead is lit by electric lights, but we're still standing in relative darkness because the beams don't penetrate this far. The wall is ringed with tiers of semicircular portals, and cascades of sewage erupt from them into the knee-deep pool in which we're standing. The liquid seems to be constantly draining through similar openings lower down on the wall, but they're harder to see in the darkness. The chamber is suffused with the drone of running water, and the chill air reeks of excrement and garbage.

Dyer has to shout to be heard over the din. "It's here!" he says. "I can feel it!"

Moscowicz puts up his light and unlimbers his Tommy gun, snapping one of the cylindrical magazines to the base. A metallic CLANK! penetrates the water noise.

"Come out, you motherfucker!" he shouts. "Come and get it!"

The surface of the muck in front of him undulates, then explodes in an eruption of dung and a cacophony of screams emitted from a thousand maws. My sweet Jesus! It's at least doubled in size since I last saw it—it towers over Moscowicz as he would over a babe. He rears back and unleashes a hail of bullets from the Thompson. The roar is deafening as it reverberates from the concrete walls, the smell of cordite supplants the smell of sewage and the muzzle flashes intermittently illuminate the chamber like a strobe. Bloody chunks of putrescent flesh fly off the shoggoth, splashing into the surrounding muck, and the volume of its screams increases, transfixing my temples like a trepanning drill.

Dyer has now brought his weapon into play as well. A bolt of liquid fire arches across the intervening space and caresses the miscreation with its orange tongue. He runs the flame up and down the creature's body, and the milky white flesh seems to boil and sizzle like gangrenous porridge. The thing's body arches into a crescent, and it dives back into the slime from which it arose.

"By God, we hurt it!" I scream.

Moscowicz detaches the spent drum from his machine gun and sails it across the chamber, extracts another, snaps it in place, then works the mechanism to chamber a round. The gun suddenly rears upward, belching lead and flame, then goes abruptly silent, spinning into the darkness as the big detective is jerked backwards under the surface of the filth. A second later, a spherical object is launched from the muck, nearly hitting me in the face as it flies by.

Moscowicz's head!

"Get out of the water into a tunnel!" Dyer screams. "We're dead if it remains under the water!" He suits action to words by wading towards the nearest wall, then climbing into an opening about three feet above the surface. Other of Moscowicz's body parts are ejected from the vile pool, splashing nearby as I head for a similar refuge on the side of the chamber opposite from Dyer.

At least he and Sally are together again.

I clamber into a slimy tunnel and turn around to face the room just as the thing erupts from the muck not five feet in front of me! The shock causes me to lose my grip on the tunnel lip, and I start to slide backwards down the slope. That likely saves my life, because the thick pseudopod grasping for me barely misses my head! I'm scrabbling to avoid slipping back, but then I realize that fleeing this place is my only reasonable alternative. I throw my arms over my head to make my torso as narrow as possible to facilitate my slide into oblivion.

This tunnel is more steeply pitched than the one we came through to enter this place. I'm accelerating as I slip backwards to I know not where. I've no idea how long it takes before I'm summarily ejected from the tube into another electrically lighted tunnel with a hemi-cylindrical channel of sewage running between two brick walkways. I do not know whether the shoggoth is pursuing me or if it remained to deal with Dyer, about whom I feel vaguely guilty for deserting. But he at least has a weapon to defend himself. I decide it's the better part of valor to get as far from here as I can. I begin walking rapidly away.

I hear it scream as it comes out of the side tunnel into mine. I don't even look back—I just begin running for my life! The tunnel curves ahead, and I as I round the bend, I spy a crack in the wall that might be big enough for me to slip into. Dare I try? I know that I can't keep running in my weakened state. But if I hide in the crack, maybe the obscenity will pass me by.

I ease myself in, and cool air that carries the smell of the subway—an acrid, electrical odor—washes over my face. I'm inside a wall that separates the two systems—a common architectural feature of the underworld that I've encountered before. I press onward—if I can get into the subway, I can find a station and ascend to the world above. Suddenly, I desperately want to see the daylight once more!

I step into the subway tunnel, nearly tripping over the deadly, wood-sheathed third rail. Maybe enough electricity flows through it to kill the thing, but I have neither tools to safely remove the cover, nor the time. I choose a direction and start trotting, hoping that a station is not far off.

Again the screams! It's in my tunnel! How is the infernal beast tracking me? It doesn't really matter—now my only hope is to get to the surface and lose myself in the City's multitudes. I realize that I am probably condemning some to an untimely, horrible death, but the possibility of escape overrides any altruism.

A low rumble interspersed with squeaking is building. Dammitall, it can't be! Two lights wink on low down up ahead. It is! A goddamned train!

I wheel around to face my pursuer, and the star-shaped amulet that Dyer gave me bounces on my chest. Fat lot of good that did me! The tunnel brightens and I can see the shoggoth about twenty yards away, closing fast in a sinuous, snakelike motion. I can't bear to look at it. I turn my head to side, and in the glare of the headlights I notice the man-shaped hollow in the tunnel wall. Just maybe...

I rip the amulet from around my neck and fling it at the horror, which is now twenty feet away. The tunnel is as bright as noon and the air thrums with iron discordance. The amulet hits the shoggoth and disappears inside it. The train's horn blares behind me with futile urgency, an earsplitting squeal erupts as the brakes take hold, and the wheels slide along the tracks in the inevitable grip of momentum. I wheel and throw myself at the hollow, cracking a tooth as I slam into stone. The screams of the shoggoth momentarily intermingle with, then drown out the squeal of the brakes, then the world itself explodes.

Silas K. Henderson

CHAPTER 32
November 21, 1931—The New York Evening Graphic

52 Confirmed Dead in Subway Crash

The death toll from this morning's horrific subway crash continues to mount, with at least 52 fatalities confirmed by the New York Police Department. Most of the dead still have not been identified. A police spokesman, Inspector William Henderson, declined to answer when asked how high he thought the toll might go, and threatened this reporter with incarceration when the issue was pressed.

Few details about the cause of the accident are available. The 1 Express train derailed between the Houston Street and Canal Street stations at 8:12 a.m. this morning at the height of the morning rush. Mr. Charles Keller, who was waiting at the Canal Street Station, told the Graphic, "It was the most unearthly noise! The train horn was sounding and you could hear the brakes squealing, but I swear I could hear all those poor devils on the train screaming too! It was just awful! Then the crash came, and smoke and dust poured out of the tunnel into the station. The walls were shaking and somebody shouting that it was caving in—there was a mad rush for the exits! I saw a few people go down beneath the crowd, who didn't get back up."

IRT officials and police quickly arrived at the scene and cordoned off both the Houston and Canal Street Stations, which are still closed with no projected time of opening available. Rumors of foul play have surfaced, leaving the Graphic to wonder if the City is under attack. Perhaps some timely information from the NYPD would go a long way toward alleviating those fears.

November 21, 1931—The New York Evening Graphic

Notice of Remembrance Service—Sally Marie Barton, 35, New York City

Ray and Stella Barton, the parents of Sally Marie Barton, have announced that a remembrance service for their daughter will be held at St. Catherine's Catholic Church at 1642 Parker Avenue in Maplewood, New Jersey, from 7 p.m. to 9 p.m. Miss Barton was born in Maplewood on May 24, 1896 and attended St Catherine's Elementary School in Maplewood, Archbishop O'Connor High School in Newark and the Pace Institute in New York City. She was a distinguished reporter for the New York Evening Graphic for the past two years. Miss Barton vanished on or about October 5 of this year. While Mr. and Mrs. Barton have not given up hope of their daughter's safe return, they want to allow her many friends and relatives the opportunity to meet and remember her life. Please do not send flowers, as this is not a funeral service.

CHAPTER 33

The Statement of Dr. Ebeneezer Warman
Manhattan State Hospital, Ward's Island, New York City
January 31, 1932

Here endeth the tale, as the bard says. Somehow, I was spared in that awful wreck. I crawled through the debris, the fire, the mutilated and the dead, and made my way back to the world of men. A police officer found me wandering aimlessly about Lower Manhattan, just as Dyer was found a few weeks before, and brought me to Bellevue. When Henderson heard that I was there, he wanted to charge me with all manner of things—burglary, arson, kidnapping Sally, and murder. They would have incarcerated me at Bellevue, but Dyer, who also survived the Armageddon, informed Dr. Oglethorpe, who, when he heard of my predicament, asked if I could be placed under his care. That is how I came to share a ward with Danforth, another pathetic victim of the shoggoth.

Oglethorpe assures me that there is hope for me. From a purely physical point of view, I'm sure he is correct. I've largely recovered from my injuries and I think I have many more years in front of me. My mental state is another matter entirely. The good doctor tells me

I'm experiencing delusions brought on by shock and trauma that will go away in time. He thinks that the charges against me will be dropped because of the terrible ordeal I had to face, and that I will be able to take up the threads of my life again.

But I know better. I know that the horror was real. I know that it was spawned by Colin in some anathematic manner from the tissue of the aborted fetuses of prostitutes and the women whom he'd murdered. The shoggoth was as human as I am. We are brothers under the skin.

Reverend Shoemaker says that humans were created with an immortal soul in the image and likeness of God. I have always believed that. But Colin, ever the scientist, proved that Eldritch creatures from beyond the stars could have created us on a whim, as their slaves. So much for the vaunted dignity of man! Even if there is a God who created the Elder Things who in turn, created us, I want no part of such a being, or a universe in which such obscenities are allowed to exist.

One question still haunts me—*was Sally still alive inside of that atrocity*, when she emerged from it to desperately plead for help?

I know that I will never see Evie, Sally, Moscowicz, or my beloved Harvey again in some eternal hereafter. All I have to look forward to is oblivion. And right now, oblivion does not sound all that bad.

CHAPTER 34

The Casebook of Dr. Hiram Oglethorpe
Manhattan State Hospital, Ward's Island, New York City

February 1, 1932

I'm sorry to report that the body of Dr. Ebeneezer Warman was found early this morning by a nurse. Dr. Warman committed suicide by hanging himself from a steam pipe with his hospital gown. It was not a quick or easy death, as he sat on the floor and slumped over to allow the weight of his body to tighten the noose and close off his airway. The other patients in the ward at the time did not intervene. May God have mercy on his troubled soul!

My prognosis for Dr. Warman was good, so his death comes as somewhat of a shock. He had experienced some devastating losses of late, but in my opinion, he still had much to live for.

He has left a lengthy handwritten statement, which I will review and file with this report.

CHAPTER 35

March 15, 2020—The New York Daily News

Headless Body found in SoHo

The headless body of a homeless man was found on Canal Street early this morning by a city sanitation crew. The body has been sent to the City Morgue for identification and a precise determination of the cause of death. Police sources say that it is too early to tell if the death resulted from foul play.

— The End —

BEFORE YOU GO...

Writing a novel is a lonely endeavor. Feedback, both positive and negative, is very important to an author. So, if you liked *The Legacy of the Unborn*, or even if you didn't, please go to the book page on Amazon and leave a review. One sentence will do if you don't have time to write anything more, and it will be greatly appreciated.

Silas K. Henderson

ACKNOWLEDGEMENTS

I want to thank the following people who were instrumental in the completion and publication of The Legacy of the Unborn.

My beta readers Craig Chapman, Ilia Davidovich and Samuel Leeman Munk provided many helpful suggestions and encouraged me to see this project through.

The Legacy of the Unborn

ABOUT THE AUTHOR

Silas K. Henderson is the grandson of Inspector William Henderson of the NYPD.